822
OR
21

JEALOUSY

A Strange Company Keeper

JEALOUSY
A Strange Company Keeper

A NOVEL

Marsha D. Jenkins-Sanders

STREBOR BOOKS

NEW YORK LONDON TORONTO SYDNEY

Strebor Books
P.O. Box 6505
Largo, MD 20792
http://www.streborbooks.com

ISBN-13 978-1-59309-180-4
ISBN-10   1-59309-180-X
LCCN 2008920029

First Strebor Books trade paperback edition April 2008

Cover design: www.mariondesigns.com

10   9   8   7   6   5   4   3   2   1

Manufactured in the United States of America

For information regarding special discounts for bulk purchases, please contact Simon & Schuster Special Sales at 1-800-456-6798 or business@simonandschuster.com

DEDICATION

To My Dad, James Jenkins, Jr.—
my greatest inspiration, and with the exception of Jesus,
the only one who has loved me unconditionally.

ACKNOWLEDGMENTS

Nothing is impossible when you trust in God!

To Jehovah Jireh, my Provider—Thank you for continuously doing just that! You have blessed me beyond my expectations! Jesus the Christ, I have come to realize—through you, I can do all things!

To the love of my life, my husband—Know that no one can get in the way of what I feel for you! Watching you undergo a Spiritual Metamorphosis has been my greatest joy. I look forward to God taking you from the pit to the palace!

To my sons—God blessed me with you and the opportunity to love you unconditionally as granddad has loved me! Thank you for testing that love…you've helped me to grow!

Dad—Words cannot and do not convey how much I love you and how truly grateful I am for having the kind of "old school" father who knows how and when to pray! God broke the mold when he made you!

Tank (Terence L. Jenkins) —The baby boy "I raised." You've always held a special place in my heart. As we've grown older, I am thankful for the wisdom and insight to no longer call you "baby boy"—but friend!

Corn (James C. Jenkins) —You've become the "big brother" I can look up to and admire—thank you for showing me the way!

Dedra Jenkins—Your selfless act created the avenue and freedom I needed to accomplish so many dreams! Forever, I am grateful.

Felicia Cromartie and Tanya Freeman—That I know you're there is enough. Thank you for being a true friend!

To Tami Wilson, Valencia Edner, Lily Milner, Andrea Richards Scott, Rose March, Yolanda Branch, and all my new DSHU's— God in all his wisdom set our feet on paths that were destined to cross. That we recognize this is a DSHU (Divine Sistah Hook Up) is the best reward! I am truly thankful for each of you in my life.

To my sistahs who took time away to *grow*: Debbie Culp— You are always in my heart and prayers! Welcome back, you have been missed! Yolanda Cheatham—God will not and cannot fail! I thank Him for answering my prayers and allowing us to reconnect. Vida Gude—we have not missed a beat. Thank you for being a real friend!

James (Jimmy) Hunter—A little became a whole lot! Your kind gestures were from the heart and were much needed and greatly appreciated.

Nelson A. Henry—Many volunteer, few are called, and some are chosen. I am speaking of friends…and I am thankful God has seen fit to bless me with such an anointed and powerful one. As a Life Coach and Motivational Teacher you deposit many positive Life Lessons into my Spirit. As a friend you allow me to work them out. Thank you.

Mayor Hilliard Hampton—It is not often someone reaches back "just because"! Thank you for pursuing your passion to help others. You have blessed me tremendously.

To those book clubs, journalists, readers, reviewers, and book stores who have supported me—Thank you for welcoming me into your world! I am humbled.

To Zane and Charmaine—Without you this would still be a dream. Thank you so much for yet another opportunity to "spread my wings and fly"!

To my Strebor Family, like the stars at night there are far too many to name, but thank you for the insight, encouragement, and guidance.

Lastly, I humbly acknowledge myself for trusting God when I couldn't hear Him, feel Him, or see Him!

CHAPTER 1

As the judge's gavel hit the block, Dakota's heart quickened. In that instant what seemed like an eternity of sheer hell was over. The cancer of deception and deceit that would have broken the spirit of the average person was now reduced to memories. The life she had hoped to live comfortably and happily with the man she called "husband" could now become a reality. Finally, she would go home and enjoy the comfort of her loved ones in peace; a peace that had escaped her for the past four years.

Still in shock, Dakota grabbed her attorney's hand to steady her as she slowly rose from her seat. The tears forming in her eyes fell as she closed them and exhaled.

"I can't believe this is over," she whispered.

"Trust me, knowing this fruitcake, it ain't over," her attorney said sarcastically as he ushered her from the courtroom.

Driving home was relaxing. Dakota could vaguely remember the last time she'd done anything freely without looking over her shoulder in fear. It was surreal. For once thoughts of the good times replaced her continuous thoughts of the bad times. After all, things were good—once—and she once was very happy.

Arriving home safely, the strangeness of the moment hit her like a brick and kept her from entering the house. Stopping short of the door, she stared at it as if she'd never seen it before. Rain began to fall. Looking up at the gray sky she allowed the tears to freely flow, mixing with the raindrops that met her velvety smooth skin. Slowly, they both streamed down her face. Recalling the horrible chain of events that nearly destroyed her life, a plethora of emotions overcame her, forcing her to her knees.

In anguish, Dakota cried out, "How could you do this to me?" She paused; the mascara was beginning to burn her eyes. Wiping them with the back of her sleeve she continued.

"When no one else was there for you, I was. I believed in you…"

The stifling pain silenced her voice for what seemed like an eternity. "I hate you!" were the only words she could muster before bursting into tears once more. Truth of the matter is, as much as she tried to hate her nemesis, it was hard. Despite the pain, Dakota found it difficult to close the door on this saga and move forward.

Tears and mascara blurred her vision. Slowly rising from the pavement, she struggled to see the keyhole and fumbled with the key trying to open the door. As the contempt she felt toward someone she once loved and trusted poured from the depth of her soul, she cried out in anguish and leaned against the door, frantically twisting the knob back and forth.

Once inside, loud wails laced with moans echoed against the stillness of the living room. Leaning against the wall, she folded her arms close to her chest and rocked back and forth, whispering to herself.

"From the beginning you deceived me!" Taking a deep breath, and gathering her thoughts, she continued.

"Well, it's over now…you're out of my life. Wonder what it'll be like *not* pacing the floor wondering *if* or *when* you're going to do some crazy thing to hurt me?"

Her voice began to rise to a high pitch as she sobbed and gasped for air in her lungs. She could not find the strength to go on…it hurt way too much. Shifting her weight, Dakota leaned back on the wall and slid down to the floor, spreading her legs in front of her. After several minutes of crying the room fell silent. A broad grin consumed her face. Following another few minutes of silence, she burst into hearty laughter.

"It feels good! This whole thing feels good…what you meant for my harm, God has turned around for my good." A schoolgirl giggle trickled out and then tears began to well up in her eyes again. Feeling stronger, she wiped them before they fell.

"Know this—what goes around, comes around!"

CHAPTER 2

Those who know me—friends—call me "Ro." Dakota North, my cousin and best friend, chose to call me by my moniker, Rochelle. She felt "Ro" was not gender-specific and Dakota wanted me to own my femininity; something I earnestly tried to do but found challenging most times.

Part of the challenge was overcoming my looks. Being born Rochelle Jackson meant little or nothing when I looked exactly like Rodney Jackson, my dad. Coming into the world a woman—not man, but looking every bit the latter was a bitter pill to swallow. Five feet eleven inches in height, with hands the size of a six-foot man and feet that require size eleven shoes to house them did not spell *feminine!* At my height with no hips, no waistline and 32-A breasts, it was difficult to embrace the womanliness I obviously lacked. It's fair to say I had a hard time liking what I saw in the mirror day in and day out, especially when Dakota had the flip side of the mirror that declared her the "fairest of all." Growing up with Dakota shaped my life. I lived in my cousin's shadow, never knowing what it felt like to notice women pull their men close when I walked into a room. Envying her, I obsessed about feeling like "Cinderella" at least once in my life. But the one time I tried to fit that "glass slipper," I realized the fairy tale was not written for size eleven feet!

Life for me was at a very low point when I decided to make the effort to get to know Dakota better. That decision may have saved my life. Prior to that, things had not gone well. A rear-end collision from a milk truck, shortly after healing from an unexpected emergency surgery to remove a fibroid cyst as large as a tennis ball, and the infections that followed the surgery, left me unable to work.

Plans to move out of my parents' home after thirty years were once again on hold and my zeal for life had completely faded. At times life was so painful I found it difficult to go on. Suicide was never far from my thoughts and something I contemplated with more and more frequency during this time.

Rodney was getting on my last nerve, controlling my life as he had done since I took my first steps. Now a grown woman, I wanted and needed to experience life without his jealous interventions, which surfaced whenever a man showed interest in me. Added to this equation, Val, my wanna-be-diva mom, continuously attempted to live the life she never had through the life she tried to force me to have.

Nothing about my life made my parents or me happy. Many were of the opinion I needed to see a professional—a shrink! But who wanted to admit that there were serious issues in the first place, then subsequently have to deal with the stigma associated with having been diagnosed with a "psychological disorder"?

It was easier to hide behind extravagance; a trip to Canada every Christmas to purchase a new fur to add to my collection that now expanded twenty; shopping trips to Atlanta and California, twice a year, to purchase the latest St. John knits; First and Last Call at Neiman's to find shoes to match those St. Johns, and a new luxury automobile every other year. Even with all of this, I was never happy!

Finding someone to talk to who would understand and accept me with all my issues drifted on the side of impossible until I really got to know my flesh and blood, Dakota.

With my life in shambles and nothing to lose I decided to look past the things I'd heard whispered about her throughout our lives—egotistical, bourgeoisie, prima donna—and find the truth for myself by accepting an invite to the affair that would change my life's course and perspective.

An invitation delivered by courier, a first in my mundane life, left me shocked and even more amazed when I realized I was included among the list of numerous VIPs and celebrities asked to attend. This unexpected "honor" made me feel really special—important. Another first! In that instant I discarded the biases I had toward her, and the joyous moments that followed opened the windows to my soul and allowed my whole world to open up.

The custom-made invitation was penned by a calligrapher on beautiful Oriental hand-made rice paper, with Rochelle E. Jackson embossed in gold leaf. It read like a fairy tale:

"Once upon a time a person I'll call me, decided to celebrate a momentous event in the life of a person I'll call Collin. The person who I'll call Collin signed a new NBA contract with the team that I'll call the New York Knicks. The person who I'll call me realized the celebration of this occasion would not be complete without the presence of the person who I'll call you."

Included were the date, time, and location. I was asked to keep it a secret, wear white, and RSVP within two weeks.

Not one to do anything half-heartedly, Dakota had put all her talents and skills to work to ensure this huge surprise going-away party for her "celebrity hunk" of a boyfriend was a success. Mr. NBA Star had just been traded to the New York Knicks from the

Atlanta Hawks, after signing a phenomenal deal for mega-bucks. True to her fashion, Dakota was sending him off in style. Only those who could appreciate the amount of time, effort, and of course, money, that went into this production were invited. So, it would be only natural to wonder—why me?

Although first cousins, we were never close growing up. Dakota, six years older than me, was perceived to be a *prima donna*. Family members and those friends she did not stay in touch with after she married into wealth gave her the label. Always totally outgoing and fearless, she had an air about her that made people feel inferior. An enterprising person, she never allowed anything or anyone to stand in her way. If they did, she consequently figured out how to move beyond them or simply go around. Those qualities combined with her financial means made her a fierce force to be reckoned with.

At the time, I felt everything whispered about Dakota made her sound more like a smart woman than a *prima donna*, but jealousy and ego never allowed those whispering behind her back to call her that to her face. All of this transpired when I was a teenager. I barely knew Dakota but concluded if some of the stories I overheard were true, she graciously lived up to those expectations and I found that extremely captivating! Living large was something few people from our hometown experienced. That my cousin did daily, left me strongly desiring to do the same.

Nobody knew this, but I often listened to the gossip about my world-traveled cousin from my bedroom, which was just a sheet of drywall away from the kitchen where my mom and her friends gathered. If I placed my ear against the heat register in my room I could clearly hear every word spoken. Many of the things they said about Dakota formed lasting impressions in my mind; the majority of which left me wishing my feet were a size eight so I could wear her shoes.

One thing was certain—Dakota was a topic everyone loved to discuss. On the top of the list was how she managed to do so well in life—"screwed her way into money" was the exact term. Those women who were less opinionated referred to her good fortune as being "blessed"; a term that infuriated me because by the time God got done blessing Dakota, not much was left for me!

Anywho…the one special something He did give me I was exceptionally good at. With unmatched skill and expertise, I could interpret a song into sign language and leave a captive audience in tears, often receiving a standing ovation for my performance.

Problem is, that's not a popular form of entertainment, and even though I was paid handsomely, requests to perform were far and few in between. Although thankful for this talent, which never failed to pay my bills, my income did not always meet my outflow, and that left me bummed out most of the time.

A true shopaholic, I found comfort in buying "any and every color it comes in," routinely spending above my means and maxing out my credit cards. Then it was a game of "robbing Peter to pay Paul" until my next interpreting engagement. Yearning to experience Dakota's financial status and social prominence (certain that would solve all my problems), I prayed for my "Bill Gates" to come along. Why not? It worked for Dakota!

Granted, we were cool growing up, no thanks to me. All credit had to be given to Dakota who routinely took the high road when I intentionally hurt her feelings in an attempt to make her feel as ugly as I believed I looked.

Dakota was always happy to see me come and I was always happy to see her go. For me, being around my cousin was as painful as wearing a pair of shoes that were two sizes too small. Everything Dakota touched turned to gold. Conversely, whatever I touched turned to dust. I could do nothing right and Dakota did nothing wrong. Our differences were astronomical and greatly magnified whenever she was around. Being in her presence with *all her glory* only made me feel worse, so I avoided being around her as much as possible.

Our families did not have the same affluence. Rodney made a lot more money as a foreman in the factory than his brother who worked on the assembly line. His income combined with the money Val made as a nursing assistant made our lifestyle much more comfortable than his brother's. As a result, my dad felt obligated to help out wherever he could. The "wherever he could" meant a well-cooked meal for his brother and children at least once a week, usually on Sunday. That put Dakota up close and personal, in *my* face and space, more times than I wanted her to be—until now.

Getting to know Dakota changed my opinion of her. Realizing I missed so many fun and exciting times made me contrite and I regretted the mean things I'd done to her. Unable to turn back the hands of time, I went out of my way to be endearing in an effort to make amends.

As with most things I do, I went overboard trying to make it up to her. My efforts became borderline "door mat" behavior and caused great concern. A "take no prisoners" person, Dakota checked me.

"Hey listen, you don't have to kiss my behind to be around me. Lighten up and be yourself…we're good! I don't carry grudges and all is forgiven…deal!" Dakota smiled, extended her hand and waited for me to shake it, sealing our truce. I was so grateful she did because I'm not good at suckin' up!

CHAPTER 3

Dakota North was as easy to like as her beauty was to appreciate. Big doe eyes, evenly located over a button nose, perfectly centered in a heart-shaped face enveloped by flawless skin, made her beauty hypnotizing. Time had been kind to her breasts and butt, which both still stood at attention, even though she was rapidly approaching forty.

A woman with style and pizzazz, her presence was difficult to ignore. Not one to believe in fake hair, Dakota kept her "good hair" cropped short and softly colored honey brown, which presented a stunning contrast against her dark chocolate skin. Proud of her full lips she accentuated them with lipstick shades that drew attention and complemented her big light-brown eyes (which she did not pay to own). Her signature look was tight and she knew it!

At a very young age Dakota learned what image she wanted to portray and spent countless hours studying high-fashion magazines learning how to perfect it. Setting the bar high, she gravitated toward a European flair and closely emulated images she found in fashion magazines such as *Women's Wear Daily*, *French Elle*, *VOGUE*, and *Harper's Bazaar*.

Her mother, a highly educated woman with the poise, grace and polish of a socialite, lacked the funds to travel in that circle.

Nevertheless, that did not stop my aunt from instilling in her daughter an unwavering desire to do so. With an unusual drive to succeed in life and excel at everything, Dakota refused to settle for "good enough," and had little patience for those who did. She wanted the best life could offer and set her mind on that goal.

Raised in the backwoods of Mississippi, her father, a factory worker with little education, lived in church. A God-fearing man, he was head of the Deacon Board, sat on numerous church committees, and served as an alternate Armor Bearer for his pastor of twenty years.

Jimmy Jackson, my father's oldest brother, wanted his children to love the Lord as much as he did. From birth they were in church several times a week and all day on Sundays. The only time they did not make it to church was when Uncle Jim had to work. Overtime in the factory was more than a day's pay and something he could not afford to turn down. So if offered, even though it meant missing church service, he gratefully accepted.

God's influence over Dakota's life was very noticeable throughout her childhood, into her teens and college. In high school most of her classmates were sexually active, some finding themselves pregnant before graduating. By graduation, Dakota and a minute handful of her classmates were the only remaining virgins.

College, a setting that lends well to freedoms and choices, did little to change her actions. Dakota held firm to her "I'm saving myself for my husband" mindset, but eventually fell short of that goal when she met her first love, Ricky Tolbert. Hailing from Ecorse, a suburb just twenty minutes from her home, he charmed her drawers off her behind and slipped his erection in before she cried out, no! By then it was too late. Virginity is not an afterthought!

Thankful she did not get pregnant, she vowed to be an "almost virgin" when she met her husband, another vow she failed to keep when she met and fell in love with bass player, Paul Butler. Now fully aware that maintaining her virginity was a sentimental notion, she kept her panties on and steered clear of situations and settings that seemed to help her fall short of her desire to wait until marriage before having sex.

Old fashioned, Dakota's father raised her and her four brothers to respect themselves and their elders. I remember them always responding to adults with "yes, sir" and "yes, ma'am." Never was "yeah" or "uh-huh," an affirmative, nor negative head motion or any form of non-verbal communication accepted. And, addressing adults by their first names, like I do, was unheard of. Prefixes such as "Miss," "Mr.," "Aunt" or "Uncle" were mandatory.

A firm believer of the old scripture, "Spare the rod spoil the child," Uncle Jim disciplined my cousins with a very stern hand. Punishments included butt whippings that were rendered when the action warranted, or weeks of being grounded. As a result, like soldiers Dakota and her brothers fell in line and straightened up whenever he entered the room. Fully aware he would give you *something to remember* if you got out of line, they seldom did—at least not in his presence.

In sharp contrast, my Aunt Miriam found his military approach to raising their children harsh, way over the top, and hard to live with. A philosophical supporter of the "time out" form of discipline, she often allowed them to say and do whatever they pleased, short of cursing, which always caused confusion for them and tension between my aunt and uncle. It never failed to create contention in their household, which always led to Uncle Jim leaving the house to take a drive to cool off. This pattern of dissension eventually led to their divorce and my uncle being granted custody of my cousins.

Prior to the divorce, most of Dakota's childhood was spent in modeling and finishing schools to enhance her self-confidence and social etiquette. These classes made her acutely aware of breeding and class, something the rich seemed to have in abundance. As her knowledge of class, wealth, breeding and social status increased, so did her appetite to be around those who could appreciate the hard work and effort it took to become "socialite worthy."

A city girl from the suburbs of Detroit, Dakota never felt she belonged in the tiny town of Romulus. Many of the women were passive and lackadaisical and an equal portion of the men were uncouth and outclassed by her finishing school decorum. As soon as she graduated from college she left Michigan and its ho-hum lifestyle, taking up residence in Atlanta—a city on the move with the energy she craved.

Atlanta, home to Delta Airlines, was expanding and looking for flight attendants. A college degree in marketing did not deter Dakota from applying for the position. Few understood her decision to throw four expensive hard years of college education in the toilet, and Dakota cared less about those few. She loved sophisticated classy people and relished the thought of exploring exotic places. Working in the airline industry guaranteed she'd do just that.

CHAPTER 4

Traveling around the world was the answer to Dakota's prayer. Working on international flights became her preference because it gave her the opportunity to meet and mingle with people of all ethnicities and backgrounds. The male species, especially Italian and French, captivated her the most.

On one of her trips she met a recently widowed Duke who found her delightfully enchanting. Twice he sent his private jet to bring her to his palace in the outskirts of England and twice she sent the jet back, empty! Not that she didn't want to play— she just wanted to play in her own sandbox. No fool and well schooled, she remembered Henry VIII had his wives beheaded, rather than divorce them. Uncertain if that same insanity ran in the Duke's blood, she took no chances!

Two years after joining the friendly skies and making them her best friend, Dakota became a household name among those who were well-bred. The lifestyle of the rich and famous was everything she imagined and she enjoyed being in the company of those with wealth. Likewise, they enjoyed her company and found her exciting.

Socialites were unconcerned with Dakota's lack of money because she was polished; her grace and beauty abound. Adding wit and zest to an otherwise mundane event, they welcomed her on their turf. Shortly after being accepted into the "circle," these women of means made it customary to ensure "their girl" Dakota was present at all of their functions.

It was at one of those events she met a newly signed NBA phenom who would quickly become her closest friend and ally. What made her so special to him was her realness—her down-to-earth temperament. Though world renowned, when in his "play sister's" presence he felt anchored and relaxed.

The strictly platonic relationship made attending events with her on his arm rewarding. It kept the groupies at bay (most of the time) and gave him time to safely test the waters of super-stardom. If he saw someone he wanted to get to know better, he did not have to worry about how Dakota might feel. He knew she had his back and she did. As a matter of fact, when he did meet someone he wanted to spend more time with, she had to be screened by Dakota before he took it to the next level.

Routinely spotted with her NBA "hot topic" garnered instant fame and press for Dakota. Smart and calculating, she utilized this fifteen minutes of fame to the fullest. It was just a matter of time before that fame would land her a "hot topic" to call her own.

News travels fast, and the A-T-L is not really that big. People talk, and although those people talking lived in Atlanta, many were originally from Detroit (or its suburbs). In time, Dakota's whirlwind romance with a two-time MVP for the Atlanta Hawks spread like a wildfire all the way back to Romulus.

Rushing to buy up every tabloid I could find, I like'na died when I saw her infectious smile beaming radiantly all over the covers. Years had passed since we'd seen each other. Not because she never returned to Michigan, but because when she did, I left.

Now looking at her chocolate complexion, which had darkened and taken on a bronzed glow from the Caribbean sun, I realized Dakota was more beautiful than I had remembered.

A front-page photo of her five-foot-seven-inch, 120-pound frame with every curve just where God intended, housed in a barely there tankini, was jaw-dropping gorgeous. The photos of her romping and playing on the beach with her man made me jealous. And when my phone would not stop ringing with "inquiring minds" wanting to get the 4-1-1 on Dakota's relationship with Mr. MVP, I turned a dark shade of emerald green…filled with envy!

Although Dakota was long gone from high school when I got there, people often said she was the kind of person you always remembered and still called "friend." Dakota, on the other hand, remembered your face, forgot your name, and never called you "friend." It was an endearing term that she did not use loosely. However, it was some of those so-called "friends" that were now calling me for the 4-1-1 and that pissed me off!

"Why call me? Call *your friend* Dakota," I grumbled after hanging up the phone.

Don't get me wrong, gossiping was my thing, but it had little reward when the subject matter was so "perfect."

With Ms. North, you either liked her or hated her, no in-between. If you liked her, it was because you could appreciate her self-assurance that was often mistaken for arrogance. If you disliked her, it was usually because her "arrogance" made you feel insignificant. Men found her self-confidence alluring and that allowed her to routinely hit the jackpot. Judging by the tabloid cover page, she'd obviously done it again.

Applying great restraint I made it past that drama, but weeks later when ET showed the new "power couple" attending the Espy

Awards in Vegas I couldn't take it! Boiling with contempt, I worked hard to stay composed and push my jealousy aside. Try as I might, watching Dakota walk with the confidence and grace of a polished socialite who knew the world was her playground was just too much to digest.

She always seemed to know just what to do to make my life miserable…a living hell. *Here we go again! No way can I hide every tabloid in every grocery store from Val. Rather than allow her to bring this news to me I'd better take it to her first.* Handing my mother the tabloid, I leaned against the kitchen island and waited for her reaction.

"See…this is what I'm talking about," Val said emphatically, pointing at the picture on the cover. She stared at the photo for what seemed like an eternity. Angry and disgusted, my mother tore the tabloid in two, then turned and stared angrily at me. As expected, I got a verbal beat-down fit for someone my mother hated.

"Just how stupid can you be? See…this could be you!" she yelled. Fighting back tears, I did not say a word.

"Get that RSVP to this girl's party and send it now," she barked.

Val threw the pieces of the torn tabloid in the trash and stormed off mad. Mad at me for not living the life she wanted me to live. Mad at Dakota because she did. Mad at "father time" for cheating her out of that life when she was young and able to snatch a "hot topic" of her own.

CHAPTER 5

The party was overwhelming! Seeing all the celebrities and rich people frightened me out of my wits. Three times I ran into the bathroom feeling as if I had to vomit. Normally I could handle anything. Living in Dakota's shadow taught me how to wear a façade. However, tonight I could not get it together. I was a nervous wreck!

On the other hand, Dakota was in her element and it showed. Watching her like a hawk I tried to take a page out of her book, but failed poorly at my vain attempt to be charming. That sent me rushing back into the bathroom, this time to run cold water on my wrists in an effort to slow my heart rate.

Emerging still frightened, I walked straight to the bar and ordered a drink. Not an experienced drinker, I had no clue what to order but followed the choice of the diva in front of me—Sex on the Beach!

Miss Thang had it goin' on. Bling up the yang-yang. Gorgeous, exotic, and sexy, with features similar to that of the owner of Baby Phat—she was absolutely stunning. Upon closer examination, I concluded it could have been her twin. When the diva turned and complimented my hair, which looked just like hers, I almost passed out.

My hair, some of which I bought, was slammin'—compliments of my stylist and only friend, Lisa, who'd been in the hair business since we graduated high school. Well- known in Detroit for creating new looks for very wealthy clients, she added two extra layers of ten-inch jet-black "silky strait" hair to my own tresses, which made the mane cascade down my back. Although I played my new look well, it did little to make me feel more secure about how God made me.

Vicki (Victoria's Secret) helped my 32-A boobs by adding extra fullness and cleavage with a padded push-up bra. St. John gave just enough sheen on a two-piece cream knit pantsuit to complement the bling on my wrist, fingers, neck, and ears. The suit jacket was a custom fit, thanks to my secret weapon, my tailor Vesta, who altered everything I put on my size four frame. She worked overtime to have the pantsuit ready with only a one-day window. Thankful, I lifted my glass in a silent toast to her and took a huge gulp.

The taste of the liquor made me gag. One more swig and things began to settle down. Resting on the bar, I casually picked up a couple cherries and ate them. Eyeing the barstool where the other lone female at the bar was sitting, I claimed it as my own once she left to dance. Leaning on it and making eye contact with the bartender I studied him for a few seconds. Appearing to be harmless, I sat down and engaged him in light conversation.

Gay, he had a unique twist on things and an extremely funny way of expressing himself. Animated with lots of slang, he spoke rapidly, with his hands flailing. Fun and entertaining, the bartender made me feel at ease as we swapped stories about our interests. Feeling the effects of the alcohol, I spoke freely, revealing I made a living interpreting songs into sign language, and had recently been selected from a long list of candidates to interpret for the hearing-impaired at a funeral service for a prominent political figure in D.C.

Impressed, the bartender asked me to interpret the song that was playing. I convincingly explained that an uptempo hip-hop mix was not easily interpreted. Letting me slide, he made me promise to interpret the next slow song played. Agreeing, I hoped he'd forget.

A bartender for several years, Dante was seasoned with "wooing" strangers. It was part of the trade and a practiced skill that routinely filled his tip jar. Tonight though was different; he really enjoyed my company and the conversation we were having was genuine.

"You are too funny. I'm glad I sat down."

"Me too, you make an otherwise boring night interesting." Dante winked at me and then smiled. Returning his smile, I paid attention as he pointed out some of the full bottles of liquor—waiting for me to make a selection, on the house. Shaking my head no, I grabbed a few peanuts and nibbled on them as our conversation continued.

Sharing openly, we discovered our many similarities. Both of us loved Shrimp on the Barbie from Outback Steakhouse and Jack Daniel's Grilled Salmon from Friday's. We also loved the same sweets, same boutiques, and the same kind of men—tall, dark and handsome.

Lots of those men were present tonight. Dante, my "new best friend," pointed out the ones he personally knew had skeletons, adding, "I know where the bodies are buried." His timely wit kept me laughing.

Several of them with secrets nodded in Dante's direction, but avoided him at the bar. Down-low brothers, many of them athletes, were in abundance at the party tonight and he generously pointed out those he'd slept with. Each had beautiful women on their arms. He also informed me some of the women, feminine and gorgeous, were intimate with each other when not on the arms of the athletes.

When the athletes were on the road these bewitching women kept one another's beds warm. Not to be played, also while on the road Mr. Athlete often sent for the one he did not live with. No one told the other and no one felt obligated to do so. This triangle, though complex, was intriguing and I wanted to know more.

"Do they ever sleep together? I mean all three of them?" My new friend sensed more than mere curiosity.

"You go both ways or what?" Shocked by his blunt insinuation, it took me a minute to answer.

"No. Why?"

"Maybe you do and don't know it!" His frankness and the subject matter made me feel uneasy. Squirming, I looked away to regroup.

"I have never gone the other way and I am not interested!" I retorted matter-of-factly. Certain I was lying, Dante stared at me. A pause, a long stare followed by a snap thing with his hands, preceded a sassy, "Alrighty then!"

All that drama was hilarious. Now two Sex on the Beaches later, I was in out-of-control giggle mode. We laughed hysterically at everything either of us said. Each time Dante said something that might be funny it became downright sidesplitting. At one point I laughed so hard I toppled off the barstool.

Helping me up, Dante realized I had consumed too much liquor and cut off my drinks for the night. The cup of black coffee that he poured for me was freshly brewed and piping hot. Placing it on a saucer, he slid it in front of me and laid some packets of sugar and cream on a napkin next to my spoon.

"Yuk! I hate coffee." Looking at me with disgust, Dante rolled his eyes and continued to wait on his customer. Slowly raising the cup to my lips, I sipped a little and gasped.

"It's too hot and it tastes awful." Ignoring me, Dante dropped an ice cube in my coffee and went back to tending bar. After it cooled, I guzzled the entire cup and sat there numb waiting to sober up. An hour later, a little more sober and a lot more tired, I decided to look for Dakota. Before walking away we exchanged numbers, excited about keeping in touch.

Finding Dakota was easy. I simply followed the noise.

"To the love of my life...consider this a beginning, not an ending." The room erupted in "here-here" as everyone present raised a glass to toast the man of the hour. Not wanting to be left out, I grabbed a glass of champagne and lifted it as well, but refrained from drinking a drop.

Working her way through the crowd, Dakota walked over and hugged me. I froze. I could not remember if or when we had ever embraced. The affectionate gesture made me uncomfortable and the moment was awkward. At first I thought my cousin had consumed too much liquor, but upon closer examination I realized that was not the case. With her arm still around me, she spoke and there was no hint of alcohol on her breath. The fact that she embraced me by choice was endearing; a moment I never forgot.

"You having a good time?" Still reeling from the embrace I simply nodded.

"So, you meet anybody special tonight?" Dakota asked coyly.

"Uh, I got a few numbers," I lied, too embarrassed to admit that with the exception of one or two lesbians, no one even glanced my way.

Dakota grabbed me by the hand and pulled me in the direction of the guest of honor who was surrounded by his boys and several of his former teammates—laughing and teasing him. As we got closer, I tensed up. Sensing I was nervous Dakota gripped my hand even tighter and glanced at me reassuringly.

Once in the area where the guys were huddled we joined in the laughter. To my surprise, they were nice and really friendly, including me in their conversation about life and their careers. Enjoying the camaraderie Dakota and I hung around and chatted for a couple minutes with the group, and then she stepped away to cut the cake.

When she did, a very tall, very handsome teammate of Collin's began to talk to me about my height and athletic abilities. Quite nervous, I conversed with him for a couple minutes and then excused myself, retreating to the restroom to call Val. Fumbling through my itty-bitty clutch bag that Val made me bring (I prefer purses large enough to carry my life in) I located my cell and dialed the number.

"Hey, Ma. Wake up! You gotta hear this! Ma…you sleep?" Val grunted and mumbled something inaudible. The line went dead. Staring at the phone, I flipped it closed and then looked in the mirror. Pressing my lips together, I wiped the mascara smudge from under my left eye and took a deep breath.

After smoothing the edges of my hairline, I returned to Dakota's side and fell right back in with the crowd. This time some of the divas engaged me in conversation, but I found it difficult to focus because my mind wandered back to the conversation I'd had with Dante. While I pondered if these women were gay, it dawned on me they might be wondering the same about me!

Trying to clear my mind, I struck up a conversation with another woman who walked up. During a brief lull in our discussion, I looked around and noticed Dakota standing behind me chatting with a well-known ball player and waved. In a split second I overheard him say something so cruel it sent me bolting from the room.

"Dakota, you lyin'! You talkin' 'bout the one with the zits? That's a woman? Get outta here! No way," he said adamantly. Putting her hand over his mouth to silence him, Dakota elbowed him in an attempt to keep him from going any further. Inebriated, he moved her hand and continued.

"I thought that was a man in drag. This is unbelievable!" Pulling Dakota over to his boy, who happened to be standing closer to me, he pointed in my direction and said, "That's Dakota's cousin... I mean, first cousin, and it's a woman!" He burst into laughter at the expression on his boy's face. An expression of disdain and disbelief!

Stunned by what he'd said, Dakota turned to look at me. Amid the chuckles and gasps, I broke the heel of my shoe as I hurriedly pushed past the bodies that were now blurred from the tears I forbid to fall.

Flashbacks of these same painful times in my childhood forced me to my knees the second I entered the ladies room. Bolting the door behind me, I sobbed uncontrollably.

"Rochelle, my God, I am so sorry!" Frantically twisting the doorknob Dakota begged for access. "Please let me in," she pleaded. Ignoring her pleas, I continued to cry.

"He was drunk! What he said doesn't matter. Ignore him...

please...ignore him!" Waiting for me to open the door or at least respond audibly to her pleas, my cousin leaned on it and listened. Realizing she was not going to gain access to console me and she had guests waiting, she decided to return to the party. But before she did, she turned once more to the bathroom door, leaned into it and through the crack spoke ever so softly just above a whisper.

"Ro, I love you for you," hoping that would be of some consolation. As in the past the only thing that would be of any consolation to me was time—alone!

CHAPTER 6

Throughout my life people wondered if I was a girl or a boy. Kids—outspoken, honest and curious, did not hesitate to question my gender. The majority of them teased me and called me names (ugly included), and they still echoed in my mind.

Coming out the womb almost the height of an average one-year-old, I had a difficult time adjusting to being six to ten inches taller than anyone comparable to my age. It was a hard task and one I never mastered. A loner, my imaginary friends became my solitude.

When I turned six, it was those imaginary friends who comforted me after I became painfully aware of just how unattractive I was. Often times people fail to realize the power of their words. Whether or not the words spoken by my mother while gossiping with her friends were spoken from her heart did not matter to me. Her words made me very aware of how unattractive my own mother thought I was and that revelation scarred me for life.

"I hope that girl grows into her looks or she's going to have a hard time gettin' a man." Nodding in agreement, Val's friends also offered equally scathing accounts of how dismal my future looked if I didn't outgrow my "ugly duckling" appearance.

"Why she had to come out so black and looking like her daddy is beyond me," my mother said sounding very disappointed. One friend reached over and sympathetically patted her hand, assuring Val she understood how painful it must be.

"She's young. Her looks might change…besides, she can always get plastic surgery."

"Yeah…," Val answered unconvinced, as she contemplated the reality of that thought. "Even if she did, what can be done about that *dark* skin?"

Although young, I knew what plastic surgery was. I'd seen plenty of stories about it on TV. The fact that this woman thought my looks needed surgical enhancement to make me pleasing to the eye, especially a man's eye, left me mortified. And if that was not enough pain to heap on a young child, Val spoke of my skin complexion with such disdain, it left me wishing I were born white—not a lighter-skinned black person, but pure white.

My mother was a very attractive dark-skinned woman who had her own issues. The only "darkie" with kinky hair in a house full of light-skinned women with long "good hair" left her scarred and jaded. Unaware of her own beauty, she married the first man who came along, daily regretting her decision.

When a new wave of black consciousness invaded the psyche of African Americans, Val woke up and realized she was a very sexy and attractive woman. But by then it was too late to take back her decision to marry a very dark and unattractive man whom she cared about, but did not love.

My dad was a good man, a great provider and very predictable. Boring was how my mother often referred to him. As wonderful as he was, she secretly wished she'd married an attractive man with means, preferably light-skinned. Ugly, dark children would be teased and tormented like she was growing up; something she could not bear to see her offspring endure.

Her first birth resulted in a medium complexion, very attractive boy who favored her. Less than a year later the stillborn birth of her second child, a dark-complexioned boy who looked just like my dad, did not affect her at all. Relieved he did not live to be tormented about his color, she thanked God for sparing him. Nine years later she birthed me. So imagine how devastated she was when she first laid eyes on her third child, a very dark, very masculine-looking girl.

Sadly, realizing I was the ugly duckling in a family of swans made me wish I had never been born. With my one real friend, Lisa, seldom home due to a shared custody agreement between her parents, I turned to my imaginary friends for comfort. They always knew just what to say to make me feel better and they could care less about the color of my skin or how I looked. That made our times together so much fun. Our conversations and adventures were private and never discussed with anyone, Lisa included.

My imaginary friends were smart and calculating. Their influence over me was powerful, often times encouraging me to make costly decisions I later regretted. Such was the case the night I overheard my mother's account of my looks!

The scratchy sound of the toothpick-looking stick with red on the tip that smelled like sulfur each time I dragged it across the rough surface of the cardboard box that contained it, and many more like it, was intriguing. Several times I slowly scraped the stick along the sandpaper path on the side of the box and watched as it shot small flashes of light followed by billows of smoke rings.

"Wow!" I exclaimed as I watched the stick begin to turn into a beautiful orange and red flame. Lifting the burning match in the air and watching its colors change continuously as it burned down the shaft toward my fingers, I stared at it in amazement.

"Ow!" was all I managed to scream when the flame reached my fingers. Letting go of the burning match I watched it fall to the floor, immediately igniting a pile of rags nearby. The rapidly moving orange and red flames frightened me.

"What have you done now," I asked myself in the same tone and manner my mother would (whenever I messed up) before grabbing me by the arm and beating the life out of me with a belt.

Rather than be subjected to that abuse, I quickly moved away from the flames to the far corner of the laundry room, cowered in a corner under the laundry tub, and began to cry. Smoke and the intense heat took my breath away, forcing me to pass out.

Moments later, yellow arms pulled me from my hiding place and carried me from the flames to a waiting gurney. Gasping and coughing incessantly from the smoke inhalation, I fought hard to find air in my lungs as the fireman attached an oxygen mask and began to check my vitals.

Half frightened from the realization of what I'd done and even more frightened from the realization of what Val would do to me, I pee'd my pants and then burst into tears. Consumed with fear, I pulled the mask away from my nose and mouth and screamed for my dad.

Hearing my piercing cries for his presence, Rodney unsuccessfully tried to push his way through the police officers who were keeping him at bay from the flames and me. In an effort to comfort me and assure me he would be by my side soon, he called out to me. The sound of his voice calmed me and my tears began to subside. Whimpering, I sat up on the gurney and looked around frantically for him; hopeful he would rescue me.

That hope quickly faded when I saw my mother standing in front of me without an ounce of compassion in her facial expression. With my heart beating rapidly I began to cry, certain the beat down I feared was now just seconds away.

Plopping down on the gurney I covered my eyes and wailed. The firemen refused to allow her to approach; informing Val she could comfort me once they were done treating me. Fully aware my mother's wrath would be worse than having died in the fire, I could not help but wish I had perished with our home.

Fortunately for me, the only memory of the physical and emotional upheaval I suffered that night is that of being smacked in the face by Val moments before Rodney rushed over to hold me in his arms. Being held by him throughout the night as I lay in my hospital bed, helped to erase the thoughts of praying for death. But his holding me did little to ease the pain of knowing my mother mistreated me because I looked like him!

CHAPTER 7

All children are born to grow, to develop, to live, to love, and to articulate their needs and feelings. For their development children need the respect and protection of adults who take them seriously, love them, and honestly help them to become oriented in the world. Children naturally expect those who love them to protect and nurture them. I held this expectation of my parents.

Children subjected to abuse develop maladaptive, anti-social and self-destructive behaviors and thoughts while trying to understand the situation and why the abuse is happening. As most abused children do, I assumed it was my fault. Rodney's silence in this matter confirmed it was; yet I hoped he'd say otherwise. He never did. Afraid to broach the subject, I opted to discuss it with my imaginary friends instead.

Our concluding it was my fault brought some sense of control and a little relief. Coming up with a list of what I did to cause the abuse and what could be done differently to avoid any future slaps or tongue lashings (lying was high on that list), I began to develop a range of maladaptive behaviors which would most definitely become pathological problems.

Avoiding contact with other children, Dakota included, caused me to become deprived of many skills necessary to navigate the social world. My entire concept of relationships started to become distorted, eventually leading to problematic interaction with schoolmates and other children. No one liked me and vice versa.

In addition to distorting my thoughts, the abuse became debilitating. I lived in constant fear. Afraid to do anything new because of the possibility it would lead to a violent attack, I withdrew from life and went into a shell. In time, I began to lose my sense of curiosity and wonder of the world. My innocence crushed, I stopped exercising my mind and trying new things.

All human beings suffer painful experiences, and some of these occur in childhood. Val's childhood demons often surfaced and left her enraged. Angry for numerous reasons, her painful childhood being one and my unattractiveness being another, she often unloaded her venom through violent physical contact with me.

A backhanded slap, a shoe thrown at my head, or skin pinched and twisted until it drew blood, were just some of the patterns of abuse I suffered at my mother's hands. Verbal abuse was also spewed twenty-four-seven. To her credit, Val never called me ugly to my face, but everything she did made me fully aware she thought I was.

Each whack across the face caused tears to flow freely, but I quickly learned not to cry out. Crying out would surely yield more whacks, so I bit my lip, ran to my bedroom, covered my head with my pillow, and then cried myself into oblivion.

The comfort I found in my dad's arms was a wonderful Band-Aid. When it was safe, usually after Val had dialed a friend to tell how I had just pissed her off once again, Rodney would tip toe into my room, wipe my tears, sneak me some candy, kiss the swollen red area where the blow landed, and tip toe out!

The joy that always followed this "knight in shining armor"

gesture made up for the rivers I cried every day! He was my hero. His comforting me kept me from hating the fact that looking like him was the reason I was constantly abused.

Rodney found great joy in knowing I was his clone. For whatever reason, he seemed to overlook the fact that my looking like him was the source of my torment. Add insult to injury, he turned a blind eye to the physical and verbal abuse his wife heaped upon me while doting on and favoring my brother.

Unable to live with knowing I was being abused *and* my mother's light-skin-dark-skin issues, my brother left home the moment he graduated high school. Marrying anything that was not light, bright or nearly white was a choice he planned to make without our mother's intervention. Feeling sorry for me, he intervened from time to time when my mom tried to beat me into tomorrow. His moving out left me to fend for myself.

A nervous wreck from constantly walking on eggshells around Val, I developed premature acne at the early age of seven. By the time I was ten the zits looked more like boils filled with pus, a gross sight that made me extremely self-conscious and of course my mom disliked me even more!

Then there's Dakota, born with the pretty gene, she came out of the womb posin' and suckin' up to the camera. The only reason she failed at being a cover girl was because she did not have my height. Her stunning beauty and poise made it impossible for me to forget what I overheard my mother say. Knowing my own flesh and blood wished I looked half as pretty as Dakota helped me loathe myself and hate my cousin.

Now more than twenty years later and tired of being lost in Dakota's shadow, I decided—no, my mother decided—if you can't beat 'em, join 'em. And I did by taking full advantage of the party invite and getting to know the person I'd grown to hate for so long. To my delight, she turned out to be quite enjoyable.

Spending time with her became the highlight of my entire "thirty-something" years on earth. Nothing compared to the thrill and power I felt when we entered a room. It was an unbelievable rush! People sat up and took notice, which made me feel powerful and important.

It's a given, all eyes were on Dakota and people literally tripped over themselves to speak to her (usually about someone famous she'd been seen with), but I could not be ignored. A stylish dresser since the age of three I gravitated toward beautiful and lavish garments; something I could attribute to my parents. Val and Rodney dressed me in very pretty and expensive things to make up for my looks. Their goal was to draw attention to their daughter and the fact that I was a girl, one way or the other. If people did not pay attention to my looks, then they paid attention to my attire.

Many people described my look as busy; Dakota was one of them. Busy or not, it served its purpose and for that reason alone, I ignored what they said. I had a "Beverly Hills Kit:" an enormous collection of cubic zirconia rings, bracelets, earrings and necklaces, all of which I never left home without. The kit, along with my height, kept me from getting lost in Dakota's shadow. And, of course it was included in my packing for the big gala.

Preparing for Dakota's event was fun. Val and I really enjoyed it. Our relationship had grown into one of fear for me and acceptance (to a degree) for Val. No longer fearful of being hit constantly, I still grimaced from the verbal thrashings Val let fly whenever she felt like it. Being belittled by her now that I was an adult hurt just as much as it did when the kids tortured me during my childhood.

Nevertheless, I managed to get past each hurtful moment with a feigned smile. These times I now spent with my mother were moments I dreamed about and never expected to materialize. The fear that now plagued me was abandonment from her "kindness" if I messed up or did not do what she commanded. To avoid being cast aside, I tread water very carefully and worked overtime to make sure nothing went wrong.

Accepting I would never be "Miss America" eventually helped Val to be more accepting of me, and my looks. In time she stopped inflicting physical harm on me, but continued with the emotional abuse—just not as frequently.

Getting to know me, Val discovered my "twisted" mind. Having someone whose thoughts were as jaded as hers was exciting and she welcomed my devious mindset and opinions, as long as they coincided with hers.

Often the two of us plotted a rival's demise and celebrated the victory through shopping sprees. Most of the *rivals* were women Val deemed a threat to her position and prominence in the community or at church. Anyone who opposed my mom's decisions on the Pastor's Aide committee (of which she was the presiding chair), or disagreed with her block club decisions (also a group she headed), felt her wrath. And I was there to assist in the twisted plot, thankful that my mother finally included me in her life.

As time went on, the daughters of these same women became targets for me, especially when one of them showed up at the church anniversary in an outfit far less expensive than the one I wore, but way more physically attractive than me.

"Do you see what she has on?" I whispered in my mother's ear.

"Don't worry about it…we'll deal with her later," Val responded assuredly and then turned to smile at the unsuspecting victim as she complimented her outfit. Without fail, within a week the unsuspecting victim was removed from the respective committee and her position was magically eliminated.

Another person we often deceived was Rodney. His relentless obsession with penny-pinching our finances was difficult to stomach. Rather than do so, we routinely excluded him from any plans or activities that involved spending money. Purchases made were placed on credit cards he had no knowledge existed. The billing statements were forwarded to a post office box and paid in secret.

Without Rodney's permission or knowledge, we went way over budget shopping for my party outfit to ensure what I wore would make those who had means think I did, too.

"Ma, you sure I should get this? It cost so much!"

"Let me worry about the cost. I want you to steal the show from Dakota!" Not certain that was possible, but hopeful just the same, I eagerly picked matching shoes and earrings.

Full of anticipation and excitement, I packed three large pieces of luggage, uncertain what other outfits and shoes to take along. Complicating the matter was the difference in the warmer temperature in Atlanta, versus the chilly weather we were experiencing in Detroit.

Safely tucked away in Dakota's guest bedroom after a long flight delay and late arrival to Atlanta, I called Val and had one of the two heart-to-heart conversations we'd ever shared.

"Hey...made it safely."

"Great! What took so long?" Val asked sounding upset. She was probably thinking that I'd done something to sabotage my arrival. Explaining thunderstorms in Georgia delayed the take-off, I went on to give a rundown of the half-hour we circled the Atlanta airport before landing, due to air traffic congestion.

"You okay?"

"Yeah, Ma, but I'm a little nervous."

"Of what? Nobody will have on your St. John...you'll steal the show."

Giggling and trying to believe her, I asked sheepishly, "You think so?"

"Yeah and you snatch one of those rich men for yourself, you hear me?"

Like a schoolgirl, I responded affirmatively, but deep down I knew few men found a woman who looked like a man in drag attractive.

From time to time I considered plastic surgery to get rid of my big nose, masculine looks and acne-scarred skin. But, when I found the courage and mentioned getting rid of Rodney's face for one that looked more like a Rochelle, my dad had a fit. Running to get his Bible, he flipped through the pages until he found a scripture that lent credence to his stance; which was I should not alter what God gave me.

One time he told the story of a woman who was nearly killed by an oncoming automobile, but God snatched her out of the jaws of death. Pleased to have a second chance at life, she decided do everything her heart desired. First she got breast implants, followed by a tummy tuck and lyposuction. Still not pleased, she had her teeth capped, a cleft added in her chin, cheek implants, eye and face-lift, and a nose job. Several months later she stepped off the curb and was instantly killed by an oncoming car. When she met God at Heaven's gate, she asked why did He not snatch her from death one more time. He simply replied, "I did not recognize you."

A somewhat religious man, Rodney often quoted scripture and "the good Lawd," but *never* failed to do so when it suited his purpose. The scripture he quoted to convince me altering what "the good Lawd" gave me was an abomination actually did not mean that at all. Later, when I read it for myself, it was clear the passage he read did not address plastic surgery. But for some reason, I could not put my dad's feelings aside to satisfy my own, so I kept the face "the good Lawd" gave me.

Somehow, Dakota made all my issues seem okay: my masculine looks, my insecurities—even my idiosyncrasies. When around her, *poof*, in an instant the pain and self-loathing was gone. She had a way of making me feel wanted and appreciated; something I'd never felt before.

And talk about fun! I was certain she created the word, capitalized it, and then put the periods behind each letter before adding the exclamation point at the end. Life—my life, now that my "big cousin" was a part of it, was more fun and fulfilling than I could have ever imagined it would be!

CHAPTER 8

The big gala Dakota threw for Collin was just the beginning of hanging with my cousin and good times yet to come. On several occasions, she surprised me with a buddy pass and we'd hop on a flight to Milan to shop. After doing damage there, we'd take a train to Florence and do more damage. A month or two later, we were off to France and the fun never stopped.

Two years later we were still jet-setting. Now senior enough to bid the better schedules, Dakota spent her numerous days off talking, laughing, and just kickin' it with *moi*. With her play brother in love and no longer available to hang, I quickly became the ornament on her side and to my satisfaction we went everywhere together.

Dakota honestly loved spending time with me. Every chance she got she sent me a buddy pass to meet her at one major event or another. Compassionate and very aware of my displeasure with my entire being, she worked overtime to try to help me boost my self-esteem and confidence.

During one of the weekends I visited her in L.A., Dakota surprised me and paid for a complete makeover to give my confidence a lift. The celebrity makeup artist took time to show me how to apply makeup to minimize the features I disliked, such as my extremely wide nose and deep-set jowls. And, she also took time to teach me how to push to the forefront my best assets—my smile and my eyes.

A stunning difference, I messed up the makeover by crying after seeing myself as an *attractive woman* for the first time in my life. That camouflage only lasted as long as the makeup did. By morning, even though I didn't wash my face the previous night, my makeup had pretty much faded, as had my confidence. But, the lasting impression of how much my cousin really cared remained.

A month after my makeover, Dakota sent me a sample of a skin care line the makeup artist recommended and suggested I try it. In less than two weeks, I saw drastic changes in my skin. Seven weeks later, my acne was completely gone. Suffice it to say I now believed Dakota walked on water and had tea with Jesus!

Hating to be away from her, I gave serious thought to moving to Los Angeles. Even though I was an adult, there was a childlike desire in me to be around someone who showed me so much compassion and kindness. Starved for attention and love, I felt completely empty when Dakota was not around.

When I mentioned my "thoughts" of moving west to Rodney, he faked a heart attack and remained in the hospital until I assured him it was a passing thought. At the time it was not, but thanks to a new husband in Dakota's life, it quickly took on that premise.

I was with Dakota when she met her husband. Kevin North was a nice guy and equally nice on the eyes. Dante was manning the bar the night she spotted him at a fundraiser in Atlanta. One of the few non African-American men in the room, he was extremely good looking, very well dressed with a European flair—something that gets her where she lives. The two of us watched Dakota cast out the line and reel this fish in.

"She'll be throwing him back in the water real soon," Dante leaned over and whispered to me. Rumor was Kevin could not be trusted when left to his own vices.

Months later, while gossiping with Dante on the phone, Dakota's relationship surfaced in the conversation. It was then Dante revealed Dakota's husband had skeletons; lots of female drama with lawsuits crawling out the woodwork. Most of the lawsuits were for sexual harassment, but a female who claimed to have contracted an STD from him also had filed.

"You think I should tell her?" I asked Dante sincerely.

"You have to decide that one."

"Honestly, I don't see this going very far," I admitted.

"Well, guess that answered it!" Dante quipped.

Uncertain what to do with the delicate information, I chose to keep quiet and let fate take its course.

Kevin's office was located in Houston and he and Dakota shared a commuter marriage for nearly a year. When he landed a contract for one of the Lakers' newest superstars his office relocated to Hollywood, which meant he was home all the time—*and in my way*.

Prior to his living in Los Angeles, I had become very comfortable with spending nearly all my free time with Dakota, usually in L.A. However, in recent months, excited about having her husband home, she spent as much time with him as he would allow. That meant little or no time for me. Frustrated and hurt, I called Dante to complain.

"Look, I know I shouldn't have…but I took it personal when I called to say I was on my way to hang, and Dakota informed me it was not a good time. Without saying how I really felt, I pretended to understand and told her to call me when it was okay to come. I never imagined two months would go by before she called and when she did, it was just to say 'whuzzup'!"

"Umph!" Dante said in disgust. "You going to tell her how you feel?"

"Naw, if what you told me is true, then like you said, she'll be throwing that fish back in the water real soon." We laughed and switched the conversation.

A year later, Dakota found out the hard way her husband could not be committed to her and their vows. From time to time rumors would surface that tied her mate to one female after another. The latest buzz was his very public affair with a reigning beauty queen from Michigan, who happened to be black. "Once black, you never go back" must be true, she mumbled.

Catching him not once, but several times with evidence that indicated he was cheating, confirmed what she'd been hearing. Suspecting her handsome husband who makes a living keeping the dirty laundry of the professional athletes he represents out of the press, had been doing the same scheming himself. Not willing to take this lightly, Dakota set out to find answers by hiring a private detective.

Weeks, then months, went by. "Nothing to report," the detective told her. Several months later when her female spy still had nothing concrete to share, she terminated their contract. That's when the newly hired male detective found out Kevin was sleeping with the female spy Dakota had just fired, and he really was having a very open public affair with the beauty queen.

Blindsided because she thought the voluptuous six-foot-one black female would be the professional her card stated, she was taken aback to discover differently. No doubt, Kevin was wonderful eye-candy and fantastic in bed, but she had not realized until now how much and how often he manipulated those attributes to get what he wanted. "Is nothing sacred?" She sighed as she sat down to look at the photos her newly hired detective had taken.

Days after that revelation, the bottom fell out of the extremely comfortable life Dakota enjoyed. An anonymous letter arrived with a newspaper photo of her husband holding hands with the beauty queen at a quaint SoHo restaurant in New York. The caption referred to her as his *new love* and questioned whether wedding bells were on the horizon. Not waiting for the answer to that question Dakota immediately filed for divorce. Bitter and not about to give up her lifestyle, she asked for Kevin's balls on a silver platter! That request guaranteed a long and hard-fought battle with him.

Excited about the possibility of having Dakota all to myself once more, I could not have been happier when I heard she decided to call it quits, vowing never to be tied down again. Hiding my elation, I called to confirm the rumor.

"You sure you want to do this?" I asked, half-heartedly.

"I can't take it anymore. Blind, yeah, I might be. But stupid I'm not!"

Confronted with his wife's demands Kevin retaliated. Without any explanation offered or a question asked, Mr. North moved out of their luxury home and discontinued all communication with his wife. To ensure his soon-to-be ex did not get his balls on a silver platter, he emptied out his personal bank accounts, cashed in his entire stock portfolio, and liquidated the majority of his personal assets.

At their divorce hearing, he never glanced her way and fought every dime she asked for. Devastated by his treatment, Dakota bit her lip and made every effort to stay composed throughout the proceedings. Ending her marriage on such a sour note hurt tremendously. However, the hefty sum the court ordered him to pay her eased her discomfort more and more with each monthly check she received. Now this!

Nine months after the divorce and weeks after finally beginning to enjoy the single life, Dakota's ex-husband disappeared. "It will be a rainy day in hell before you get another dime of my hard-earned money," was the last thing she heard him say on the phone before the line went dead and he went missing. Up to now she had dismissed what he said as just mere words—an empty threat. How wrong she was!

Kevin had not been seen or heard from in over three months. His staff, close friends, and the sheriff attempting to arrest him for contempt of court failed to locate him. He'd simply fallen off the face of the earth, and for Dakota, who depended on that hefty spousal support, that was not good news.

The Norths' mutual assets had been divided by the court in Dakota's favor, but it took a steady cash flow to maintain her spoils. In an effort to stay afloat, she'd sold their luxury autos, downsized to a more affordable used Benz for herself and pawned all the diamonds, platinum and gold he left behind. Selfishly she held onto her twelve-carat diamond bands. For now, this was her insurance policy; if needed she could pawn them for cash later. Of course, she would rather have them re-set in a cocktail ring, but necessity would dictate which way that situation unfolded.

In the meantime, Dakota spent a lot of time waddling in misery. When in the midst of a party for one, most call it a pity-party, the right ambiance is necessary. A dark room, a gloomy song softly playing, old pj's, a comfortable bed, favorite alcoholic beverage and a shoulder to cry on are mandatory. Thankful she felt my shoulder would do, I caught the next flight to Los Angeles.

❤❤❤

The slightly parted window blind failed to keep the glare of the sunrise from entering her cocoon. Dakota, annoyed that I disturbed her doom and gloom ambiance by opening the blind, pulled the covers over her head in a futile attempt to shield her eyes (swollen twice their normal size) from the daylight that was beckoning her back to life. Try as it might, she wasn't having it.

Two days prior she would have eagerly rolled out of bed, put on her sweats and running shoes, grabbed her keys, effortlessly completed a two-mile power walk, hopped into her Benz and driven for a cup of java and a paper.

Returning to the comfort of her luxury home, she would have reclined on her chaise in the oversized master bedroom and turned on her favorite soap, *The Young and the Restless*. But that was two days ago.

Money now very short, Dakota was faced with having to find gainful employment. It had been quite some time since she'd labored in the work force. Success—her husband's—had not necessitated she do anything other than be a lady of leisure and that she did quite well.

"So what are you going to do?" I asked. Dakota stared at me and then motioned once more for me to close the blind. Ignoring her, I continued to unpack the overstuffed luggage I'd brought with me. After several minutes of silence, she sat up and answered my question.

"Not sure. Fortunately, I have plenty of designer shoes and clothes to keep me *looking the part*. But I have to eat and I gotta keep a roof over my head. How, is the question?"

Flopping back on the pillow, Dakota stared at the twelve-carat band she still wore on her ring finger. Playfully she held it to the sun that continued shining brightly through her bedroom window. A slight smile formed on her lips and then quickly disappeared when the telephone rang.

"How bad is it?" she asked her attorney.

"Let's just say, he needs to be found quickly. Your financial situation is grave and your time in that palace you call home is limited."

"I appreciate your honesty. Talk to you later."

It was apparent Kevin had been planning his departure for quite some time. All the bills, including the mortgage payment were in arrears. Dakota was facing foreclosure and had no resources to stop the process. She did not share the conversation she'd just had with her attorney, but it was obvious from her demeanor things were not going well. Drained of all emotion and tired of fighting a hopeless battle, she rolled over and pulled the covers over her head. Dakota knew what she had to do.

CHAPTER 9

The quaint bedroom she adored as a little girl seemed much smaller than it did back then. It had not changed and that made Dakota smile. Her heart warmed knowing her father had kept her room just the way she liked it. To her surprise, it felt good to be home!

"Dakota, get the phone," her father called out from the lower level.

"Okay, Dad, give me a minute." Dropping her purse and bags on the aqua carpeted floor, she lay across her bed to answer the phone.

"Hello? Oh hi, Auntie, you okay?"

Her favorite aunt was on the phone welcoming her home. It had been years since she'd seen her mother's only sister and she was happy to hear from her. They finished their brief conversation with Dakota wondering how her aunt knew she was back in Michigan. It didn't take long to learn the answer.

"I called your aunt to let her know you had come home," her father volunteered. "She always asks about you and I knew she'd be upset if she heard it in the streets first."

This infuriated Dakota. Her unshakable pride had not allowed her to tell anyone (but me) she was facing foreclosure and was penniless. She wished her father had not been so zealous and given her an opportunity to let the entire situation settle in her spirit. Realizing he meant well, Dakota simply smiled and went back to her room. Once there, she slowly began to unpack her life, which had been reduced to several small boxes and a few pieces of luggage.

After three days of unpacking and sulking, she called me with hopes I would want to go out.

"Hey! When did you get here?" I asked.

"Three days ago," Dakota responded dryly.

"Three days ago! Why are you just now calling me?"

"Unpacking and trying to come to grips with all of this."

Although I understood, it genuinely hurt that my cousin had been in town for three days and had not notified me. Feeling left out of the loop, I questioned whether Dakota really cared about me like I hoped. Afraid of the answer, I dropped it.

❤❤❤

Ginopolis on a Tuesday night was the spot. The Detroit Pistons were known to congregate there after home games and the skeezers were there to meet and greet them. Always wanting to go but too afraid to do so, I suggested we try there.

Donning a brand-new Tracy Reese outfit, I added a fabulous pair of chandelier-style earrings that closely resembled the rhinestone and crystal accents in the jacket to complete my look.

Using the technique learned from the California makeup artist, I shadowed the corners of my nose and highlighted the bridge to make it look pointed. Eyes and lips painted to perfection, I felt beautiful as I stared in the mirror. Excitement and anticipation took hold as I imagined the Pistons player I had my eye on asking me to dance. In anticipation, I popped a mint in my mouth, grabbed my keys and headed to my car to pick up Dakota.

That exuberance lasted no longer than the time it took me to make the five-minute drive to my uncle's home. The instant I saw Dakota emerge from the house my euphoria vanished. We had on the same outfit in the same color—black. Problem was, Dakota's curves filled her two-piece pantsuit with sexy lumps and bumps in the places mine did not. Suddenly my desire to party disappeared.

Pretending not to feel well, I used that as an excuse for my lack of desire to hang and apologized. Disappointed, Dakota offered to follow me home in her car to make sure I made it okay. That made me feel like a louse. Caught in a lie, I agreed and drove home with her following behind. Once there, she got out and helped me to the door.

Curious, I asked about her plans for the night (now that I had backed out) and quickly backpedaled when she told me she was still going. Making a miraculous recovery, I rushed inside and changed clothes while Dakota waited in the car. In a flash I was fully dressed in a fresh Baby Phat outfit and hopped into the passenger seat to accompany my cousin to a night of sheer fun and excitement.

Many of the professional ball players seated in the VIP section were familiar to Dakota; a result of her days of hanging with her "play brother" on the NBA set. Greeted by the starting center, she hugged him and accepted his offer to join him and several other players at his table. Ill-prepared to be thrust into the heart of the action, I froze and became very introverted when we were seated.

When the player I imagined I would marry and have babies with joined us at the table, I became nauseated from the anxiety that continued to mount. Although he had to maneuver around a few bodies, Teddy Dunlap sat next to me and extended a hand to introduce himself.

Striking up a conversation that did not include more than the two of us, Dakota excused herself to dance, leaving us to a private moment. I was so nervous I couldn't breathe. Returning to find us slow dancing to Keith Washington's classic, "Kissing You," Dakota smiled and made herself scarce for the remainder of the night.

That was the beginning of the endless nights we spent at Ginopolis. Two months later, we were considered regulars. A table was always waiting for us along with our first round of drinks— on the house. Every Tuesday night we hung at Ginopolis and sometimes managed to squeeze in a Friday or Saturday. Short on disposable cash, Dakota worked the room and seldom paid for her meal or any additional drinks. Sometimes I benefited as well.

Whenever there was a home game, I took extra time to apply my face with hopes *my man* would pick that night to ask for my number. After walking me to the car three months from the night I met Teddy, he did. Opening the driver door, he waited until I was seated and had started the engine before popping the question. Dakota wisely stayed back until he left.

"Girl...did I just see you pass him your number?"

Eyes bucked, I did not answer. Instead, I burst into laughter and pointed to my lap.

"What? What are you laughing about?"

Still laughing in between gasps for air, I admitted in the excitement of the moment I peed in my leather pants. Laughing heartily, we sat and replayed what happened over and over before driving home.

Wisely, I kept my secret lover from Rodney and Val. Our three-week telephone romance had blossomed into a real courtship by week four. On the road, he called me several times a day. In town, he called less frequently, but called just the same.

When we spoke, our conversations were warm and affectionate. The mutual attraction between us was obvious.

Dakota thought it strange that he never asked me out on a date and never spent time with me other than when the *three of us* met at Ginopolis, but she kept her thoughts to herself because I was so happy.

This whirlwind romance continued for five months and my confidence level exceeded even Dakota's expectations. Always dressed in a new designer outfit, I played the part of wealth and affluence well. So well, I began to tell lie after lie to keep up the façade.

Inevitably my lies caught up with me the night Teddy asked to stop by and chill at "my place" as we were about to leave Ginopolis. Having told him I lived in a luxury three-bedroom condo in Bloomfield Hills, I was at a loss as to how to deal with his request. Also absent from the truth were the numerous sexual encounters I led him to believe I had experienced; resulting in his thinking I had been around and knew how the game was played.

A fast thinker and quickly becoming a skilled liar, I told him Dakota was spending the night with me and offered to stop by his place instead. Rushing Dakota home, I broke speed limits getting to his condo off the water in downtown Detroit.

Since he'd wined and dined me for quite some time, Teddy needed some recovery from his investment and set the tone for the night by lighting scented candles, playing his favorite Kenny G jazz CD and chilling a bottle of Te Whare Ra Riesling.

Arriving just twenty minutes after he'd put the wine on ice, I nervously hugged him as I entered his place. The view of the Detroit River was breathtaking. His condo was on the penthouse level, which opened to a phenomenal panoramic view of Canada on the opposite side of the water.

Handing me a glass of wine he leaned in and kissed me before releasing his grip on the glass. Mouth closed, I allowed a peck on the lips and then gulped some wine as I turned to look out the window at the view and gather my wits.

Nervous and regretting coming, I focused on the view, but my mind tussled with a way to exit before he tried to take this romantic encounter any further. Sick to my stomach about the possibility of sleeping with him, I excused myself to the bathroom to buy some time.

A virgin who had never been kissed or held by a man, I felt disconnected. Although I had truly dreamt of this moment, the thought of him on me and in me made me ill. Bile rose to my mouth, followed by a burst of fluids mixed with my last meal. Shocked, I stood at the sink and stared at the mess in complete silence.

Minutes later a knock at the door jolted me back to my senses and the tears flowed. Concerned, Teddy knocked on the door again, opened it and peered in when I did not answer. Realizing I was ill, he sat me on the commode, ran a face cloth under cold water and began to dab my face, removing the pieces of food that had splattered on my cheeks and around my mouth.

Handing the cool rag to me, he left to retrieve a T-shirt and some of his sweats so I could change. Confused, frightened, and inexperienced, I dashed to the living room, grabbed my purse and ran to my car. Once there, I frantically searched for the car keys. Finding them, tears kept me from clearly seeing how to insert them into the ignition. Once I did, I sped out the parking garage.

Instead of going home, I drove straight to Dakota and woke her from a sound sleep. Too embarrassed to admit I'd been lying for five months about who I was and what I was about, I explained what happened, omitting my deception.

Unaware of my lies, my older and more experienced cousin tried to talk sense into me, pleading with me to reconsider my decision to leave Teddy hanging without attempting to offer an explanation. Silence filled the room when I snapped at Dakota and demanded she drop the entire subject.

Startled by my outburst, Dakota did, and did not broach the subject or hanging at Ginopolis again. A month later, we began to hang at Floods—a new set with fresh faces: doctors, lawyers and other high-profile professionals; none of them ball players.

Without missing a beat, we had a wonderful time. Wednesdays were the night of choice at Floods, and we were there religiously. More seasoned at being a social butterfly, I quickly made friends. The dance floor was a very comfortable place for me, especially after one or two drinks, so I often spent the majority of my night dancing.

After receiving a personal invite to a fundraiser being given by the Pistons' wives, Dakota asked me to attend, neglecting to inform me who was sponsoring the event. The entire club had been rented for the fundraiser and it was held on their usual Wednesday night.

An hour after arriving at Floods, Teddy walked up to me and

pulled me by my arm off the dance floor to a corner of the room. Angry, he accused me of being a tease, called me a few choice words and left as people watched.

Humiliated, I dashed to the ladies room, hid in a stall and tried to compose myself. Trying not to mess up my face, I fought back tears, dabbing them instantly as they formed in my eyes.

Once the ladies room fell silent, I exited the stall and slowly emerged, perusing the club in search of Dakota. Spotting her, I grabbed her arm and insisted we leave. Tired and ready to head home herself, she gladly agreed. En route, I told her what Teddy had done intentionally failing to give the reason why. Feeling awful about the encounter, Dakota pondered how to make it up to me for failing to tell me he might be there since it was a Pistons' wives event.

The fact that Dakota knew people in high places was a benefit to me most times, but this was not one of them. Contacting a friend, she managed to get Teddy's number. Assuming my lack of dating led to this blowup, Dakota convinced him to apologize and give it another try. Reluctantly he agreed, adding he did think I was a fun person to be around and maybe we could be buddies if nothing else. Jotting down my address, she gave him directions to our home before hanging up.

Rodney, apparently stunned that a man would be at his door asking to speak with his "pride and joy," did not offer Teddy a seat. Leaving him standing in the foyer, he informed me I had a guest. Unaware Teddy knew where I lived, I unsuspectingly walked to the door unkempt and without my face on.

Eyes meeting, we both stared in disbelief; me, because I was so busted; Teddy because he'd never seen me without makeup. Taken aback by my appearance and certain I was a man, he turned around and left feeling angry and deceived.

Realizing who he was Rodney returned to the foyer and began to question me. Unable to think up another lie, I did not answer, pushed past him, and retreated to my room where I remained for the rest of the day.

In the stillness that enveloped the atmosphere, I dealt with the situation by talking it out with my friends—the imaginary ones that came out to play whenever I needed them.

CHAPTER 10

Coming home to Romulus was strange. It had changed tremendously. Single-family home developments ranging in the upper $100's were springing up on every corner. The once lower-middle-class, all-black neighborhood had become an upper-middle-class neighborhood of mixed marriages—mostly black men with white women.

Dakota laughed at the irony as she wondered how Romulus would have greeted her if she'd returned with her white husband. Though wealthy, he was still white and many would perceive her as being a sellout!

Once beleaguered, Detroit had re-elected a young mayor whom the newspapers dubbed "Detroit's Hip-Hop Mayor," a label he did not find endearing. Under his leadership, things had changed primarily for the good (depending on who you asked). The biggest change was to be found in "The Village."

Indian Village, not quite on the level of Beverly Hills but prestigious nonetheless, was experiencing a transition. The "old money" was moving toward the more affluent suburbs, leaving their 3,000- to 12,000-square-foot sprawling mansions to be inhabited by the "new money"—baby boomers.

Located on Detroit's East Side and a comfortable distance

from the heart of downtown, historic Indian Village boasts a number of architecturally significant homes built in the early twentieth century. Most of the homes were built by prominent architects such as Albert Kahn, Louis Kamper and William Stratton for some of the area's most prominent citizens, including Edsel Ford. Many of the homes exceeded 12,000 square feet. Several were equipped with a carriage house, with some even being larger than an average suburban home.

A fun little neighborhood with presence, no other area of Detroit compared. It's unlike the suburban sprawl where everyone has a big garage dominating the front of the house and a little steel front door with a peephole, and a bunch of neighbors they've never even seen, let alone met. People here take time to get to know each other and often congregate at local block club meetings to catch up on what's going on in the neighborhood. Because baby boomers were taken by its ambiance "The Village" was rapidly becoming the place to live, work and play.

On every corner once abandoned shells were now thriving meeting places for young up-and-coming power players. Those in the know were gobbling up these "eyesores" and turning them into swank coffee and jazz houses, or chic hair salons with smoothie and espresso bars.

The latest trend—resale shops—were springing up in every neighborhood that had income levels averaging above six digits. Vintage clothing was in and though old, the new blood charged a small fortune for these previously worn threads and the players did not think twice about the asking price. This high price tag came with the territory and was part of the thrill of kickin' it in "The Village."

Brownstones were in demand. They sat on the outer boundaries of the streets that led to the sprawling mansions, lending prestige to their presence as well. The one that sat on the corner of Kercheval and Parker wasn't much to look at and needed a whole lot of fixin' up, but if one had avision you could see past the caved-in ceiling, rotted floors, peeling paint, and broken windows and doors.

This quaint historical structure reminded Be-Angeleke of a past relationship. He too wasn't much to look at, but if you could see past his exterior, he was a diamond in the rough. With a little TLC and a whole lot of fixin' up, he had major potential.

Moving him into her home and investing quite a bit of time and money in making him over, Be-Angeleke made him her new project. However, his need for fixin' outlasted her desire to fix him and she quickly booted him out and turned her energy toward a venture that was more of a sure thing—C'est Shee…With a Little He!

Be-Angeleke Lately, aka BL, always dreamed of owning a re-sale shop. She'd been unable to fulfill this dream on the salary she received as a manager for Blue Cross. Consequently, the quarter of a million dollars she received from a botched abortion presented the opportunity to make her dream a reality.

The grand opening of C'est Shee…With a Little He was the talk of the town. Its canopied entrance embraced oversized double doors with stained-glass panels, framed by massive columns that lent elegance and class to the otherwise mundane brick structure. Walking through the striking entrance, the interior was equally impressive. White fixtures and furniture accented the hand-painted metallic pewter walls.

In the center of the room sat a fabulous piece of workmanship, an oversized antique sofa that had been reupholstered in off-white ultrasuede. Given the name "The Couch," this work of art had been pitched for rubbish pickup by its previous owner, but a well-skilled craftsman restored it to its original grandness and now it majestically rested on its throne—an expensive hand-crafted white, silver-and-gray leather area rug.

Be-Angeleke had big hopes for this area of the boutique. If all went as planned, the couch would become a much used fixture within the walls of C'est Shee. It, coupled with the welcoming ambiance and relaxing aura, would hopefully become the meeting place for hours of "Shee Time"—a time set aside for girlfriends, new and old, to congregate, shop and then relax on "The Couch," unwinding and swapping stories before going home to retire for the evening.

Daydreaming, Be-Angeleke jumped when she heard the door chime and turned to see who was arriving a bit early to the grand opening festivities.

"What's up, Ro?" she exclaimed as she greeted me, the first to arrive. Towering over five-foot-four Be-Angeleke, I leaned down to meet her European-style greeting—a kiss on each cheek. After a momentary pause to look around, I gasped in awe. The interior was nothing like the first time I'd visited during the renovations.

"This is breathtaking! I can't believe it's the same place. Look at what you've done to these walls…this floor, oh wow, the entrance…" Moving farther into the room, my words tapered off as I focused on "The Couch." Pointing to the enormous centerpiece, I continued, "Tell me this is not the ugly duckling you found out back." Not waiting for an answer I ran my hand along its lines, reflecting on how it formerly looked.

"Yep! It sure is," Be-Angeleke affirmed proudly. Smiling, she handed me a glass of champagne and escorted me to a decadent display of food. As more people arrived, I sampled a few appetizers before moseying over to "The Couch" to get acquainted with the other guests who had now gathered to chitchat.

"Rochelle, I'm glad you could make it!" Looking in the direction of the voice that had just formally addressed me by my name, instead of Ro, I recognized my cousin. Standing to hug her, I watched Dakota work her way through the crowd paying close attention to her attire. As usual she looked fabulous, causing me to feel a little envious. Swallowing hard and taking a deep breath, I managed to suppress my resentment and smiled broadly.

"Girl, who you calling Rochelle?" I asked playfully, looking around as if Rochelle did not exist. "You know I prefer Ro," I reminded her as we hugged and then burst into laughter.

"So what do you think?" Dakota asked.

"This is so you…first class all the way!" Pleased everything turned out so wonderfully for the boutique, I hugged her once more.

"Well, let me just say for the record this was no day at the beach!" Dakota laughed and looked around the room feeling a sense of pride as she continued to speak. "BL and I worked our butts off to make this dream a reality." She smiled when her eyes rested on "The Couch."

Nodding in agreement, I chuckled as I thought about previous times I had stopped by to bring lunch. Dakota's rag-hag appearance on those days was very different from the glamour queen appearance she now displayed. Before I could tease her about that, Be-Angeleke grabbed her by the hand and led her to the rear of the boutique.

I felt a twinge of jealousy as I watched people in the room

admire Dakota as she walked by. Almost six years my senior, she looked a lot younger than I did. Her slim waist, round-tight butt, flat abs and sexy-cool style, gave the next generation—my peers and me—a run for our money. Adding her seniority to the equation, her poise and refinement were unmatched. When it came to Dakota, feelings of jealousy came easy to even the most confident women.

The media, well represented, asked question after question. Some centered on the unique name *C'est Shee* and what *"a little he"* meant. Be-Angeleke explained she loved the French language and *C'est Shee* meant she or female, and of course, *"a little he"* meant just what it said—a little somethin'-somethin' to draw in the male clientele. In hopes of capitalizing on their bank accounts as well, unique items like gemstone cuff links; croc, gator or stingray belts; and handmade Italian silk ties were housed separately in a handsome masculine display case for the men.

One reporter asked why Dakota and Be-Angeleke formed their partnership, while still others questioned what they hoped C'est Shee would bring to "The Village." Aware that Dakota was more seasoned at handling the press, Be-Angeleke eagerly deferred all questions to Dakota, the designated C'est Shee spokesperson.

"Tag, you're it," she said as she playfully tapped Dakota on the shoulder. They chuckled and the press joined in the laughter, finding Be-Angeleke's wit cute and catchy.

Dakota offered a brief synopsis of her friendship with Be-Angeleke, which began before they were teenagers. The nucleus of a friendship that had lasted over thirty years was formed when they both experienced the trauma of suddenly losing their mothers as young girls. Childhood dreams of owning a business gave them the fuel to overcome what seemed like insurmountable odds. A stick-to-it mindset and being in the right place at the right time made the boutique a reality.

Being at the right place at the right time was pure luck for Be-Angeleke. She frequented "The Village" and kept her eye on the brownstone she now leased. The concept for C'est Shee…With a Little He, an upscale clothing boutique, was birthed from Dakota's best friend's defunct venture, Tara's Closet.

Tara, an unhappily married mother of four, met Dakota shortly after she moved to California. Married to a street hustler for over a decade and with only a high school education and four kids, Tara felt trapped and hopeless. Dakota's positive outlook on life and her caring and easygoing demeanor made her easy to talk to. In no time Tara was pouring her heart out to Dakota and over the years a lasting friendship was forged.

Pre Dakota, Tara made shopping her best friend. To fill the void her routinely "missing in action" husband created, spending money gave her a sense of pride and accomplishment. Paying a professional to come in and revamp her double-wide walk-in closet gave her a rush. She felt comforted each time she hung her designer threads in the very neat, well-organized space that closely resembled an upscale boutique.

Post Dakota, things changed. Tara still shopped frequently, but purchased fewer things because she found her time and attention was being better served by focusing on improving herself. Dakota motivated her; so much so that she began to work out.

The changes she sought in her figure did not transpire overnight and with no change in her "love life" she gave up working out. No longer a shopaholic she found a new companion—food.

Constantly alone with only her two boys and two girls to keep her bed warm at night, she ate herself to sleep. In less than two years her four-foot-nine frame ballooned from 110 pounds to 190 pounds. Suffice it to say sizes two, four, six and eight sat in her closet on hangers with the tags still attached.

In denial about her weight, Tara continued to buy clothing that was excessively small, until one fateful night. Walking in her nightgown past the floor-length mirror, she caught a glimpse of herself and reality set in. Deep cellulite dimples played connect-a-dot on her behind. Her sagging breasts were hard to define from her protruding stomach. Disgusted with her appearance, this reality check brought her shopping momentum to an abrupt halt.

Unfortunately, after a short respite she was back in the stores, only this time she was shopping for someone new; the four-foot-nine, 190-pound Tara. Not certain of her size and in too much denial to find out, she bought an entire new wardrobe, all size twelve. Afraid to try them on, the new garments sat in her closet along with her used-to-be buddies—sizes two, four, six and eight—and her shopping addiction resumed.

By the time Tara and Dakota were best friends, Tara could not fit into sixteens. Depressed, tired and plagued by tons of health issues (heart palpitations, high blood pressure and borderline diabetes), Tara was still not motivated to seriously drop the weight. However, with her dear friend always obsessing about working out she decided to try it.

For motivation, Dakota hung one of Tara's favorite photos of Halle Berry on her refrigerator. In the photo, Halle was wearing an outfit similar to a size six one that Tara had hanging (unworn) in her closet, tags attached. "Seeing is believing!" Dakota reminded her daily.

After several months, the brainwashing began to yield some results. One day, Tara went to the fridge at least ten times, opened it, grabbed something unhealthy to eat, and closed it. Halle's photo slapped her back to reality and she returned her ill-fated selection back eight of the ten times. Not bad. Now consciously aware of her eating habits, gradually she began to shed the pounds.

Most of the expensive designer pieces were purchased at full price and could have been returned, but once in her closet Tara was not about to take them back. From time to time she'd remove them from the hanger, hold them to her body and stare at herself in the mirror, wishing she were that small once again. Her imagination would take over placing her at a concert, front row and drop-dead gorgeous in the outfit she was holding, and on the arm of her husband. In her mind, she was the envy of all his *hoes* who would be scattered throughout, *but not in the front row.*

Tara did a great job of losing most of her weight. Thrilled with her new size-ten frame, she decided to say "bye-bye" to her closet of mixed sizes by having a garage sale. However, the night before the sale she sat and pondered what she was doing. When she finally drifted off to sleep she had a dream; the result birthed an upscale designer resale shop, Tara's Closet.

The money Tara's husband gave her as a weekly allowance was tucked away while she looked for a building. When she found a location in the 'hood that sat on a corner with a large parking lot, she signed the lease agreement and began to decorate.

Finding a sense of pride and independence, she plunged into her new venture without depending on her husband's financial assistance. Dakota was with her from the inception to the grand opening.

Tara's Closet was an instant success. Women were thrilled to be able to purchase Hilfiger, DKNY, Gucci and Versace at rock-bottom prices. Other women, most in Tara's former weight predicament, brought in their designer threads to be sold on consignment. Thriving for three years, Tara's Closet became a hot spot for great fashion finds. Her sense of pride and accomplishment gave her a different outlook on life and she became quite content with her husband not being around.

Sensing her independence, he began to intimidate her and create arguments that usually escalated to physical contact. Much of the abuse consisted of slaps and punches. However, one day in an intense argument, he put her face through a wall. Her cheekbones and nose were shattered. A very lengthy hospital stay and the time it took her to heal abruptly ended Tara's Closet and Tara's emergence from dependency on her husband and his B.S.

Unwilling to see her best friend fall back into a submissive role with an abusive mate, Dakota tried desperately to save Tara's boutique. Although unsuccessful, she learned how to operate in the world of resale.

After completing his two-year jail sentence for spousal abuse, Alex returned home. Reluctantly Tara took him back. His commitment to be a better husband to her and more of a father to their kids lasted long enough to wipe out any thoughts of independence she had. In time, she fell back into the old routine of eating and shopping.

It was painful for Dakota to watch her girlfriend lose what she had worked so hard to win—her freedom! Years later, she was still being abused as her children watched.

With hopes she'd wake up, Dakota stayed in touch even though the relationship had become very lopsided with Tara only responding every now and then to the numerous messages she left on her voicemail. Informing her she was opening her own boutique and thanking her for allowing her to gain the requisite experience, Dakota left a very endearing message on Tara's voicemail. It, too, fell on deaf ears. The congratulatory phone call she hoped for never came.

Although hurt by the slight, she maintained the belief that the knowledge and experience she gained at Tara's expense would pay off for C'est Shee!

CHAPTER 11

Dakota and her sister-in-law, Elly, got along well. Prior to moving back to Romulus, Dakota's time spent in Michigan was limited and Elly looked forward to her visits. Each time she came, it was an opportunity to catch up on what the "Hollywood set" was doing.

Even though Dakota returned home often, lately her stays were short and that left no time for her to sit and chat with her sister-in-law about what the stars were or weren't doing. Two years later and hundreds of stories behind, Elly suggested all of us get together for a private "Shee thing" at C'est Shee so Dakota could bring us up to date on the lifestyles of the "rich and famous."

"The Couch" was the perfect setting for this gathering. With no men around and no strangers in our midst, Dakota was guaranteed to dish the real dirt. Fall had set in so I brought apple cider to be heated in the microwave. Be-Angeleke already had the cute mugs and cinnamon sticks; Elly brought a dozen decadent assorted pastries.

With the smooth-jazz station playing softly in the background, we each grabbed a spot, kicked off our shoes and settled in. Like small children about to hear a captivating bedtime story, we hushed and focused our attention on Dakota.

For me this was as exciting as the basketball games I attended with Dakota in L.A. During those times I met a number of her rich friends who lived in mansions, had limos, servants, and enjoyed lavish lifestyles. Because I was with Dakota, they treated me special. Memories of how important I felt being in such prestigious company made me smile.

Thinking back, I could clearly recall being in L.A. when Dakota received a phone call from the sister of a very famous Chicago Bulls player. The Bulls were in town to play the Lakers and the sister was inviting us to attend the game with her. After the game, we returned to his hotel suite. Around three a.m., with everyone famished, he placed a phone call to a well-known restaurant owner who happened to be a huge fan. Without hesitation he opened his establishment. Arriving in a stretch limo, we were greeted and served breakfast with a full wait staff. The NBA star paid the entire bill and tipped the staff handsomely. Needless to say, I was impressed!

Returning home, I shared the details of my exciting trip with Elly, Be-Angeleke and Val, finding great pleasure in knowing they envied my relationship with Dakota.

Be-Angeleke looked up to Dakota. She admired her beauty and poise. Pretty in her own right, a warm caramel brown with striking features, Be-Angeleke Lately never seemed to be satisfied with her looks, often changing them to rival Dakota's. To enhance her looks, she spent tons of money on managing her professionally colored honey-blonde hair and hazel-brown disposable contact lenses. And to maintain her well-endowed curvaceous size-six frame, she smoked half a pack of cigarettes daily.

Having issues of abandonment as a teen by her father left Be-Angeleke blinded by her own beauty and self-worth. Subsequently, she had issues with men throughout her adult life resulting in repeated failed relationships. An easy lay, men stayed long enough to hit it, then they were gone. Be-Angeleke equated their rejection to not being pretty enough or worthy of being with them.

Knowing Be-Angeleke quite well, I believed she envied Dakota's life as a rich man's wife. Often referring to it as "make-believe" and Dakota's association with famous people as having "gone Hollywood," she seemed to enjoy putting her down and gravitated toward people and conversations that did the same. She incessantly mimicked Dakota's walk, charm and dialect, but swore she was not jealous.

I always thought she was lying. In secret, I believe Be-Angeleke wanted to live as Dakota and resented her for never giving her the chance to experience that lifestyle. Hearing Dakota's take on the life of "Champagne Wishes and Caviar Dreams" was the closest Be-Angeleke would ever get to living it, and that made her extremely envious.

Truth is, though in-laws, Elly was not much different. Dakota didn't know this, but Elly had a hard time digesting all her "pomp and circumstance." Although she eagerly waited with baited breath to hear what it was like attending the Espy Awards or being in the company of well-known athletes and celebrities, it only made her wish she enjoyed that lifestyle, too.

Loving Dakota's brother, Jeff, and recently tying the knot made Elly happy, but she wanted more. Longing to leave her lower-middle-class lifestyle behind, her heart's desire was to own one of the contemporary showstopper homes being built down river that everyone was talking about.

Solo, she could only sell her modest thirty-year-old, three-bedroom home for a nicer previously owned four-bedroom that ranged in the $100's. Jeff owned a comparable size home that would garner approximately the same value, but he wasn't willing to sell a home that was paid for at his age, only to assume a new mortgage. This made no sense to him, especially when the mortgage Elly wanted them to assume was in the $400,000 range. This created serious tension between them, which was enhanced when Dakota came around talking about her friends' guesthouses that were larger than the 4,000-square-foot home Elly hoped to build.

As a computer engineer, Elly made a substantial amount of money and if she chose to stop traveling and eating out, she could manage the mortgage on her dream home by herself. But she was not willing to give up the accoutrements that had become a normal way of life for her, so she needed her husband's share of the mortgage payment.

Money was not often spent on her looks or in stores. This striking chocolate fudge-brown beauty stood five feet seven inches and had a flawless set of white teeth that highlighted her deep-set dark eyes. Her head full of thick, naturally black hair was precision cut and always coiffed. Lean and well cut, she had soft curves but often hid them under tailor-made attire.

A tomboy since birth, Elly seldom wore heels and makeup. To her credit she was one of few women who could pull off the *au natural* look. Working in her profession did not allow for long fingernails, which gave her the reason she needed to forgo "girlie" things like well-manicured hands. She liked the look of groomed hands and feet, but seldom indulged; blaming it on the job and her past tomboy lifestyle.

Prior to Dakota's return, Elly had no problem being just another pretty face in the crowd. Since she'd resigned herself to saving every dime to build her dream home, with or without her husband's help, she had tightened her budget and cut back on spending money frivolously.

However, the attention and compliments Dakota's presence garnered made her feel somewhat inadequate. In time, she found herself adding a little more lip-gloss to her lips or a coat of clear polish on nails that had not been pampered in months. Rather than go shopping for new attire, her outdated tailored suits were updated with form-fitting waistlines and tops that showed a little cleavage, and awesome two-inch pumps.

These changes helped draw more attention to her—if Dakota was not around. Figuring out how to hold on to the attention in Dakota's presence was still a mystery, but Elly planned to figure it out!

CHAPTER 12

Initially the "Little He" portion of C'est Shee attracted very few men. However, after a couple months of being open, word spread about the attractive and available women who frequented the shop, and men began to come, as well. Actually, the men began to stop by so often, they became comfortable with the setting and eventually "took a load off" on "The Couch."

Most of the men who were brave enough to sit on "The Couch" found the conversations enlightening and of course biased, but few who sat there were able to resist offering the male perspective on whatever topic was being discussed, and at times debated.

Time and again, Dakota had an opinion that differed greatly from those of Be-Angeleke, Elly and me. The lessons she learned from her previous marriage taught her to take time to find herself, and in the process she let go of any bitterness and hurt that lingered. Emerging as a much more understanding person who saw the old adage "it takes two to tango" in a different light, Dakota accepted her responsibility in the failure of any relationship, male or female. This awakening released her from being S.O.S. (stuck on stupid), and afforded her the ability to be open-minded on most relationship and life issues. Her stance often left her friends aggravated.

"Wait a minute! What did you just say?" Be-Angeleke asked Dakota, with attitude.

"Oh! I didn't stutter!" Dakota quipped. "He could not have continued to cheat if you didn't let him. Think about it. A man cannot have an ongoing affair with another individual and you not have some clue. Now the real question is, what do you do when you get the clue?" Dakota said pointedly.

The lone male present on "The Couch," Officer Griffin, a bicycle police officer on patrol, chuckled, looked at Dakota, smiled, winked and then added an "amen." Be-Angeleke rolled her eyes and shifted her body to face those with views that were similar to hers. Accustomed to this kind of behavior from many of the females who were "still asleep," Dakota chuckled and excused herself. Officer Griffin followed.

"You're not the typical sistah!" he whispered as he leaned on the display counter near the front door.

"Why are you whispering?" Dakota asked.

"Sh-hh! Don't want to get that group of piranhas goin' again." He broke into laughter and Dakota joined him.

"Piranhas, huh? What makes you call them that?" she asked facetiously.

"Haven't you been listening? They really don't like men!"

"My motto is live and let live. An open mind will take you a long way, know what I mean?" she said staring at him, waiting for a response.

"Like I said, you're not the typical sistah."

"What does that mean?" Dakota asked a little annoyed with his terminology. Before he responded, she continued. "What exactly is a 'typical sistah'?" she asked as she did a *sistah girl* move—with hands on her hips, rolled eyes and popped neck.

Officer Griffin pointed to her. "That's 'typical sistah' and so is what they are doing over on that couch." He spent the remaining twenty minutes of his "break" explaining to Dakota his take on women—black women in particular—and their need to continuously sing their chosen anthem: "all men, especially black men, are dogs."

Dakota wisely lent a listening ear and refrained from offering an opinion or advice. He left in a good mood, vowing to return to shop, and in her mind that was twenty minutes well spent. Cha-ching!

CHAPTER 13

Winters in Detroit last through spring. When summer finally arrives the natives are restless. Sunshine and warm temperatures are guaranteed to draw people off the sofa and "out to play." Every day filled with sunshine and an elevation in temperature was a guarantee women would come out to be seen and men would be out looking. This eighty-degree Friday was proof.

Shoppers and loiters crowded the sidewalks. The Grind, a very popular coffee house, was on jam. Tables and chairs were scarce inside and out as the patrons lingered, sipping their iced coffees or latte creams and taking in the sights.

Halter-tops, tube tops, mini skirts, and booty shorts were in abundance. Ladies were sporting "fresh did" do's and the guys had just been clipped to perfection. In the background you could hear "My Name is Charlie..." playing while the smell of ribs wafted through the air.

It was an eclectic mix of people, most with money, but all there to meet and mingle. "The Couch" and C'est Shee were crowded. Be-Angeleke and Dakota moved constantly trying to make every sale possible. Three hours before closing, I dropped by. Elly met me there.

"Wow, will you look at this crowd?" I squealed, shocked at how many people had squeezed into such a small place. Without responding, Elly put her purse behind the counter and began to help people find their sizes or a different color. Strapping my LV backpack on my back, I did likewise.

"You need a size larger. Hold on…" With no clue where to find a size twenty-two, I located Dakota and allowed her to assist the full-figured customer standing in front of her, annoyed that the size ten she was holding would not fit. As Dakota assisted her, another patron requested assistance from me as the shopping frenzy continued.

Twenty minutes remaining before the store would close, things began to settle down. Unwinding from the daylong hustle and bustle, we slowed our pace. With Elly's help, and me, gettin' in where I could, sales for the day were larger than the grand opening's total. Amazed at the phenomenal day they'd had, Dakota and Be-Angeleke hugged each other in excitement.

"C'est Shee…With a Little He is a success," Be-Angeleke shouted as she twirled and did the "it's your birthday dance" in the center of the floor. For the first time in the eleven months and four days since its doors opened, the owners could exhale.

Most of the women stayed after closing for an impromptu "Shee Thing." Tonight they were treated to a visit from "Ms. Harriet Tubman" who stopped by to say hello and explain how she freed the slaves via the Underground Railroad.

In full period attire, Gail Jones, a regular on "The Couch," recounted the events of the runaway slaves step by step. She sang, and then translated the hidden messages in what have become known as Negro spirituals. By the time she finished this soul-stirring vignette everyone was speechless and in tears. Gail's hidden talent was received with rousing applause and a standing ovation. Overwhelmed by this unexpected response she cried and made a confession.

"I am thirty-six and I have yet to pursue my dream of acting. Not that I don't believe I can act but various circumstances have always kept me from pursuing my passion, wholeheartedly." Pausing to gather her thoughts and fight back the tears, she looked around the room in amazement at the women staring back at her and clinging to her every word.

"My only son will be eighteen. Married to his father for only two years of his childhood, I gave up my acting dream to take care of him. Single parenting took precedence over my dreams and what you saw me do tonight was something I have rehearsed for eight years, but never performed publicly."

Once again the room exploded into loud cheers and applause. Gail began to cry and walked to the corner of the room. Dakota approached her and took her by the hand. Holding it tightly, she raised her free hand to silence the group and get their attention. Looking into Gail's eyes she said, "You have a gift. The world would be robbed if you did not share it." More applause erupted. Silencing them, she continued, "Remember, age ain't nothin' but a number. Step out on faith; trust God and watch the world make room for your gift."

Embracing Gail to congratulate her made her cry harder. Many of the group gathered to offer support and kind words, reminding Gail not to forget them when she "made it." One by one each "Shee-friend" approached Gail and offered encouraging words or a hug. She basked in the moment, not sure if it would ever happen again.

When the last guest left, we all gathered on "The Couch."

"A perfect ending to a perfect day." Dakota sighed.

"Yeah, nights like this make the long hours and hard work worth it," De-Angeleke chimed in.

"This is proof that what you have here is needed," Elly stated as she made eye contact with Dakota and Be-Angeleke. "Look at the women who were here tonight instead of at a club…and what about the bonding that took place? Women need an outlet, someone to talk to…"

Sniffles were heard and everyone looked around to see where they were coming from. I was crying and it caught everyone off guard. Looking up, I met their gaze and looked away trying to gain my composure. The intense urge to talk about some things that had been bothering me was suffocating. Scared, ashamed, and afraid of what my friends, especially Dakota, would think if I told them, I pressed the tissue to my eyes, cried some more and said nothing.

Not sure how to handle this unexpected breakdown from the one who always made everyone else laugh, no one responded or moved. Dakota, seated next to me, slowly lifted her arm and guardedly put it around me. Melting into her embrace, I wept. Be-Angeleke and Elly sat in silence until I spoke.

"Sorry! Guess I got caught up!" I admitted shamefacedly.

"You want to talk about it? We're all ears," Be-Angeleke offered.

Shaking my head no, I tried to blink away the tears. *How can I talk about what I can't understand?* I had been wrestling with some strange thoughts and feelings that this group would not be able to handle. Truth was, neither could I!

Trips to Atlanta to visit Dante had started out as weekend getaways every couple months. However, time spent with him had become way more fun than the recent times I had been spending with Dakota.

Being incognito was exciting and enlivening. No one in Atlanta, Dante included, knew who I was or anything about me, so creating who I wanted to be was electrifying—even intriguing. Of course, I chose to be the person I daily dreamed of becoming—beautiful, a shade lighter and a Coke-bottle figure—Dakota.

None of these characteristics were within my immediate reach, but I imagined they were a part of me just the same. Those attributes I could "lie about"—wealth, fame, material gains, lovers, I did. Pulling off the lie was easier to do at a distance. I thoroughly enjoyed living the lie.

Tired of being "mothered" by Dakota, I gravitated to the free spirits of my new friends, who, with the exception of a few—Carol, Latrice and Don—were gay or bisexual. The parties they threw were like none I had ever attended. The evenings ended or mornings began by one or more couples engaged in an orgy or steamy sex. If you did not care to participate, you could watch.

At first I was miffed. My serious Christian upbringing forced me to steer clear of this kind of behavior or thought process. Not the least bit homophobic, I was guilty of using labels like *butch*, *dyke*, *fag* and *lesbo*. I said them often and meant them in the most demeaning way. The fact that I was now more than curious, made me seriously question my morals. A major tug-of-war developed inside my core, and I constantly wrestled with my physical desires and my moral issues for months before I attended another party.

With the ability to push my confused thoughts to the back of my mind, I found the second party more relaxing. Observing the sexual activities from connecting rooms via camera helped put me at ease. Groups of onlookers gathered in different rooms to watch, while Dante and I sat and watched from a private room on the lower level. Sipping on Mimosas, I chuckled from time to time as Dante made comments or jokes about the participants. Inwardly I felt uncomfortable joking about something I had never experienced, but I never revealed those feelings.

It was not easy to admit watching women kissing or interacting sexually was very stimulating; but it was. There were varying sexual escapades to view, but I gravitated toward those that were bi or all lesbian. Eventually I loosened up and found staying in the room to watch an orgy or a threesome, especially when it did not include a man, pleasurable.

The last time I flew down, the party was a twenty-four-hour event on a luxurious yacht. Although e-vites were sent, I never received one but became aware of the details from Dante. The theme for this party was "Hedonism: a celebration of nature in its most magnificent form—nudity." Very simply put, anything that would shock your mama was included. If it felt good, then you could do it and if it was delicious, then you could taste it.

New to the concept and unable to pronounce or spell the word, I eagerly anticipated attending the event, unaware that the education I'd receive would begin to change the course of my life.

Arriving oblivious to the expectations for participants, I was taken aback when I was informed I'd have to disrobe. Scoffing at the request I attempted to walk past the hostess posted at the entry. Stepping in front of me, the hostess tactfully explained if I did not acquiesce, I'd have to leave the yacht. Dante walked up just as I was about to depart.

"What's up?" he said, greeting me gingerly.

"I'm outta here!" I snapped, annoyed and angry.

"Why?"

"Dante, why didn't you tell me what to expect?" Shocked by my question and attitude, he remained silent while I vented. Looking past the anger in my tone, he listened to me rant and rage about how I was ill-prepared to walk around naked in front of people I did not know.

Nodding because he understood how I felt, Dante asked me to wait while he worked it out. Exiting the yacht, I waited at the docking area. Upon his return I was given one option; disrobe to my underwear. That still did not sit well with me but I felt more at ease when he told me everyone would be wearing a mask throughout the entire event. That safety net made it easier to deal with because no one would know who I was, and vice-versa.

Once on board, I reluctantly stripped down to my strapless bra and panties by imagining I was wearing a two-piece bikini—something I'd never worn. The bright-colored mask each person wore was decorated in varying designs, some with glitter and rhinestones, and others with feathers. Of course I picked one with loads of sparkle.

Vibrators, dildos and other sex toys in varying colors and sizes were available at no cost and scattered throughout the entire ship for those who wanted to indulge. Condoms in numerous colors and sizes were strategically placed in all the bedroom suites along with flavored gels and lubricants. Those into group activities had board games to play and the necessary accoutrements to help elicit their desires. Porn movies were being played in different rooms on the boat and for those less inclined to partake, there were card games like bid whisk and of course, strip poker.

Never in my wildest dreams had I imagined something like this actually happening; sure in movies, but not in real life. The big dildos were frightening. Ill-experienced with having an orgasm by any means other than my own finger, I stood in a corner hoping Dante would come and rescue me. When he didn't I walked over to the bar and ordered a Sex on the Beach.

An extremely beautiful and voluptuous woman approached me

wearing a thong and pumps. She had an edge, a way about her that emanated despite the mask. Exotic and erotic all mixed up in a gorgeous five-foot-eight frame. The platform stilettos she wore added another three inches bringing her to eye level with me. Standing at the bar and chatting about nothing in particular, she told me her name was Sundae. Before I could ask why, she told me.

"I like to lick and be licked." Staring at me *in that way*, she lowered her eyes slowly making her way to my crotch. Sundae's blatant stare made me squirm.

"You like sundaes?" she asked. Nervous, I chuckled and looked away; unsure if she meant ice cream sundaes, but suspected she did not. Sundae moved closer, intentionally brushing against my body. Leaning in, she sniffed my neck and let out a soft moan. Uncertain of what to expect and unsure of what to do I gripped the edge of the bar and guzzled my drink.

Gently, Sundae took my hand and led me around the corner where it was quieter. Guiding me, we entered an empty bedroom, but I stopped at the door frozen with fear. Letting go of my hand, she smiled and walked toward the bed.

Picking up a hot pink vibrator from the nightstand, she slowly licked it, intentionally leaving a layer of saliva on the tip. Staring at me, she placed it between her legs and moved it back and forth. Enjoying the sensations, she moaned and arched her back while I looked on.

Lying on the bed Sundae directed her pelvis toward me and spread her legs. Pulling her thong to the side, she enjoyed the penetration of the toy. A throbbing wave cascaded through me causing my crotch to moisten.

Curious, I watched Sundae lie on the bed and play with herself, holding the vibrator in place. Turned on by what she was doing, I began to perspire as my heart rate increased. Rotating her hips, Sundae slowly moved the vibrator as she increased the friction with her finger. As her moans and breathing increased, so did mine. Fully aware she was about to have an orgasm, I tried to look away, but was too caught up in the moment. Embarrassed to be watching something so private I thought about bolting from the room, but my curiosity was hard to ignore.

Twitching and quivering, Sundae let the sensations consume her as she climaxed. Slowly she removed the vibrator and licked it as she stared at me. To run was my first inclination as she approached me, but my feet would not move. Heart racing, my entire body shook from the trembling in my legs. Sweating profusely, I wiped my brow and tried to get it together!

With one of her exposed breasts touching my body, and one of her hands on my behind, Sundae placed the toy on the front of my panties and turned it on. Slowly she circled my stomach, then rubbed it between my legs, holding it there. The feeling was unbelievable. Squatting, Sundae licked the seat of my panties with her tongue, applying pressure in certain spots to heighten the sensation.

Replacing her tongue with the vibrator sent shock waves through me. Yearning for more, I slowly rotated my hips as my body began to quiver. The sensation was overwhelming. The continuous pressure and slow motion of the vibrator made my body erupt into convulsions, bringing me to my knees as I climaxed.

Mission accomplished, Sundae smiled, laid the vibrator on the floor and left me enjoying repeated "after shocks." The waves upon waves of spasms sent a pleasurable feeling to my toes and then reversed itself. Mustering the strength that had escaped me, I slowly crawled to the bed and pulled myself up. Two hours later I woke to Dante rubbing my face with a wet cloth.

"You okay?" he asked sincerely. I smiled but did not answer.

"Yep, you're good!" he teased and reached to give me a drink of water.

"Want to eat?"

Not the least bit hungry, I sat up and told Dante what had happened. He teased me about bursting my cherry and then listened as I repeated the story. Before the night ended, I admitted I enjoyed the encounter and looked forward to another, which is why tonight's outburst in front of my friends was difficult to explain.

The guilt and embarrassment, coupled with the pleasure and excitement I felt on that yacht, was stirred up when Gail slipped me her number and winked. Offended and scared, I wondered if I was that transparent. As far as I was concerned, I was neither gay nor bi—or was I?

CHAPTER 14

The majority of the men who walked through the doors of C'est Shee were patrons by default. Although they entered under the guise of checking out the carefully selected array of men's items that sat ever so neatly in enclosed glass cases, their true objective was to check out the two female owners who skillfully arranged those enclosed glass cases.

The head "Shees in charge," Be-Angeleke and Dakota, knew they were often the draw for men continuously popping in and out of their boutique. The ladies' daily serving of well-dressed "face" and form-fitting outfits on toned bodies, which were sprinkled with a sexy fragrance, was an appetizer few men turned down. Relentlessly, they unsuccessfully attempted to woo the sexy owners trying to get in their heads (and beds).

Be-Angeleke was not interested because she had decided to finish a "project" she'd started over a year ago. Leotis, Mr. Diamond in the Rough, was back in her bed and she liked the changes she saw. With her no longer being on the market, men essentially turned their time, interest and energy on trying to land what most thought was clearly the best catch of the two—Dakota.

Don't get it twisted; this was not just about looks. It went deeper, way deeper. Four to six weeks into any quality time spent with Be-Angeleke left a man running in the opposite direction. Always on the edge, with her guard up, she exuded lots of bitterness and insecurity. A bitter and insecure control freak is a formula for a witch on a broomstick at any given moment. Those men who had been around, knew the signs and were wise enough to steer clear. Others brave enough or foolish enough, to test the waters anyway, never came back to Be-Angeleke or C'est Shee.

In contrast, Dakota was easy to talk to and be with. She was way wiser than her thirty-plus years on earth and she called a spade a spade. Her open and sometimes brutal honesty set the stage for like conversation and many stepped onto that stage. The "truth will set you free" motto she had etched on a silver key chain was a creed she lived by, and it afforded others a chance to be open and honest with her—not feeling ashamed or judged.

A Christian who "church hopped" for years before settling into a non-denominational setting, Dakota was careful not to stand in judgment of anyone. Her slate was not clean and her life was far from perfect. Not taking time to worship the Lord or serve Him like she did growing up, she often felt guilty for allowing life—hers, those of her friends, and things she deemed more important take precedence over attending church service on a regular basis.

From time to time she went to bible study through the week. Once she settled into her dad's home, she managed to squeeze in a Sunday morning eleven a.m. service once a month. But totally committing to a disciplined pattern of seeking God and all He had to offer was not on her list of priorities.

Although she loved God and as a child had accepted Jesus as her Savior, praising and worshipping from her bedroom on

Sunday or through the week by way of the Internet or television brought the same consolation and peace to her life that attending church every Sunday as a little girl did. And even though she felt guilty from time to time for not having church *in church*, that guilt was short lived!

People were drawn to Dakota. Something about her made them curious and often left them wanting to get to know her. "Smooth" was her nickname, coined by some of the regular brothas who stopped by. Dakota was refreshing, fun, strong-willed and always positive, yet she was disciplined enough to stop short of forcing her opinions or will on a man; admonishing him like a mischievous child (a habit of Be-Angeleke's). Having spent years of wasted energy "raising and chastising" her former husband in an effort to control him and make him do what she wanted, she'd learned a valuable lesson: you cannot raise an adult and you cannot change a grown man.

Her *live and let live* outlook on life allowed any person, not just male, to be whomever and whatever they chose. It was then her responsibility to decide if she liked whomever or whatever, then make a decision to continue seeing that person or change shoes. Staying in that relationship or leaving was her right and she exercised the option to change shoes often.

Those she chose to leave were always told, "We can still be friends." Most took her up on her offer of platonic friendship: anything to have the opportunity to spend time with such a "breath of fresh air."

"Smooth, real smooth!" one of the patrons said under his breath to Officer Griffin as he watched Dakota handle her customers.

"Yeah, she is," he agreed, staring at her. A regular at the store, Officer Griffin had never approached Dakota about her number or going out with him. He respected her and their friendship too much to ruin it by trying to date her, but he'd also grown very fond and protective of her. So when the patron mentioned getting the digits, he immediately sized him up and chuckled.

His gator-wearing butt won't make it to first base with Dakota, he surmised. Like most of her suitors he would not even get a phone number. Officer Griffin watched as he approached her.

"Uh, Dakota, I believe it is?" he said, extending his hand.

"Yes, and you are?" she responded, making eye contact and firmly shaking his hand.

"David, David Smith." He smiled and put one of his hands in his pocket as he flexed his wrist to look at the time, intentionally displaying his diamond-encrusted Rolex. Dakota smiled, ignoring the watch, and guided him to the glass case that housed the items for men. He balked and chuckled, and then turned to face her.

"It's not that I am not interested in the items you are selling. It's just that I am more interested in you."

"Really?" Dakota said facetiously.

"I'd like to take you out to dinner sometime. You game?"

"Thanks for the offer. I'm flattered, but I am so busy with the store I don't have the time."

As David tried to find a different way to approach the subject, Dakota excused herself promising to return to show him some ties. Not interested in seeing anything other than her phone number, he left.

Officer Griffin hung his head and laughed, then drew a line with his finger on the glass top. He'd just won another bet with himself. Having studied Dakota for quite some time, he was pretty good at predicting what she'd do. Her MO (modus operandi) was to accept any and all flowers, boxed lunches, and bottles of non-alcoholic bubbly sent to the boutique in her name. Graciously she'd respond with a handwritten note of thanks. But few notes ever included her number. You really had to have it goin' on to get to know her. Not just monetarily, but socially, mentally, emotionally and of course physically. However, a brotha wearing brightly colored outfits with matching gators would never darken her doorsteps because she liked a man with class and panache.

Big bellies, tires for waistlines, and fat butts were not given any consideration. Those with bad credit and living with their mommas never stood a chance. If a suitor scored a ten in all the categories that mattered, he might get her number, but most times she asked for his.

A married man was tossed in the trash immediately. Men who had outside children *they did not support* were never called again and those with children they supported were approached with caution. Baby daddies and their babies' mamas were not on her list of things to experience in life.

"So, why you break the brotha's heart?" Officer Griffin teased.

"Oh see, don't even go there! By now you should know what I like and that was not it!"

"Boy, you're hard on a black man, but I understand. You like what you like."

"Exactly! His shoes told a story I did not want to read!" She had to laugh at her own wit. Officer Griffin joined in fully aware of what she meant.

Having overheard labels whispered—"Playette" being one of them—behind Dakota's back, Officer Griffin often wondered if she was. Her game was good. Fully aware she dated frequently, he could not help but wonder if she slept with all the men she dated. Realizing it was a personal matter, he put the thoughts out of his mind until the day he walked into the boutique and overheard Be-Angeleke accuse Dakota of being loose.

Apparently envious of how often and how many men asked Dakota out, Be-Angeleke voiced that envy through a put-down, insinuating the constant flow of men in and out of the store was a setup to rob it. She suggested they might pretend to be interested in Dakota but were actually casing the store and setting it up to be robbed. Most times Dakota ignored her comments and found something to do to keep from having Be-Angeleke's stupid remarks escalate into an argument. Today was different; she responded firmly.

"Duh! Part of our name is *A Little He* and we do carry items for men," Dakota snapped with her hands on her hips, glaring. Before Be-Angeleke could respond she let her have it.

"Listen, BL, whenever you and Leotis have a fight, you bring that B.S. in here and I'm tired of it. Not that I owe you any explanation about my love life, but you should know the men I meet here in the store, we both benefit from. I get dinner, dancing or a movie and we both get them as repeat customers. I never mix sex with my bread and butter, but I am wise enough to play it so they keep coming back. Think about it, how many men do you see leave our store empty handed?"

Because she knew Dakota was right, Be-Angeleke stared at her refusing to answer. The times men did come in the store to pursue her, they spent their money freely to impress her. With no defense for her untimely diss Be-Angeleke backed down and dropped the entire topic; that is until Liar Liar walked in.

Be-Angeleke could not stand him from the instant she met him. High-yellow with an unusual swagger, he was Billy Dee smooth;

that came off too rehearsed for her taste. Even though he had all the right credentials—a last-year resident at Detroit Medical Center with an offer to join the staff upon graduating—something about him did not ring true.

"Dr.-Dr." knew all the hot spots in town and everyone knew and seemed to like him. Conversations with him were enlightening and enjoyable because of his quick wit and humor. Without a doubt, he was very different from the men who constantly pursued Dakota, which is why she enjoyed his company.

"Ro, she's your cousin. Can't you talk some sense into her?" Be-Angeleke pleaded.

"You see how she is…what makes you think she'll listen to me? I don't even have a man. She'd receive it better from someone who does. You talk to her!"

"Last time I tried she went off on me…like she thought I was jealous or something."

"It did come off that way. Are you?" I asked. Be-Angeleke looked at me with contempt, but did not answer. Certain she was, I smirked fully aware this time my cousin had a right to be pissed. Although Be-Angeleke was concerned, it was obviously fueled by jealousy.

Dakota and the *wannabe* doctor became an item quickly. She kicked all her other suitors to the curb, making him her focus. A man about town, he held her interest with his "not a care in the world" demeanor. One day he was calling her from a friend's yacht and the next day he was wining and dining her at a trendy restaurant.

Two months into their dating, Be-Angeleke began to complain about his being around the store *all the time*.

"Hold up, you're griping about my slice coming around all the time, but you don't seem to mind that *Mister Diamond in the Rough* is always here. At least my man has a J.O.B.," Dakota snapped.

"Let me explain where I am coming from," Be-Angeleke begged, realizing she may have crossed the line. Dakota stared at her as if looking through her, but shut up long enough to hear what she had to say. "Something is not right…I can't put my finger on it…but something is just not right. I think he's lying to you…" Dakota cut her off.

"Listen! To *you*, all men are liars. You don't even know him and you have determined he's lying? About what?"

"It's not just me, Ro agrees," Be-Angeleke interjected and glanced at me. Hurt that her business had been discussed previously and behind her back, Dakota frowned at me and rolled her eyes.

"Look at the signs, Dakota," Be-Angeleke pleaded. "What doctor goes around with a stethoscope hanging from his neck when he is not in the hospital? And the hospital scrubs…is he on call every day, twenty-four-seven? I think not! So why does he not have any clothes to wear and why does he stop by to use your car? Where's the Hyundai he was driving? It's a smoke screen. He wants something and he's hiding something," Be-Angeleke said adamantly.

Fuming, Dakota slammed her fist against the glass display case.

"You seem to have it all figured out…so let me put it this way. You have your own life to worry about and maintain; let me handle mine. As far as his coming around…when Leotis disappears, so will *fake doctor*." Angrily, she grabbed her purse and walked out of the boutique, leaving Be-Angeleke and me to close the shop.

Staring at each other and fully aware what had just happened was not what we'd hoped for, we waited for her to leave before speaking. Regretting getting involved but unable to ignore her gut feeling, Be-Angeleke wanted to discuss it some more. Not wanting to be perceived as talking behind Dakota's back, I dropped it and hoped Be-Angeleke would as well. Grabbing my purse and keys to leave, I listened to Be-Angeleke ramble on about her suspicions as I headed to the door.

"Ro, what if he is an ex-con or murderer or one of those types that dopes a woman and then rapes her?" Not wanting to hear another word, I waved and left.

Continuing with her thoughts, Be-Angeleke spoke out loud. "What if he is hanging around to learn our system of operation with the intent of setting us up to be robbed? What if..." Pondering the "what if's" brought her to tears.

The last thing she wanted was something to happen to Dakota or their boutique. Fearful of that possibility she felt obligated to pursue her hunch. But she couldn't afford to have her partner walk out, permanently. Short on personality and patience, Be-Angeleke knew Dakota was a real asset to the profit margin of the boutique. With an inherent gift of gab, she could talk a snake out of its skin and into a Japanese silk top in seconds. People bought just because she said it looked good, and if you hesitated for a second, she sold you two. Besides, they were friends—life-long friends.

Wishy-washy people got on Be-Angeleke's nerves. Time was a commodity she respected and those who wasted it were on her list of things to avoid. Rather than coax them into buying not one scarf, but three, Be-Angeleke would rather they hurry up, pick one, pay and leave. Rent would never be paid like that and she knew it!

CHAPTER 15

Dakota's two-week unplanned vacation was costly to the boutique. The weekly sales totals declined and the absentee male clientele was very noticeable. This reality left Be-Angeleke shaken and angry. Suffice it to say, the tension in the air was thick enough to slice when Dakota returned.

"So, how was your vacation?" Be-Angeleke asked sarcastically.

"Fa-aa-bu-lous!" was all Dakota offered. The silence following her response lingered for over an hour, only to be broken by the timely visit of Officer Griffin.

"Hey-yy, whuz-up? Where you been?" he shouted as he entered the door; coffee lattes and cinnamon rolls in tow. Dakota reached to grab the "goodies," but he leaned in and gave her a peck on the cheek before handing them to her—a first. Caught off guard, but delighted just the same, she responded in kind. Be-Angeleke rolled her eyes. *There she goes again! Is no man safe from her claws?*

"You're an angel," Dakota squealed as she bit into one of the cinnamon rolls.

"I missed your face in the place. You have a good time? Everything okay?" he asked smiling and genuinely concerned. Before she could answer, Be-Angeleke butted in.

"Ain't this some mess? And just how would you know if anyone or anything for that matter was missing? You have not been around yourself!"

"What you mean?" he asked guardedly, uncertain what the scowl on Be-Angeleke's face meant.

"Last I remember seeing you was the day before my so-called partner decided to take an unscheduled hiatus."

"Not true!" he shrieked, sounding defensive. "I have been here every…"

"You can stop testilying," she snorted. "Don't you think I'd know if you were here? The uniform, badge and gun stand out like a sore thumb. I'd say that's pretty hard to miss *and* it's not like we've been so busy I would have missed you," she added, glaring at Dakota. Officer Griffin took offense to what Be-Angeleke said and let her know it.

"Now hold up," he piped in, raising his voice. "I *was* here and I do not appreciate you insinuating I'm lying. I rode by daily, sometimes twice a day. I didn't see my girl; saw nothing unusual— no crime transpiring, so I kept going!"

"Oh…so, Miss Missy is not here and you can't stop to holla at me?" she asked angrily.

Wisely, Officer Griffin remained silent. No rocket scientist was needed to figure out Be-Angeleke was in a bad mood. Rather than let her continue to use him as a punching bag, he faked answering a call on his radio and then apologized for having to depart abruptly.

"Duty calls," he explained as he backed out the door.

Not willing to allow Be-Angeleke's rudeness to pass, Dakota spoke up.

"What did he do to you to make you treat him so rudely?" Be-Angeleke turned and stared at her, saying nothing. She looked like a rabid animal.

Certain she was crazy, Dakota retreated to the stock room and began to log in the new inventory and unwrap what had arrived via UPS. The day was exceptionally slow, so shortly after one p.m., Be-Angeleke left without saying a word and did not return until one hour before closing. The scene that greeted her when she pulled up in front of the boutique made her even angrier.

C'est Shee was packed! Most owners of a small business would be thrilled, but Be-Angeleke realized the patrons had returned because her partner was back. Naturally she wondered if they were in the boutique because of Dakota's return or her own absence. Either reason stung, adding fuel to the already raging fire inside her belly.

Once inside she nearly exploded with anger. The majority of the patrons were men. To add insult to injury, they were the regulars who had been irregular the entire time Dakota was gone. Enraged, Be-Angeleke spoke to no one, turned around and forcefully pushed open the door, allowing it to slam behind her. Startled by the loud clang, everyone turned in time to see her burn rubber as she sped off. Within seconds things returned to normal.

What's good for the goose is good for the gander! Taking time away to regroup and pay Dakota back, Be-Angeleke took a short respite. Two weeks and a day later, she returned to a well-stocked, well-maintained store with profits galore. A time to be happy was not a happy time for her. It was obvious things ran well without her.

Not feeling wanted or needed awoke the sleeping giant from her childhood. Unresolved issues, especially those dealing with rejection, can be like illnesses that go into remission and surface at a later point, unannounced and unexpected. How one chooses to handle it is so vitally important to how well they will survive. Be-Angeleke did not handle it well at all.

The following morning when Dakota put her key in the lock and turned it, the door did not open. After several attempts, she called Be-Angeleke on her cell phone.

"Hey, I can't get the door to open…"

Bluntly, Be-Angeleke responded, "I changed the locks and I'm on my way!"

"You did what?" *Click!* The line went dead. Dakota removed her cell phone from her ear and stared at it as if she expected it to offer an explanation. Shocked and bewildered, she sat in her car and waited for Be-Angeleke to arrive. While waiting she tried to imagine what would make her partner nut up like this.

Changed the locks? Is she crazy? What's she trying to prove? Question after question raced through her mind. Dakota tried hard to answer the questions, but couldn't.

Two customers came and went before Be-Angeleke arrived. When she did, three people were standing waiting to get in.

"Hi ladies!" She smiled and greeted them gleefully as she unlocked the door. "Come on in."

Be-Angeleke held the door for the customers and made it a point to allow the door to slam in Dakota's face. To avoid any confusion, Dakota remained silent as she opened the door and walked to the office to wait for the sales transactions to be completed. The door chime rang three different times, indicating everyone who had entered should have also exited. Waiting ten more minutes, she went out to confront her partner.

The sight of her casually chatting on the phone made Dakota's blood boil. She slowly walked over to the counter in front of Be-Angeleke and stared. Turning her back to Dakota she continued to gossip with her sister. Within seconds the call ended. *Snip!* Dakota had taken a pair of scissors and cut the telephone line.

Enraged, Be-Angeleke threw the phone at Dakota who ducked just before it hit her head. In an attempt to leap over the counter, Be-Angeleke cut her knee. For Dakota that was enough proof that she was crazy. Grabbing her purse she headed for the door as each exchanged expletives. Well aware she was trying to make a quick getaway, Be-Angeleke ran to the door and blocked the entrance. Then she tried to grab Dakota's hair to keep her from pushing past her, but missed her entire head.

Frustrated, Be-Angeleke tried to grab her throat. Feeling threatened and very frightened, Dakota pushed her to the floor and ran out, leaving the door wide open, never looking back to see if BL was hurt.

The finality of the blow-up hit Be-Angeleke shortly before the fake doctor showed up looking for Dakota. Bitter and ready to sling dirt, he took advantage of her absence to bash her and Be-Angeleke willingly listened. Shocked to learn Dakota discovered he was a fake after taking her advice and digging into his personal and professional lives, she became numb.

As he ranted about her digging into his background, Be-Angeleke tuned him out. It hurt her to know she'd not given her girlfriend time to share that tidbit. What she'd just done to Dakota hurt even more when Be-Angeleke realized she'd actually listened to her.

Doctor wannabe informed her that Dakota showed up at the hospital and asked a lot of questions about him. When she found out he was just an orderly, she dumped him. He was angry because he was now the buffoon the real doctors made fun of. Labeling her materialistic, selfish, self-centered, and stuck-up, he bashed her and made excuses for his lying to her.

Acknowledging what he'd just said, Be-Angeleke thought about what she'd just learned. *An orderly! I was right about this lying piece of trash. I knew it!* Pissed off and now blaming him for her blowup with Dakota, she picked up a pair of scissors and rushed toward him, chasing him out the door.

"If you ever come back, my oldest brother will make you wish you'd never known Dakota, me or C'est Shee!" she screamed as he ran for his life. Seconds later the entire morning's events came crashing down on her.

"What is wrong with me? I could've hurt her. I probably would've killed that lying S.O.B., but why? Why? Wh…?" She burst into tears, slumped on the floor just short of "The Couch" and cried for over an hour. When she thought about the consequences of her actions and the probability of Dakota never coming back, she wept some more!

This acting-up and acting-out behavior had been under control for years. The anger management classes she'd been ordered to attend when she snapped and cold-cocked her boss, seemed to be working. She'd only had one "episode" (her slang for a mental lapse in judgment) since completing her class, and none in recent years. The last episode yielded few consequences—minor things like broken glass, nothing too costly.

This time her episode could cost her dearly. How much remained to be seen.

CHAPTER 16

Unfortunately, desperation has a way of forcing one to make decisions in haste. At the time, the partnership with Be-Angeleke seemed like a good idea. Dakota realized she'd acted hastily in going into business with an old friend *of the female persuasion*. Previous life experiences taught her entering into business with a friend, especially an unstable female friend, could be volatile. But, in an attempt to hang on to her only insurance policy—her twelve carats, she jumped at the opportunity hoping it would be fruitful and multiply.

"Girl, can you believe how she nutted up on me?" Dakota squealed, still sounding shocked that Be-Angeleke had reacted so irrationally.

"What set her off? You've been friends forever," I asked.

"She was obviously jealous of how often guys asked me out, but *she* chose to take herself off the market by shackin' with Lee-oh-tis!" Dakota explained, exaggerating Be-Angeleke's boyfriend's name. I laughed and listened intently. This was juicy.

"Have you thought about what you're going to do now?"

"Well, since I'm no longer a partner in C'est Shee, I have time to take a long overdue break from the 'same ol-same ol' of Detroit. I hear Cali calling!" she gushed.

Caught off guard by her announcement, I fell into silence pondering how she could afford the trip. Based on what I knew, Dakota had little or no cash. Then I remembered Dakota wouldn't need money once she got around her wealthy friends, and envy quickly consumed me.

It had been a long time since we'd hung out with Dakota's whosey-whosey friends. Although she'd been back to L.A. several times since moving home, Dakota never asked me to go. The feeling of being snubbed like this cut like a knife and left a deep open wound. I wanted to reach through the phone and choke her.

What I didn't know was not being invited by Dakota was intentional. Her affluent friends did not want me around. They found me nosey, messy, and gossipy and their business was not something they wanted to see land in the tabloids.

Lately, Dakota and I were at odds. My constant lying about who I was and what I had got old to her. On several occasions, she took time to have frank chats with me, admonishing and warning me about the consequences of living a lie.

"Hey, what you're doing…the lying…it's going to get you in a lot of trouble. God does not make mistakes. You are who you are; why not embrace that instead of trying to mirror me. You're fabulously witty and so much fun to be with. Your value is determined by who you believe you are. I can't elevate that for you."

Taking offense to the "mirror me" part of this ill-timed advice, I became furious with Dakota. In my mind there was not a word of truth in that comment. How dare she say that to me. In hindsight, there was some truth and I only resented the statement because it hurt!

Blinded by jealousy, I began to perceive everyting Dakota did as a personal affront toward me. Mistakenly, I interpreted anything my big cousin said as if it was connected to what she thought or felt about me. I read meaning into her words that were never intended by what she said or did.

Over time, I chalked up these heart-to-heart chats as jealous rants; certain Dakota was envious of my newfound independence and my own new set of wealthy friends.

Months later, our friendship began to unravel when Dakota learned I was still lying and telling people I had been involved with a well-known ball player for over a year, dumping him when I caught him with his current girlfriend.

Well aware if left unchecked, my lies and jealousy could set me on a course of self-destruction, Dakota made an effort to talk some sense into me. Confronting me, she pleaded with me to stop lying and making up tales that might hurt me, or those I lied about. But my real nails-scratching-on-the-chalkboard moment came when she told me I "needed to find Jesus!"

I could not help but wonder, when did she start sitting on his throne? Suffice it to say her warning fell on deaf ears. "Mind your own business," is what I said and that was mild in comparison to what I was thinking.

Jealousy makes people most unattractive. I became guarded and defensive after the confrontation, turning our relationship from amicable to acrimonious. Poisoned by what I believed was Dakota's jealousy—not love, I set out to prove it!

When this jaded in thought, there are no positive rewards except the temporary illusion of power jealousy offers. Fully convinced Dakota meant me no good, I decided to respond in kind.

Not long after that "blowup," my demeanor became very confrontational and defensive. So much so, Dakota avoided me as often as possible. Tired of Romulus and me, Dakota decided to get away from it all.

Fun and sun calling, she made an appointment to meet with a longtime family jeweler to sell her twelve carats. That process was relatively quick and much less painful than she imagined. The hefty sum she received from her investment produced a wide smile.

"Thanks, Kevin," she said sarcastically, feigning blowing a kiss to her ex. Sitting down at her computer, she stared at the ring finger that once housed the diamonds and smiled widely while she waited for it to boot up. For a second, her mind drifted to her former husband but she forced herself to focus on the Internet to find the next available flight.

"Seems like I'm not the only one who wants out of this place," she murmured, observing the numerous sold-out flights. Searching over an hour, she was unable to find a flight into LAX. Each one was sold out forcing her to switch from her routine of flying into one of the nation's busiest airports to something smaller. Ontario's airport was a good choice and it was in close proximity to Tara.

Selecting an overnight flight left her a couple hours to gather her things and get a ride to the airport. Packing was easy; she took several pairs of jeans, pumps and an assortment of tops and jewelry. Living only ten minutes from Detroit's Metro airport, she conveniently called a cab, which dropped her off curbside at the airport. The skycap informed Dakota she'd have to check in at the counter, which made her thankful she'd arrived earlier than the required two hours.

Surprisingly, Dakota found flying into Ontario's airport a refreshing alternative to LAX. The short distance from the loading bridge to baggage claim and the main terminal was less than a mile walk, unlike the marathon walks at LAX. Swollen feet and "lead-heavy" legs made her grateful Tara had suggested this terminal.

Tara only lived twenty minutes from the Ontario airport and happily offered to pick her up. In most instances this would have been a great plan, but thanks to the "cheap seats" airline Dakota chose, her flight landed seven hours late, which placed Tara's journey to the terminal in the middle of rush-hour traffic and of course late, leaving Dakota to wait curbside.

"Aw man, the brotha gotta be a fool," the skycap blurted out as he stared at Dakota. Tired from the long flight and not in the mood for uninvited conversation she opted to ignore him.

"So, you waitin' on your husband?" he asked, looking for a wedding band.

"Nope," she answered dryly, not bothering to look his direction.

"Whoa! Got frostbite from the chill," he grumbled as he walked away.

Sitting on a nearby bench, Dakota sighed and looked at her watch. She'd been waiting close to an hour. Remembering Tara was always late and drove very slowly, she nestled up to her luggage and exhaled wondering how long she'd have to wait—this time.

CHAPTER 17

Anticipating seeing Dakota for the first time in nearly a year gave Tara a sense of joy she had not felt since her best friend left. Dakota's divorce, though well deserved, had left Tara with mixed emotions. Initially she was happy her girlfriend had found the strength to end her nightmare. But as her own nightmare continued, Tara felt envious of Dakota's freedom. The longer Dakota was absent from her life, the more Tara felt abandoned by someone she'd grown dependent on.

"Ma, why you so quiet?" her youngest son asked.

"Just thinking."

"'Bout what, Momma?" her oldest daughter asked.

"Your Aunt Dakota will be here shortly. I was just thinking about how much I've missed her." Several yelps and squeals erupted as her tribe began to celebrate the news of the long-awaited arrival of their favorite "aunt." Always patient—sometimes overly so—Tara allowed this celebration, although loud and nerve wrecking, to continue until the first school bell rang.

Shortly after the last child was safely in the school doors, Tara turned off the ignition and sighed. Thinking about her girlfriend, she found herself slightly envious of how happy she sounded when she called to say she was coming to visit. Dakota had changed, but that was not news to Tara. The change, though gradual, had been apparent for some time, which is why Dakota's announcement that she was ending her marriage came as no surprise.

Tara wondered what that kind of freedom felt like. The momentary "jail break" she experienced when she owned her resale boutique gave her some inkling, but to really be free…"Lord, what I wouldn't give to be as brave as Dakota," she whispered. Tears welled up in her eyes and choked her voice. She laid her head on the steering wheel and let the tears fall.

Married to Alex since her teens, Tara ran to his arms to escape her mother's rage. An abusive woman, she physically took her anger toward Tara's absentee father, and men in general, out on her sons and once done with them, she verbally abused Tara.

The only girl, Tara desperately wanted to please her mother. When years of attempts to win her love, praise and adoration failed, she sought those needs in the arms of the neighborhood bad boys. Low self-esteem and lack of self-worth made it possible for any male individual who paid her a compliment or showed her an act of fleeting kindness, to end up in her bed.

Alex, at age eighteen, was already an established street hustler. He'd been around the block hundreds of times and knew how to get what he wanted. Shortly after he met sixteen-year-old Tara, he began to buy her trinkets her mother's state assistance could not afford. Instantly smitten, Tara dumped all the other bad boys she'd been sleeping with; certain this was the man of her dreams.

Nine months after they began dating, she ignored seeing him driving down Crenshaw Boulevard with another female in *her* seat of his new BMer. It wasn't until she became pregnant at age eighteen with their first daughter and they said, "I do," that these "sightings" became an issue.

"Who was the slut you had in your car? And don't tell me it was your cuu-zin!" Tara yelled angrily.

"Look, chill wit dat. I ain't feelin'…" Tara cut Alex off before he could finish, still screaming at the top of her lungs.

"I ree-ee-ly don't care what you feelin'. Who was the 'B'?"

"Tara, look! Don't have me put my foot up yo…" *Click!* Tara hung up the phone, not wanting to hear the rest of what he had to say and very aware hanging up on him would piss him off. Alex called right back, and got even angrier when the line was busy. For thirty minutes he hit the speed dial and for thirty minutes he got a busy signal.

Looking at the clock, she smiled. It had now been two hours since she'd hung up on him and taken the phone off the hook.

"By now he should be good and mad. Any plans he had tonight with that heifer should be ruined."

Pleased with herself, she waddled to her bedroom, placed the phone back on the hook, turned off the ringer, switched on the answering machine, turned down the volume and climbed into bed for a good night's sleep, which never came, thanks to unexpected labor pains.

Labor and delivery was hard. Her daughter's early arrival was life threatening because she was breech. Complications during delivery forced the two of them to remain hospitalized for several days. Alex was not there for the birth but paid his one-hour-a-day token visit to the hospital. The day Tara left the hospital and brought Alexis home, he purchased her a new Benz as a homecoming present. A week later they wed.

Shortly after settling into a luxury apartment with her new husband he began to disappear—again. The more Tara complained about his disappearing acts the more trinkets he bought her. Unhappy and lonely, she stopped eating and quickly lost the thirty-plus pounds she gained during her pregnancy. Immediately she went on a three-day shopping spree.

Nearly every Baby Phat, Gucci and Juicy garment or shoe available in her size, an eight, she bought. The two closets that existed in their two-bedroom apartment failed to house the three hundred or more shoes she amassed, most of which still lay in unopened boxes. Her enormous clothing collection required her to change a minimum of five times a day to wear all of it in a year; something she'd never do.

Alexis also reaped the benefits of her mother's anger with her dad. Her small bedroom closet and drawers were packed to the brim with designer baby gear, many mimicking what her mother purchased for herself. As she grew, Tara spent lavishly on her hoping to ease the pain of being married and alone. Most times the "shop 'til you drop" thing helped, but when reality set in she'd lose it, throwing temper tantrums and ransacking her home. Consequently, Alex was never around to see it, leaving her to clean up the mess she'd made—alone.

Two years into her shopping sprees she became pregnant. Unlike her first pregnancy, Tara was now well aware of her husband's infidelity and found little solace in shopping. She longed for the comfort of his time and affection and hoped another child would "tie him down." However, time would prove the only one "tied down" was her.

Frustrated and lonely, Tara reached out to her mother. A grandchild had already opened that door and with a second one on the way, the possibility of a reunion became a reality.

"Hi, Momma." Tara smiled as she stepped aside to allow the door to the cleaners to close behind her.

"Tara, what a surprise!" Winifred squealed, placing a quick peck on Tara's cheek as she reached to take Alexis from her arms. Tara, winded and tired, felt her baby kick and grimaced.

"Here girl, sit down. Why you carrying this chile? Let her walk!" Winifred barked as she pulled a chair close for her daughter to sit in.

"You better let this girl gain some independence so she can get out the way for that one you carrying." Leaning over to take a closer look at her daughter's face, Winifred gently rubbed Tara's abdomen.

"Baby busy?" she asked, wiping the sweat from Tara's brow. Tara nodded and smiled.

"Thanks, Ma. I'm okay now." She looked around the room and shook her head. It was a mess as usual, but the filth was a real concern.

"Momma, how come Johnny hasn't cleaned up this mess? Why is this old food left in the trash like this? You gonna end up with roaches if this is not cleaned up!" Tara said, slowly rising to her feet to clean.

"Sit yo behind down, girl! Ain't no roaches comin' in here and you ain't got no business pushing no broom." Tara sat down and looked at the photo on the wall over the sorting table. It was a picture of her mother, grandmother, and grandfather standing in front of the abandoned building, which had become their family-owned dry cleaning business.

Expert Care Dry Cleaners was a present to Winifred from her mother who'd done well playing street numbers over the years. She invested her money in real estate and the building that housed the cleaners was one of her investments. An only child, Winifred's mother made sure her single daughter would not need the help of a man to sustain her. However, it was not until

Tara and her mom parted company that Expert Care sprang up under the ownership and management of Winifred Henry—Tara's mom.

Set in the heart of the hood, business thrived because no one else dared to brave the daily onslaught of drive-by shootings and robberies known to take place. But, Winifred did not have to worry about those issues; her son-in-law was a man to reckon with if you crossed him or his family.

Less than two years after the birth of Alexis, business had doubled without the manpower to sustain the increase. As with any understaffed business, something will suffer. For Expert Care, it was the back end where all clothes were sorted for cleaning.

All clothing was still treated with the utmost care and concern, but often times they were mixed up with the wrong owners, which took more time, and manpower to sort through to correct. As a result, promised due dates were missed resulting in customer complaints and some loss of revenue. Since it was a family-owned business, Winifred refused to pay a salary to someone who was not family, so she tried to manage the increased workload with just herself and her son. Tara saw the result of that poor managerial decision and with nothing better to do, went to the cleaners two days a week to help out and do her own laundry and dry cleaning at no charge.

Working in her family business was a rewarding experience. After adjusting to the challenges being a working mother presented, she eagerly looked forward to Wednesdays and Saturdays, which were her days to work at the cleaners. This time away from home, her child and her husband not only took her mind off her misery, it also gave her an opportunity to meet and mingle with the customers. It was one such busy evening that one of those customers helped deliver her second child.

"Ma, something is wrong!" Tara yelled as she fell to one knee and then lay on the floor on her back. The pain intensified. As she wriggled on the floor of the sorting area, she screamed for her mother to get help.

"Oh my God, what is it?" Winifred called out as she ran to her daughter's side. Taking short uncontrolled breaths, Tara whispered "call 9-1-1" before she slipped into unconsciousness. Johnny, her brother, was manning the front end of the store at the time and was waiting on a repeat customer who was also an emergency medical technician. Winifred's screams alarmed them both. Looking back and seeing Tara on the floor, Johnny raced to her side, the tech following closely behind.

Blood now covered the seat of Tara's white linen capris. Her head rested in Winifred's lap, as she lay dazed. The tech checked her pulse and immediately called for an ambulance; her vitals were weakening. Appearing to be going into shock, she began to drift in and out of consciousness. In an effort to spare one, if not both lives, the paramedic determined the baby had to be delivered.

Winifred was given the responsibility of keeping her daughter awake. At times Tara was alert enough to follow his instructions to bear down. Each time she did the baby's head poked out a little more. When he could see just below the neck the problem became clear. The cord was wrapped around the baby's neck and she was discolored and not breathing. Quickly he unwrapped the cord, reached his hands around her tiny chest and gently pulled her from the birth canal, handing her to Johnny while he looked for something to cut the cord. Using a nearby pair of scissors, he freed the infant from the stranglehold and she began to breathe, but her breathing was labored. Johnny continued to hold her while the technician tended to Tara who had now begun to hemorrhage.

The arriving paramedics worked to save the baby's life and prepared Tara for transport. Winifred held sleeping Alexis close to her bosom as she prayed.

"Lawd, don't leave this baby here without a momma...spare her life and make her whole." As she stood by and watched helplessly she continued to pray and hum her favorite hymn, "His Eye is on the Sparrow."

Carely Goodwin, Tara's new bundle of joy, showed no lasting signs of the battle she'd fought to live. On the other hand, her mom did. Tara lost a lot of blood and had to receive several pints through a transfusion. She lay comatose for two days, eventually waking to the sound of her newborn's cries.

"Oh God, thank you!" Winifred screamed when she saw her daughter open her eyes. Alex gripped his wife's hand and kissed it as he stared at her.

"Thank you for giving me this wisdom," Winifred whispered to God, grateful He gave her the idea to lay the baby on Tara's bosom. She pressed the nurses' call button.

Tara's parched, cracked lips tried to form a smile, but she was too weak to do that. Her eyes focused on the tiny little girl lying on her breast as she slowly reached to touch her.

"Hold up, baby," Alex said, gently taking her right hand and placing it on Carely's small body. A tear fell from Tara's eyes as she drifted off to sleep. After a thorough examination, her physician determined she had indeed regained consciousness without suffering any long-term effects from the hemorrhaging.

Certain his wife would live, Alex left the hospital in a hurry to return to hustling the streets and his women; content with his mother-in-law at his wife's side. Days later Tara was released from the hospital. Still weak she needed help with the baby.

Winifred agreed to take time off from the cleaners, if Alex hired someone in her place. He instructed one of his sidepieces to show up daily at ten a.m. As instructed she was there on time, and spent most of the day flirting with Johnny and the male clientele.

More than one good thing came from Tara's three weeks in the hospital. She not only had another beautiful and healthy baby girl, but she had her old body back, without working to get it.

"Not bad," Tara said as she looked at her figure in the mirror. "Hemorrhaging and a coma is not a diet I'd recommend to anyone, but it definitely worked," she joked. Winifred rolled her eyes, not finding the humor in what she'd said.

This near death experience gave Tara a lot to think about. Dropping out of school when she discovered she was pregnant with Alexis had not bothered Tara in the past. However, lately, her repressed dream of becoming a fashion designer kept pushing its way to the front of her brain to an unusual extent, aided by the hundreds of commercials airing for academies offering payment plans. Bored with her marriage or lack thereof, she decided to take the first step and enroll in a GED program.

Upon hearing the news, Winifred offered to keep the kids while Tara attended her classes at night. With classes ending after her daughters should be in bed, they were usually asleep when she arrived to pick them up. After a couple nights of fighting to get two sound asleep toddlers safely home and tucked into bed, Tara decided to leave them at her mom's on class nights, which gave her time to go home and study.

Being away from her daughters actually felt good. She'd never spent a night without them, but it gave her the opportunity to spend quality time with herself. Learning was stimulating. Tara enjoyed being around other young adults who had similar life challenges, but making major strides to change their situations. She especially found interesting the life changes Noel Higgins was making.

At sixteen Noel got his high school sweetheart pregnant. Raised to do the right thing he dropped out of school, married her, and went to work to provide a home for his wife and child. Life was not easy, but they were happy. His wife, Michelle, gave birth to his namesake, Noel, Jr. and stayed home just under a year to nurse him. Noel continued to work to support the three of them.

In late December, two months after returning to her job, Michelle and her son were hit head on by a drunk driver en route home from work. Noel, also en route home from work, happened upon the accident scene moments after impact. The tangled mesh of metal kept him from recognizing his wife's car, but he assumed the injuries were serious. A compassionate person and always willing to help, he pulled to the side of the road and raced to the driver's side hoping to find someone still alive. Someone was—his son. Junior was frantically crying, still safely strapped in his car seat. Michelle died upon impact.

Years later, Noel would still wake in cold sweats from the trauma of seeing his wife's lifeless body slumped over the airbag, blood dripping from her face. In an effort to maintain his sanity and give his son a stable environment, Noel and Junior returned to his parents' home. With his mother's help he was able to work and take care of his son, who had grown into a rambunctious, well-rounded, handsome little boy. A scholastic achiever, Junior routinely needed help with his homework in many areas where Noel fell short. Proud of his son and wanting to set a good example for his child, he returned to school to get his GED and further his education.

"So will you ever marry again?" Tara asked.

"I hope so, but right now this little boy is my life," Noel said as he took his son's photo out of his wallet and handed it to her.

"Oh wow! He is so cute...looks just like you," she said sincerely. "You've really accomplished a lot. You should be proud."

Handing the picture back to Noel, her eyes met his and her heart skipped a beat. The spark she felt caught her by surprise and forced a nervous smile. Pausing long enough to really notice his facial features, she was captivated by his boyish looks, broad grin and deep-set dimples. Nervous, she dropped her eyes but not her thoughts of what might develop between them.

A couple days later Tara got a professional makeover and dumped her "ho-hum housewife" look. The new Tara went to class looking more like a confident twenty-three-year-old college student. Anxious to get to class to see her friend Noel, she allowed herself plenty of time to brave rush-hour traffic, arriving at least twenty minutes early every day. In those moments she and Noel chatted about their lives, problems and sometimes they reviewed their homework.

One night, certain Alex would not be home and would not miss her if he were, Tara stopped by Noel's house so they could work on their homework assignment together. His parents were asleep, as was Junior. Not long after they completed their assignment Noel leaned over and kissed her. Not a good kisser, she enjoyed it just the same. Truth is, having not been kissed in such a long time, Tara would have thought the kiss was good even it came from a seal. Folding her arms around his neck, Tara allowed her tongue to dance with his as he guided her to his bedroom. Once the door gently closed behind them, she had a change of heart.

"Noel, I can't do this." He stopped kissing her but continued to hold her close.

"I got condoms," he whispered, reaching to pull one out from his dresser drawer.

"It's not that." Tara paused and leaned back a little to look in his eyes. "I—I'm married."

Lifting her chin he kissed her gently on her lips letting go of his embrace but still holding her hand.

"You okay?" he asked, feeling her body tremble. Tara nodded as tears filled her eyes.

"Let me walk you out." Tara hesitated, then slowly gathered her things and allowed him to escort her to her car. He leaned down and pecked her on the cheek.

"See you next week," he said as he winked and backed away from the car door.

Tara smiled half-heartedly before backing out of the drive. She thought about Noel all the way home. They had bonded in the manner in which she'd hoped, but she was not emotionally ready to take that bond to another level, even though her wet panties were contradicting her thoughts. Feeling euphoric about what had happened she drove home in a relaxed state, which quickly dissipated the second she opened her apartment door. Alex was home and that made her flesh crawl.

Asleep in a sitting position with the TV on, Tara sneaked past him without waking him. Safely behind the bedroom door she quietly slipped out of her clothes and climbed into bed, hoping to fall off to sleep before he joined her. Waking to him trying to dig her a new vagina, she fought to free herself but he was too heavy. After several failed attempts to push him off, she stopped trying and let him have his way. Tears fell as she lay numb, while he pumped up and down sounding like a moose in heat! When he finally got a nut he rolled off and began snoring. She showered and then rolled up in a blanket on the couch for the night, repulsed by what had just happened.

Pregnancy number three, a result of that night, was unwelcomed, as was the gonorrhea. Until now Tara had ignored what was staring her in the face—her husband was sleeping around without protection. His infidelity was not a surprise but that he was doing it unprotected was unforgiven!

Undercover in a rented car, Tara and a close friend followed Alex for several hours observing his comings and goings. She saw him with not one, but two different women; both with children and both showing great familiarity and affection toward him. Seeing her husband openly hold them, caress their huge butts, breasts and stomachs or tongue-kiss them, hurt. It was easy to conclude he was sleeping with them both and that truth sent her over the edge.

Returning home, Tara threw a temper tantrum that left very few items in their apartment whole. With her daughters safely asleep at her mother's, Tara waited up for her husband. Just before day he quietly entered their apartment, turned on the light and yelled several choice expletives. Shocked, he walked through the clutter and took inventory of the damage.

Listening as his footsteps drew closer, she suddenly became alarmed by what the consequences might be. Afraid of his wrath, she locked herself in the bathroom and began to cry. She'd never been on the receiving end of his anger, but had witnessed those who were and that scene replayed in her mind scared the life out of her.

Calmly, Alex approached the bedroom door.

"Open the doh, Tara!" he demanded. She said nothing and did not budge. Breathing shallow and at times holding her breath afraid he'd hear her exhale, she lay still on the bathroom floor. Forty minutes passed. Hopeful he'd fallen asleep, she stretched out on the floor in front of the door and drifted off to sleep.

BOOM! The explosive sound of the door being kicked in startled her. Before she could get her bearings, Alex grabbed her hair, dragged her out of the bathroom, through the bedroom and into the living room as he berated her with profanity. Crying and worried about her unborn child, Tara tried to free herself. Begging for him to let her go she clung to every piece of furniture he pulled her past. When they arrived at the largest pile of debris, he tossed her on it, head first.

"Get it up now!" he barked.

Shaken and frightened, she sobbed as she began to pick up the mess. Moving slower than he wanted, he kicked her on her behind.

"I will f' you up if you don't get your fat behind movin'," he shouted as he approached her and hit her on the side of her face with an open hand. Tara fell forward onto the pile and sobbed. Alex grabbed her hair, pulled her head back and gave her a look that instantly stopped her tears. Barely able to speak, she begged him to stop.

"Ple-eez, don't h-h-hit me again, please!" she pleaded. "I-I'll be good. Just don't hit me again…"

More afraid than hurt, Tara balled up on the floor, sobbing softly. Alex left her there and went to bed, slamming the bedroom door behind him. Quietly, Tara did as he commanded, but slowly died inside.

Alex Jr.—affectionately called "JR" by his mother who could

not stand to call him by the name of the man she loathed—and her second son, Romney, were easy deliveries. However, JR lived at the doctor's office, a result of being conceived while she was infected with gonorrhea.

After being raped and conceiving JR, Tara never returned to school but often thought about Noel. Secretly she held on to the few happy times he brought to her life and retreated inside the recesses of her imagination for the comfort his touch or smile rendered to her hopeless situation.

Fourteen years later, her marriage to Alex was worse than ever, but she'd grown numb to it all. Dakota's impending visit forced her to exhume what she'd managed to bury. Wiping her tears, she started the car and headed home to clean it and herself before her Best Bud arrived.

CHAPTER 18

Flying from the East Coast to the West Coast will wear you out. Especially when seated in the middle between full-figured passengers who snore when they sleep! Tired and jetlagged, Dakota slept in and never heard Tara leave or return from taking the kids to school.

"Hey girlie!" Tara said cheerfully as Dakota walked into the kitchen.

"Hey yourself. Thanks for not waking me." They both chuckled, knowing Tara's kids were not a quiet group.

"You sleep well?"

"Like a log!" Dakota responded before she yawned, stretched, and turned to face her girlfriend. This was her first good look at Tara since arriving and what she saw shocked her. Tara looked tired and had gained a lot of weight.

Self-conscious of her Humpty Dumpty frame, Tara moved around the island to hide her body.

"You not walking?" Tara asked, hoping to draw her girlfriend's attention from her butt to her eyes.

"Nope, not today. My feet feel like I have on cement shoes." They both laughed and the chill that hovered vanished.

Walking into the great room of Tara's four-bedroom home,

Dakota was blown away by the spectacular view of the mountains that butted up against the fence protecting her backyard.

"Once my feet feel better, I'll test my stamina and see how far I can climb...wonder if I still got it," she mumbled.

"Tara, your home is beautiful," Dakota shouted, trying to talk above the loud TV in the kitchen.

"What?" Tara said as she rounded the corner.

"I said your home is fabulous. I'm impressed with what you've done." Tara smiled and leaned against the wall that divided the kitchen from the living room.

"You really like it?" she asked sincerely. Dakota made a panoramic sweep of the room and nodded, assuring insecure Tara she'd done a wonderful job. Pleased that her girlfriend, whose taste she held in the highest esteem, liked her decorating techniques, Tara retreated to the kitchen to fix something to eat. In an effort to hide her flabby belly, she donned an apron and pulled her oversized T-shirt down over her oversized butt.

With age Dakota had become even more beautiful. Divorce looked good on her; a fact that did nothing for Tara's lack of self-esteem. Being around her best friend made Tara feel awkward. Slowly that green-eyed monster, jealousy, began to creep in.

Focusing on her friend, Tara noted Dakota's decision to cut her lion's mane was a good one. Her cute cut, which she wore in a straw set with light-brown highlights, took nearly twenty years off her and really accentuated her brown eyes. When she smiled her cosmetically corrected pearly whites lit up her face. Her baby-bottom smooth skin had lightened from a dark chocolate to a warm milk chocolate since she'd left the California sun, but was still a rich color brown.

Tara thought about the skycaps at the airport when she picked up Dakota. They nearly broke their necks watching Dakota walk past them to her car. Seeing her "in the raw" (a term Dakota used for no makeup) and sweats, Tara clearly understood what they saw. She longed for those days; days when men like Noel or even Alex found it difficult to keep their eyes off her.

Sensing something was not quite right, Dakota moved closer and leaned on the island. When she did, Tara quickly moved to the far side of the island—still hiding!

"Listen, I'm hanging out with Sonya Lee today. She's coming to get me to spend the day with her. Want to come along?"

Tara felt her already unstable temperament take a turn for the worse. *Dakota had just arrived and she already had plans with someone else.* Tara had missed her tremendously and really needed her time and attention. Feeling less than important, she became angry.

"You know I can't!" she snapped. "Lil' man gets out of school soon." Consumed with ironing her outfit, Dakota missed the anger in Tara's voice. Her lack of concern infuriated Tara even more.

"Oh, that's right. I forgot. Kindergarten means half-days," Dakota responded absentmindedly. A few seconds passed and then Dakota offered a solution to the problem.

"Tell you what, why don't I have Sonya Lee come later, and then you and Romney can hang with us?"

"What an asinine suggestion!" Tara barked. In a nice nasty tone, she added, "Then who will pick up the rest of my kids? Did you also forget about them?"

Feeling awkward and not sure what she'd done to upset Tara, Dakota stopped ironing, sat down on the bar stool and stared at her. Tara kept her back to her, avoiding her gaze.

"Tara, everything okay?"

"Just tired, why?" Tara responded dryly. Dakota pressed the issue.

"Let me re-phrase my question. Are we okay?" Tara looked at her strangely but did not answer.

"You seem on edge and since we're on the subject, you've been noticeably unavailable by phone." Dakota chose her words carefully and waited for Tara to respond.

Silence.

"Have I done something? Is there something you need to say to me? What gives?" Tara looked at her but still did not respond.

Before Dakota could broach the subject again, Alex came in from the garage door. His clothes were mussed; he looked like he'd been screwing all night. He seemed shocked to see Dakota and looked sheepish when she eyed the clock as he walked in. Half-heartedly he spoke, avoided eye contact, and went straight to bed.

Realizing she too felt embarrassed, Tara excused herself from the room to check the laundry. Once safely behind the closed laundry room door, she fell apart.

"What is wrong with me? Why am I trippin'?" she asked herself, continuing to take deep breaths to calm down. Pacing the floor she continued.

"Dakota knows all my business and even more of Alex's. Why am I feeling like I need to make excuses for him being out all night?" Tara leaned against the door and tried hard to sort through her emotions.

Alex coming home just after sunrise was not new to anyone in present company; for the first time in this long-term friendship, Tara was not comfortable with Dakota witnessing his infidelity. It was different when they had this kind of drama in common.

At one time, they spent hours comparing war stories about their spouses sleeping around. Every now and then, they plotted what they would do it they caught them in the act, and then burst into laughter never intending to carry out those plans. But that was then, pre-divorce. Now, none of this was funny and since Dakota was so "happy" there was no hope in them once again plotting Alex's demise.

While Tara dealt with her issues in the laundry room the doorbell rang. No one to silence the ringing, Dakota headed toward the front door. Peering out the peephole she could not believe what she saw. In "full drag"—made up from head to toe—at eight a.m., stood Sonya Lee.

"Let's get this party started," she squealed in her country-western drawl as Dakota opened the door. Sonya Lee grabbed her and held her in a tight bear hug. They both held onto the embrace as they giggled like schoolgirls, failing to notice Tara lingering in the distance.

Staring at the two females in her living room who could easily be contestants in a beauty pageant, Tara became consumed with jealousy and rage, nearly bursting into tears. Her head began to spin as she tried to maintain her composure and hide her feelings. She found it difficult to ascertain if she was jealous of Dakota's happiness or envious of the two gorgeous bodies standing in her living room. Needing time to figure it out, she backed out of the room unnoticed and retreated to the laundry room once more.

Sonya Lee had known Dakota several years more than Tara, but the two of them had lost touch for a very long time. They met while both worked for the airline industry and remained friends over the years. Theirs was a friendship born out of significant commonalities. Sonya Lee was married to a man as drop-dead gorgeous as she, and Dakota was dating an equally handsome man. Both men loved to sleep around.

A wannabe country-western singer, Sonya Lee possessed great unrecognized talent. Eventually she landed a casino club gig in Las Vegas and her fame soared. As it did, so did her need for someone who could take her career to the next level. She left her unfaithful dark-chocolate "eye candy" for a blond-haired, blue-eyed "European" sponsor named Stefan, thirty years her senior who worshiped the ground her ebony feet walked on.

Marrying the European and moving to Europe caused the friends to lose touch. In Europe, her husband was a well-known, well-respected man with financial status and prominence. In spite of that, the thousands he spent on demo tapes and recording sessions to launch his wife's career were to no avail.

Years later, after running into each other at a trendy nightspot in L.A., the ladies exchanged numbers and eventually rekindled their friendship. Once Sonya Lee met Dakota's well-connected husband, she decided he could be instrumental in opening doors to her career so she stuck to Dakota like glue, with hopes of having an opportunity to place her demo in the hands of the "powers that be"—something her rich husband's money had not been able to do.

Of course, Dakota's decision to leave her husband left Sonya Lee with very little use for her company, so she spent weeks on end away from L.A. at the home her husband owned on his private island off the southern tip of Washington. Dakota never took Sonya Lee's disappearance, at a time when she needed her emotionally and financially, as a slight. Dakota knew that's just the way she was.

Tara got herself together and returned to her living room. This time she spoke to Sonya Lee.

"Hi, Sonya Lee," she said just above a whisper.

Sonya Lee spun around and walked briskly toward her.

"Ta-aa-ruh, gurl! Give Sonya Lee a hug," she gushed in an exaggerated Southern drawl. Leaning into Tara she did the European thing—kiss-kiss on each cheek. Stunned by Sonya Lee's attire, Tara did not reciprocate. In utter disbelief, she gawked at Sonya Lee who wore a lemon-yellow leather halter-top with plunging center, showing lots of cleavage.

No bra, her breasts stood at attention and made her size-zero frame very sexy. Bright fuchsia leather hot pants perfectly matched the ankle strap Manolo Blahnik sandals which were equipped with a three-inch stiletto heel. On top of her head was a huge lemon-yellow cowboy hat with fuchsia feathers and turquoise stone accents. Her twelve-inch-long, jet-black, handmade human hair wig drew attention to the turquoise-and-silver choker she wore around her neck. Indian and Moor, Sonya Lee was dark in color and wore very dark eye shadow and lipstick, which made this brightly colored ensemble even more alluring.

Once Sonya Lee released her embrace, she caught a glimpse of Tara's rear-end as she looked around the living room, admiring the décor. Cringing at Tara's huge booty she thanked herself for being disciplined enough to stay on a strict diet to avoid such a disaster. *That might be contagious*, she thought to herself and chuckled.

"I lu-uu-ve your home. It's so comfortable. The culurs are my favorite, ya know!" she said to Tara without looking her way. As she ran her hand across the off–white-and-aqua ultrasuede furnishings, she was shocked to discover the ultrasuede was real. That had to cost a pretty penny and she never thought Tara had it like that.

"Ultrasuede…you pick this ya self?"

Unsure of what to make of such a stupid question Tara did not respond. She'd only met Sonya Lee once before and found her to be phony and pretentious. Dakota's friendship with her never added up and always seemed lopsided, with Sonya Lee reaping all the benefits. Nothing had changed. A lull in the conversation between them made Tara, who was already feeling like a fish out of water, excuse herself.

"I have to put a load of clothes in the dryer. Have a seat. I'll be right back," she said, motioning for Sonya Lee to sit down.

While Dakota went to retrieve her purse and a jacket, Sonya Lee continued to admire Tara's surprisingly good taste.

"Who knew?" she murmured. Sitting down on the edge of the off-white sofa, she was careful to not get the "leg makeup" she wore on her bare legs on the exquisite piece of furniture. The family photo on the end table, though charming to look at, made her thankful she was on the pill; a secret she had yet to share with her husband who believed they were trying to have the one child she had promised him.

Admiring how clean and neat the living room was, Sonya Lee wondered how Tara kept everything so white with four *bad* kids. The sound of the dryer running and the washer filling with water, made her quiver. The thought of having to do dirty laundry made her even more thankful she had Maria, the housekeeper she paid to do her laundry and clean her home weekly, because "stars don't do those kinds of things"—something else she kept from her husband who believed she did the housework.

Sonya Lee lived in a home built in the '40s by Frank Lloyd Wright. Nestled in the hills just above Universal Studios, she and her husband enjoyed their more than comfortable lifestyle. They did not entertain often, but often found Sonya Lee's eclectic mix of friends entertaining. Money drove her and money decided who stayed and who went. Here today, gone tomorrow was her creed and she lived it well.

While discussing where and what to eat, Dakota witnessed a change in Sonya Lee that bothered her. In times past she and Sonya Lee jumped at the chance to eat down-home cooking. Expecting the same, Dakota set her sights and taste buds on eating at her favorite soul food joint, M & M. Now anyone who is a real soul food connoisseur knows to get real soul food you got to go to the 'hood. That never bothered Sonya Lee in the past, but things had definitely changed.

"Where you wanna eat?" Sonya Lee asked.

"M & M of course," Dakota responded.

"What is an M & M?" Sonya Lee asked facetiously, showing just how out of touch she was with black people and the real world. Annoyed, Dakota quipped, "The best soul food in L.A., but you'd have to venture to the 'hood to know that."

"Well, there you have it! You know mah husband would just die if he knew I was hangin' with the common folk, goin' to the 'hood or the Wal-Mart or somethin'."

Not sure she was joking, Dakota turned and looked at Sonya Lee. Her stoic face answered the question.

"Wait a minute…you're serious? You too good for your own people now?" Dakota asked angrily.

"My 'own people'; what does that mean? My people are not just black. I happen to be equal part Cherokee. And just because um part black don't mean I gotta act like 'em…"

"'Them' who?" Dakota cut her off.

Very aware of Dakota's unwillingness to come up from where she was and "hobnob" with those of means, Sonya Lee changed the subject.

"Listen, I've got an idea. Why don't we eat a light breakfast on Sunset, and then hit some of the boutiques? That'll work up an appetite for a huge lunch, which we can work off shopping before taking in dinner at the marina. You game?"

Despite her disappointment in Sonya Lee's transparency, Dakota agreed. A mile from the restaurant Sonya Lee stopped at FedEx to mail a package.

"Listen, be a dahl and run this in for me." Sonya Lee plopped a small box in Dakota's lap, expecting her to do as ordered.

"Hold up, which of your legs is broken?" Dakota snorted. Sonya Lee laughed, Dakota didn't.

"Seriously, where do you get off ordering me around? I'm not your maid, Maria!"

"Gurl, if it's that big a deal, ah'll do it mahself. Ah just hate bein' seen doin' things like this. Stars don't run errands for them-selves, ya know!" Angry, Sonya Lee snatched the box from Dakota's lap and sauntered into the building.

While waiting for her to return, Dakota thought about the time Sonya Lee's husband pulled her aside and asked if she thought Sonya Lee married him for his money. Dakota answered no. After today's revelations, she was sure the answer to his question was an emphatic, yes!

The rest of the day went downhill quickly after Sonya Lee com-mented that the cheesecake Dakota wanted them to share would look better on Dakota than on herself. Dakota found it impossible to enjoy Sonya Lee's company after such a put down. The remaining time spent with her was enlightening and disappointing. On the ride back to Tara's home, Dakota sat silently wondering if money had brought about the change in Sonya Lee. Or, was it time and distance that now allowed her to see her friend for what she really was, plastic and full of herself?

CHAPTER 19

The two months Dakota spent in California gave me time to perfect a business plan I had secretly been working on. My decision not to share this business opportunity with anyone was not selfish; it was smart. Dakota had great business savvy and she never let an opportunity pass her by. Only a handful of business proposals would be considered for this moneymaking venture. Dakota was more skilled at what it would take to formulate and sell a business plan, and I could not risk her beating me to the punch and submitting her proposal first.

A month before Dakota left for her vacation to Cali, I overheard two people seated on the church pew in front of me talking. One of them I knew, the other I did not, so I remained inconspicuous. Leaning forward pretending to be reading my Bible, I listened and made notes. The discussion centered on continuing education funds for employees of the big three automotive companies—Ford, Chrysler and GM. Enough information was exchanged between the two chatty women for me to follow up on.

Monday morning after investigating what I'd overheard, I realized I had stumbled upon a gold mine. Any company whose proposal was accepted by all, or even one of the big three, stood to make hefty sums of money. In need of a well-formulated business plan, I called Lisa's husband, Joey, and asked him for help.

Joey was VP for an extremely successful marketing firm. He created an impressive business plan for me and gave me step-by-step instructions on how to proceed. Business plan complete and well prepped for the presentation, I carefully followed Joey's instructions and landed contracts with all three corporations, which made Dakota's untimely and lengthy trip to the West Coast a problem.

After a couple weeks of leg work, filing and posting a fictitious business name, and hours spent researching and purchasing supplies and textbooks, I launched my new sign language company, United Hands.

The classes were structured to educate thirty students at $695 per student, once a week for six weeks. All classes would be made available to the day and afternoon shifts, Monday through Friday, at every interested factory site.

Income earned from my sign language classes was dependent on the employees registering and attending at least three classes. That put me in a position of needing my cousin's help. Dakota's beauty, charm, and charisma would help secure a full registration roster with most of those registering—men of course—attending at least three classes with hopes of getting to know her.

Fully aware of Dakota's financial need, I offered her substantial pay to conduct all registrations and attend the first three classes at each location. Not working and with nothing better to do, she accepted the offer and requested half her salary up front. Thankful to have her onboard, I agreed to pay her and we agreed once the classes made it past the third week, the remaining salary would be deposited into Dakota's account. Sealing our verbal agreement with a hug, I eagerly dipped into my savings to pay her, certain I'd earn it back.

Popularity for the class was tremendous, as was the money

made. Attendance increased so much after the first week I had to hire a part-time instructor who demanded a pretty hefty salary. A well-thought-out budget had not taken this glitch into account, forcing me to rethink things.

Unable to find the extra funds in the budget to pay the teacher, I decided to go back on my verbal contract with Dakota—without informing her. Week four, pay week for Dakota, and the instructor came and went. The instructor got paid, Dakota did not.

"Rochelle, where's the rest of my money? This is the last message I'm leaving you…call me!" Dakota slammed down the phone, angry and disappointed. Even though I knew I owed her, it was hard to face her, so I decided not to return her calls until the checks cleared from all three automotive companies; my books balanced and I bought a new car—a 500SL Mercedes.

Classes were thriving and the more I made the more I did not see the need to pay Dakota the amount I originally offered. No longer in need of her services, I blew her off a few more days and then called and offered half the original amount to ease my guilty conscience. Dakota went ballistic screaming, "The last person I expected to screw me was a family member!" and then hung up. What I did to her obviously hurt; it was an emotion she did not care to re-visit. Lesson learned from past experiences, she immediately cut ties with me and my parents, who excused my actions.

Since we were family I really believed Dakota's temper tantrum was temporary—some pouting, harsh words and then she'd come around. If for no other reason, she needed the money. But she didn't come around and avoided my entire family like we had the plague; refusing to return any of our phone calls.

Dakota felt used. And to a degree she was right. Even though I never planned for things to turn out this way, I made little effort to correct it, opting instead to look out for myself. My mindset and lack of desire to do the right thing created adverse effects on our friendship and relationship as cousins.

Realizing she was not going to come around I took the matter to our parents. As is customary, they called a mandatory family meeting. I attended. To my dismay, Dakota did not.

Uncle Jim explained her absence and asked me to pay Dakota what was due to end the rift. Ignoring his request, I explained why I reduced my offer and tried to convince my uncle the new offer was fair. But, unable to explain why funds were available to purchase my new Mercedes, yet unavailable to pay my cousin, my uncle did not waiver in his support of his daughter or his stance on the issue at hand.

"A deal is a deal," he stated and then waited for me to agree to fork over the cash. My blatant refusal to do so resulted in him leaving on a sour note, blaming me for disturbing the peace the family had experienced all these years.

The fact that my uncle supported my cousin was no surprise and expected. He always supported Dakota, which got on my nerves. In his eyes, she could do no wrong. However, in fairness to him, he drew the line when she was wrong, and believed his brother and sister-in-law would do the same with me.

When my parents chose to defend my refusal to pay Dakota the full balance of her salary, citing "we were family" and Dakota was just being greedy, Uncle Jim cut ties with all of us. Shocked he would react this way, we decided his reaction was proof his daughter had him wrapped around her finger—something we always suspected.

Dakota's sudden disappearance from any family function I attended aroused everyone's curiosity and people began to inquire about our friendship. Not willing to come off like the bad seed,

I explained her disappearance from my point of view whenever opportunity presented itself. In a short amount of time, the family gatherings became my podium to do so.

"...naw, let me tell you what happened. I paid her, but she wanted more than we agreed to once she saw the kind of money I was making. You don't do family like that, so I let her go."

On other occasions, I explained Dakota's behavior in one simple word—jealous. Jealous of my new success, jealous of my new money, and jealous of my new independence. A select group of family members accepted and believed me. And they would; it would be easy to suspect Dakota of being jealous of me, especially because she'd fallen from her "prima donna" pedestal, lost her wealth, and had been reduced to driving a ten-year-old broken-down Benz while residing at home with her dad. Anytime there is a perceived inequality or imbalance, the door is open for jealousy.

"Anybody surprised?" I asked sarcastically at a relative's birthday dinner. "It's obvious she's jealous of my success. Think about it...for the first time in both our lives, I'm the one on top—stylin' and profilin.'" Several of those individuals in attendance nodded in agreement and added their two cents.

Through a distorted reality, I saw Dakota as being larger and more powerful than she was; a rival who was now threatened by my newfound popularity—something I absolutely loved! This threat needed to be fed quickly. By design, I forced confusion and division amongst family and friends and relished my moment in the limelight.

Dakota's absence made me the center of attention and it was thrilling and addictive—the more attention I got the more I wanted Dakota gone, for good! Not having her around to steal my glory made me feel valued. Those who frequented the events I attended were my loyal supporters who could appreciate my bling and material gain. Having them around was so rewarding and fulfilling. They were full of praise—"oohing" and "ahhing" at every new trinket, designer outfit or other item I showed off.

In the midst of my successful business boom, and just months before our big family reunion, I purchased a luxury contemporary condominium in a swank new subdivision fifteen minutes from my parents' home. Never living on my own, my knowledge of decorating, accessorizing, or organizing my home was zilch. So, I toyed with the idea of calling Dakota for advice and help. She had mad skills in this area and decorating was at the top of her list of accomplishments.

"Hello?" Dakota held the phone and waited for a response. Chickening out, I hung up the phone, glad I'd blocked my number.

"Yeah, Momma, I called her but I hung up!"

Val laughed.

"After I thought about it, I don't want to give her any reason to rain on my parade. Next thing you know she'd be braggin' about the work she did, claiming that I did not pay her. Besides, she'd probably sabotage my place out of spite."

Simultaneously, we burst into laughter and finished the discussion about "jealous Dakota" before retiring for the night.

Pleased to be on top looking down on my cousin, I lay in bed and imagined snatching Dakota's crown from her head, placing it on *my* head as I took my "Miss America" stroll down the aisle. Upon my return to center stage, I'd slowly turn, smile, and perch my narrow behind on the pedestal that once belonged to her. Accepting a dozen flawless red roses, I would bend down to accept the sash, which held the title I once detested—"Prima Donna." Jealousy is a strange company keeper!

CHAPTER 20

Necessities demanded a change in mindset. With very little funds left from the sale of her twelve-carat diamond wedding bands, Dakota had to find gainful employment. A college education did very little to mask the fact that she was in her late thirties and unemployed for years. Companies hiring in the salary range her marketing degree should garner were reluctant to offer her a position. After all, she'd never worked in her field and only worked for a couple years as a flight attendant before retiring to her "leisure princess" lifestyle.

After two months of searching and interviewing, she realized the pay level she sought would have to be lowered *tremendously* if she planned to be employed in the near future. All other avenues exhausted, she agreed to work for a temporary personnel agency for $10 an hour.

"I made more money than this when I graduated from high school," Dakota murmured as she kicked off her pumps and sat on the bed to think about the plight of her current situation. Life had taken a drastic turn for the worse and she had no clue as to what her next move would be. Until she figured it out, $10 an hour would be better than nothing.

The personnel agency was a thirty-minute drive from Dakota's father's suburban home. She left early to beat the traffic and get a cup of java en route.

"Hi, I'm Dakota North. Come on in," she said as she motioned for the inappropriately dressed applicant sitting in the lobby to follow her. Once inside her office, Dakota got a better look at what the young female was wearing and was flabbergasted by her appearance. She looked like she was headed to a nightclub in a gold lamé tube top, skintight jeans and gym shoes. One of her oversized rhinestone hoop earrings was caught in a strand of her bright gold ponytail. Dakota smiled and extended her hand to greet her, but the gesture was not reciprocated.

"O...ka...aay! Why don't you tell me a little about yourself so I can get a better idea of how I might be able to help you."

A neck pop and a glare preceded the applicant's response.

"Duh! I need a job!" Not even two minutes into the interview and Dakota found herself highly annoyed with the inarticulate, uneducated, "ghetto acting" female applicant slouched in the chair in front of her. Compassion was in short order, as was her patience. It had been eons since she'd dealt with such ignorance and it tested her countenance. However, during the last minute of the interview, Dakota had a flashback of the time she spent with Sonya Lee in California, and remembered how she accused Sonya Lee of being out of touch with "her people."

"Ouch!" she said just above a whisper and chuckled. That subtle slap snapped her out of her funk and she took control of the situation. Turning to the young lady, Dakota spoke sternly.

"Listen, I'm not here to judge you or be your friend. I'm here to help you get a job and I assume because you walked through those doors you at least realize you need to work." The young lady bucked her eyes and prepared to pop her neck again, but Dakota checked her.

"You can chill with the 'tude! I ain't feelin' it. I cannot get you work if you don't make the effort to apply yourself." She stared directly into the young lady's eyes that promptly looked at the floor.

"Sit up straight, give me eye contact, and when I send you out to interview I want you to dress appropriately. Deal?"

To Dakota's surprise the young applicant smiled and nodded. That reaction softened Dakota's approach because she saw her in a different light. They both needed to take breaks; Dakota to get some coffee and the young applicant to use the restroom. What was originally a five-minute negative interview evolved into a thirty-minute positive interview and pep talk with Dakota scheduling the young lady for three interviews. Smiling, she walked out feeling upbeat and positive about herself and her outlook on life.

Watching the meek female who walked into her office with her head low, dejected and no spunk, leave with her head upright, shoulders back and pep in her step, made Dakota feel energized. The entire experience made her realize she was not working for $10 an hour, but for people with little or no hope.

In the world where "ghetto fabulous"—bright blonde pony tails, weaves or braids, extra-long busy and brightly colored nails, excessive amounts of gold or silver jewelry and club attire—is perceived as appropriate, most of her applicants came ill equipped to thrive in the real world. Dakota took time to educate those who cared to listen on the acceptable attire and persona needed for gainful employment. Those who listened and learned were employed in a short amount of time, many moving on to permanent placement; the young female applicant was one of them.

Word that Ms. North could get you a job spread around town quickly. Unskilled and former prison detainees constantly filled the lobby, insisting on seeing her. Substantial numbers of applicants were hired, filling long lists of available positions with companies the personnel agency held contracts with. It was exciting and invigorating to see these individuals begin to have hope about their circumstances. However exciting it was, the excitement did not last long when Dakota sat down and figured out how to make ends meet on her low-paying wages.

With gas prices at record highs, additional mileage and wear and tear on an already tired car, she found the job to be no more than an even trade-off. Outgoing expenses and the real possibility of her "old lady" needing some things of her own: brakes, tires, oil change, or you name it; she routinely questioned her decision to stick with her low-paying job.

Several months into this position, things did not get better. Dakota found herself pinching pennies and this frustrated her enormously. Before leaving for work one morning, she decided to have a little talk with Jesus.

"Okay, Lord! Don't know what's going on…don't know what you're doin', but I need a breakthrough. I'm not feelin' this ten bucks an hour and I've hung in here, but this is getting old. Need some help from you real quick…" She left for work feeling less depressed than when she woke up that morning, but depressed just the same.

One hour after the personnel agency opened the next morning, a very attractive, coal-black young man walked into the lobby. Dakota's niece, Seanny, was the agency's secretary for the summer and was very efficient. She instructed the young man to have a seat, while she checked to see who was available to interview him. He refused.

"Naw, I want to see Ms. North. She available?" Seanny knew her aunt was preparing workbooks for the afternoon training session and did not want to be disturbed, but she knocked on her door and peeped inside. Agitated, Dakota looked up but did not acknowledge her.

"Hi, uh-hh, a guy is here looking for a job, but only wants to see you. What do you want me to do?"

"Why me?" Dakota snapped.

"Don't know!" Seanny responded, keeping her cool. She stared at her aunt and waited for instructions. Dakota exhaled, frustrated. There were three other interviewers available; she knew because she could hear them chatting in the office next to hers. Why one of them would not offer to help this young man eluded her and made her furious.

Heaving a sigh, Dakota counted to ten, then looked up at Seanny and instructed her to send him in. She cleared her desk, sipped her decaf and took out the necessary papers for him to complete.

Instantly after he entered her office, she was impressed. Extending his hand to greet her he exuded charm and charisma. Very animated and comical, he controlled the flow of their conversation, immediately winning her over. His well-spoken and polished demeanor made her wonder why he was in her office looking for a minimum wage job. As they communicated further, she found out.

"My girl is in labor with my son. I gotta get some funds flowin'—quick," he said anxiously. "Don't have time for interviewin' and stuff. You got anything for me?"

Dakota chuckled at his facial expressions and hand gestures. She did have a position that would be perfect for him and the pay was more than she made—$11 an hour with anticipated overtime. She offered him the position and he gladly accepted. His training was scheduled for that evening with him starting the next day.

"Bet! Thanks, Ms. North. I won't let you down! See you this evening." He jumped up, spun around twice and then jumped to his toes, like Michael Jackson in "Beat It." One more spin and he walked out of her office, smiling. She smiled too; he was enjoyable and she was glad she could help him.

Thirty minutes before training was to begin, she saw the cute little chocolate applicant bounce through the front door. Meeting him at the lobby desk she smiled.

"You're early. I'm impressed. How's your girl?"

He smiled. "Still in labor. Uh, listen, need to talk to you...got a minute?"

"Sure, come on in my office."

Dakota motioned for him to be seated and she shut the door.

"What's on your mind...something wrong?"

"Naw, nothin' like that. You married?" he asked, catching Dakota off guard by his question.

"Why? You trying to push up on me?" she asked coyly, bursting into laughter. Now don't think it's too far-fetched. Robbing the cradle was not beyond her dos and don'ts. On more than one occasion Dakota ventured into the land of "tenderonies," a back-in-the-day slang New Edition made famous, and a term Dakota clung to even though it was dated. Although she found him attractive and in his own way quite alluring, Dakota would never mix business with pleasure.

"Aw naw..." he said, joining her in laughter. "I'm not askin' for me...see I got someone I want you to meet." He waited for her to respond, but Dakota just stared.

"Don't you want to know who?"

"Not really," she answered bluntly.

"Listen, it's my play brother…" She cut him off.

"Your play brother? What is a 'play brother'?" she asked joking. "You playin,' right?"

"Your play brother?" Dakota paused, absorbing what he said. "You want me to meet your play brother!" She sat back in her chair and stared at him, puzzled.

"Before you say no, hear me out! I got this play brother who is all that. He got money, he's single and he is an ex-football player. He got it goin' on. You gotta meet him!"

Dakota smiled. "If he's all that and got it goin' on, then why is he available?"

He smiled, leaned in and laid his elbows on her desk. Staring directly at her and making eye contact, he said, "Ask yourself the same question!"

She burst into laughter, motioned in the air "a point" for him and sat back in her chair once more. This breath of fresh air was right. She knew she was all that and she was available. His point was made and well taken.

"You get points for that one…but no, I am not interested in meeting him or anyone else. I'm just not dating at this time in my life."

He looked at her completely bewildered.

"You gay?"

Dakota laughed heartily.

"No, not even…just not dealing with the dating thing right now!"

"I wish you'd think about it…"

"No thanks," she responded. "But I appreciate you thinking about me and it's flattering to know you think I'm all that!"

"Yeah…why?" he inquired.

"I'm old enough to be your mother, so that says a whole lot for me. An attractive young man like you thinking an older woman like me 'got it goin' on!'"

A wide grin, encased between two beautifully deep-set dimples, showed off flawless white teeth. He continued to stare, trying to guess her age.

"I probably shouldn't ask…"

"Don't," Dakota said playfully, knowing he was about to ask her age.

"Well, whatever age you are, you got it goin' on. No joke!" he exclaimed, rising to high-five her. They both slapped five and burst into laughter as they exited her office to begin the training session.

Two days later, Seanny interrupted an interview Dakota was concluding.

"Sorry…you have a call on line one you might want to take!" She winked at Dakota and smiled.

"Excuse me!" Dakota rose from her seat, walked out to the desk where her niece was stationed to find out what was going on. Seanny explained there was a call holding for her that she was certain was not business. Perplexed, Dakota took the call on the lobby phone.

"Ms. North speaking, may I help you?"

"Yes, you may…have lunch with me!" His voice was smooth and sexy. Dakota froze, lost for words.

"Are you there?" he asked.

"Uh, yes I am. Who is this?"

"You interviewed and hired my play brother on Monday. Remember?"

"Well, yes I do and I also remember I told your play brother I was not interested in meeting you!"

Ignoring her, the voice continued.

"How's your day going? Did you like the flowers I sent?"

"Flowers, what are you talking…" The lobby door opened and a floral delivery guy was carrying a beautiful dozen of flawless yellow roses. Baffled, Dakota placed the phone down, went to the front door and looked in the parking lot to see if "the voice" was lingering nearby. She noticed no one.

Seanny signed for the delivery and Dakota instructed her to put his call on hold. She rushed through the remainder of her interview and walked the interviewee to the door. Hurriedly, she picked up line one to thank him for the roses and continue their conversation. She found herself genuinely disappointed when she discovered he'd hung up.

"Must not have been that interested," she said to Seanny as she walked back to her office. Before she could sit down, she heard "uh-hum" and turned around to see who was trying to get her attention. It was "the voice," packed in a five-foot-eight muscular frame with a six-pack, going on eight-pack—all abs, arms and thighs.

An obvious body builder, he had strong Indian features, a very dark complexion, and thick, shiny, and semi-straight black hair. Blindian comes to mind; a mix of Indian and Black!

"I'm very interested. May I come in?" he asked, handing Dakota the roses she'd left on the lobby desk.

Dakota took the roses, smiled and motioned for him to have a seat. Softly exhaling, she sat back in her chair and let him talk. As he did, she listened intently; surprised she was so attracted to him. Short men were not her thing. That usually meant a short penis as well and that equaled short on pleasure. *It's been a long time since I've given it up and I'm not about to give it up and be left on the short end of the stick!* Her short end of the stick reference tickled her and she chuckled! It just so happened he'd said something funny, so her giggle was timely.

"You like that, huh?" he asked, Dakota nodded and giggled again. He joined her, oblivious to her real thoughts.

Genuinely attracted to his voice and cockiness, Dakota took time to really pay attention to him. When she stopped fantasizing about the size of his penis and listened to what he was saying, she realized they had a lot in common. Both were single, both were tired of B.S. and both were looking for a long-term monogamous relationship. He explained he'd been hurt by someone he loved and hoped to marry, but caught her with another man. Dakota nodded understandingly and sighed. "Been there done that." She rolled her eyes.

Four times Dakota tried to break away from his captivating charm and wit—four times she failed. He sat charming and wooing her for quite some time, while prospective employees waited to be interviewed.

"I know you need to get to work, so I'm going to go. I've taken up two hours of your busy schedule and I only stopped by to meet you and see if you liked the roses."

Dakota gaped at him, realizing she'd forgotten to thank him for the roses.

"Wow, I totally forgot to thank you...they are exquisite!"

"You free later?"

"Depends on what you have in mind!" Dakota teased.

"Dinner, nothing more." He leaned over her desk and kissed her forehead. "Call me when you're done here and we'll set a time for me to pick you up!" He laid his card face down on her desk and walked out.

Watching his behind, Dakota said softly, "Nice butt!"

"Thank you, glad you like it!" he said, looking back at her when he reached the lobby door. Dakota covered her face and chuckled. He winked, walked out and blew her a kiss as he walked past the lobby window. Her heart was racing and skipping beats; excited about their date and looking forward to more conversation. With lots of work waiting in the lobby, she scooped up his card and dropped it in her purse, moved her flowers off to the side and went back to work.

Thinking about this "smooth operator" on her drive home, Dakota realized she'd never asked his name. Reaching in her purse, she pulled out his card. His name was

Chauncey. It was hard to accept she'd spent over two hours with him and was so engrossed in the conversation she never asked his name. She could not help but wonder if he was "healthy" for her peace of mind, horny body and fragile heart. Time would tell!

CHAPTER 21

Battered, bruised, and unable to see clearly from her half-swollen eyes, Tara fumbled for the telephone.

"Hello!"

Dakota, not able to ascertain if she was speaking to Tara, one of the kids, or if she might have dialed the wrong number, hesitated to answer.

"Uh-hh, did I dial the Carroll residence?" she asked apprehensively.

"Yeah! Who is this?" Tara asked just above a whisper.

"Tara? Is that you?" Dakota could barely understand what the person on the line was saying.

"Oh...yeah, Dakota, it's me."

"You sound funny...everything okay?"

"Um fine. You okay?" Tara responded weakly.

"Long time no hear. Seems like I don't hear from you if I don't call you, so I'm calling. What's going on? Why are you talking funny?"

"Had some major dental work and I'm still swollen."

Dakota wanted to believe Tara, but she'd always had perfect teeth, not a cavity to be found. Last time she remembered her girlfriend sounding like this, her abusive husband had put his massive fists in her face and her lips were swollen and hindering her ability to speak distinctly. She prayed this was not the case but was not comfortable broaching the subject.

Things had not been the same between them since her visit. Dakota could feel the distance between them; their conversations were generic, light and airy—shallow. Their relationship had always been fulfilling and full of substance. Each of them housed some life-altering secrets, told to the other in confidence with the assurance it would go to the grave before it was spoken.

Not certain what brought about the change and unwilling to let go, Dakota made a sincere effort to stay in touch with her girlfriend, even if she had been reduced to occasional three or five minutes of the superficial chatter you'd have with a stranger. Today's conversation was no different. After three minutes of what grades the kids got on their report card, the laundry she still needed to complete and what errands she needed to run, Dakota volunteered to hang up first.

"Listen, gotta go. Just wanted to connect and let you know I miss you and love you. Answer the phone when I call, Tara. You're making me work way too hard to be your friend." They both laughed, but Dakota was quite serious. Their friendship was strained and she was getting tired of being the only one trying.

Sitting on the edge of the bed, she suddenly felt alone and sad. She had wanted to talk about her dating Chauncey but realized only one person would be excited to hear she finally was seeing someone, and that one person would not be Tara.

Uneasy about their brief conversation, Dakota decided to call Kizzie, Tara's mom. She loved Kizzie, and valued her advice and friendship. Kizzie helped Dakota through some rough times during her failing marriage and she shed light on Tara's unexplained disappearances. Both situations were unnerving and hard to deal with, so Dakota reached out to Kizzie for comfort.

Thanks to her mom, Dakota had a full understanding of the terror and drama Tara lived on a daily basis. She never told Tara she knew about the times her husband used her for a punching bag and she never told Tara she'd shared some of her marital secrets with her mom; that would create a major breach in their long-term friendship. Sharing the nightmare Tara was living with her mother was not something Dakota did with malice; she shared a few of the most horrific and traumatic events out of concern. Concern that if Tara did not leave him, one day she may not live to make that choice.

The last event which occurred just weeks before Dakota moved back to Detroit was very frightening. Alex hit Tara and knocked her to the floor while she held one of their sons in her arms. In a torn nightgown and no shoes, she fled with her children to Dakota's home. When Alex showed up at Dakota's door looking for them, she denied they were there and refused to let him in. After a day passed Tara returned home to him; two weeks later Dakota returned to Detroit. Tara's mom never mentioned the incident and she would have if she knew, so Dakota kept it to herself. She hoped she'd not live to regret it!

"Mom, you okay?"

"Dakota, is that you?" Tara's mom squealed gleefully. The two of them giggled and caught up on each of their lives before they delved into the drama in Tara's life. As suspected, Alex had once again resorted to taking his anger and frustration out on his wife. He had beaten her quite severely this time and with a warrant out for his arrest on another charge, he fled the state when the oldest daughter dialed 9-1-1. To date the cops had not found him, nor had Tara heard from him.

Though not new, this information was alarming and hurt Dakota deeply. She stopped and prayed for her girlfriend hoping she'd find the strength to leave this nut before he took her life. Thinking about what she must look like and how she must be feeling, Dakota burst into tears and lay on her bed in a ball, crying out in anguish for her girlfriend whom she regarded as her sister. Sister-less, there was no other woman Dakota felt this close to. Tara was the sister she was never blessed to have and she loved her as such.

A timely phone call from Chauncey woke Dakota. She'd fallen asleep and slept through the night clothed and on top of the covers.

"Hey, baby. You okay?" Hearing his voice and this question brought it all back to her and she sobbed again.

"No, I'm not. I could really use a hug," she whispered.

"Consider it done. I'm on my way." Chauncey was already en route to her father's home when he called from his cell phone. Arriving at their home in minutes, Dakota opened the door and fell into his arms.

Whispering in her ear words of encouragement, he wrapped his arms around her and waited for her to tell him what was wrong. Dakota held him, cried, and said nothing. They stood in the doorway until her father walked into the room and interrupted.

"She okay?" he asked Chauncey with concern filling his voice.

"She will be. How are you, sir?"

"Oh, I'm alright. My arthritis is actin' up, but other than that I'm fine. In here gettin' my dinner started," he said as he waved and returned to the kitchen to finish cooking his Sunday dinner. Chauncey managed to keep a straight face, but wanted to laugh when he thought about the conversation he'd recently had with Dakota about her dad. They found it humorous that he cooked his Sunday dinners on Saturday morning at six a.m. and then ate that "Sunday dinner" two to three times by Saturday evening.

A divorcee for thirty years, Dakota's retired father, who everyone referred to as Jimmy, had lots of time on his hands and no female companionship. He did what he wanted when he wanted and followed his own agenda. Whenever Chauncey was around, he hogged most of his time by holding one-way conversations about life, religion, politics or whatever the current news headline happened to be. Never waiting for Chauncey to respond, he rambled on and on, thus the one-way conversations continued. Quite simply, as most elderly people do, he enjoyed having a living breathing body in his company.

To accommodate him, Chauncey usually arrived early to pick up Dakota, which gave her father time with him. She was thankful Chauncey was so accommodating and really admired him for spending that time with her father. Prior to working, she filled that void; however, that got old. Working and dating Chauncey left little time to spend with him and that bothered her.

Most times Dakota was dressed before Chauncey arrived; this morning she was not. While he entertained her father, Dakota retreated to her room to dress and regroup. Once inside the privacy of his car, she opened up and shared with him the hurt and frustration she felt toward her girlfriend's plight

"She's a grown woman, baby…making grown-folk choices. You can't make her do for herself what she is not willing to do."

Dakota knew he was right but it did not make her feel better about the situation. For now she'd let it go, but she hoped she would get the opportunity to "talk some sense" into Tara before her husband killed her.

Very absorbed in Tara's difficulties, Dakota had not thought about where Chauncey was taking her. He was always full of surprises and unusual outings, which they spent with no one but themselves. Every waking moment in his company was unbelievable and she enjoyed not sharing him.

Whenever he had something special planned for her, he went out of his way to make it a surprise. One moment they were cruising the Detroit River on a yacht, the next they were attending a thoroughbred horse race. Today was no different; they were attending the world renowned "Dream Cruise."

An annual event that began in the summer of 1995, the "Dream Cruise" was the place to be and be seen. Expensive hot rods and classic cars of all makes and models were "dressed to impress" those who lined the streets of Woodward Avenue to view them as they slowly cruised by.

En route, Chauncey stopped at a warehouse and entered alone. After five minutes of waiting in the truck, Dakota watched the garage door slowly lift, followed by a loud engine revving, which caused the truck to vibrate.

Seconds later, Chauncey appeared smiling from ear to ear in a 1956 convertible Corvette that had been converted to a hot rod. Dakota feigned a smile, hesitant to be excited about riding in such a loud mode of transportation. As the car idled, he approached the passenger side of the truck, kissed Dakota on the nose and smiled.

"You ready?" he asked.

"Uh, for what?" she responded nervously.

"To ride...we're headed to the Dream Cruise."

Looking like a child awaking on Christmas morning after Santa had left, Dakota sat befuddled. She was well familiar with the Dream Cruise because she'd attended it once as a spectator with her brothers, but her heart's desire was to attend one day as a participant. Although she had mentioned this to Chauncey in a past conversation he never indicated he was interested in attending or participating.

"Is this your car?" she asked.

"My baby...until I met you, that is!" He kissed her on the forehead.

"Chauncey, why didn't you tell me you had a classic and a hot rod at that?"

"Wanted to surprise you...kinda make your dream come true."

"Wow! This is unbelievable," Dakota gushed as she climbed out of the truck.

"So what's under the hood?"

Chauncey looked at her in amazement, shocked she would ask about the guts of the car. Popping the hood, he showed her his fully restored, 300+ HP, chrome engine.

"That many horses, huh?" Dakota said with expertise as she leaned in to take a good look at the workmanship.

"I'm impressed!" she said in approval as she walked around the car checking out the paint job.

"Me too," he said softly, really blown away by this ultra-feminine woman who had tomboy tendencies. Her knowledge of cars, paired with her feminine mannerisms, was an aphrodisiac that made him hard. Leaning on the fender, he successfully hid his erection until it subsided.

"You ready to go, baby?" he asked, holding the passenger door open. Dakota nodded and climbed in. Before shutting her door, he gently kissed her on the lips and winked.

"Buckle up, you're in for a ride!" he shouted as he gunned the engine and took off. Dakota squealed, put her hands in the air and giggled, certain they were going to have a wonderful day fulfilling her *dreams*.

Today they were "outing" themselves. Chauncey was the first to suggest they stay away from friends and family, so they often stole away to private locations and spent time in public away from the places their friends and family might frequent. Like Dakota, he too had family drama and he did not want to expose her to it.

Explaining his family was messy and constantly causing confusion in others' lives, especially his, Chauncey did not want to allow them to mess with her mind as they'd done to numerous ladies in his past. The only one in his family who had successfully reached some level of prominence and financial wealth, they fought over him and his money on a constant basis. Any woman he brought around did not last long—a threat to *their* inheritance, they'd run her off!

For Dakota, his lack of desire to meet and mingle with her family was perfect. The ongoing feud between us had climbed to what appeared to be insurmountable levels—leaving the entire family divided. Those who believed Dakota was jealous and envious of me on one side and those who believed she had too much on the ball to be jealous of me, on the other side.

The second day of the Dream Cruise was more fun than the first. Chauncey and Dakota spent the day cruising in his customized hot rod and ended the day by winning third place in the judging. To prove *chivalry ain't dead*, he gave the trophy to her.

That night, she stayed with him as they explored each other's bodies after waiting for months to consummate their relationship. He was a passionate lover and a sensual man; slowly and methodically loving every inch of her small frame. Once she came, he started over, and made love to her until she begged him to stop. Only then did he join her in one final climax and the two of them fell asleep holding each other.

Because Dakota had to be at work the next morning they were forced to check out of the hotel early. During the ride home she wondered why they spent the night in a hotel instead of his home. She assumed he was not married because he did not wear a wedding band and he spent most of the time he was not working with her, but she'd never asked if he was. His cell phone did not ring continuously and when it did he answered it freely without checking caller ID first. She had no reason to think he was hiding anything from her, but the hotel thing bothered her. Afraid of the answer, she decided not to inquire and fell into a melancholic mood.

"Somethin' wrong?" he asked, reaching for her hand. Holding it tight, he waited for her to answer, concerned she might not be pleased with the way he made love to her. She said nothing, but a gentle tug on her hand forced her to look at him.

"Hey, talk to me! What's up?"

"Why did you take me to a hotel?" she asked softly. Chauncey was silent for quite some time and that made her feel uneasy. When he pulled into her father's drive, he explained.

"I just sold my home and moved back to my father's house to take care of him. He's sick and his 'live-in' could care less…no one else cared enough to be there for him. Living in his home is awful, a dump…I'd never take you there."

Silence lingered until she leaned over and kissed him gently.

"You upset with me?" he asked, just above a whisper, the concern very apparent in his voice.

"No," was all she said before she kissed him passionately. Dakota understood and appreciated him even more. Any man who would sacrifice his own freedom, privacy, and comfort to care for an ailing parent was the kind of man she wanted to grow old with.

"So what was the home like you just sold?"

Chauncey explained it was a white, ultra-contemporary, five-bedroom bachelor pad; a knock-off of the one in the movie *Scarface*. He built it for his dad and his three-year-old son.

Dakota gasped. "Son? You have a child?" They had been seeing each other for three months and he'd never once mentioned a child, nor had she seen him with one. She was shocked.

"His name is Kelsey. I've had custody of him since he was six months old. His birth mom did not want him and I did," He could sense Dakota tense, so he let go of her hand and looked out the window.

"Why haven't you said anything? A son…"

Chauncey's heartbeat quickened; he'd feared this moment.

"When you told me you did not have kids, I was reluctant to admit I did. But when you said emphatically you did not want any children, I was just plain scared to tell you. I didn't want to lose you!"

Although there was truth in what he'd said, Dakota was angry and felt betrayed. Three months ago she *would* have "abandoned ship" if he had revealed he had a child, especially a young one. But that was three months ago and prior to her falling in love with him. This was hard to accept. Mommy material she was not and she was not looking forward to filling those shoes.

Without saying a word, Dakota opened the door and shut it gently. Never looking back she entered her father's home, shut the door behind her and got ready for work. Three days went by before they spoke again. Chauncey broke the ice by sending her flowers. Calling to thank him, the conversation ended with her agreeing to meet him for dinner that evening.

Punctual as always, Chauncey picked her up in a new Jaguar. Something he bought himself to make him feel better during her absence, he told her. Even though she smiled at his comment, she found it a little weird and irresponsible to run off and purchase such an expensive automobile just to feel better. Besides, he did not need it; he already drove a current model Escalade. Up went the red flag in her mind, which slowly changed to yellow and then green by the time they were done eating.

Dinner was fun. They laughed and talked about their feelings for each other and future goals. Chauncey offered to introduce his three-year-old and Dakota agreed to give "getting to know him" a try. Back at her dad's, he declined to come in and kissed her at the door. While holding her he reached into his breast pocket and pulled out a sealed envelope, handed it to her and instructed her to open it once she got inside.

No sooner than she closed the door, she carefully tore open the envelope and dropped it after reading the contents. Inside was the bill of sale for a new (not previously owned) 420 Mercedes-Benz. Dakota ran to the bathroom and vomited.

Of course he knew she would call, so Chauncey turned his phone off. As predicted, Dakota tried speed dialing him for over an hour. Drained from the shock of this situation, she lay down to rest hoping he would call. The next morning she woke, realizing he did not!

CHAPTER 22

Things spoken in private are expected to stay private. Tara knew she could trust Dakota and she needed to talk to someone before she lost her mind. Even though their friendship had been strained lately, Tara had no one else she could share such a horrible thing with and trust it would not be repeated.

"Can you talk?" she asked, almost whispering.

"Tara! This is a surprise. Everything okay?" Dakota asked, wondering what earth-moving event had occurred to make her call.

"Need to talk to you…real bad…"

"Hold on a minute. Let me change phones." Dakota had Elly, who was over visiting, hold the phone while she picked it up in her bedroom.

"Okay, you can hang it up, Elly…thanks!" Tara called out from the stairwell leading to her bedroom and waited for her to get off the line before she said anything.

"What's wrong?"

Again, just above a whisper, Tara said, "Something really bad has happened and I don't know what to do…" Tara burst into long hard sobs. By the time she was strong enough to continue, Dakota had bitten her lip so hard it was bleeding.

"This freak, this pervert…oh God, I can't believe this has happened!" Tara screamed.

"What? What happened? What are you talking about, Tara? Please tell me…you're really scaring me!" Dakota pleaded.

"My baby…he hurt my baby," was all she managed to scream before she burst into uncontrollable sobs once more.

Of course Dakota thought the worst. Her mind raced all over the place. Was her child dead? Had her M.I.A. husband come home and killed one of their children? Not knowing was unbearable. As a last-ditch effort to learn the truth, Dakota screamed her name.

"Tara! You're not making sense! What happened?"

Tara contained herself, then methodically told Dakota the unthinkable.

"Over the past four months, JR's physical education teacher has been sexually molesting him." A long pause followed and then a deep breath. She continued.

"Apparently after gym the teacher would keep JR behind to show him different basketball techniques. You know how much JR loves basketball, so he was game. This freak would get behind JR and caress and fondle him while having him hold the ball or focusing his aim to shoot. It started with him caressing his butt and his balls, but eventually he unzipped JR's pants and gave him head."

"Oh no!" Dakota inhaled and slowly let the air out, trying to get past feeling faint.

"It wasn't until he asked my baby to give him head did it become an issue. My baby ran for his life and hid in the janitor's closet. When he did not show up for his last period class, the staff and security began to look for him. Mister Neely, the janitor, found him in the janitor's closet crying."

Tara explained that the police had been called and the teacher had been arrested. She met the police at the school and drove her son home. After he bathed, she fixed him his favorite drink, hot chocolate with extra whipped cream and marshmallows, and held him until he fell asleep.

Nearly holding her breath, Dakota clung to every word as Tara discussed in great detail the repulsive act over and over again. Amidst a long silence, Dakota began to pray. She immediately realized that the trauma this perverted act heaped upon JR, Tara and his siblings would require more than police intervention.

"Thanks for praying. I am going to need God's strength. Tomorrow I have to take him to the doctor to see if he was penetrated. If he was… then he has to be tested for a ST…" Agonizing screams could be heard as Tara broke down at the thought of her innocent child possibly being infected with HIV or any other sexually transmitted disease.

Dakota held the phone waiting for her to return. The line stayed open and she could hear Tara moaning at times and then burst into screams of agony once more. Helpless, she held the phone, rocked and cried. For a second she thought about calling Kizzie, but Tara made it clear she wanted no one else to know— that included her mother. Before she finally hung up the phone, the sun had set causing all light to fade from Dakota's bedroom.

In the darkness, a feeling of gloom overcame her. Realizing Tara was handling this alone made her quiver. She wished at this instant Tara had a loving caring man like Chauncey in her life to lean on and help her get through what she was facing. Two hours passed before she emerged from the darkness. When she did, she missed seeing Elly dart from the bottom of the stairs where she'd been camped out eavesdropping

"Girl, you been upstairs a long time. I stopped by to see Dad *and* you. Why you leave a sistah hangin'?" In no mood for company or conversation, Dakota faked a smile and walked past her to the bathroom.

"You okay?" Elly asked when she emerged.

"Fine…fine," Dakota lied, waving her hands as she disappeared up the steps to her bedroom.

The nightmares that accompanied the horror of the news she had learned about her "play nephew" were indescribable. Dakota tossed and turned all night, waking in a sweat. Bolting upright, she looked around her room making sure she was safe. Knowing her father was just one level below brought a sense of relief, reminding her of how safe she felt as a child.

Reflecting on her healthy, loving, and wholesome upbringing, despite her parents' divorce, Dakota pondered what kind of monster could abuse a child. More importantly, she wondered what scars the child would retain. Thankful she never knew such horrors, Dakota went to her father's bedroom and hugged him.

Returning to her bedroom she dialed Chauncey's number and was disturbed when it rolled to voicemail. When they first began dating, he was always available. They enjoyed whispering sweet things to each other late at night and falling asleep to each other's words.

Conversely, lately he was less and less available when she called him in the middle of the night. His lack of availability was most noticeable after he thought she should be asleep. If she left a message, it took over an hour for him to call and when he did he seemed rushed and distracted. Dakota made a mental note to ask him about this, but tonight she only wanted to talk to him about Tara. She finally drifted off to sleep wondering where he was.

CHAPTER 23

Was it love at first sight? Perhaps! But ten carats made a believer out of Dakota. Eight months into a serious monogamous relationship and no baby mama drama from Kelsey's birth mother made her secure and comfortable enough to say yes to Chauncey's marriage proposal.

There was nothing special or romantic about the way he popped the question. No getting down on bended knee with roses and a speech. He simply walked into her office, announced God had confirmed she was his wife and opened a small box that housed ten, nearly flawless carats. And when he did, Dakota lost her mind. With the ring still in the box, she ran through the office screaming and showing it to everyone. Excited and elated, Seanny burst into tears. Applicants applauded and the "haters" in the office rolled their eyes and shut their office doors.

"Ten carats! Can you believe it? He gave me ten carats, one for me, one for him and one for each month we've been dating," she shrieked as she ran back to her office and hugged her fiancé.

"You like it?" he asked.

"Love it!" Dakota cooed.

Good news travels fast. Then again, the recipient of the news determines if it is good or bad. Days after agreeing to become

Mrs. Chauncey Bentley, Dakota began to plan her engagement dinner. With Chauncey's blessing, she planned a lavish occasion and included Val, Rodney and me as part of the invitees so she could gloat and rub her happiness in our faces.

"Gurl-ll, did you get an invite to this charade?" I asked Elly as I read the invitation for the third time.

"What invite? To what charade?" Elly asked.

"From your sister-in-law? She's getting married to that fake."

Speechless, Elly listened as I read the invite to her.

"Jeff and I were just over there. She didn't have a ring on her finger! This has to be a joke. No way would she marry *him*."

"Well, you're wrong. Her name is Dakota North—right?" I asked sarcastically.

"Quit playin'! You know what her name is. What's goin' on? Where's an engagement ring?"

"It's probably so small you can't see it and I bet she's embarrassed to wear it."

The truth was, Dakota chose not to wear her rings around her brother and his wife because of all the flack she took when she decided to turn down the Mercedes Chauncey bought her. One week after Chauncey gave her the bill of sale; he called to tell her it was ready to be picked up. Uncomfortable with such an elaborate gift so early in their relationship, Dakota declined to accept it. Although she never told her brother and sister-in-law she did not accept the gift, she regretted she told them about the bill of sale. They believed he never bought it for her; surmising the bill of sale was fraudulent. "An old street trick, straight out the playah's handbook," Jeff suggested.

For months she listened to their suspicions and negative comments about Chauncey and said nothing in his defense, but she did not forget their negative reaction or what they'd said. So, she was in no hurry to tell them about her ring or the engagement. The last thing she needed was more berating and negative feedback about her future husband, or whether the ten carats were real.

Recently, Dakota had shared her previous wealthy background with Chauncey, something she'd kept to herself until now. Up to that point he was unaware she'd come from luxury and she hoped his knowing that would enhance their relationship and stop him from trying so hard to impress her with material things. Her belief was his choice of ten carats (instead of something smaller) came from that conversation. With that in mind she could not help but wonder whether all ten of them were his way of proving to her he could well afford to restore her to her previous pedestal of wealth.

Dialing her husband's number, Elly put me on hold, clicking me into the call when he picked up.

"Hey, I got Ro on the line. Did you know your sister is engaged to that fool?"

"What fool?" Jeff asked.

"The fake Mercedes bill of sale nut!" Elly squealed.

"What? Ain't no way...sis wouldn't fall for him! She can see right through him...where'd you hear this?"

"Ro, am I lyin'?" Elly asked, seeking confirmation from me.

"Jeff, she's tellin' the truth. I got the invite in front of me. Want me to read it to you?"

He answered yes and I slowly read the entire invitation to him. Hurt and in disbelief he did not utter a word. After a couple seconds of silence, he excused himself from the conversation, unable to digest the news.

Certain Chauncey was a penniless fake; Elly and I spent the

next few hours laughing and debating about the cost of a two-carat cubic zirconium, certain that's what he had given to Dakota.

He who laughs last, laughs best! Running into Dakota days later at my favorite java stop, I spilled my entire cup of coffee when I saw Dakota stirring her brew with a huge diamond on her ring finger. Although I never gave her the satisfaction of asking to see the ring, I could not help but stare at it from afar.

While she waited in line to pay for her coffee, I darted to my car to call Elly and Val. Conference call connected, I spoke rapidly, full of disbelief and dismay.

"Ma, you there?" Val answered yes.

"You there, Elly?" She too answered yes.

"Sit down…that heifer got a diamond on her finger big as your head. I mean hu-uu-ge! Now where'd this loser get that kind of money?"

"How you know it's real?" Val asked.

"Ma, I know diamonds. It's real!" I snapped, perturbed my mother questioned me as if I were an idiot.

"Drug dealer. He's gotta be…that's the only valid answer," Val said emphatically.

"Wait a minute. Why he got to be a drug dealer? Anybody find out what he does for a living?" Elly asked.

"Nope. Been asking around, but nobody ever heard of him. If he were somebody, I would know," I said matter-of-factly.

As Dakota walked to my Benz, I turned away pretending not to see her. Tapping on the window to get my attention, she smiled a huge smile, gave me a "Miss America wave" with her left hand, making sure the ring was in full view, said "nice car," and then walked away.

"Oh, no she didn't! That witch! You are not going to believe this. She just walked over to my car and tapped on the window. When I looked up, she did the 'Miss America' move—smile and a wave, with the ring in my face, and walked away."

Val gasped and Elly burst into laughter. Not enjoying the egg on my face, I made light of the situation by bringing up the cubic zirconium again. We all laughed and finished our conference call by debating whose theory about his wealth was correct.

Dakota's drive to work was extra special. Flashing her real ten carats in my face was fulfilling. To have the forethought to gloat by waving it "Miss America" style was a long overdue orgasm.

Misery loves company and when you're not miserable your company can be limited. Not many responded to her engagement invitation, Tara was one of them. However, with the exception of a few, me included, those who did respond were those who really cared about her and wished her well.

❤❤❤

Elly and I arrived very late. Dinner had already been served and a toast was underway when we walked in. Seanny, head hostess for the evening, consulted with Dakota first, and then had the wait staff bring meals for us.

As we sat to eat, Jeff looked at Elly and frowned; disappointed her late arrival interrupted his toast. Raising his glass once more to give the last toast of the evening, the moment never arrived. Seconds before he spoke, a short, stodgy, dark-skinned woman (looking and sounding a lot like comedienne Cheryl Underwood, minus the purse), burst through the door with five people trailing behind her. She went straight to Chauncey and Dakota's table and began to speak a well-rehearsed speech.

"Hold up! Ain't gonna be no engagement celebratin' here tonight!" she proclaimed. With hands on her hips and shifting from side to side she continued. "How can this man be engaged to you when he gave me a ring just three months ago?" she asked Dakota, obviously grandstanding.

Gasps filled the room. Glasses were lowered as everyone looked on in disbelief.

Chauncey's ailing father moved toward the woman, fist balled with all intentions of knocking her out. Rushing to his side, Chauncey pulled him back. She continued.

"I know this baby ain't about to call you momma. That's what he calls me," she said as she reached to take Kelsey from Chauncey's arms. Three-year-olds don't lie."

Kelsey, with a frown on his face, pulled away from her and screamed, "I not call you ma!"

Some of the guests chuckled and others whispered as her well-weaved tale began to unravel. When she stepped to Dakota to show her ring, Dakota smiled at the tarnished piece of cut glass. Shocking the woman and everyone looking on, Dakota grabbed her hand and flipped it over, exposing the adjustable band that had been pinched together to fit her finger.

Although she was humiliated, the woman continued ranting until she informed the invited guests she was a pastor and was engaged to Chauncey. To prove her story true, she'd brought some of her congregation to accompany her. However, embarrassed by this tirade, one by one they backed out of the room. When she turned to them for confirmation, only one person remained by her side, her sister. Shaking her head, the lone "church member," walked past the pastor and approached Chauncey and Dakota. Apologizing, she explained they had been led to believe they were coming there for a very different reason. After a sincere apology once more, she walked out the door leaving her sister, the pastor, all alone.

While everyone else focused on this out–of-control woman Dakota perused the room. The only two people not appearing to be surprised or disgusted were Elly and me. She wondered why, and why were we so late?

CHAPTER 24

Fall was approaching and "Old Man Winter" was fast on its heels. Temperatures were rapidly falling in Detroit and Chauncey wanted to get out of Michigan before it got any colder.

As soon as he mentioned fun and sun, Dakota jumped at the chance to enjoy both on a beautiful sandy beach. Her thoughts immediately centered on a tropical island. Although the Bahamas, Jamaica and Aruba all guaranteed fun and relaxation, her heart longed to visit St. Croix; an island she'd yet to pay homage. To sell this Caribbean paradise to a man afraid of flying, she needed some backup.

Over lunch and right after giving him exceptional head, Dakota showed him several beautiful brochures she'd picked up from the hotel lobby en route to the restaurant. Each brochure presented a different side to the allure of St. Croix. Unfolding three, she placed them in front of Chauncey while she placed her bare foot on his crotch and slowly moved it back and forth, arousing him instantly.

"So...what do you think?" she asked.

Chauncey looked at her, smiled and gently grabbed her foot.

"You got my attention!"

"Well, have you seen such a beautiful place?" she cooed as she removed her foot from his hand and placed it back in her shoe.

"Never! St. Croix, huh? That's near St. Thomas, right...the Virgin Islands...surrounded by all that water?" he asked nervously. Noticing the concern in his voice, she attempted to calm his fears.

"Baby, it's not a long flight! Think about it, okay?" she begged.

"I suppose driving is not an option?" he joked.

Not one to let an opportunity pass, Dakota explained they could drive to Florida, catch a flight from there, and be in St. Croix in a couple hours.

Chauncey folded the brochures and returned them to Dakota.

"Let me think about it, baby..."

Disappointed he did not say yes, she remained hopeful. Since he didn't say no, she tried one last time to win him over.

"Okay, just know I really want to make love to you on a secluded beach. You've made some of my other dreams come true...make this fantasy happen, baby!" she whispered seductively.

That evening, excited and certain he would agree to vacation in St. Croix, Dakota discussed her plans with her father. Seeing her smile and so full of joy made him happy but he was apprehensive about encouraging her to go. Seldom did he ever voice an opinion on her personal life; this time he did.

"I like Chauncey...seems like a nice guy. But do you know him well enough to run off to some island with him?"

Dakota laughed at his question. Her father was always suspicious of people— "too many movies" is how she dismissed what he said.

Smiling, her father chuckled and then shot her a "think about what I said" look before going to bed. A week later, at Chauncey's suggestion, she submitted a "leave of absence" to her manager, with no intention of returning. Seanny had returned to college and the new secretary was a terror. Two of the three account reps had resigned. Overworked, Dakota looked forward to leaving $10 an hour behind.

Two days prior to their scheduled departure, Chauncey surprised Dakota with a call just after midnight informing her he'd be there in a couple hours to pick her up. Puzzled by his sudden need to leave early, she questioned why. Assuring her they would discuss it on the road she did not hesitate to finish packing and get dressed. Just before walking out the door, she wrote a note to her father explaining they'd left and included her new cell phone number.

"I packed several of my swimsuits...you?" Chauncey smiled and kissed her hand as he pulled out of her dad's driveway.

"Hey, who's keeping Kelsey?" she asked.

Chauncey explained he'd left him with his favorite aunt who adored him and spoiled him rotten. Thrilled about getting away to some sun and fun, alone with her man, Dakota's heart rushed. Days prior to this departure, she'd not slept well full of anticipation about finally going to St. Croix. An hour into the ride she dozed off and slept for five hours. Stopping for gas woke her.

"Where are we, baby?" she asked groggily.

"Ten more hours and we'll be there." *Ten more hours*, she thought to herself. She'd assumed they were driving to Florida to fly to St. Croix. Well traveled, Dakota knew enough about traveling to know his announcement of "ten more hours and we'll be there" did not mean Florida or St. Croix.

A bit presumptuous, she had not discussed her version of a good time with Chauncey since their one and only conversation about leaving town focused on St. Croix. Why should she? He'd always done everything in his power to grant her her every wish. When he told her to take a leave from her job and he'd handle her bills, she assumed he was going to make her dream of running off to St. Croix a reality—"assumed" being the key word.

"Chauncey, where exactly are we going?" He smiled broadly and winked. She was not feelin' this game of "tag."

"Okay…I know *you* like surprises, but you know I don't. Where are we going?" she asked firmly. Heaving a sigh, Chauncey answered her question.

"I'm taking you to meet my mother and sisters. They've been waiting to meet my future wife and I thought this would be a good time."

All her excitement about relaxing in the sun on a beautiful sandy beach faded instantly.

"Don't they live in Alabama?"

"Yeah, and there are some beautiful sandy beaches there," he joked. Dakota frowned, sunk into the seat and stared out the window. Alabama and meeting his messy family was not her idea of a good time. Granted, she had not met them, but that could be accomplished in a weekend—by air. Driving fourteen hours to say "hi," be put on display, and get grilled about their future wedding plans was not something she looked forward to. After a long deep sigh, she drifted off to sleep.

"Hey, baby, wake up. We're here," Chauncey said as he lovingly rubbed her cheek.

Incoherent and groping for her sunglasses Dakota bumped her head on the sun visor as she gathered her bearings.

"Ma, this is the love of my life," she heard Chauncey say as she leaned down to rummage through her purse for a breath mint.

Opening her car door, he helped her out and she extended her hand to greet his mother.

"Hi, Mrs. Bentley. I'm Dakota."

"You can call her Mo!" Chauncey offered as he put his arm around Dakota. His mother extended her hand and Dakota gently held it and then spontaneously hugged her. Caught off guard by her spontaneity, his mother froze and began to chuckle. Dakota laughed as well.

"What's so funny?" Chauncey asked. Dakota did not know and his mother did not say, allowing an obvious awkward moment to quickly pass. Hungry, he suggested they all go to his favorite restaurant, Golden Corral.

"If Man had told me ya'll were comin,' I would've fixed some dinner."

"Man?" Dakota squealed.

"That's what we call him...been callin' him that since he was one," Mo explained as she fondly looked at him, remembering how much she enjoyed him as a child.

"So, you *really* didn't know we were coming?" Dakota asked, wondering why Chauncey had not informed his mother they would be visiting. Concern and anxiety started to take hold. Leaving two days early like "thieves in the night" began to bother her. In retrospect, she wondered why he rushed to leave, especially since his family was not expecting them. Realizing they had not discussed it "on the road" as promised, her mood changed.

She could not stand confusion and lack of organization and Chauncey seemed to thrive in it. This was not the first time he'd shown he might not be capable of being "President of the Entertainment Committee," a position he promoted himself to. Prior to now, she'd allowed him to be in complete control. It genuinely felt good to let a man *be the man.* But more and more she was becoming disenchanted with his inability to get it right; the letdowns were becoming quite frequent.

Chauncey avoided eye contact with Dakota; he knew he'd messed up. Surely she'd have questions, she always did. Problem was he did not have answers. The late-night telephone call he received from a Detective Jones frightened him. According to her, a "Pastor Cross" had come in and filed a written complaint against him, claiming to be in possession of two checks he had her cash for him that were written on a closed account.

That bogus claim did not bother him. He knew he had not written any checks to Pastor Cross, who happened to be the woman who intruded on his engagement dinner. However, the outstanding warrant he had for failing to pay child support was of great concern.

Suffice it to say if the detective knew his home phone number she probably knew where he lived. He was not going to wait around to find out. Getting arrested was not something he wanted to deal with; the end result would be losing Dakota. Losing her was not an option; running from the law was. Alabama seemed like a safe place to be—for now!

CHAPTER 25

Minors are not photographed and their names are not printed for public review. For now, Tara's son's secret was safe. Rumors had begun to circulate around the school and the school district, but no one knew of whom the rumors spoke. In an effort to ensure anonymity, Tara removed all her children from that school and enrolled them in a neighboring school district.

Not one word had been heard from her husband or his friends and family. Tara was never their first choice for him; her spending habits cut into their spending habits. None of that was important to her now; she needed her husband. More importantly, her son needed his father.

Placing a call to the one sister she did get along with, Tara asked her to please get in touch with Alex and let him know there was an emergency at home. When she pressed for more information Tara lied and said it was related to her mother. His sister denied knowing his whereabouts, but Tara knew she was hiding the truth. He was a momma's boy and to keep from worrying her, he never left home for any length of time without letting her know he was fine.

Lost and in need of some solid advice, Tara went to see the

one other person she could trust with this information—her play dad. This sixty-five-year-old "playah" was best friends with the most prominent high-profile attorney in criminal law, JC, better known as Jesse Crowe. Every mega-star and celebrity hired him when they got in trouble. To date he'd not lost a court battle and her play dad doubted he'd start with JR's case.

Meeting such an icon was earth moving for Tara and her son. During their lengthy consultation he agreed to handle the case and assured her it would end with her, her son and her other children set for life. She left his office feeling much better about receiving vindication for their heartache and pain.

Most children who are molested have a tendency to falter at some point in their lives. Scars, guilt, psychological and physical issues haunt them. Many never find their way back to a stable life and many become child molesters, themselves. Jesse wanted to eliminate that possibility for JR and to get the ball rolling in a positive direction, he immediately arranged for him and his mom to begin counseling.

JC felt it was his responsibility to ensure his client and family members had a jump-start when he reached adulthood. That jump-start—millions—would get him on his feet and carry him the rest of his life.

In Tara's mind, no amount of money could make this horrible nightmare go away, but knowing her child would have a chance in life, and all the professional assistance he needed, helped her relax. For the first time in months she was able to sleep, without having a nightmare.

Dakota's untimely call woke Tara from a sound sleep. Alabama was just as boring as she thought it would be. Frustrated with being there and disappointed there would not be a St. Croix vacation, she called her best friend to check on her and vent.

"Hey, you okay?" Dakota asked as Tara answered the phone sounding groggy.

"Yeah girl, lots goin' on, but we're makin' it. What about you?"

"I'm good. Need to talk though…you got a minute?"

"Uh…can you call me back in about a half hour?" Tara asked sounding distracted.

"Okay…talk to you then." Dakota hung up the phone disappointed. Going home immediately would make her happy, but Chauncey had a stubborn side and when she brought it up he ignored her. Enjoying his family would be normal if he had not already stated that he did not like or enjoy being around them. His wanting to stay made her curious. Something just did not seem right!

Talking it over with Tara might help shed some light. Back in the day they made an awesome two-some. No mystery went unsolved. They were the best at busting their wayward spouses and relished those moments. Thirty minutes passed and Dakota called back and let the phone ring fifteen times before hanging up. Catnapping, Tara rolled over and looked at the caller ID. Not recognizing Dakota's new cell phone number she let it ring.

"Wonder what is going on," Dakota mumbled as she flipped her cell phone closed. "It's not like her to not have her answering machine on." A mental flashback to the molestation JR had suffered made Dakota nauseated. She popped another chip in her mouth to make the awful bile taste disappear.

Each chip she bit into was soothing. Chauncey sat next to her watching mindless TV—*The Three Stooges*. His mom and sister sat with him, laughing and enjoying this time together. Wanting out of purgatory, Dakota leaned back on the sofa and took advantage of the "down time" to make some critical decisions. Leaving Alabama immediately was something she'd have to persuade Chauncey to do. How to accomplish the exodus was a major task she gave herself twelve hours to figure out. Falling asleep on his shoulder eliminated the possibility of formulating her "escape."

CHAPTER 26

No one knew where Dakota was, nor had anyone heard from her. Age had begun to affect her father's memory and he totally forgot she'd mentioned the vacation with Chauncey. The note she'd left him explaining where she was and with whom, also contained her new cell phone number. Although he noticed the neatly folded piece of paper on the floor, without glasses to read it, he assumed it was trash and tossed it—failing to notice the writing and never reading what it said.

Panic set in causing genuine concern amongst Dakota's family. Tara was the one person I was sure would know Dakota's whereabouts. Problem was, no one had her number. Two days went by before someone thought to check Dakota's phone bill for Tara's number. Finding it in a stack of papers in her room, I volunteered to call since I had personally met Tara.

"Tara...hi, this is Dakota's cousin Rochelle." Unable to recognize the voice Tara did not respond. "Are you there?"

"Who did you say this is?" Tara asked guardedly.

"Dakota's cousin Rochelle...from Detroit."

"Oh! Yeah, I remember...is everything okay?"

"Well...something has happened and I really need your help."

"My God, what is it? What's happened?" she asked, her voice rising from fear.

"It's Dakota. Have you heard from her?"

"Not lately, why?" Tara managed to ask as tears formed in her eyes and rolled down her cheeks.

Explaining Dakota was missing, I informed her of my suspicion that she was possibly with Chauncey. Giving her my spin on who I believed Chauncey was and what I thought about him, frightened Tara. By the time I finished painting that Picasso, she was ready to call the FBI.

Agreeing to work together on finding Dakota, we called each other all day and into the night trying to piece together what could have happened to her and to learn if the other had heard from her. Forty-eight hours later, Dakota called her father. By then I had taken advantage of the crisis and my desire to launch an all-out campaign of unveiling who Chauncey Bentley might really be.

Pastor Cross was the first person I contacted. We had not spoken since meeting in the lobby of the hotel on the night of Dakota's engagement dinner to discuss how she'd barge in and interrupt the occasion. That night, with Elly in tow, I quickly reviewed what was expected of Pastor Cross and paid her my half of her asking price of $1,000 in cash. Elly had to get $300 from the lobby ATM to complete her $500, which is why we arrived so late. Parting company the moment she was paid, we agreed to never discuss what transpired and never contact each other again.

This emergency warranted going back on our agreement, so I called her and arranged to meet her in the church office. Behind closed doors Pastor Cross admitted she'd had an affair with Chauncey and he'd been spending days and nights with her for the past six months. Suspecting he'd met someone after he began to withdraw from any physical intimacy, she kept a close watch on him.

Smitten and afraid of losing him she attempted to buy him with money. Church money was spent on him and she felt he owed her for what she spent. Clothing for him and toys for his son, Kelsey, were purchased with tithes and offerings from her church. Several of the car notes for his Escalade were paid from her own personal account.

Two years prior to his meeting Dakota, the pastor met Chauncey when she made a service call to his company. In need of an air conditioning unit for her church, a fund-raiser had garnered close to $5,000 to make the purchase and ensure it was installed on top of the building and not on the ground. The seedy area her church was in would have allowed for some thief to steel the unit in the middle of the night once installation was complete.

Over a period of time Chauncey's company also handled several other church maintenance and contracting issues. Spending hours around him, she became very attracted to him and their business relationship quickly evolved into a physical one.

Living in his ailing father's dilapidated home kept her at bay, but she wanted him around on a more permanent basis. Eventually she began to "buy" his affections and with hopes of making him a permanent fixture, she suggested he "move in." Bitter about his leaving her for Dakota, Pastor Cross admitted she went through his things he never retrieved from her home and found a checkbook in a duffle bag.

As payback for all he'd put her through she made two checks out to herself, forged his signature and then deposited them. To leave a paper trail she withdrew the cash and waited several weeks before reporting she'd been scammed to the police. Such a brilliant scheme should not be wasted. I made a mental note to use it in the future.

Pastor Cross knew some of Chauncey's business partners but

had no numbers on them. However, she did know what church one of them attended. In her pastor capacity she called the office of the presiding pastor's congregation, and ended the conversation with contact information for one of the partners. We called him and arranged a meeting.

Elly was recruited and we all met the business partner for cocktails. Guarded, he listened to our suspicions and became alarmed when the pastor showed him the returned checks from Chauncey. It frightened him because they shared a business checking account. The wealthy and influential clientele he conducted business with would not be forgiving if he were connected to such illegalities.

Realizing we had him just where we wanted him, I accused Chauncey of being a money launderer for drug dealers and a con who used unsuspecting women for their hard-earned money and life savings.

Feeling a need to explain his relationship with Chauncey, the partner admitted only knowing him a short time and being clueless as to where his wealth came from. Short on cash when he met Chauncey, the partner accepted funds from him without question. The fact that the money could be "dirty" left him shaken and vulnerable. A recently married man with a newly pregnant wife, he admitted he wanted no trouble.

Like a shark smelling fresh blood in the water, I began to feed his fear. Pretending to be concerned for my "wealthy cousin," I made the partner believe Dakota was in danger, as were her affluent friends in California. This opened the door to question him about his business dealings with Chauncey. Scared to death he told us everything he knew, including what banks held the other accounts he mentioned.

Panicked, he left the meeting vowing to cut all ties with Chauncey and close all bank accounts. After he walked out the bar, Elly, Pastor Cross and I ordered a round of champagne to toast our success.

Funny, the frantic search for Dakota was pushed to the back burner with no one in a hurry to find her.

CHAPTER 27

Arriving in Los Angeles was a tremendous relief for Dakota. She hated riding anywhere in a car that a plane could carry her. This five-day journey was the epitome of hell and she decided during her turn driving, Chauncey was going to drive back to Detroit alone.

After checking into a hotel and taking a long hot bath to relax, she felt better about Chauncey's impromptu suggestion to forgo returning to Detroit and driving to LA instead. Missing her friends, she jumped at the opportunity to see them and did not regret her decision until she was asked to take over the driving while Chauncey crawled into the passenger seat to rest. Fourteen hours later, cramps in her legs, a stiff neck, and very groggy, she realized her desire to see her friends overruled sound judgment.

While Chauncey showered, Dakota reclined on the bed and dialed her father. It had been nearly two weeks since she'd seen or spoken to him and she wondered how he was doing. His tearful outburst the moment he heard her voice was alarming. Her heart racing, she sat up on the bed certain someone had died. With baited breath she waited for him to compose himself to tell her who had passed.

"Wh-wh…" Her dad was so shaken he could not speak.

"Daddy, what's wrong?" she asked softly and waited for him to answer. It took a few seconds for him to speak. Once he blew his nose, he cleared his voice and spoke softly

"Where are you? Are you okay? If you can't talk just say so!" Confused and at a loss as to what her father was talking about, Dakota became frightened. Never giving her time to answer he continued babbling about her being in danger.

"Dad! What are you talking about?" she shouted. The shouting got his attention and he stopped talking and let her speak.

"Listen to me…I'm fine. Why would you think I wasn't?"

"That guy you're with…he ain't who he says he is. You don't know him. He's with you to try to get money from your rich friends. Y'all not in California, are you?"

Flabbergasted, Dakota began to cry. Not for her or Chauncey, but because she thought her elderly father was losing his mind; Alzheimer's or something! Hearing her cry made him cry, and neither said a word.

Chauncey listened through the bathroom door, but decided to leave the two of them to their conversation while he showered. My uncle explained I had investigated Chauncey and found out he was a money launderer and a con artist. Prior to dating Dakota he had someone check her background and knew her good friends included a wealthy circle of individuals. His ultimate goal was to drain her friends' bank accounts through contrived business transactions.

"What!" Dakota shrieked. "Let me get this straight. Everything you just told me you got from Rochelle?" Exhaling slowly to calm the anger that was beginning to rise, she composed herself and chose her words carefully. "Dad, why would you listen to *her?*"

Crying once more, her father explained he had not heard from her and no one knew where she was. I offered to help locate her and in doing so met with people who knew Chauncey, and these individuals shared terrible things about him. Out of concern, I brought the information to him and with nothing to go on, he believed me.

This is B.S., Dakota decided after carefully considering the source—me. Knowing my twisted behind like she did, Dakota knew not to put one minute of thought into what she'd just heard from her father. Dismissing it was instantaneous for her and she wished her father could do the same. The next hour was spent trying to reassure him Chauncey was who he said he was and had what he said he had.

"Dad, listen. We are in California and he has not met any of my friends…but I doubt he'd harm any of them."

Not as certain, her father pleaded with her to leave him and come home. "I'll pay for your flight. Just please come home!"

Listening to him choke back tears and try to mask the fear in his voice, Dakota became alarmed. Realizing how frightened her father was and concerned about his fragile health, Dakota did not end their conversation until she felt comfortable that he'd calmed down. Curious why he had not called her before now with this information, her father told her the cell phone number he had for her was not working.

"What do you mean it's not working? I just called you from my cell phone! What number are you dialing?"

"The one I always dial," he snapped.

"Dad, I left you my new number and my whereabouts before I left. Didn't you get the note?"

"Left a note where?" he asked, genuinely concerned about his daughter's state of mind.

Backtracking, Dakota walked him through where she left the note and helped him remember what he did with it. By the time they hung up, her father was laughing and feeling better. Although he still wanted her to come home, he was okay with her being gone as long as he could contact her.

Prior to hanging up the phone she begged him to stay away from me and my overactive imagination.

He agreed to her terms, *in word only.*

CHAPTER 28

Cali was just like she remembered. Hot, crowded and smoggy. Since it was Chauncey's first time there, Dakota agreed to do the tourist thing and show him the sights— Mann's Chinese Theatre, Hollywood Boulevard, the Walk of Fame and Sunset Strip. They ran into quite a few stars, some she knew.

Most people would show some sort of excitement. Not Chauncey. Dakota was thoroughly impressed with his poker face and laid-back demeanor when introduced to someone famous. He had that "I'm just as important as you are" arrogance that she'd not seen on a "commoner" and she liked it!

Continuing to be a tour guide, she pointed out more well-known places as they slowly drove to the beach.

"So, what do you want to do now?" she asked as she playfully kicked sand on his leg and darted off down the beach. Chauncey did not chase behind her; it was too hot! Instead he watched her run and frolic in the sand, enjoying the role of observer rather than participant.

Famished, Dakota returned to the rock he was seated on and pulled him to her. The restaurant, which hosted her last birthday bash, was a short walk away. After a long passionate kiss, he placed her hand on his crotch and agreed to join her if she'd do something about the rise in his shorts.

"Deal. Feed me and I'll do whatever you wish," she said giggling and bowing.

"Okay...enough of that. You know I don't see you as a slave or anything other than my equal. Beside me, remember?" Chauncey winked and blew her a kiss, watching her walk ahead of him to the restaurant.

Pretending to catch it, Dakota skipped the rest of the way to the entrance. Winded and tired by the time he arrived, she sat on the bench in the front entrance and rested while he got their table.

Grilled salmon had been one of the entrées at her party and if memory served her correctly it was delicious. Allergic to seafood, Chauncey got his usual T-bone steak and baked potato. While the waiter served their appetizer, Dakota excused herself and went to the ladies room. Upon her return she was surprised by the nearby sound of a voice she'd not heard in quite some time. Turning around to locate the voice, she spotted Sonya Lee and her "European bank account" seated with a record industry mogul Dakota knew quite well.

Rather than interrupt their conversation, she sent a bottle of wine to their table, compliments of Mr. and Mrs. Sanders, a suggestion of Chauncey's. Where Sonya Lee and posse were seated shielded them from the prying eyes of the public and blocked Dakota's ability to watch their reaction. Curiosity almost got the best of her, but Chauncey, a master at playing the game of "tag," kept her calm.

"Wait. She'll come over. The fact that someone acknowledged her *stardom* will make her curious to find out who sent the bottle."

How right he was! As they looked at the dessert selections, that Southern drawl in Manolo Blahniks, a halter top and mini skirt worked its way to their table, greeting each person along her path.

Approaching from the rear of the room, Dakota's back was to Sonya Lee as she approached. Instantly her eyes focused on the bling on Chauncey's ring fingers. Assuming he had money and status, she extended her hand to thank him for the bottle of Chablis, without paying attention to Dakota.

"What a kind gesture. Have we met?"

"*We* have not, but you and my fiancée have!" he replied, motioning to Dakota. Sonya Lee shifted her eyes to Dakota's ring finger and grabbed her hand, never once looking at her face.

"Mah goodness…someone sure loves you," she quipped. Dakota responded by pulling her hand away and standing up.

"I know!" she said and reached to hug Sonya Lee. Startled, she pushed her back and then realized who she was and screamed. People in the room turned to see if something was wrong.

"Duh-ko-dah! Is that you?" Sonya Lee squealed as she grabbed her and hugged her tightly.

They both giggled and jumped up and down. Chauncey laughed. The sight of Sonya Lee half naked, bouncing up and down and nothing on her jiggling or moving was hilarious.

"Plastic—inside and out," he mumbled.

Her European sponsor moseyed over to where the commotion was and burst into a hearty laugh when he saw Dakota. The two of them were pleased to see her happy and anxious to know more about Chauncey; each for different reasons. Sonya Lee, because she hoped he was a wealthy music tycoon; and her husband because he hoped he could talk him into investing in his new real estate business venture. And perhaps while they talked he'd also get some guidance on how to get Sonya Lee out of his checkbook.

Chauncey and Dakota followed them back to their home. Their guesthouse was vacant and they graciously extended an offer for them to stay. Dakota declined the offer and disappeared to the office with Sonya Lee, leaving the guys alone to talk.

"Now gurl-ll, you sure what ya doin'? Is this what you really want to do?" Sonya Lee asked, mincing no words and wasting no time getting in Dakota's business.

"What do you mean?" Dakota asked, already disturbed by the direction this conversation was heading.

"You come from money...I know he must have some. You in this for his money?" Before Dakota could check her, she continued.

"Marriage ain't necessary in today's day and time, ya know... shack with him and git to know him," she suggested.

Counting to ten before she responded, Dakota calmly gave her a long overdue tongue-lashing, reminding Sonya Lee she met and married her European sponsor in less time than Dakota knew Chauncey. Six weeks of wining and dining, *she* asked him to marry her and had drained his pockets since.

Before this could escalate into a full-blown argument, Chauncey interrupted them, speaking through the office door.

"Baby, I'm tired. We should go."

"Come on in. We're done," she answered as she stood and picked up her purse. Sonya Lee stood as well, and European-kissed Dakota. Approaching Chauncey to do the same, he kept her at a distance by extending his hand for a shake. Slapping his hand away, Sonya Lee hugged him instead. He laughed, finding her pretentious; she did not, finding him uncouth!

On the drive back to the hotel, Dakota asked Chauncey what he and Sonya Lee's husband talked about.

"He's looking for some financial investors for a new real estate venture he is about to undertake."

"How much?" she asked half-heartedly.

"A mil," Chauncey said dryly.

"As in a million dollars?" Dakota exclaimed.

"Yeah…he needs each investor to put up a million and he needs thirty investors."

"That's thirty million dollars! I know you told him no," she said emphatically, waving off the conversation as if she were dismissing a servant.

Chauncey never responded, allowing her to believe he turned the deal down. In truth he was very much interested in doing business with Sonya Lee's husband. There was a ton of money to be made in real estate and this was an opportunity of a lifetime. He wrote him a check for $100,000, the down payment minimum each investor must pay.

Experienced in real estate investing, Chauncey knew a good deal when he heard one. He'd done well in amassing his small fortune from buying and flipping properties in and around Detroit. And although he'd invested his money well and had some funds tucked away, a million dollars was steep for his pockets, which did run deep—but not that deep. If he pulled out a million from his finances, he'd have to live like a pauper for years waiting for the payoff.

His fiancée did not impress him as the type who would agree to living on a shoestring budget—long term, and this venture was no quick flip and run. Street wisdom convinced him to keep his mouth shut and see what happened.

CHAPTER 29

"Oh my God!" Tara whispered, staring at her caller ID. Without hesitation she picked up the phone and began to scream and yell at her best friend.

"What is your problem? Do you know how many people are looking for you? What is wrong with you…why would you let your father and brothers worry about you like this? You're so selfish…anything for a man. That's you; always has been, always will be!"

In disbelief, Dakota held the phone and listened to the ongoing verbal abuse. There were no words to respond to what had been said. Things Tara had secretly felt and thought oozed out of the top of this erupting volcano, crept slowly through her insides, scorching every inch of Dakota's feelings. Once the "hot lava" stopped flowing, Dakota hung up, speechless and numb. Tears filled her eyes as she slowly turned and looked at Chauncey, hoping to find comfort in his eyes.

Pain—unexpected, unwarranted, and uninvited—consumed her. The love she felt for Tara was matched only by the love she felt for her father and siblings. Tara was the only "sister" she'd known and she expected her to always be on her side—no matter what.

As if in slow motion, Chauncey watched her turn pale as the cell phone toppled from her hand. Strong legs, which dutifully offer support, became limp noodles forcing her to her knees. Dizzy and unable to catch her breath, Dakota collapsed on the floor.

Seconds later, still breathing but clammy, she tried to get up but could not. Chauncey was in the process of dialing 9-1-1 when she reached for him to help her up. Rushing to her side, he gently lifted her to the bed and felt her pulse. Initially it was faint, but in seconds it began to strengthen.

"You okay?" he whispered, holding her in his arms.

"What happened?" she asked softly.

"I think you fainted. I'm not really sure. It all happened so fast."

Lifting herself to her elbows, she looked around the room in an attempt to gather her thoughts. As her memory returned she began to whimper. Harsh words had never been exchanged between her and Tara. In their entire twelve-year friendship, they'd never had an argument or even a "friendly disagreement." They loved each other as sisters and respected each other's love. No—they did not always get along, but they always got past issues peacefully, lovingly and amicably.

With every intention of calling Tara to find out why she behaved with such hostility, Dakota rolled over on the bed to recover her cell phone from the floor. Before she could, Chauncey grabbed it and tossed it across the room. His behavior startled her. Already an emotional wreck, she burst into tears once more.

Remorseful, he retrieved the phone and handed it to her. Placing it on the nightstand, Dakota covered her face with a pillow. Unable to breath, she tossed the pillow on the floor and stared at the ceiling trying to figure out what was going on. Nothing made sense anymore. Tara's disturbing behavior had to be fueled by some other source. But what, and why?

Exhausted, Dakota drifted off to a much-needed sleep while pondering those questions. Chauncey took advantage of this quiet time to sort through some issues he knew he would face when he returned to Detroit. In pursuit of answers, he stole away to the bathroom and made several phone calls to some well-connected close friends: a police captain, a prominent attorney, and a cousin who made a living street hustling.

Their conversations centered on the recent unexplainable occurrences with Dakota's father and her best friend. Less than two hours after he began to pick apart *the what*, he was certain he had the answer to *the who*, and *the why*. Well aware I was jealous of Dakota, he was certain I was behind this drama. Although he had no concrete evidence, he was determined to prove himself right.

A couple days after the incident, Dakota secretly called Tara with hopes of finding out what happened. What she learned tore her heart out! Tara took pleasure in telling Dakota how much I hated her and continued to inform her that the hatred stemmed from childhood and had been hidden for years. Giving great detail, Tara recounted numerous family events and affairs that left me scarred. These scars created a very deep and very dangerous desire to see Dakota dead.

Tara found it amusing that Dakota was completely unaware of how I was extremely jealous of her. Explaining I had endeared myself to her out of envy with hopes of becoming her, Tara burst into laughter. Each new hurtful tidbit she shared with Dakota pierced her soul. Hoping she caused her as much pain as she felt Dakota's betrayal caused her, Tara continued. The one-way conversation lasted over an hour and only became a two-way conversation near the end when Dakota asked why?

"Tara...I need to know why? Why did *you* do this? Why would you go out of your way to hurt me? What did I do to you?"

"Call me Judas," she quipped. The line went dead and so did their long friendship. Dakota sat on the floor of the bathroom and quietly cried, not wanting to wake Chauncey from a sound sleep.

Returning to his side she lay there and reflected on the details of what had been revealed. Per Tara, when I first called her she was guarded. The one and only time she'd spent in my company, she found me to be gossipy and messy. After my initial call, my cousin Jeff called crying, greatly concerned for the well-being of his sister. Lying, he told Tara he had no idea where Dakota could be or who she could be with.

"Why would he do that? Before I left I told him where I was going and who I was leaving town with," Dakota mumbled.

There was a method to his madness. Seeking Dakota's personal information, I tried to coax Tara into revealing Dakota's deep secrets; things from her past that had no relevance regarding what was before them now. Tara kept quiet, so I recruited Dakota's brother for assistance. When he called and revealed through tears their father was taking her disappearance really hard, Tara felt compelled to help.

Keeping her best friend's past a secret was maintained for three more days. However, on the fourth day when I called and dropped a bomb, Tara broke their code of secrecy instantly.

The molestation of Tara's son was a secret Dakota swore to never discuss with anyone else. "I'll take it to my grave," she'd assured her. And she would have, but the secret did surface, therefore Tara decided to bury Dakota and her betrayal in that grave.

Months earlier when Tara phoned Dakota to discuss her son's sexual molestation, Elly eavesdropped on their entire telephone conversation on the cordless phone which was housed on the main level of her father-in-law's home. Sitting at the bottom of the stairwell, she hung up the phone the instant she heard Dakota end the conversation and ran to return the phone to its mount before Dakota came downstairs. That night, Elly called Val and me and repeated this very personal and private conversation word for word.

When I called Tara and did the same, omitting how I learned the information, Tara assumed Dakota betrayed her and their friendship. Because she believed Dakota had already stabbed her in the back, Tara felt no guilt in betraying her best friend. One good stab deserved another!

Angry and hurt, Tara spent two hours listening to and dishing out the details of very personal and hurtful things from Dakota's past, like the abortion she had from a fling with a married man. And the fact that not one sin, but two, haunted her for years: the abortion and he was married.

This was an abomination she'd fought hard to overcome, buried and planned to never exhume. Tara knew this would literally destroy Dakota and her "good girl" reputation and it felt good; so good, she embellished the situation, adding details that never existed for added drama!

Well, Ro knows drama. The queen of it, I couldn't help but get caught up in the details of Dakota's less than stellar past. Hanging up from Tara, I called Elly and Val.

"Gurl, just like I thought! That heifer is just as phony as they come. Miss 'I'm blessed' got lots of dirt out there. 'Celibate' is a word she just learned and obviously seldom practiced. Bet you didn't know she had an abortion after sleeping with a married man."

Val gasped. Elly whispered, "What?" The captive audience instantly hushed to avoid missing any of the details. A great liar,

I embellished the facts, mixing truth with fiction because in my heart I knew my cousin could not "walk on water" like everyone thought. Now I had the opportunity to prove it. Pleased with successfully spearheading her demise, I retired for the night looking forward to the chaos I'd cause in the next twenty-four hours.

CHAPTER 30

Returning to L.A. for an extended stay was the farthest thing from Dakota's mind. Staying there permanently was attainable, but only in her dreams. When Chauncey offered to make her dreams come true, she quickly accepted his offer.

"Baby, why don't you call some of your friends and find a real estate agent? Set up some homes to look at, but make sure they are thirty-day closings or less. I'm going to the front desk to pay on our room and then I'll run to get us something to eat. Want anything in particular?"

On cloud nine, food was the farthest thing from Dakota's mind.

"No bay, whatever you pick up is fine. I'm going to get busy on my homework assignment. See you when you get back." Blowing him a kiss, she reached for her laptop and looked around the room for a telephone book. While her computer booted up, she called a couple friends that she was still in touch with.

Seven were dialed, none contacted, but each was left a wonderful voicemail. An hour after she called her goddaughter's mother, she received a return phone call.

"Hey girl…long time no hear. How are my babies?" Dakota squealed.

"Not babies anymore," Reese answered, chuckling. "They are all grown up, very mature for their ages." Dakota's goddaughters were beautiful fraternal twins, who looked identical. Nothing about their personalities was the same. Night and day they fought: each vying for her own space, time and attention from their mom.

This behavior originated before they ever entered the world. While in the womb, Kayla and Kylee jockeyed for position. Kayla won out on the best spot; upper abdomen and she ate the most. Kylee accepted what was left—lower ab and thumb sucking to compensate for the lack of available groceries.

Giving birth to the twins was difficult. They were delivered by C-section two months early with each weighing just over two pounds. Kylee, mad at her sister from the time she breathed air, was placed in the incubator, feisty and full of life. Despite being born with a hole in her heart she fought hard to live.

The doctors pulled Kylee out of the birth canal first, allowing Kayla to position herself to come out, but she got stuck. The fattest, she was the last to be pulled from the womb, blue and not breathing. The doctors worked hard and long to bring life to her limp body. Both girls survived their difficult entry into the world and were growing into beautiful young ladies. Dakota last saw them when they were entering elementary school. Now in lip-gloss and nail polish, they were popular students in middle school.

Reese was a very striking five-foot-eight, high-yellow bombshell. A cosmetologist by trade, her real talent was in the fashion industry. With an adept ability to take a tablecloth, wrap it around her slender yet curvy frame, cinch it at the waist with a rhinestone belt, add some three-inch designer stilettos (with rhinestones, of course), matching clutch, and rhinestone chandelier earrings and come off looking like she's wearing a haute couture original, Reese made the most of her limited budget.

Her naturally jet-black, waist-length hair was always perfectly coiffed to complement her striking African-American and Asian features. Makeup kept to a minimum was routinely applied flawlessly and with perfection. The end result of this process yielded strolls down Rodeo Drive that were as eye-catching for her as those women of real wealth and prominence.

Men wanted her and spent big bucks to have her. As a single mom, she had a lot to deal with and her cosmetology skills paid the bills, but not all of them. It took more than her salary to keep up appearance which meant everything in L.A..

Not one to sleep around, Reese was selective. Before any man got in her bed, she'd been romanced, well fed and a bill, or two, was paid. "Can you pay my bills?" was the only question on her mind whenever she met and agreed to date a man. Her two-door Benz coupe and luxury apartment payments were difficult to handle alone. If a man planned to set foot in either, he had to pay BIG to play!

Dakota met Reese through Tara and quickly befriended her. Reese was smooth and independent. Stylish with class that matched or excelled most of the Hollywood set she hung around, it tickled Dakota to watch the *haves* (her rich Hollywood friends and acquaintances), envy the *have not* (Reese), all the while thinking she did.

Happy to hear from Dakota, Reese did not want to wait to meet her new fiancé. Unable to understand Dakota's reason for leaving her husband, she still hoped things would go well for her. In Reese's mind, infidelity was par for the course in any marriage, but being married to money made that infidelity less important.

Unfortunately, she knew a thing or two about both ends of the infidelity spectrum. She'd been played and she'd done some playing. Her heart still belonged to the ultra-fine, body-building fitness trainer dad of her twin daughters, who, when around, kept her in the finer things life offered. Their long-term relationship was off and on due to his inability to commit and her inability to realize he wouldn't. When they were "off" she played, netting healthy paydays!

You could tell from her facial expression, Reese was shocked to meet Chauncey. Not at all what she expected and very different from Dakota's ex, she faked being excited to meet him. A low-key dresser, jeans, a T-shirt and Timberland boots—no matter what— was not Dakota's style. Reese knew enough about her friend's taste in men to know this Lil' Abner throwback had to have a whole lot of money for her to be seen in public with him.

To a degree she was right; he was not Dakota's style. All the men she dated in the past had panache. Her preference had always been someone stylish, taller, and slimmer. But that was before her failed marriage knocked her into the real world. No longer hung up on looks and material things, Chauncey's style was of no consequence. She'd changed and very few knew it; count Reese as part of that few!

"Reese, meet Chauncey. Baby, this is my dear friend Reese, who is the mother of those two little girls I am always talking about," Dakota said proudly. Chauncey extended his hand and shook Reese's as he sized her up.

High-class "'round the way" girl was his conclusion. If she'd been raised on the other side of the tracks, she would have been married to wealth for the sheer pleasure of the wealth. Love would have nothing to do with it!

For Chauncey, lunch was enjoyable. Reese was down to earth, smooth and easy to talk to with a street edge that made her alluring and challenging. Chauncey liked a challenge, but his fiancée's friend was off limits and much too light for his taste. Unpretentious, he found her a refreshing change from Sonya Lee.

Listening intently to her conversation, which centered around sipping Mimosas on private yachts and shopping on Rodeo Drive, he accepted a different challenge; figuring out if the life stories she was sharing with them about her hanging with Hollywood and money was a figment of her imagination.

When he excused himself from the table, Reese took advantage of his absence to quiz Dakota.

"So how'd you meet him?" Reese asked sincerely concerned.

"You sound like you don't approve!"

"It's not that…you know that's not me. I just don't put the two of you together."

Dakota patted Reese's hand, which rested on the table.

"*He* found *me* at a time when I could care less about a man." Staring at the table, she pondered her next words and chose them carefully. Frustrated with feeling like she always had to defend her decision of being in love with Chauncey, she said very little. "He's good to me and I have never been happier."

Feeling guilty for posing the question, Reese apologized and rose to leave, explaining she had to pick up the twins. Knowing Dakota like she did, Reese believed Dakota thought she was happy and for that reason she wanted her to be. However, she knew Chauncey was not Dakota's flava.

Flava was everything; you had to like what you spent day in and day out with, or then there had to be an ulterior motive for being there. Dakota had not revealed the ulterior motive that Reese was certain existed. Wisely she left the subject alone. Time would tell.

The valet attendant pulled Chauncey's vehicle curbside first. "Nice Escalade," Reese offered, breaking the silence.

"Thanks," Dakota said half-heartedly, knowing Reese expected a Bentley or something. Once again, feeling like she should apologize for not rolling in one and meeting Reese's expectations, she bit her lip and looked away.

"Call me later," Reese called out as she climbed into her Benz. Noting it was new and certain it was quite expensive, Dakota wondered how she afforded it and the new boob job she was sporting. In search of answers, she called a mutual friend of theirs seeking information she felt Reese omitted during lunch.

In an effort to work her way up to inquiring about Reese and her high-profile lifestyle, Dakota chitchatted about nothing for a few minutes. When she finally broached the subject, the friend responded as Dakota hoped. The revelation was shocking. Reese was sleeping with one of the Los Angeles Lakers on the *down low*. Apparently they only met at night on scheduled days at his home, when his fiancée was out of town. But that was not the shocking part. The shock was learning Reese really thought she could steal this man from the mother of his two children—a woman he'd been with over eight years and had been living with for six.

Being nosey was not her style and learning this about Reese did not give Dakota pleasure; it actually hurt. Concern for her goddaughters and their mom ruined her mood. Closing her eyes to think while Justin drove them to their first meeting with a realtor, she vowed to have a heart-to-heart about this with Reese. If for no other reason, Reese needed to know her *down low* secret was not *down low*, nor a secret!

CHAPTER 31

Tara's confirmation that Dakota was now in California with Chauncey created a sense of anxiety and envy in me. Fully aware I would never live those California fun-filled moments again with my cousin, I made the decision to make her stay there as miserable as possible.

First on my list was Dakota's former pastor, B.B. Winston; his wife, Shelly Winston; and her "celebrity Bible study" group. Placing a phone call to his office at their mega church, I made no headway on my quest to speak with him. Contacting the pastor was more difficult than I imagined. His secretary screened the call with efficiency and informed me he was unavailable and unless the call was urgent, he'd have to call me later.

After waiting four hours for that call, I called back and stated the situation had grown to an emergency status and I needed to speak with him immediately. Fully aware who Dakota was, the pastor accepted the call and listened to my heartwrenching tale of Dakota's perceived mental breakdown and the family's concern for her well-being. Our conversation ended with his assurance if he spoke with or saw Dakota he would contact me.

Next, after waiting until seven p.m., Pacific Standard Time, ensuring all Dakota's Bible study sisters would be there, I contacted Barb Anderson, head of the "celebrity Bible study" group. Initially Barb spoke with me in private, but after I gave her the same heartwrenching tale I'd shared with the pastor earlier, the call was transferred to the conference room where the Bible study took place.

To ensure I'd get to speak with the entire group, I spiced it up a little by telling Barb several of the celebrities in the group could be in danger of having their personal finances compromised or their identities stolen.

Once on loudspeaker I repeated the now well-rehearsed story to the group and placed emphasis on Dakota's declining mental state and each of them possibly being Chauncey's target. Everyone in attendance was stunned by this news and very concerned. One, Tabitha March, a well-known actress who was very close to Dakota, gave me her number and asked me to call if I heard anything.

The next morning I called and chatted with the actress who shared personal information about Dakota and asked more questions about Chauncey. After hearing my alarming account of who Chauncey really was and what he was capable of, Tabitha became very concerned. Before hanging up, she assured me I would immediately be informed of any contact with Dakota. That evening she kept her promise by informing me Dakota called to say hello and locate a real estate agent.

"Hi, Rochelle, it's Tabitha. I wanted to let you know I just heard from Dakota."

"What? Is she okay?" I asked, pretending to be concerned.

"She sounds fine. Actually she seems very happy…are you sure you're not overreacting? Nothing in her voice or our conversation alarmed me."

Concerned I might lose this connection to my cousin, I began to choke up and faked a cry.

"I'm glad you think she's okay, but what we've noticed is…it comes and goes. One minute she's fine, the next she's doing something strange or totally out of character…I mean, think about it. When have you known her to run off with a complete stranger?"

"Well, she is going to call me tomorrow so I can meet Chauncey, but I found it strange that you alluded they barely know each other, yet she addressed him as her fiancé and said they've been dating for almost a year. Is that true?"

"Too embarrassed to tell you the truth is my guess…," I offered as an explanation to the inconsistencies Tabitha noticed in my story.

"To my knowledge she's never lied to me…I wonder why now? Anyway, she's going to meet me at my realtor's office…"

"Realtor!" I shrieked, sounding quite alarmed. "Why does she need a realtor?"

"She didn't say, but I'll call you tomorrow and let you know." Without confirming a time, I hung up and pondered why Dakota would be looking for a realtor..

Realizing she might be considering making L.A. her home once again—without me—I became bitterly jealous and with a renewed fervor, set out to ruin any chance of that happening!

Rising early the next morning, I located the check I kept from Pastor Cross and called the branch. Chauncey's personal banker was a difficult person to locate. After explaining to several different individuals I suspected he might be conducting illegal activities using an account drawn on their bank, my call was finally forwarded to a Ms. Wright who had been his personal banker for years.

In a disguised voice, I tried to discuss his banking habits and the details of his account by informing Ms. Wright I suspected he was laundering money for illegal individuals. Before Ms. Wright could or would dismiss the conversation as a hoax, she listened and took notes, so she could investigate the possibility of the claim. Thanking "Ms. Hingle" (the name I gave) for calling, she asked for a contact number, which I promptly rattled off—bogus, of course.

Ten o'clock that evening was seven o'clock in Los Angeles; plenty enough time for Dakota and Chauncey to have met with Tabitha and her realtor. Even though Tabitha promised me she'd call after the meeting, I did not wait for the promised phone call. I called her. No answer. I left a voicemail asking her to call, no matter what time she got the message.

Panic began to take hold when my call went unanswered for two days. Feeling out of the loop I started calling everyone all over again, beginning with the pastor and his wife. Unable to speak with either, I called Tara who did not answer and then I called the actress, seven more times, but only leaving a message once.

Four days after promising to call with information, the actress finally called.

"Hi, Rochelle. This is Tabitha. I'm a little concerned about Dakota and your version of things. I agree, she seems quite taken by Chauncey, who is a nice enough fella…"

Interrupting, and not wanting to hear this garbage, I cut to the chase. "Did you find out why she wanted a realtor?"

"I did and I also saw her fabulous ring. Were you aware they *are* engaged?"

Busted, I lied. "Engaged! Since when?"

The actress went on to explain what she'd learned while spending two days house hunting and dining with the two of them. In her opinion, Chauncey seemed credible and harmless.

"On the surface he can be, but don't believe what you see," I warned.

Tabitha informed me they met with her realtor and set up appointments to view several homes in Northridge. What concerned her about the entire two days were the homes they chose to view, all selling for no less than $1 million. According to her, they'd chosen two: a very contemporary 10,000-square-footer with detached guest house and game room with asking price of $1.5 million; and an ultra-contemporary 8,000-square-foot home with elevator, indoor pool and attached guest house. The latter was on the market for $2.7 million. Flabbergasted, I stayed calm and collected long enough to get the realtor's name, number, and more information about the homes they were considering purchasing.

A pretty good judge of character, she did not feel Chauncey was financially able to handle such an undertaking.

"As I indicated earlier, my concern is Dakota is so enamored by him and seems so happy that she may not be thinking straight. And quite frankly, I don't know if he can afford such opulence. I would hate to see her get hurt in all this."

"Well, at least I know I'm not crazy. I felt this way about Chauncey the instant I met him and it escapes me why Dakota can't see him for the fake he is!"

"Love can be blinding," was all the explanation the actress offered, which made me want to puke!

"If anything else develops, I'll let you know and you do the same. She's your cousin. You may hear something before I do."

Assuring her I'd call if I did hear from Dakota, I hung up and checked the time before dialing the realtor's office. No answer, I dialed his cell phone. Still no answer I called Tara and left a detailed voicemail.

The following morning, Tara, shocked by the information she'd learned from the message I'd left, called to get more details.

"They're buying a house?" she shrieked.

"Gurl…not just a house, try a ten-thousand-square-foot house!"

"No way!" Tara screamed.

"Got it straight from the horse's mouth." I took the next hour carefully repeating each detail about the two homes. Neither of us believed it possible for him to have the finances to pull this off, but we agreed he was slick enough to try. Waiting to find out was not an option. We laid a plan to immediately uncover the underlying source of his supposed wealth.

After speaking with the realtor and informing him Chauncey was laundering money, I convinced him to send me his paperwork and give me the name of the bank where the funds were to be wired. Repeating the same routine I had successfully used on Ms. Wright, I created enough concern with the Los Angeles bank manager to cause her to freeze his incoming funds until the bank had time to investigate the claim.

That afternoon, when Chauncey and Dakota arrived at the bank to pick up the cashier's check for their earnest money deposit, the manager was waiting to speak with them. As she guided them to a private conference room, they were informed there was a concern regarding the legitimacy of the funds that had been wired and until the concern was clarified, the funds would remain frozen and in possession of the bank.

Fear consumed Dakota! Things her father had said to her, though learned from me, were beginning to haunt her. Sweat broke out on Chauncey's forehead as he fought to control his temper. Demanding more information than he was being given, he stood up and started yelling at the manager who called for security.

Dakota, afraid of being arrested, grabbed Chauncey by the hand

and begged him to leave and get an attorney to handle the matter. Although it took a couple minutes for him to acquiesce, he did, vying to return for his money with an attorney. Seconds after they left, the bank manager called the legal department to find out her options in case he made good on his threat.

Licensed to practice law in Michigan, Chauncey's attorney could only advise him via phone. He suggested Chauncey return to Michigan where he could then intervene on his behalf and work on finding the underlying cause of this situation. The end result of that advice was his loss of both properties due to well over $500,000 of his money frozen and hanging in limbo.

Unsure what to believe, Dakota took out her fear and frustrations on her fiancé, who returned her tirades with venom of his own, blaming her meddling cousin for the situation. The ride back to Michigan would prove to be long and miserably silent, resulting in the couple agreeing to put their wedding on hold!

CHAPTER 32

A four-day Hedonism break in Jamaica was the frosting on the cake to a well-executed plot. The actress's phone call to inform me Dakota and Chauncey were unable to produce the funds needed to complete the transaction on the house was gratifying.

Dante called, last minute as usual, to invite me to a private party that was being held on the island of Negril in honor of a very wealthy friend. In an effort to avoid any misunderstandings, he informed me any and everything could (and probably would) happen. Without hesitation, I accepted the invite and immediately booked a flight.

Relaxing on the three-hour flight to my connection in Florida, I took great pleasure in strategically calculating the next surprise I would heap upon Chauncey and Dakota. Coming up with the drama was easy, but executing it would be tricky. Certain they would return to Detroit within the next few days, I'd have to recruit others to help pull it off, and that would take money— quite a bit!

Negril was more than I could have imagined. Its beautiful shimmering beaches stretched over several miles of crystal white sand, was breathtaking and created a relaxing atmosphere. Taking it all in, I sat on the deck of my villa sipping on an island drink recommended by Dante. Reading over the well-thought-out plot to f' with my cousin's head, I pulled it close to my chest when I realized Dante was peering over my shoulder. Catching a glimpse of the list, his curiosity was aroused.

"What is that, Missy?" he said, reaching to take the pad from my lap. Defensively I gripped it tightly. Giggling, I waved it in the air before responding.

"Remember 'Mr. Man' my cuu-zin is engaged to?"

"The fake?" Dante sneered.

"You got it…this is for him—and of course, her."

"Um, do tell!" he said, pressing his lips and bucking his eyes as he pulled up a chair. Carefully I explained my plan to ruin Chauncey's life and Dakota's—by default. If calculated correctly, I was certain I could pay people to do what I planned and that money would be well spent if I could get him permanently detained by the law.

"That ought to make that prima donna dump his fake butt like a hot potato."

Listening intently, Dante nodded in agreement, but chose not to express his true feelings, which were—I was jealous *and* wrong!

Together we fine-tuned the plot. With Dante's input I added some unexpected twists that would definitely wreak havoc in both their lives. Over drinks at dinner, we chuckled at the thought of Chauncey being carted off to jail. Even more pleasurable was, knowing that Dakota would be forced to return to a life of ten bucks an hour and living at her father's home.

On the private beach after sunset, the reggae music was bumpin' and drinks were flowing. Many of the partygoers were topless and some were completely nude. Light intimate touches could be seen from time to time as couples engaged in dancing or other social activities.

Fully clothed in beach appropriate attire, I casually walked around the bar area while I waited for Dante. Several of the people in the crowd looked familiar; regulars from some of the other events I'd attended back in the States.

Off in the distance I caught a glimpse of someone familiar, but could not place the six-foot-four chiseled frame with the face that was perfectly molded by God's hands.

I know him! I thought, but could not remember who he was or how I knew him. Sitting on the bar stool farthest from the dance floor, trying to be inconspicuous, I stared at him trying to place his face with the place I was certain we'd met. His dance partner, a striking six-foot-two, caramel-colored male with piercing hazel eyes, confounded me because the man I thought I recognized was not gay.

"What can I get you?" the bartender asked, breaking my concentration.

Turning momentarily to acknowledge him, I absentmindedly responded, "Nothing just yet." While my back was turned, the familiar face left the dance floor with his dance partner. When I turned back to stare they were gone, leaving me bewildered.

"There you are…," Dante gushed as he plopped down on the empty stool next to her.

"Thought you said to meet you here over an hour ago. Am I late or is it you?" Normally that question would evoke a humorous response because I was always late. This time it did not. My thoughts were still on the "familiar face" that had now begun to haunt me.

"You okay? Look like you've seen a ghost."

"I may have. I'm certain I saw someone I know...the thing that's bothering me is I can't remember who he is or why I know him."

"I'd say it's a former beau, but we know you haven't been there or done that!" Dante quipped. Even though we both chuckled, I found little humor in what he said. Hiding the hurt, I ordered a round for both of us as I downed the remainder of my Sex on the Beach.

Drinking most of the day and all the night, I retired to my room relatively early, three-thirty a.m. Although Dante was my roommate, I returned alone and fell on the bed fully clothed, still pondering the familiar face.

Dante chose to stay on the beach with someone he found enchanting, leaving me to deal with being drunk on my own. With my head spinning most of the night, I woke in a sweat and ran to the bathroom to vomit. Head hanging in the commode, I suddenly remembered *the face*, and how I knew him.

That six feet four inches of fineness, who obviously preferred men, was Dakota's missing ex, Kevin! Crawling back to the bed, I rested until the room stopped spinning and then ordered a light breakfast to help me feel better. With more energy, I grabbed my cell and dialed Dante, certain he'd be able to shed light on my discovery. No answer—not wanting to leave a message, I hung up.

Hung over, I popped a couple of aspirin in my mouth and downed them with water before showering. Questions and more questions bounced around my brain while I scrubbed, but answers evaded me. Where had he been? Why did he disappear? His disappearance put Dakota in financial ruin—could that have been intentional? Pondering these questions, it was pretty obvious what he was hiding was his sexual preference. This realization made me chuckle.

"Bet he'd pay handsomely to keep that quiet." I smiled at the thought and then realized what I'd just said. Kevin, a man with means and a real secret to hide—would probably be willing to pay quite handsomely to remain *missing*...

"Wonder what that prima donna would do if I told her I saw her man? Bet she'd die, especially if I told her *with whom*!" I murmured as I dried the beads of water running down my long legs. Slowly my mind began to hatch a new plan to f' with Dakota's head, namely Kevin and his re-emergence. But first I had to make sure it was really him.

Without inviting Dante, I ventured to the same bar area a little earlier than the time I'd seen him the previous evening, with hopes of running into Kevin and his "friend." I had not yet determined if they were a couple, but I knew Kevin was either bi or gay because he fondled his dance partner more than once. *That alone is information that would net me a pretty penny*, I said to myself.

Comfortably seated at a table angled toward the dance floor I lay in wait for Kevin to appear. To my dismay, the wait was lengthy and wasted. Once again quite drunk at approximately one a.m., I stumbled to my room surprised to find Dante entertaining several of his friends.

"Hey, where you been?" he asked half-heartedly, too busy dancing to really care or notice I was drunk.

Without answering, I kicked off my shoes and plopped face down on the bed falling into a deep slumber. Dante and his guests partied until the sun came up. Unfortunately, I never noticed one of the guests was the six-foot-two, caramel-colored, hazel-eyed male I'd seen with Dakota's ex.

CHAPTER 33

Dakota's California friends were all abuzz about her new beau, and thanks to the actress, their failed attempts to purchase a luxury home. Was Dakota the butt of their jokes? Perhaps, but not all of them found her plight humorous. Those who did not attempted to contact *her* (instead of me) to make sure she was okay. Others—Tara, Sonya Lee and the actress—bypassed the source and went to the storyteller—me.

By the time Dakota learned her business was all over Cali and most of it was not good, two months had gone by. Her three-week hiatus from Chauncey, after returning from the West Coast, was much needed. It gave her time to sort through some feelings of uncertainty; one of them being her impending marriage.

Time and distance did not change her mind; she truly loved him. But she did heed the small voice in her head and decided to slow her roll until she felt certain she was doing the right thing by saying, "I do!"

Chauncey did not accept rejection well and panicked when Dakota asked for some time alone to think. A product of a broken home, he often witnessed his father and mother battling, the end result being his father absent from their home for days on end. Those heated confrontations eventually led to his mother packing up and permanently relocating with his sisters to Alabama, leaving him to be raised by his street-hustlin' father. Missing his mother and the closeness of his family, Chauncey vowed his marriage would not be volatile and his wife would never leave him.

Normally he was not one to rush into anything. However, he'd done a lot of that lately. This time his reason for making hasty decisions was warranted. Nothing and no one could or would be allowed to keep him from an answered prayer—Dakota North.

Custom ordered she was everything he had asked God for. A perfect figure—not messed up by giving birth to tons of kids. Mature, educated, independent, fantastic personality, a go-getter (not sitting home collecting welfare checks) and beautiful to look at and make love to. Who could ask for anything more!

He'd had scallywags all his life; that's what the *way East side* of Detroit produced. During his brief stint in the pros he'd been with all sorts of women, many with class and breeding. But none measured up to Dakota.

There was one who caught his eye, an older woman who was a real estate investor with means. And even though he was now engaged to Dakota, she was still around. Full figured, Pam was very attractive but Chauncey had a hard time making love to "all that" and only did so when all else failed! Tied to her in ways that were paramount to his survival, he kept his pending nuptials a secret.

Nights he spent warming her bed became far and few after he met the love of his life. Creeping out of the condo he shared with Pam to answer Dakota's late-night calls became increasingly difficult, but he managed to do so successfully. Keeping her at bay and not making love to her was the challenge that he'd not managed successfully.

Angry and feeling threatened because he'd been gone for quite some time with no real explanation to his disappearance, Pam did not hesitate to let him know who held the trump card in this bid whist game. "Mo-fo, listen! I don't know where you been for the past month, but let me get one thing straight. *That* Escalade you rollin' in got my name on it! Don't make me snatch those wheels, 'cause we both know your no-credit behind will be catching the bus!"

While she quickly reminded him her Jag was now off limits, Chauncey slammed the bedroom door, cutting off the rest of her tirade and climbed into the Jacuzzi to relax and think. Pam was right; he was tied to her financially. His money was no good when you're a man on the run and unable to purchase anything in your name.

A huge portion of his wealth was attributed to investments he'd made with her that yielded healthy paydays. When he met her, he was down on his luck after having blown the settlement he received from being injured as a kicker for an upstart pro football team. During a scrimmage, his successful bid to make the pros as a walk-on ended one game into the season. Walk-ons do not yield hefty paychecks, but the settlement with the team and his insurance company made up for the plastic that now held his working knee together.

With less than $50,000 of his $750,000 settlement left, he met and immediately liked Pam. Sassy, street, and a hustler, she was very knowledgeable about real estate law and financial investing. Anxious to regain his status of financial means, he quickly latched on to her and learned how to buy and flip real estate.

Their four-year relationship had made them both quite a bit of money, but he had a difficult time enjoying any of it because The Friend of the Court was looking for him. Years of running with and bedding scallywags had resulted in a tribe of kids he'd failed to pay for, a fact he'd yet to reveal to Dakota.

The first year of his relationship with Pam, the po-po showed up at his father's home with a warrant for his arrest for back child support. Three years later, Chauncey had not returned to his father's home unless it was in the middle of the night and he left before the sun came up.

His investing in a condo with Pam's name on the deed made that little drama go away. A wanted man, he had no choice but to disappear and obtain everything that required "paperwork" be put in her name, thus tying him to her for life. At the time, that was okay because he saw whomever he wanted whenever he wanted. As long as she did not feel threatened, Pam kept quiet.

Meeting and falling in love with Dakota changed his mind-set and his ways. Now he faced a quandary that did not have an easy fix. Add to that equation, I was getting very close to the *real* Chauncey and making his life miserable.

"She's got to go," he said emphatically to his street-hustlin' cousin. "How is my challenge, but I got to get that ho off my butt before long, or she'll have me behind bars."

"F' that, cuz! What you need me to do?" Glen asked as he clutched the handle of his glock, which was tucked in the right side of his pant waistline.

"Naw, nothin' like that. I just got to figure out how to get her off my butt. Everybody got a price…she's greedy, she can be bought!"

"Aw right, cuz, but be careful. The *ho* sounds like a loose cannon. You know you ridin' dirty, watch yo' back!"

"Bet!" Chauncey threw his cousin a half-cocked glance as he walked away; well aware no truer words had been spoken. Certain I was a loose cannon, one that could do major damage if not brought under control, Chauncey realized figuring out how to accomplish controlling me would be his next challenge.

CHAPTER 34

Grosse Pointe Shores is one of Michigan's white affluent coastline suburbs. The home community of the Edsel and Eleanor Ford House, it is located north of Detroit, along the St. Clair River and far enough away from Romulus to give Chauncey a false sense of security from my prying eyes. Although a small village that butts up to Grosse Pointe and Grosse Pointe Woods, "the Shores" boasts waterfront homes and condominiums with breathtaking price tags to match their splendor.

Freedom from her father's home and the ability to take in a waterfront view of the Detroit River, day and night, was unbelievable and welcomed. Dakota was speechless when Chauncey put the first year's rent in an account for her and put the three-bedroom luxury condo's lease in her name. Thrilled to be a "home owner" she did not give his generous gesture a second thought. Quite frankly, it endeared him with her. She'd never met a man who would do such a self-less thing; most men would at least want their name on the lease to ensure their turf was pee'd on!

Moving in was fun. Together they picked their furnishings: black ultrasuede sectional with reclining end units, and two off-white, overstuffed, leather side chairs. Chauncey left the accessorizing to Dakota.

Their first night in their new home was wonderful and very peaceful. Kelsey spent the weekend at his granddad's home allowing them privacy. Things flowed smoothly over the weekend, thanks to the lie he'd told Pam.

"I have to go look at some lakefront property in North Carolina," he said. To make his story more convincing, Chauncey added he'd been watching it for some time and it had been drastically reduced. Ensuring it was a good investment and viable for home building he wanted to have the soil tested.

That lie bought him two to three weeks of being away from Pam and in bed with Dakota. He'd worry about the remaining forty-nine weeks when that time came. For now he wanted to enjoy "playing house" with the love of his life.

Unfortunately, the serenity he enjoyed with his future wife came to a quick halt one month after he moved in. A female—short, squatty and fitting the description of Pastor Cross—appeared at Pam's real estate office demanding to speak with her.

After completing a business conversation with the seller who was seated in her office, Pam excused herself and escorted the woman, who identified herself as Ida Thompson, to the conference room.

Behind closed doors, "Ida" revealed she'd been bamboozled by Chauncey for quite some time and produced a copy of a check she'd written to him for a real estate investment that had never yielded any results. The check amount was $100,000 and appeared to have been cashed by Chauncey. Pam listened as the woman described how their business relationship had teetered on the brink of something more on several occasions, but she resisted his charm. Enamored by his charisma, good looks, and gift of gab, she foolishly gave him cash over extended periods, failing to get receipts.

Fuming, Pam took notes and the woman's number, vowing to get her money back. It took her several hours to reach Chauncey, but when she did, she threatened to castrate him and he did not take the threat lightly.

Lying to Dakota once more, he blamed his staying away from home, another night, on his father's health and told her he'd see her in the morning. Speeding, Chauncey cut the drive time in half, arriving in twenty minutes to a fighting-mad Pam. Yelling, screaming and throwing things, she repeated the "facts" as presented by "Ida" and demanded the truth.

Clueless to whom the woman was or how she found Pam, Chauncey struggled to find a satisfactory response. Because he was so careful, he was certain his past flings never knew she existed nor where his office was located. Alarmed, he became paranoid, uncertain who found him, how and why. Jail time and the possible loss of his freedom made bile rise in his throat. He opened a bottle of water and took a long swig to erase the taste.

"Pam, I swear I have no idea who this woman is and I never took any money from her or any other woman without your knowledge. Think about it, why would I? We got bank…plenty of it! I don't need to hustle nobody. What bank was the check drawn on?"

That question got her attention long enough for her to stop yelling and think.

"I have no clue…come to think of it, we don't have an account that is not joint…wow…my name was nowhere on the check."

"Okay…and what address was on the check?"

"Uh-hh, I think your dad's."

"Does that make sense? When's the last time I lived at my dad's?"

Pondering the question, she calmed down. In retrospect, she realized he was telling the truth.

Four years have passed since he's lived with his father...said he couldn't get along with Daphne (his father's "live-in") so he moved out and then we got a place together; He's been with me since! Why am I trippin'...?"

Very convincingly, Chauncey whittled away at the woman's story until there were no doubts left in Pam's mind. Sorry she'd acted such a fool, she fixed his favorite meal, fried pork chops and fries, doused in hot sauce.

While he ate, she showered and put on a new negligee, crawled into bed and waited for him to join her. The thought of making love to her made him almost regurgitate. Not wanting to "bite the bullet," he ate ever so slowly, hoping she'd fall asleep. Before crawling into bed with her snoring carcass, he turned off the alarm clock, ensuring she'd oversleep and be too rushed in the morning to get what she did not get that night.

The next morning as planned, Pam overslept and woke discombobulated. Frantically she dressed, blowing a kiss to Chauncey as she ran out the door still gathering her thoughts.

An hour later, Dakota welcomed her man into their bed and her body. Making love while Kelsey played in his room was challenging, but they both managed to reach a climax before answering his cries of hunger.

"How's Dad?" she asked, genuinely concerned.

"He'll be fine…"

"Called your cell, it went straight to voicemail. I was worried about him."

"Turned it off so he wouldn't be disturbed," Chauncey said just above a whisper, hating himself for lying to her.

"Thought so…," Dakota admitted and continued.

"Listen, where do you keep the Jag? I'd like to drive it sometime!"

"Uh-hh, no problem, babe, but most times I leave it at Dad's so he can have transportation to get to the doctor."

Dakota turned and stared at him with a "that makes no sense" look. Chauncey knew it didn't, so he cleaned it up quickly.

"They have a garage that locks and when it's not being used, he keeps it in the garage."

"Oh-hh, because I remember you said it was a rough neighborhood which is why you don't want me there, but a Jag would not last a couple hours sitting out in the open."

"I know you right," he added as he grabbed his keys to leave, pleased he wormed his way out of that question unscathed.

Now a stay-at-home mom, Dakota had extra free time on her hands and very little "things" to fill that "free time." Chauncey had her on a tight budget, which eliminated impromptu shopping sprees leaving her to spend her days being a mom and "wife." Very happy and adjusting to motherhood quite well, she planned each day and included her dad and Kelsey in those plans.

Before leaving home, she called Chauncey to see if he could meet them for lunch. However, on second thought, she decided to take lunch to him; she simply needed his office address. Leaving that message on his voicemail, she drove to her dad's house and waited for him to call with directions.

Hungry and not very patient, Kelsey began to complain and fret, forcing her to eliminate lunch with Chauncey as part of her day. But, she still wanted to stop by his office, since she had yet to see it. After being seated at the restaurant and looking over the menu, her dad ordered his favorite—grilled salmon—and Kelsey asked for Buffalo style chicken strips. Watching her weight, Dakota chose a salad with lots of croutons and hot bacon mustard dressing.

Just before they were done with their meals, Chauncey called.

Happy to hear his voice, she neglected to get directions because the thought escaped her. Not wanting her at his office or aware of its location, he never brought it up.

Returning to her father's home to drop him off, she backed out the drive and headed toward her home failing to notice the car parked across the street that was now following her.

CHAPTER 35

J amaica was relaxing and the hedonism experience was invigorating. Still reeling from the tryst I shared with Natasha, a Colombian hottie I met on the beach, I un-packed before implementing the well-thought-out scheme Dante and I concocted.

Obtaining copies of the rest of Chauncey's paperwork from the Los Angeles realtor proved easier than I imagined. Contacting him with a contrived story of a real estate scam Chauncey was linked to, he gladly faxed copies of the entire portfolio with pertinent bank account and personal information blotted out!

Upon careful review of the numerous documents, I discovered his social security number still visible on one of them and jotted it down, along with other information I deemed relevant to my plan. Now that I had his full name, social security number, previous addresses and birth date I contacted Elly, who helped me run his credit through her niece—a real estate agent. Although the information was a couple years old, Chauncey had impeccable credit and an impressive credit score. Reviewing his Experian report, much more information was learned about this mystery man and to her dismay, it was all good.

"That will have to change," I said, circling the information with a highlighter. Making a note to f' with his credit, I moved on to my next task: "f' with Dakota."

"No need to check her credit. I know It's busted and she's too broke to pay attention!" Laughing heartily at my comment, it tickled me so much, tears began to run down my cheeks.

"Can't pay attention…whoa…that was funny." Doubting the truth in my statement, I became curious about Dakota's credit background, as well. Browsing the documents once more, I failed to locate any information on Dakota other than her name. Without her social, I couldn't check her credit.

You lucked out, Missy, I thought as I placed the documents in my file cabinet.

"I'll deal with your behind later…I got bigger fish to fry right now!" I quipped.

An offer to translate in sign language at a two-night, sold-out concert for a prominent gospel singer just days after returning from my vacation tremendously hampered my plans to assume Chauncey's identity. After resting for a day I put that plan into motion by placing an Internet order for a new kidney-bean-shaped sofa, and a high- heel-shaped side chair, both purchased on a replacement credit card I received in the mail.

Two weeks after taking delivery, I went out and used his card as Mrs. Chauncey Bentley on a spending spree for "girlie things" like my favorite fragrance, Hermes. Sharing the bounty with Elly and Val, I treated them to their favorite perfumes as well— both unaware I obtained the goods illegally.

When the first credit card payment was due, I smiled as I ripped the billing statement in half and tossed it in the trash. I did like-wise with subsequent billing statements. Each one included a written warning informing Mr. Bentley he risked damaging his current credit standing by not paying the balance in full.

With great delight, I ignored them, tossing them in the trash each time I visited my post office box to retrieve the mail. Months later, my final purchase before his account went to collections was a knee-length, honey-colored, swing mink coat.

Totally oblivious to the ruse, Chauncey continued his daily activities, with one added precaution—continuously looking over his shoulder, fully convinced I was out to get him. Street connected, he'd done a little investigating of his own, and what he discovered about me was not good. Three women had been granted restraining orders against me in a period of seven years. The complaints, although similar, were registered in three different counties in Michigan: Oakland, Wayne and Washtenaw.

Each document he read clearly listed irrational behavior that included possible stalking. One woman complained she'd been a close platonic friend with me for three years and when we fell out, I began to taunt her and appear in public at places she would frequent. The judge did not rule I was stalking her, but because I produced a crow bar and threatened bodily harm when my friend refused to return a pair of earrings I'd given her, he granted the restraining order.

As Chauncey read the other females' accounts of twisted behavior, it was nerve- rattling. They accused me of bugging their home phone lines, placing listening devices in their homes, and spreading defamatory and slanderous information about them. Even though some of the "slanderous things" I said about them were true, a huge portion of it had been embellished or made up!

"Aw man, this fool is crazy!" Chauncey mumbled as he continued to read the documents. Wasting no time he called Glenn and his attorney, Frank Girgenti, and scheduled a time to meet both that evening.

Three hours were spent with his attorney going over the information the documents contained. He warned Chauncey about being in possession of the documents and advised him to shred them immediately. Fully aware he was dealing with someone who could at any moment "nut up," Chauncey ignored his warning and advice and put the documents in his safe.

Meeting with his cousin was quite informative. Glenn had done a thorough job in digging into my past.

"Man, prior to her hookin' up with your woman, she was pretty much a loner. She had people she hung out with, but they were far and few. What's odd is…no man. This ho gotta be a dyke."

"Really…" Chauncey smiled a lecherous smile, realizing this might be the ammunition he'd need to get me off his back. Relieved and feeling much better about the outcome of his plan to rid his life of my meddling, he called Dakota and asked her to meet him at his favorite spot, Steve's Soul Food.

Sitting at the corner in the dark away from any streetlights, I watched as Dakota started her Benz and drove out of the garage. Waiting for her to get a safe distance ahead, I pulled off and followed.

"Ma, I'm following her now."

"Rochelle, what is wrong with you? Leave that girl alone. If she wants to be with that nut, let her!"

"Ma, you don't understand. He's a fake…a liar and I can prove it!"

"Suppose he is. Why is that your concern?"

Not wanting to hear anymore of this lack of support, I told Val I'd call later. Hanging up, I dialed my favorite support system, Dante.

"How's it going, Missy?" he asked, answering the phone quite chipper.

"You won't believe what I'm doing," I whispered.

"What? And why are *we* whispering?" he asked just above a whisper. Realizing we were both whispering, I laughed and went on to explain I was trailing Dakota and had been for a couple weeks.

"I now know where they are living and it's fabulous from the outside. How is that nut able to pay that high rent? Trust me, he does not have a dime!"

Taking advantage of my momentary pause to breathe, Dante cut in.

"Be careful, little one…you're playing with fire. From what you've told me, Mister Man is not the one to be messed with!"

"Please, I'm not scared of him. Besides, what's he gonna do… sue me?"

"Maybe…just be careful…and don't say I didn't warn you!"

Disgusted with his lack of support, I suddenly remembered I had to make a very important call.

"Listen…gotta run, I need to make a really important call. Talk to you later."

Dante agreed to check in with me later in the week, but issued me another warning before hanging up. That angered me even more and I vowed I'd keep the rest of the dirt I did to myself. My call to Elly went unanswered and I did not leave a message. On second thought I decided I would not share my shenanigans with her either.

Steve's Soul Food did not have many windows, so watching from the parking lot or street side was unfruitful. Even though I was uncertain what I'd hoped to accomplish by watching them meet for a bite to eat, I decided to wait just the same. Two hours later, they emerged. Watching Chauncey passionately kiss Dakota before walking her to her car made me cringe. After she safely pulled away, he climbed into the Jag and pulled off.

Puzzled, I pulled off and followed him.

"Jag? When did he get a Jag?" At the light, I jotted down his license plate number and the model of the car.

Twenty minutes after leaving Steve's, Chauncey pulled into a luxurious gated condominium complex in West Bloomfield. Using an access card, he gained entry and disappeared before I could squeeze through forcing me to wait for another car to exit or enter before I could gain access. Once inside the complex and uncertain which direction he drove, I made a right turn at the first corner and slowly drove through each section of the huge community, hoping to spot his car.

"Who lives here?" I wondered admiring the homes. "Nice, very nice." Taking in the ambiance, the well-manicured grounds and the high-profile luxury automobiles, it was easy to surmise money lived inside the walls of these lavish homes.

Spotting the Jag I went to the end of the cul-de-sac, turned around, parked, and waited for him to come out. At times it was difficult to stay awake, but I successfully fought off nodding. Morning came before anyone emerged from the condo. Pam was the first to exit, locking the door behind her. Entering the Jag, she pulled out of the drive and drove off. Chauncey's Escalade emerged from the garage seconds later.

"What the…?" Stunned by what was unfolding, I forgot to start my car. Reaching for the phone, I hurriedly dialed Val as I tried to shift into gear to follow him. Flustered and unable to focus, I dropped the phone and the car key. Retrieving it from the car mat I fumbled for the ignition and managed to start the car, speeding off without locating my cell phone. In the distance, I could hear Val speaking.

"Hello? Hello?"

"Ma, you're on speaker and I can barely hear you. I dropped my phone, but listen to this. I just saw that fake come out of some fat chick's house and he spent the night."

"Wha-aat?" Val shrieked. "Rochelle, you been watching that man all night?"

"Ma, don't start! I got him…I got him. Busted, wait 'til Dakota finds out!"

"Rochelle, you listen to me. You wrong and you need to leave them alone!"

Not wanting to hear it, I did not respond. Reaching the front gate, I put the car in park and retrieved my cell. Without acknowledging what Val said, I hung up and exited the complex quickly, hoping to catch up to Chauncey.

One streetlight away I spotted his Escalade and slowed down when the light turned green to give him time to pull off. He parked in front of a real estate office. Trailing a safe distance behind, I pulled off and waited for him to enter. The instant he shut the door, I pulled into an adjacent lot so I could see and wrote down the address to the building and the license plate to the Escalade.

Pleased with my "James Bond" adventure, I went home and took a hot bath before making a couple phone calls to find out who owned the condo, the real estate office, the Jag and the Escalade; certain that would not be Chauncey.

CHAPTER 36

Nine months after living in peace and quiet in beautiful Grosse Pointe Shores the serenity came to an end. A detective left his card with the guard at the front gate of their exclusive community, requesting he give it to Dakota. Chauncey had paid the guard handsomely to keep him informed of anything or anyone suspicious. His money was well spent.

"Hey, Mr. Bentley, got somethin' for you," he called out as Chauncey drove through the gate. After parking, Chauncey walked over to the gatehouse and read the business card the guard handed him. Scribbled on the back of the detective's card was a note to Dakota. *Ms. North, please call me. It's important.* Detective Burns scribbled his signature.

Waiting for acknowledgment of a job well done—a tip, the guard stared at Chauncey.

"Good lookin' out, man…thanks!" Chauncey handed him $50 and walked away. Smiling, the guard shouted, "I got yo' back, Mr. Bentley—remember that!"

Carolyn, Chauncey's sister, reluctantly agreed to call Detective Burns and pretended to be Dakota. Their discussion was brief and informative. He told her he was looking for Chauncey Bentley, and had been told he lived with her at that address. When Carolyn inquired why he needed to speak with Chauncey, the detective said he wanted to discuss a sexual assault complaint as soon as possible.

That information in tow, Chauncey went straight to his lawyer's office for advice on how to handle the situation.

"I'll need to know who filed the complaint and when," his attorney informed him and then facetiously asked, "Have you assaulted anyone?"

Shooting him a "you gotta be kidding look" Chauncey chuckled and then became stoic.

"It's that heifer, f'in' with me!" he said, certain I had filed the complaint. Three hours later his suspicions were confirmed. Attorney Girgenti, the lawyer he kept on retainer, went to the Grosse Pointe Police Department and was able to review the complaint.

It stated two weeks prior, Rochelle Jackson had filed the complaint and it included the address he shared with Dakota. Possible known automobiles Chauncey might drive were listed as a Jaguar and Escalade with detailed descriptions, license plates included. Lastly, the address he shared with Pam and the real estate office were given as additional locations to find him.

Listening to the information his attorney repeated from the report caused beads of sweat to form on his forehead and above his lip. Chauncey fought to maintain his composure, but failed miserably. After kicking over the trash basket and breaking a couple items scattered throughout the room, he sat down and took long slow breaths.

"She's got to go…I ain't goin' to jail." Looking on concerned, his attorney poured a stiff drink for them both. Chauncey, a non-drinker, sat his on the desk. Ten minutes passed before another word was spoken. Chauncey was the first to speak.

"I underestimated this nut. It won't happen again." With an

evil look, one the attorney had not witnessed before, Chauncey rose and laid three Benjamins on the desk.

"Sorry for the implosion…this should cover it."

"You thinking straight?" Attorney Girgenti asked.

"I am now…and she will have hell to pay!"

"Be careful, Chauncey…"

Cutting him off, Chauncey simply said, "I got this!" and exited his office.

With three months left on their Grosse Pointe Shores lease, Chauncey began to look for a new place for his future wife and son. Because Dakota's credit was now in great standing (thanks to him and his friends who knew how to get things done), he chose an investment property in Indian Village he'd recently acquired, without Pam's knowledge, to "give" to his future wife.

The home was four levels with a library, a great room, formal and informal dining areas, a maid's quarter, and a nursery. No guesthouse, it had a massive gated backyard and garage, which you entered off the alley. A six-foot-tall decorative wrought-iron fence and two massive entry gates restricted entrance to the front of the home. Unless invited, access to the home and its yard was nearly impossible.

Christmas was spent in their new home with a huge celebration that included Dakota's entire family, with the exception of Val, Rodney and me. Elated to see Dakota back on top and doing extremely well, her relatives celebrated the purchase of her new home well into the night.

A warm fire kept the main level inviting. The children played on the second level and the third level was off limits, because the radiator heating system needed repair. Anyone who smoked was asked to step out onto the garden terrace or retreat to the basement. It was a wonderful night for everyone but Chauncey.

Unaware Dakota had planned the occasion, he felt ill at ease with her family members knowing where they lived. It would be only a matter of time before I knew as well and that would surely mean more drama.

He was right. One month later their peace and tranquility quickly turned into endless nights of hell. Their telephone rang constantly throughout the night interrupting their sleep. Afraid it might be me and trying to ensure Dakota was not enlightened about his checkered background, Chauncey turned the ringers off on the phones at night and turned them on in the morning before she woke. Next he tried forwarding the house calls to his office, which worked for a while, but that Band-Aid was short lived. Although he managed to keep me at bay within his home, he had no control over the outside!

Sirens blaring and lights flashing, police cars surrounded Dakota who was driving the Escalade, one block from their home. She'd noticed the cop car following closely behind her for several blocks but thought nothing of his actions. Guns drawn, they ordered her to exit the car hands up and wrestled her to the ground when she did. Seconds after handcuffing her, they informed her she was driving a stolen automobile.

"Stolen, what are you talking about? This is a mistake…," she pleaded. Ignoring her pleas the police placed her in the back of the squad car and took her to jail. The one gratuitous phone call allowed was placed to Chauncey. Through his connections he got her released to her father with apologies, six hours later.

Once Dakota was safely home, Chauncey's attorney met with him and revealed Pam had turned in the stolen car report. Dealing with Pam and this stunt would be the ending to their relationship and his rolling in the Escalade or Jag. Covering his bases, he used Dakota's Benz to stop by the bank prior to confronting Pam and cashed a check for the amount of "his share" of the funds sitting in Pam's account. Although they jointly used the account, only her name was listed as the account holder. Tucked away in his wallet was a blank check he'd held for years, signed by Pam in case of an emergency. This was an emergency!

Full of rage, Pam waited for him to arrive. When he did, she threw a shoe toward his head and charged. Ducking the shoe Chauncey jumped out of her way allowing her to ram the door with great force; knocking the wind out of her. While she gained her composure, he hurriedly packed some of his things and then returned to check on her. Holding her wrist, she moaned and rolled on the floor.

"I think it's broken…call an ambulance."

"In a minute. What did you do, Pam?" he asked unsympathetically.

"What did I do? Mo Fo', what did *you do*?" she screamed.

Looking around the room, he saw papers lying on the dining room table. As he walked over to look at them, Pam screamed out in agony, "Please, Chauncey, call an ambulance."

Ignoring her, he picked up the folded pages and read them. Like a well-written story, they gave details of the life he was living with Dakota, including their current address in Indian Village.

"Where'd you get this?" he barked.

"You should know; it's your woman."

"Dakota brought this to you?"

"You're so stupid, not that woman; the tall skinny one that looks like a man."

"And her name would be?"

Writhing on the floor, Pam sat up long enough to examine her wrist, ignoring his question. As she carefully palpated the tender area around her wrist, she realized it was not broken and reached for Chauncey to help her up.

Lifting her from behind, he hoisted her to the nearby entry seat and stared at her, waiting for an answer. Knowing he was not leaving without one and wanting him gone, she blurted out my name and walked to the bathroom, where she stayed until he left.

In the safety of their home, which Dakota had fled, he reviewed the documents taken from Pam. He was scared to death. For the first time he realized I had been spying on him for quite some time; the fact that he did not know shook his foundation. Finding out how I accomplished this and what I really knew was mandatory and immediate, and would take reinforcements.

Glenn met him at his home within an hour. Giving him time to look over the papers I left with Pam, Chauncey called to check on Dakota who hung up on him. When he called back, her cell was turned off so he tried to contact her at her father's number. Answering, her father informed him she was there and did not want to speak with him. Reluctantly hanging up, he called his father to make sure Kelsey was okay.

Fifty thousand dollars can buy a whole lot of information. Chauncey offered to double that if Glenn came back with answers. In the meantime, he had to work on getting another car before Dakota retrieved hers.

CHAPTER 37

Remorseful for her part in helping to deceive Dakota, Elly thought long and hard about telling her what was going on. However, the consequences her actions might have on her happy marriage outweighed the guilt she felt and she remained silent.

"Here's your money," I said and smiled broadly as I handed her $500.

"They work like a charm! Girl, I can hear everything he says," I boasted, speaking about the listening devices I paid Elly to plant throughout her sister-in-law's home on Christmas.

"You know what, this is eating at me and I don't feel good about it!" Elly admitted.

"You'll get over it. Stop by tonight and listen…it's fun!"

"Is Dakota home yet?"

"Nope, maybe she left his butt for good," I gushed and then giggled.

"Has it ever dawned on you she may be happy?"

"Nope! She can't be happy. She doesn't know him." Still consumed with guilt, Elly shook her head, sorry she'd gotten involved.

"I'm outta here. Next time, you're on your own…this is wrong and I won't do it again!" Standing to leave, Elly picked up her money, folded it and placed it in the secret compartment of her wallet. Living with what she'd done was difficult, but explaining it and the money to her husband would be impossible.

For a month, I parked in the alley behind my cousin's home and monitored the conversations Chauncey conducted inside. Unhappy with my inability to hear what the other party was saying on the phone, namely Dakota, I sought a device that would allow me to do just that.

After three weeks of researching my options and deciding on two, I realized I needed deep pockets to make it happen. Kevin's offer in Jamaica to keep his former wife from being happy with Chauncey had suddenly become an offer too good to refuse. Digging out his number, I phoned and left a voicemail, which included my number and the time I could be reached.

Answering his call on the first ring, I greeted him eagerly.

"What's up, Kevin?"

"*Not* on the phone!" he responded. "There will be a ticket in your name on the same airline at the same place, tomorrow morning. Be on the flight. We'll talk then..."

Suddenly afraid and not certain I was doing the right thing, I thought long and hard about meeting Kevin in Jamaica—alone. Tossing and turning throughout the night did little to help my physical and mental state. Restless, I became fidgety during the flight and popped a sleeping pill to help relax. With the exception of my connection in Florida, I slept the entire flight and relived the conversation I'd had with him my last night on the island.

Very curious about Dakota, he arranged to meet me. Little explanation was offered about his current living status or why he disappeared. What was divulged and very noticeable was his disdain toward his ex-wife and her continued quest to locate him and his money.

"So that was you the first night I saw you on the dance floor?"

"Yeah, I wasn't sure you saw me, nor was I sure I was ready to be outed, so I skipped out."

"Why'd you change your mind?" I asked cautiously.

"Curious…about your cousin," Kevin admitted. "See, without a pre-nup, I had little ground to stand on during our divorce. It pissed me off to see her gain control of so much of what I'd achieved."

"Did you say no pre-nup?" I asked shocked.

Embarrassed by his stupidity, Kevin nodded yes.

"Why not?"

"Thinking with the wrong head," he reluctantly admitted. Sitting back in his chair, he reflected on the night he met his wife. Stunned by her beauty, he calculated how to approach her. White and not certain she went that route, he struck up a conversation about the fund-raiser they were attending. An hour into that conversation it became pretty clear they had a connection— mental and physical.

Even though he'd been exclusively dating black women for several years, none had turned him out like Dakota. A freak between the sheets, she introduced him to tricks he had not known. Mind blown, a month later he asked her to marry him and in a matter of weeks, they said, "I do," in Vegas, without a prenuptial agreement. Recalling his stupidity angered him.

Skillfully he changed the subject to what had been transpiring in his ex-wife's life over the years and I gladly contributed what I knew. Our conversation lasted for hours. Parting company when the bar closed, we exchanged numbers. I actually never expected to hear from him.

My flight landed on time and a driver waited for me curbside. Arriving at the same hotel, I went straight to the bar. Incognito in a baseball cap and dark shades, Kevin waited for me at a small table in a remote area off to the side.

Following a brief and somewhat formal greeting, he got straight to the point by angrily admitting he messed around on Dakota, but justified his actions by pointing out how well she lived. In his mind, that was a fair trade-off. Because his public persona was his lifeline to his clients—athletes, the majority of whom were straight—he had to hide the fact he was bi or risk losing his bread and butter.

Marrying someone as refined and beautiful as Dakota gave him the persona he needed and the ability to keep up the charade. Life was going well for them until he met the man of his dreams on one of his trips to South Africa. Secretly dating for nearly a year, his partner, whom he'd fallen in love with, demanded a monogamous relationship and insisted he dump *the wife*.

Despite his wife continuously professing she loved him, it was not enough to keep him from the love of his life. P-whipped and for the first time happy, he took no chances. Doing as told, Kevin concocted a plan to get rid of his betrothed. His very public affair with a reigning beauty queen was well planned and calculated.

A woman of high morals and great sense of pride, he knew Dakota would dump him when she caught wind of the "affair." Where he miscalculated was underestimating his wife; he never thought she'd play dirty. The piranha she hired to represent her in the divorce went after everything he owned, his balls included.

To keep some of his wealth, his sanity, and his lover, he disappeared into oblivion and had been living obscurely since. With the number of years that had passed, he'd thought Dakota would have moved on and met another *meal ticket*. Discovering she had not hampered his ability to live freely, and resulted in his lover leaving.

The caramel-colored hunk I saw him with Hedonism weekend was just one of many flings he'd begun in an effort to get over his broken heart. Blaming Dakota, *and* her greed for his loss, he wanted revenge.

"She's made my life a living hell…" His words drifted off as he reflected on how difficult the past years had been trying to live in obscurity when he had millions tucked away in offshore accounts.

I informed him of her relationship with Chauncey. When Kevin's face lit up hopeful he'd soon be rid of her, I spent the next hour bursting his bubble. As always I put my negative spin on who I believed Chauncey was and how little I was certain he had, and Kevin became agitated. Realizing he was still "trapped," he finally revealed what was on his mind.

"I heard through the grapevine she's no fan of yours and vice-versa. What would it cost to make her as miserable as she's made me?"

Smiling, I digested his question before answering.

"Money! Lots of it."

"How much?" he asked, pleased I was game.

"I'll let you know, but I can tell you this: I ain't cheap!"

Kevin smiled and reached to shake my hand, confirming our arrangement. We agreed I'd contact him with updates on a weekly basis and as needed he'd wire the funds to my account from one of his offshore banks. I left him one of my voided checks and made sure he had my cell and home numbers. To secure the deal, he gave me $5,000.

Rising, I put the money in my purse, smiled and walked to the lobby where the driver waited to take me back to the airport. Now that money was no issue, Dakota was going to live in purgatory for a long time.

CHAPTER 38

Certain I would end up behind bars Val made a sincere effort to get me some psychological help. With Rodney's insistence, I agreed to meet with Dr. Lui, someone our pastor recommended while I was off meeting Kevin.

Because Kevin and I agreed I'd keep his whereabouts and the fact that he was alive a secret, I never shared with my parents or anyone else his emergence. But his being alive was "juicy" gossip and keeping it a secret was proving to be hard. Needing to tell someone, I dialed Dante. However, remembering Dante's last act of insubordination, I rethought my momentary lapse in judgment and changed the topic when he answered the phone.

"Hey you!"

"Hey yourself," Dante responded dryly.

"Listen, I got a gig that's going to keep me pretty busy for awhile. Just don't want you to think I don't love you if you don't hear from me as much."

"And would this be your way of saying good-bye?" he asked bluntly.

"Dante! You trippin.' Why would you think that?"

"'Cause I know you and I know you were not pleased with the last conversation we had."

"So what, you think I am trying to pay you back? Get a grip, Dante."

"If you say so," he said very nonchalantly. Try as I might to convince him, he did not believe me. Hurt by friends and lovers numerous times, he knew when someone was coming or going. He was certain I was going.

"Talk when you have time, ta-ta!" he added with attitude before hanging up on me.

Holding the phone, I stared at it and contemplated calling him back to explain, but remembered my agreement with Kevin. Returning the handset to its cradle, I sat pensive, uncertain how to fix what was obviously broken between my best friend and me.

Meeting a shrink right now was bad timing. My foul mood would definitely make him think I needed counseling and that was something I was not agreeing to. Inhaling deeply, holding it and then exhaling slowly (something I learned from Dakota's yoga classes) I began to relax. Repeating the process several more times I felt calm enough to see the doctor.

Putting on my best Oscar performance, I conversed and cajoled with Dr. Lui convincing him I was mentally sound and avoiding his recommendation I return anytime soon. Assuring my parents there was nothing to be concerned about, he recommended I return only if things got progressively worse.

Upon leaving his office, Rodney hugged me pleased with his diagnosis. Val sat quietly the entire drive home certain he'd gotten it wrong. Pulling into the garage she did not wait for Rodney to open her door. Climbing out in a hurry she retreated to her bedroom to be alone.

With lots to do and a deadline of next week to complete it, I rushed home to order the equipment I'd need to deal with Chauncey and Dakota. To my dismay, everything I wanted to order online was either out of stock or on back order. Settling for an even more expensive set of eavesdropping and surveillance equipment, I called Kevin to request more funds. A day later, my bank balance reflected the amount I'd requested.

"That was easy," I bragged to no one in particular.

After watching Chauncey's pattern of coming and going for a couple days, I figured out the best time to have Elly's daughter's boyfriend, who worked for the phone company, scale the fence and put a tap on the home phone. With neighbors that emulated pit bull guard dogs, late night preferably when no lights were on in the house would be best.

Several failed attempts finally yielded results when Chauncey inadvertently left the gate leading to the alley unlocked. In his absence, the phone technician was able to tap the line and ensure all conversations were recordable.

"Now I'll find out just what you are all about, you fake!" I squealed and remained glued to my headset, waiting for someone to speak or the phone to be used. Dakota was the first to do so.

"Hey baby," she cooed as she rushed into her fiancé's arms.

"Yuk." I snorted as I listened intently.

Dakota's return home was without pomp and circumstance. She missed Kelsey and Chauncey, but more importantly, she was tired of being in her dad's home. Taking his future wife by the hand, he led her to the garden room where he'd prepared her favorite dessert. Magnificent melon-colored roses in a crystal vase greeted her.

A wonderful cook, Chauncey spent the afternoon making peach cobbler for Dakota and ran out to her favorite florist to pick up the roses, hoping to make his long overdue confession a little easier to digest.

Coming clean about Pam felt good. Chauncey omitted numerous details about their "brief" relationship, but did acknowledge the cars were in her name, adding he paid the car notes. His explanation of having material gain in her name was re mined to include a bad credit score; something he'd recently obtained as a result of trying to help out his ailing father.

"I co-signed for a car loan for my dad, but when he got ill, he stopped paying the note. No one told me the car payments were behind until the repo man showed up to take his car—by then it was too late!"

While sitting discussing some changes Dakota wanted in their relationship, she mentioned some strange occurrences with her father's home phone.

"What do you mean?" Chauncey asked guardedly.

"His phone is designed to alert you when someone has picked up on the line. At least once or twice a week he received that warning, but neither of us were on the line."

Feds do that, he thought and made a mental note to have "his people" check her dad's home phone line. Certain they were not looking for him, he was equally certain someone had tapped her father's phone. His money was on me.

CHAPTER 39

Overconfidence can be a noose around one's neck. Not knowing who I was dealing with I put my neck in my own noose and so the game of tag began.

Every move Chauncey made, I knew it—or so I thought. Every move I made, Chauncey knew it with a few exceptions: the tap on his line and the bugs in his home. Slinging big bucks, he paid a professional to monitor my phone calls—morning, noon, and night.

Two weeks after being hired, the pro contacted Chauncey for an off-site meeting. Rendezvousing at a friend's home, he handed Chauncey a written report of what he'd discovered. Shocked, he learned I'd been listening to his entire life since Christmas. A sense of fear consumed him as he wondered how much I knew.

Within a matter of hours he arranged to have a professional crew sweep his home and remove all the bugs as well as line taps. Before his fiancée returned home, he and Glenn met to discuss how to put an end to this "problem" that was getting way too close for his comfort.

Hurriedly, Chauncey and Glenn visually inspected each room that had been swept to make sure nothing was out of place. Keeping all this from Dakota was becoming increasingly difficult, but something Chauncey felt he had to do at least until she said, "I do!" Not wanting to run into Dakota and cause concern, Glenn left just before she arrived home.

❤❤❤

Springtime in Indian Village is beautiful and Dakota took time to enjoy each day that the rain did not wash away. With Kelsey enrolled in half-day kindergarten, Dakota had that time to get her "exercise on." Belle Isle was twenty-two minutes away and had become her favorite walking spot.

Geared up with umbrella in case it rained or she crossed the path of an unfriendly dog, she stretched several minutes in the grand foyer of her home before heading out the door to power walk for the next hour.

Flowers of every sort—magnolias, begonia, petunias, name it—were in full bloom, making the neighborhood a vividly colored canvas. Walking briskly Dakota enjoyed the view as she rounded the corner, now ten minutes from Belle Isle.

Running into Be-Angeleke was not high on her list of favorite things to do, but when she saw her pull off to the curb to say hello, she stopped to chat.

"What's up, girl? Long time, no see!" Be-Angeleke squealed.

In between pants, Dakota responded in kind, allowing her to do most of the talking. Be-Angeleke looked good and seemed happy. Years had passed since they'd ended their friendship, but she kept in touch by way of Elly. Timing her heart rate with her three fingers pressed to her wrist, Dakota cut the conversation short to finish working out. Before she walked away, Be-Angeleke dropped a seed in her Spirit.

"Dakota…be careful. Everyone in your circle is not whom they appear."

Caught off guard, Dakota turned around with every intention of getting clarification, but BL pulled off before she could: keeping her promise to Elly not to divulge what she knew about my devilment.

It took several minutes to get what was said out her mind and by the time she did, Dakota was a quarter of a mile from home. Reaching her front door, she stretched and slowly allowed her heart rate to decrease. When she could breathe normally, she called Chauncey and told him what Be-Angeleke had said.

Even though he was hesitant to share what he knew about me with Dakota, certain it would alarm her, Chauncey decided he could no longer put it off. Promising to be home early, he informed Dakota he had something to discuss with her.

Pleased he kept his word, Dakota laid her head on his lap as he turned off the television to discuss the matter at hand. Chauncey methodically laid out what I was doing, when it began and why he believed I was doing it. When Dakota asked how he knew, he told her part of the truth—his cousin Glenn had investigated the situation for him.

Suspecting Elly or another family member planted the bugs in their home on Christmas, he shared that tidbit of information with Dakota who began to cry. The answer to the obvious question was simple—jealousy. Contemplating the equation of Elly and me, Dakota deduced the two did not fit. She could accept I was doing this out of jealousy, but she could not understand her sister-in-law's reason for plotting with me.

"Jealousy is a strange company keeper, baby."

Nodding in agreement, Dakota wiped her eyes and lay in silence on Chauncey's lap. Exhausted, he rested his head on the wing of the oversized sofa and fell asleep. Within minutes, Dakota joined him, only to be awakened by the sound of the front gate buzzer.

Rising, they both peered out the window and saw an unmarked police car and a plainclothes officer at the gate. Running upstairs, Chauncey peered out the side windows to see if any cops were laying in wait. None in sight, he had Dakota answer the buzzer.

Rather than let the officer in the gate, she met him to discuss what he wanted. Opening it, she extended her hand to greet him and then listened intently to what he had to say. Chauncey watched from the window in the great room, behind the one-way silhouette blinds.

Anxiety mounted as he watched her converse for fifteen minutes with the officer. The instant she waved good-bye, butterflies took over, certain she was now aware of what he'd been hiding from her for two years. Nervous, and unable to read her face, he waited for her to say something.

"Baby, you are not going to believe this. That detective says he needs to speak with you. Rochelle has accused you of fondling her breast at a restaurant last month."

Sitting down, angry and trying to absorb what she'd just said, Chauncey banged his fist on the glass table and broke it, cutting his hand and sending shards of glass cascading throughout the room. Startled, Dakota screamed and then ran to get rags to compress the wounds and stop the bleeding. As she tended to his hand, Chauncey explained this was not my first time pulling this mess. Owning up to the initial accusation that occurred when they lived in the Shores, he explained how he allowed his attorney to deal with that situation.

"What did he do about it?" she asked concerned.

"At the time, he recommended I either begin a lawsuit against her or file a complaint against her for filing a false police report. Both options would bring me gratification, but I'm way too busy for that."

Staring in disbelief, Dakota waited for him to go on.

"Listen, now that I am not working with Pam, I have to hustle a lot harder to flip properties than I used to. Starting my own business has not been easy and I'm swamped. Tying up my time—no, our time—in court with her stupid butt is not something I can afford to do right now."

"What is wrong with this girl?" Dakota screamed, tired of the entire scenario.

"Let me deal with her. I just need you to watch your back and be careful. No more going walking by yourself. There's no telling what she might do!" Agreeing, Dakota promised she'd limit her workouts to their home, yard or the gym.

CHAPTER 40

Unaware Chauncey was still turning off the ringer to the home phones at night, Dakota was stunned to learn a day after I was admitted, I was in the hospital in serious condition. Jeff tried to call Dakota on her cell phone throughout the night but could not reach her. When the sun rose, he tried her home phone and Chauncey answered half asleep. Handing the phone to Dakota, her brother explained how difficult it was to reach her. Checking her cell phone, she discovered she'd turned it off to rest with no intentions of leaving it off all night, but inadvertently did.

"What happened to her?" Dakota asked. Whispering, he explained no one could seem to get a straight answer from anyone. All he'd been told was I was injured when I ran off the road and hit a tree.

"Had she been drinking?" Unable to answer that or most of her questions, her brother promised to call as soon as he had any news.

Chauncey had already left for the day and uncertain he cared, she decided to wait to tell him when he got home. However, the news she held on to was not news to him. Since he was still paying for me to be watched, he already knew what happened, how it happened, and why.

The watered-down hospital version that I wrapped my car around a tree carried no truth. A newly evolving affair I had begun with a beautiful Chadian woman who lived in Dearborn had me sprung. New to lesbianism and having any romantic involvement, I got caught stalking the girl by her lover.

The much smaller and stronger lover tried to beat me to a pulp. In an effort to flee from her powerful blows, I jumped into my Benz and pressed the gas pedal to the floor, losing control of my car. Wiping out two small trees, my car came to a rest in the center divider wedged between two trees, airbag deployed.

Rather than admit the truth and be outed, I lied and said I lost control of my car and my injuries were a result of that mishap. Since Dakota knew nothing about Chauncey's knowledge of the situation or how he got his information, he decided to wait and hear her version before he said anything.

Later in the day, Chauncey purchased a Hummer (financed in his sister's name) as a birthday present to himself. The next morning as part of the celebration, he packed up the truck, gathered the two youngest of the four boys he mentored and headed south to Wild Adventures in Valdosta, Georgia to celebrate turning thirty-five in three days.

En route they discussed my accident and he decided to allow Dakota to live with the watered-down hospital version, rather than answer the barrage of questions that would arise by disputing that account of the incident.

A week of no me was a rewarding thought even to Dakota, despite her having to spend her down time with three, count them—one, two, three children under the age of ten.

Kelly, the oldest at seven, was mature acting for his age. Kenny, the youngest and just eleven months younger than Kelsey, had learning challenges. Settling in for what would not be a restful week, Dakota drifted off to sleep while the three of them, and Chauncey, enjoyed the ride.

Thankful to have his "wife" and "sons" with him, Chauncey took his time driving and pondered how enjoyable this time would be, particularly because I could not, and would not, be around to mess it up. A broken clavicle and fractured ribs had me restricted to bed rest. Realizing he'd get more than a week-long break from my madness, Chauncey exhaled and smiled.

While I recuperated, he planned to take full advantage of my downtime to put a halt to my meddling once and for all. His "peeps" were working overtime to locate the source of my funding and cut it off. If he accomplished that before I got on my feet, I would be doomed and his secret would be safe.

In the meantime, he decided to press Dakota to set a wedding date. Waiting to marry her, at the risk of losing her, created restless nights and long days for him. Kelsey loved her so much and she was an excellent mother. Their lives were complete with her in it and living without her was not an option.

Each new day in Valdosta was an interesting experience for the five of them. To remember the moments, Dakota made sure they took plenty pictures of each of the boys, so they'd have them as they grew older.

Chauncey's mother and sister showed up on the fourth day and surprised Chauncey to help celebrate his birthday. Although Dakota found it odd, she thought it was sweet that the boys addressed his mother as "Grandma" and his sister as "Aunt Carolyn."

On the last day of the trip, while packing, Dakota mentioned to Carolyn how much she admired Chauncey for stepping up to the plate and mentoring children he did not father. Eyes bucked, she turned several shades red and never responded to Dakota's comment. Again, she thought the behavior was odd, but it still didn't cause her any concern.

However, on the ride back from Georgia to Michigan, the cat came out the bag.

Young Kenny asked his dad when he was going to come get him to live with his brother Kelsey. Anxious to have him under the same roof, Kelsey chimed in.

"Yeah, Dad, when is Kenny coming home to sleep at the house you bought for us?"

Chauncey ignored the question and turned up the music. In a matter of seconds, the boys had forgotten what they'd asked, but Dakota did not. Feeling sick to his stomach, Chauncey pulled over at the next rest stop and got out to use the restroom. During the ten minutes he was gone, Dakota recalled the "grandma" comment and then decided to investigate the situation on her own.

"Kelsey, your mom's name is Nina, right?"

"Uh-huh!" Correcting him, she reminded him he was to answer yes or no. He responded yes. Turning to Kenny, she asked the same question and he said his mother's name was also Nina. Kelly, quite mature for his age, did not wait for her to ask him and volunteered priceless information.

Kelsey and Kenny were blood brothers and Chauncey was their father and Nina was their mother. Kelly was also his son, but his mother's name was Diane. Three other siblings, a girl and two more boys between the ages of twelve and eighteen, were also their siblings and they too had different mothers.

Mortified, Dakota began to hyperventilate. Once again she'd

caught Chauncey in a lie. Without permission, the information her father shared with her nearly two years prior came knocking and she could not help but wonder if she knew Chauncey like she thought she did.

Afraid to face Dakota, Chauncey rehearsed his explanation over and over again before returning to the truck. Rather than delay the inevitable, he planned to broach the subject once they got back on the road. Inside the Hummer, the chill in the air was thick and the boys, tired from the ride and a wonderful week, were falling off to sleep. It left an unending eerie silence, which made the ride long and uncomfortable. From time to time, he'd turn up the music to keep him company and evade Dakota's glare.

Crossing the Michigan state line eliminated any urgency he felt to admit the truth. The fear of losing Dakota kept him from owning up to his six children, by four women. After a long restful night in their quiet home with no thoughts or fear of drama from me, he'd sit her down and explain why he hid his tribe from her. Until then, he only wanted to take his kids to their mothers and go home to rest. Feeling the same, Dakota dropped it, until morning. But, restless and unable to sleep, she decided not to wait for the truth.

Smack! Startled, but fully aware of the second slap en route, Chauncey grabbed Dakota's hand and held it until she relaxed her grip. Pulling away, she glared at him through a film of tears. Slapped into a state of alertness, he guardedly watched his fiancée who did not take her eyes off him.

Opening her mouth to speak, her voice quivered, threatening to betray the tears she tried to blink away. Unable to bear watching her cry, her eyes searching his for answers, he owned up to his tribe. His silence about fathering five boys and one girl by four women was too much to handle. Admitting it now, more than a year after they'd been a couple, only added to her pain.

Without uttering a word, Dakota slipped on her house slippers, picked up her purse, grabbed her car keys, and walked out the door in her pajamas. A man's man, Chauncey fought back tears, bit his lower lip and stared blindly at the blur of photos of the two of them hanging on their bedroom wall.

"Dad, what's wrong with Mommy?" Kelsey asked groggily, fully aware she'd left angrily. Reaching out, he picked up his son and cradled him in his arms.

"She'll be home soon…I hope," he whispered as tears ran down his cheeks, landing on his son's head, which was pressed to his chest.

CHAPTER 41

Despite familiar surroundings, her bedroom did little to comfort Dakota. Numbness consumed her body and her mind was a blank palette. Betrayed and deceived, she felt like she should press rewind, but had no concept of where to begin. Who was her fiancé, Chauncey Bentley? Did she really know him?

"Six kids! Six kids and he allowed me to believe they were not his. What else has he lied about?" Baffled by the realization she'd been sleeping with a total stranger, Dakota went into a deep funk for several days, refusing to answer any of Chauncey's phone calls.

With Kelsey safely tucked away at his father's home, Chauncey, who was determined to stay out of jail, focused his energy on getting rid of my meddling behind. First things first, his attorney requested information from the branch manager of the California bank that was still holding his money. Second, Attorney Girgenti contacted the who brokered the two deals on the seven-figure homes. Lastly, his "inside person" at my bank, which he'd paid handsomely for information, was given a number to fax my bank documents so he could locate the source of my funding.

Over the month Dakota remained out of touch with him and the world, Chauncey began to unweave a skillfully woven web, starting with his money being held "captive" in California. Amid the backlash that followed the discovery of unethical practices by the now resigned branch manager were some blatant indiscretions. She, very married was having an ongoing affair with the "very married father of two" real estate agent; who, along with Tabitha recommended Chauncey open his account at that bank.

The new branch manager explained the previous manager's personal relationship with the real estate agent. It contributed to her decision to violate bank policy and freely share all of Chauncey's personal information with the real estate agent, who shared it with Tabitha and faxed it to me.

In a handwritten letter from the former branch manager, she admitted overreacting to a phone call she had received from an unknown person who stated, "Mr. Bentley was conducting illegal activities through her branch."

Reviewing this information with his attorney, they both speculated there might be a recording of the phone conversation. Most bank conversations are recorded, along with the phone numbers for security purposes. If any of this evidence existed, Chauncey was certain it would lead them to me, or one of my cronies.

Applying legal threats and maneuvers yielded much more than either Chauncey or his attorney had hoped. In a matter of ten days, they had a transcribed copy of the telephone conversation I had with the branch manager, as well as transcriptions of conversations the branch manager had with the actress, Tara, and the real estate agent regarding Chauncey's finances.

Not wanting any further problems, the real estate agent gladly spoke with Attorney Girgenti by phone as his attorney sat nearby. In that conversation he revealed Tabitha and I had contacted him. Early on, we only inquired about the homes Chauncey and Dakota were interested in purchasing. However, weeks after they had reduced their choices to the two million-dollar properties, we questioned him about the legalities of the deal and Chauncey's ability to buy either property.

After he revealed his mistress sent him copies of Chauncey's paperwork showing he more than qualified for the home, the real estate agent said he shared the information with Tabitha, but only forwarded altered copies to me. When asked why he sent the paperwork to me, he stated he was afraid of being implemented in any money laundering charges Chauncey could be facing. Once questioned about the source of the money laundering theory, he sheepishly admitted I told him.

Figuring out who was paying me a sizable amount of money to f' with his life was not an easy thing to do. Nothing in the bank paperwork Chauncey received from the insider showed who was sending the funds or where they were sent from, which led him to believe the source was an offshore bank account. A longtime offshore bank account holder, he was fully aware of the lack of paper trails those accounts rendered.

"No way is she that connected," he mumbled.

"So, what you think she's into?" Glenn asked, scratching his head in disbelief as he browsed through the documents Chauncey had handed him.

"Can't call it...but she ain't that deep, trust me!"

"Well, if it ain't her, someone's pulling her strings," Glenn deducted.

"Got that right...but who?" Chauncey asked absentmindedly.

Glenn shrugged his shoulders admitting he had no clue. Together they laid out the papers on the table and combed through them looking for a clue or something to lead them to my source. Focusing on the stacks of papers in front of him, and with his cell phone still on vibrate from his earlier meeting with his attorney, Chauncey missed Dakota's phone call.

"Chauncey, it's me...call as soon as you get this message. My dad is in emergency."

Dakota's father had collapsed at home and without waiting for an ambulance, she rushed him to the nearest hospital. While the medical staff tended to him, she stepped out into the parking lot to call Chauncey, in desperate need of his support.

Within hours family members gathered at the hospital to offer their support, Val and Rodney included. Seizing an opportunity to hatch another part of my plan, I contacted my uncle's newly estranged girlfriend, who'd just moved to North Carolina after he refused to marry her.

Jimmy and Verida had dated for ten years, long enough for her five-year-old daughter to become a teenager. With only three more years before she'd be free of children, Verida felt it was an excellent time for him to make their relationship legal and permanent—especially since she was only forty-nine and he would soon be eighty.

Bitter and still in disbelief that he broke up with her, she jumped at the chance to get back in his good graces, so when I called and offered to buy her a roundtrip ticket to come see him, she agreed.

Verida and Dakota could not stand each other. Years earlier, Verida had struck the first blow that drove a permanent wedge between them. After Dakota's much publicized thirtieth birthday party on a private beach in California, her father returned with photos and endless boasting about the wonderful occasion. Jealous and feeling slighted for being omitted from the guest list, Verida "borrowed" the photos and passed them around the hair and nail salon they both frequented, giving her scathing interpretation of each photo.

Unbeknownst to her, one of Dakota's former classmates was present and called to inform her. While Verida continued to bad-mouth and pick apart every detail of each photograph, Dakota snuck in and hid in the shampoo room to listen. Unable to remain silent for longer than ten minutes, she walked out and confronted Verida who called her a wannabe diva. Verida uttered not another word because Dakota lit into her with a verbal berating that left the entire room of patrons speechless.

In tears, Verida fled the salon, leaving her purse and the pictures. Wanting no parts of what they'd just witnessed, those who still held pictures quickly handed them to Dakota. Some patrons who had not enjoyed what Verida had done applauded as Dakota opened the door to leave. Well pleased with what she'd done, she thanked them and curtsied.

So imagine the look on Dakota's face when she returned from eating and found Verida holding her now awake father's hand at his bedside.

"Hi, Dakota," she said superciliously.

For the sake of her ill father's peace of mind, she faked being pleased to see her—waved and smiled.

Just above a whisper, Dakota's father informed her he wanted Verida to have his bedroom at the house until he got out of the hospital. His stay would be less than a week. The doctors had determined his thyroid was the problem; three tumors were attached laying side by side on his left lobe and one on his right lobe. They suspected cancer. A biopsy had been ordered and if cancer was found he'd undergo immediate surgery followed by radiation treatments.

Dakota gave Verida a disapproving frown. Smirking, she returned her attention to "her man." Later that evening just before visiting hours ended, Verida left the hospital with me, informing Dakota she had her father's door key, and she'd be "home" late.

"Dad, I know it's your house, but are you sure you want her there, rummaging through your things?"

"Ain't nothin' there for her to see. All my stuff is locked in my safe."

"Well, my stuff is not locked away and I don't trust her."

Patting her on the hand, he dozed off to sleep; groggy from the pain medication he'd just received. Right after he began to snore, Dakota rushed home to put her items she'd treasured most out of Verida's grasp and eyesight. Not enough years had passed to make her forget three of her favorite pairs of rhinestone sunglasses came up missing after she accidentally left them at her dad's home on one of her visits from California.

Right or wrong, she had concluded Verida took them—a conclusion based on nothing more than instinct and the fact that she always commented about how much she liked them. With one eye open she fell off to sleep after waiting up until two a.m. for Verida to arrive.

Sleeping in, Dakota left Verida at the house and did not set the burglar alarm so she could leave freely. Fifteen minutes prior to her father's surgery to remove the cancerous thyroid, Verida popped her head in, appeared to take inventory of who was in attendance, and announced she'd be right back.

Concerned, Dakota stopped momentarily and took stock of the room as well. Missing was Val, Elly and me. Minutes after the prayer for a successful surgical procedure was concluded, Verida joined the well-wishers avoiding eye contact with Dakota.

As they wheeled her father to the operating room, Val arrived and offered a word of encouragement. However, Elly and I did not arrive until three hours after he'd been wheeled into recovery.

A very weird feeling of déjà vu came over Dakota, one she could not get past. Flashbacks of the two of us missing from her engagement dinner and what followed our absence sent chills up her spine! Seconds later, overcome with joy to see Chauncey walk in the door, she began to shake uncontrollably and burst into sobs. Falling into his arms, he escorted her from the hospital waiting area and everyone's prying eyes to console her.

"Talk to me, baby. Did something go wrong? Your dad okay?"

"Hhh-ee's fine!" she said, trying to calm down.

"Then why the tears?" he asked sincerely.

"You got my message?" Dakota asked absentmindedly.

"Yeah, baby, I did…this afternoon and I came straight here."

"I missed you so much," she said and burst into tears once more.

"Baby…I missed you, too. Come home!"

"I'm not ready…I want to…"

Lifting a finger to silence her, Chauncey assured her, when she was ready, he and Kelsey would be waiting. Embracing her gently, he held her and let her cry. When she was calm, she asked about Kelsey. Briefly, in an effort to cheer her up, Chauncey told her a joke Kelsey had shared with him. She chuckled, but became melancholy again.

Changing the subject, Chauncey asked about Verida.

"That his ex I saw in there?"

"Uh-huh. Something is not right, baby…"

"What do you mean? What's not right?" Chauncey asked concerned.

"Her! Her being here, and her being with Rochelle."

"Rochelle?" he shrieked, taken aback by their camaraderie. Back in the day, Verida and I could not stand to be in the same room. Verida, very full figured and in denial, often wore clothes way too tight and way too youthful. Most ignored her failed attempts to be a diva, but not uncouth me. "Hot mess" was the label I bestowed upon her and it stuck! Any and all future family gatherings that included her also included her new name, "hot mess."

"Look at that hot mess" or "here comes hot mess" were just a few of the endearing terms people used to refer to her presence. She knew, and she really did not care. Assuming we were jealous, the more we talked, the more she gave us to talk about. When she learned the source of those "labels" was me, a nasty confrontation ensued and then we made it a point to avoid each other's company at all cost or both our weaves were going to be costly to repair.

"Don't take a rocket scientist to figure out they're up to something. She staying at Dad's?"

Dakota nodded her head yes.

"Aw man…bad news! You should come home at least 'til he gets out."

"And leave her to his home…alone! No way!"

Chauncey agreed it was best she stay there, if for no other reason, to guard the house. However, because he knew something was amiss, he called Glenn and had him increase my surveillance.

Recovering exceptionally well, Dakota's father was released a day early to go home. Once more, Verida, unaware he was being released, was not present but showed up fifteen minutes late for her usual visit five minutes before he was to be driven home. Dakota thought it strange when she saw Verida rush out of the hospital lobby ahead of the two of them and frantically dial a number on her cell phone.

"Dad, wait here…I'll get the car!"

Walking up behind her, Dakota heard just enough of the conversation to know she was conversing with me.

"Say hello for me," Dakota said as she walked past.

Instantly she heard the phone snap shut. Looking back, she saw Verida hurriedly return to her father's side inside the hospital lobby. Certain we were up to no good, Dakota went home guarded and kept her guard up until Verida left a week later.

As suspected, their home phone began to ring incessantly with inquiries from Verida, concerned about Jimmy's recovery. Times she was certain her father was asleep, Dakota turned the phone ringer off until he awoke, not wanting to speak with her.

Another month passed before Verida successfully convinced him to allow her to return for a visit. When she did, she suddenly began to question him about things that pertained to Dakota; things he knew nothing about.

Her weekend stay proved to be a miserable visit for my uncle. They argued the entire time she was at his home because she constantly inquired about Dakota's personal business. Angry he would not discuss the "prima donna" with her, she stormed off her last night there and spent the night at her sister's home in Detroit.

Concerned about the information Verida shared with him, he left his bed and sat next to Dakota in the TV room to discuss the things Verida had said.

"Is everything alright with you and Chauncey?"

"We're working on it, Dad, why?"

"What's goin' on?" he asked with genuine concern.

Not one to ever question her about her personal business, Dakota knew something was on his mind. Patiently she waded through his questions and picked apart the subject matter well enough to ascertain he was fishing with reason.

Several clever questions from her resulted in discovering Verida had probed him for information about subject matter she'd discussed with no one but Chauncey; some on the phone, most in person. Certain her fiancé had not shared their conversations, she called him in a panic to inform him what she'd learned.

Explaining in detail what happened, she demanded he find out how Verida knew what they'd discussed. Immediately Chauncey concluded she had to be listening to their conversations, but how she could do that long distance perplexed him. Assuring his fiancée she was in no danger and he'd handle it, he hung up and called Glenn.

Their conversation was brief, the end result being the house needed to be swept for listening devices. In an effort to avoid alarming her father, Chauncey picked up the bug sweeper from Glenn and headed to his future father-in-law's home. After Jimmy fell asleep, Chauncey spent an hour sweeping the home and was astonished to find six listening devices throughout the house, two in Dakota's bedroom (where she conducted most of her conversations).

Certain Verida planted them and tired of being f'd with, he decided he and his boys needed to pay her a visit in North Carolina.

"I'll be back in a day or two," he informed Dakota, as he pushed past her ignoring her pleas not to go.

Shopping in North Carolina's newest Wal-Mart with the $1,000 she'd gotten from me was fun. It had been quite some time since Verida had had something extra to spend freely. Money was tight now that she was no longer in Jimmy's wallet. Handing the cashier the last item in her cart, she waited for him to subtotal to see if she'd exceeded the cash she had in her wallet. Relieved she was just sixty-five cents short, she opened her purse to search for loose change in the bottom.

"Ma'am, anything under the bottom of your cart?" the cashier asked before totaling her sale. Turning to check her shopping cart for any additional items, Verida nearly passed out when she saw Chauncey standing behind her in line. Thanks to late-night gossip with me, his gangster reputation preceded him, causing her to shake in fear as she fumbled in her purse for the additional sixty-five cents. Frightened for her life, she prayed for mercy.

Oh God, please help me... don't let him kill me!

Not wanting to die, she tried to prolong the inevitable by asking the cashier for an item she knew they did not carry. Moving to the exit, Chauncey waited never taking his eyes off her. Looking around for security, Verida saw none and the senior citizen door-greeters would obviously be of little assistance in helping her deal with him. As her breathing became labored, she found it difficult to lift her legs, which felt like lead.

Taking a long deep breath, Verida exhaled and scurried past him avoiding his gaze. Outside in the parking lot she could feel him on her heels. Suddenly she stopped, abruptly spun around and blurted out what happened, hoping to stave off the beat down she believed was coming.

"Okay...listen." Swallowing hard she explained.

"Rochelle offered me a thousand dollars and a roundtrip ticket if I agreed to go to Michigan to see Jimmy and stay at his home while he was hospitalized." Silent, Chauncey stared at her waiting for her to continue.

"In exchange for the money, I had to let Rochelle and Elly into his home when Dakota was not there. They picked the day he had his surgery to come over because they knew Dakota would be at the hospital all day, giving them time to rummage through her personal things and place the listening devices throughout."

Continuing, Verida explained she was given instructions to call us whenever anyone left the room or the hospital; especially Dakota. Initially she agreed to go to Michigan because she needed the money, but when she realized how serious Jimmy's condition was, she wanted to be there for him.

Uncomfortable in his home knowing *I* could hear everything that was said, Verida admitted she found excuses to stay away and returned to North Carolina days after Jimmy was released from the hospital and safely tucked away in his bed.

"I'm so sorry for what I've done. I was going to tell Jimmy when I went back to visit," she explained, sounding contrite.

Sucking his teeth, Chauncey clenched his jaw as he stared at her. A film of sweat engulfed her body, even though the temperature was a comfortable seventy degrees. Shaking, she stood silent, afraid to speak or move. Disgusted with her very presence, Chauncey motioned for Glenn to pull forward.

"Let's bounce before I knock her out."

As a parting gesture, Chauncey gave her a "B…don't f' with me" look as he climbed in Glenn's car which was parked next to Verida's. To make sure she knew he was not playing with her, he pointed to her four flat tires and held up the knife used to flatten them. Placing it to his throat, he slowly drew it horizontally across his neck, pointed it at her and winked!

In one deep gasp, she felt the air fill her lungs and her heart stop as she imagined the knife cutting her throat from ear to ear. Leaving her shopping cart parked behind her car she ran back into Wal-Mart to safety, where she remained until the tow truck arrived to help her. Loading her shopping bags into the trunk of her car, the driver towed her to a nearby tire store where she spent the remainder of her bounty from me on new tires.

Two hours after the visit from Chauncey had ended, she was

safely home. Afraid her relationship might be doomed, Verida frantically dialed Jimmy's number to explain what she'd done and why. Forgetting the phone line was tapped, she warned him to be careful around his niece and daughter-in-law. As he pressed her for more details, Verida remembered the phone was bugged and abruptly hung up you cannot sweep phone lines!.

Too late! I had been listening to the conversation and became enraged that Verida took my money and did not honor our agreement to keep her mouth shut.

"Vengeance is sweet," I whispered as I took off the headset to my listening device and mulled over how to get even.

CHAPTER 42

Once more comfortable inside the walls of her bedroom, Dakota chatted on the phone with Roz, a former classmate who did a great job of keeping in touch from time to time. One of the few individuals who adored Dakota while they were in high school, she never bought into the post-graduate "prima donna" persona and never felt intimidated by her presence.

Down to earth, Roz married right out of high school and immediately started a family. Her husband, a drummer and minister, was pretty well known in the Detroit entertainment community for his exceptional musical abilities and his forthrightness.

"Well, listen, I've got to go, but I want to invite you and Chauncey to Family Day at our church."

"I'd love to come, and I'll see if Chauncey and Kelsey want to come as well."

"It's still hard for me to believe you're a mom. Will wonders never cease?" Roz teased. They both laughed and discussed Kelsey and his "old soul" before ending their conversation.

Missing "her son," she dialed Chauncey and asked to see them both. Busy, Chauncey suggested she stop by around noon, pick up Kelsey, and spend the day with him. "What an excellent idea!" she exclaimed, and did just that.

Extremely bright, Kelsey had changed dramatically in the five months Dakota had been absent from his life. Spending a few minutes with him here and there did little to reinforce the manners and etiquette she'd worked hard to instill in him. Gone was his correct grammar and in its place was slang—lots of it. Enunciating his words had been reduced to slurs and endings being dropped and he'd developed a new set of words—fo' (instead of four); do' (instead of door); flo' (instead of floor), and the list went on.

Disappointed and feeling very guilty for neglecting him, she made up her mind to go home and took Kelsey with her to "Granddad's" to pack.

"Granddad," he squealed as he ran through the door, arms wide open.

Excited to see him, her father scooped him up in his arms and hugged him tightly. Certain Kelsey would be kept busy long enough to allow her to call and inform Chauncey of her decision, Dakota left him with her father.

Thrilled to hear she was moving back in, Chauncey rushed home from his office and hurriedly spot cleaned. No longer a complete disaster the house still looked a mess. Underwear, socks, shoes, and dirty clothing were strewn about the bedroom and bathroom. The kitchen had dishes stacked with dried food encrusted on them and the pantry and cabinets were void of any food. Kelsey's room was a wreck with his clothing and toys everywhere.

Taking inventory of the mess, Chauncey called A Woman's Touch cleaning service and paid extra for the rush job he requested. Before evening, the home was pristine and the last load of laundry was in the dryer. Ordering out, he dashed to Steve's Soul Food to pick up dinner.

When his *wife* and son walked through the front door, Chauncey, overcome with emotion at the sight, broke down. Holding them both he allowed the tears to fall, thankful to have his family restored.

Now that Dakota had returned, life would be good and he'd do a better job at being a husband and father; something he'd promised God he'd do if He restored his home life and family.

Giving Dakota time to eat and settle in, Chauncey informed her he had a serious matter to discuss with her. Just before bed, she went to him and sat patiently as he apologized; making no excuses for all the times he deceived her and promised he'd not do it again. Next, he explained his youngest son: Kenny had been taken from his birth mother for neglect and abuse and was in danger of going into the foster care system if he did not intervene.

"Chauncey, what are trying to say? Spit it out!"

"Baby, he needs me—us. I can't let him stay in the system…I want to bring him here to live with us."

Well aware Kenny was slow, Dakota could not help but be concerned. As she sat thinking about what he was asking, and the consequences of having this disruptive little boy in her home and life, she began to cry. Chauncey left her to her thoughts.

Realizing this would be a major sacrifice and a permanent change in her life, she could not bring herself to say yes. However, realizing saying no would be a life-altering decision she would make—for him, she could not live with herself knowing she sent him into a system that is already overrun with a massive influx of children it is ill-equipped to handle.

Falling to her knees, through tears, Dakota petitioned God to give her some sign that her decision to agree to accept Kenny into their home and her life was the right one.

"God, you know me…and you know this is not what I want. I

did not have children because I did not want them... but this baby needs someone to care. Why that someone has to be me, I don't know!"

Not wanting to see the child be subjected to more neglect and abuse, Dakota prayed her decision to become mom to yet another child she did not birth (nor want) would not become a decision she'd regret. As she lay prostrate and wept, a feeling came over her of complete peace; a peace she'd never felt before. Rising, she emerged from their bedroom—eyes red and swollen, and walked over to Chauncey, hugged him, and whispered, "yes."

Tightening his embrace, he thanked her and whispered, "I love you," over and over again. Together they went to Kelsey's room and informed him his baby brother would be "coming home."

CHAPTER 43

With Dakota's absence from her father's home, he became very lonely. As his health continued to improve so did his attitude toward Verida. Two months of no one to talk to on a daily basis became unbearable for him. In need of companionship, he called Verida and asked her to come for a weekend visit.

Apprehensive because of the listening devices, and afraid of what I might do to her, she asked for time to think about it. A day later, she accepted his offer, excited about the chance to be with him once more. Men, the wrong kind, were plentiful. However, a good man was hard to come by; and a good man with means was even harder.

Living with what she'd done to Jimmy was difficult. Even though money often motivated her decisions, she had a conscience and it was whippin' her behind. Believing I was crazy, she worried about the outcome of her spilling the beans to my uncle. I had not contacted her since she'd ratted me out. For that she was thankful! But, returning to *my turf* sent a chill through Verida; especially when she reflected on my supposed mental instability.

Arriving at his home fairly early, Verida had little to say as she unpacked; unaware Chauncey had removed the bugs. Limiting what she said in Jimmy's home, she suggested they spend time together out and about. Both fond of the casinos, they decided to spend the weekend in Canada gambling.

Happy to be in each other's company, they gambled and spent quality time talking about life. Thankful to have someone to talk to, Jimmy enjoyed every second with her. Very sorry for what she'd done, Verida went out of her way to be attentive to him, hoping to make up for lost time and her indiscretions.

Sunday evening, they drove from Canada straight to the airport. Curbside, Jimmy asked to see her again. Her heart became filled with new joy and beat quickly as she responded, "yes!" Whispering a prayer, she promised God she'd not blow it again. Climbing out the car, Verida leaned in the window and told him to be careful and stay away from me. That warning scared him and stayed on his mind during the short drive back to his home.

Lying across his bed to channel-surf, he decided to call Dakota and discuss Verida's warning. Not wanting to have the discussion over the phone, Dakota promised her dad she'd talk about it when she came over on Saturday morning, her usual time to visit with him and clean his home; assuring him there was no reason to be alarmed.

The next morning, earlier than usual but not unexpected, his brother Joe arrived for his coffee-and-toast stop. A ritual of twenty years, the two of them sat and watched *Jerry Springer*, laughing at the shenanigans and fights, while debating whether the confrontations were staged.

Every noon, they drove to the corner store to play their mid-day-lottery choices. Caught up watching TV, both lost track of time and ran a little past their noon departure. Hurrying to get in the car, they were delayed again when Rodney pulled into the drive. Suddenly remembering another number he wanted to play, Jimmy hurried back inside the house while Joe spoke with Rodney outside.

Excited to see Rodney, Jimmy jotted down his number and raced outdoors to greet him with every intention of inviting him to ride with them to the store. Disappointed to see him backing out the drive, Jimmy waved his arms in an attempt to get him to stop. Rodney saw him, but rather than stop, he accelerated and sped off.

"What's wrong with your brother?" Jimmy joked with Joe.

Eyes bucked and mouth agape, looking like Buckwheat on the *The Little Rascals*, Joe stood silent.

"You alright, bro?"

"Uh-hh, naw, I feel a little lightheaded. My pressure must be up!" Joe explained.

"Okay, you go on back in and sit down. Give me your money and numbers. I'll play our horses. Be back in a minute!"

Returning inside, Joe hurried upstairs and then ran downstairs, tossing minute, flat devices that had the ability to pick up noises several feet away with perfection. Sweating, he threw the last one behind the furnace in the laundry room just as his brother entered the door.

"Joe, you alright? You sweatin' like a pig goin' to slaughter. Go sit down, man, 'cause I can't pick you up if you fall." They both chuckled.

Tired and winded Joe walked into the TV room and sat down. Cognizant of the listening device he'd thrown into that room, he sat stoically and quiet as the TV blared. Joining him shortly before the lottery airing at one p.m., Jimmy stared at the TV and jotted down the winning numbers, disappointed he'd missed by one digit.

"What'd you get?" he asked Joe.

"Nothin'..."

With such a dull reaction after losing twenty dollars, Jimmy was certain his younger brother was ill, so he offered to take him to the doctor. However, illness had nothing to do with the way he was acting. His guilty conscience was getting to him.

The previous night, Val and I had asked him to place the bugs in my uncle's home, but he balked at our request and refused. For the next two hours we filled his head with stories about Chauncey being a fraud, trying to convince him he had to help us catch Chauncey before he robbed Jimmy and Dakota blind.

Still not convinced we were doing the right thing, he told us he'd think it over and went home. Unable to accept our explanation of things, he bypassed his usual morning stop at our home and went straight to his oldest brother's home.

In need of reinforcement, we trumped up a story to convince Rodney to get his brother Joe to put the bugs in Uncle Jim's house. What we said was Dakota was crazy in love and Chauncey had her fooled. We also made him believe his oldest brother was wrapped around his daughter's finger and unaware of the danger he was in because his age kept him from thinking straight.

That lie worked and my dad drove to Uncle Jim's to solicit Joe's help. Bugs in tow, Rodney showed up and whispered to Joe, "Jimmy is old and can't think straight. You have to look out for him." Feeling a sense of obligation to do so because all his life his older brother had looked out for him, Joe did as instructed. By the time Dakota arrived on Saturday to discuss what Verida had revealed to him, every room was bugged and the conversations could be overheard clearly.

Dakota had decided to let her father say what he knew first.

Based on his conversation, she could tell he knew something was wrong, but she also knew he believed Verida took no part in the plot. As they sat and ate breakfast, he repeated the warning from Verida—verbatim.

No longer willing to keep him in the dark, Dakota disclosed what Elly and I had done to his home on more than one occasion. In great detail, she explained how Chauncey had the listening devices removed from her father's home and telephone lines, and also informed him their home had been subjected to the same thing.

Tears filled his eyes as the reality of how much he'd been deceived and taken advantage of by his niece and daughter-in-law pierced his heart! Dakota scooted close to him and wrapped her arms around him, as she assured him Chauncey had the situation under control.

Waking early because I expected Dakota's visit, I listened intently, hoping to hear anything they said above a whisper. Well aware Verida was the reason Chauncey discovered my first set of bugs, I was highly pissed off to learn she'd also betrayed me by giving my uncle a heads-up. However, I took great pleasure in knowing they were clueless I'd successfully bugged his home and phone lines again, and I chuckled when Dakota said Chauncey "had the situation under control."

Not long after Dakota left, Jimmy called Verida to discuss the warning she'd issued. Unable to stomach hearing him calmly explain how hurt and disappointed he was to learn she never mentioned this or anything else she knew until months after it happened, she broke down and cried. Unmoved by her tears, he gave her details of how Chauncey located the bugs and then removed them. He ended their conversation by informing her she'd broken any trust or confidence he had in her and their relationship would never be the same.

Begging for another chance and full of apologies, Verida pleaded with him to forgive her.

"Forgiving you is the easy part...I won't forget!" he said emphatically and hung up.

A month later, determined to get even with Verida for her disloyalty, I took my focus off Dakota and Chauncey long enough to mess with her. Pretending to be concerned about her relationship with my uncle, I contacted Verida to inform her he had started casually seeing a beautiful lightskinned woman in Indiana.

"Girl, what's goin' on? Uncle Jim was at a wedding with this new chick from Indiana. Why weren't you there?"

Verida gasped. "What? Who is she?"

Although I had met Karen before the wedding, I did not admit it. Instead, I took great joy in dishing the details of the woman's wealth, the Benz she drove and her beautiful long hair, which was not a weave.

Verida asked if he had known her long and if the relationship was serious. Baiting her, I offered to call and converse with my uncle (with Verida listening in) to get the answers. Not thinking and feeling very threatened by Karen's presence, gullible Verida agreed to a three-way call, remaining silent while I spoke.

"Hi, Uncle Jim, it's Rochelle...just calling to see how you're feelin.'" Untrusting of me and not wanting to hear from me, he was cool and aloof. Utilizing the wedding we'd just attended as the reason for my call, I mentioned Karen and how much I liked her. Striking a common chord, Jimmy admitted he liked her as well. In that same breath, I brought up Verida to make him angry. As he vented about his disgust and disappointment with her, Verida sniffed as tears began to fall.

"What's that noise...who's cryin'?" he asked. I did not say a word, waiting for the bomb to explode.

"It's me, Jimmy...Verida."

"What? What's goin' on?" he growled.

Disconnecting Verida from the call, I lied and said Verida asked me to call him on three-way so she could find out if he cared about Karen more than her. For Uncle Jim, that was the final act of deception. Vowing to never speak to Verida again, he hung up angry with her and me.

Unaffected and uncaring about how he felt, I gloated. I'd cut Verida's cord—her connection to Jimmy, and that feeling was indescribable.

CHAPTER 44

Adjusting to a structured lifestyle that did not include being beaten constantly was difficult for Kenny. Because the transition was not smooth, Dakota put her plans to launch a new clothing and accessory line on hold, a difficult decision, but one she had to make. Knowing how much she'd dreamed of owning her own label, Chauncey tried to convince her not to wait to display her talents; feeling a little guilty because she was doing this for his son.

"Listen, baby, I know you really want this...he'll be okay. I don't want to see you give up your dream."

"Bay, he needs me. The only way he'll come out of his shell is if he is given time to adjust to being loved and not beaten. Have you noticed how he flinches when I reach to hug him? And he freezes when I touch him. I can feel his body shaking...he's frightened to be a child."

Tears welled up in Chauncey's eyes as the reality of the nightmare his son had obviously survived hit home.

"Man, I had no clue he was being treated this way." Feeling responsible for not being more involved in Kenny's life, Chauncey dropped his head in sorrow and contemplated the information he now knew about the young child's abuse at the hands of his mother.

"Chauncey…" Aware he was unable to respond, Dakota got up and knelt beside him rubbing his shoulder as he wiped each tear that fell.

"When we know better we do better," she whispered. That truth made him lift his head and smile. She was right. Now that he knew better he was making sure things were better for his son.

"You're a great mom, baby!"

Dakota smiled in agreement.

After bathing Kenny, she rubbed cocoa butter on the cigarette-burn marks that covered his abdomen in such close proximity to each other you could play Chinese Checkers. Not use to such pampering, he blushed and dropped his head, holding his lips tight to avoid smiling.

Dakota slathered baby lotion on the rest of his body and helped him get into pajamas, which were long enough for his height, but way too big for his skinny frame. Pencil thin when he arrived, Dakota had to assure him he could eat slowly, without worrying about his food being taken from him as punishment for dropping a part of it on the floor. When that sunk in as truth, he slowed down and enjoyed his food, but the weight he needed to gain would take a while to show.

Pajamas were foreign to him, as was a robe and house slippers. Teaching him to wipe his face with a napkin and not the back of his hand was a daunting task, but not nearly as difficult as teaching him to wipe his behind. Four years old, Kenny did not know, nor could he retain the importance of, wiping his butt or the technique. For months, Dakota dealt with long dark skid marks in his underwear, or crusted feces under his fingernails from missing the wipe with the tissue.

Afraid of women, he did not enjoy being in Dakota's company and preferred to be with his brother twenty-four-seven. Lacking any social skills and the ability to articulate his thoughts, Dakota often had to prod him to figure out what he wanted and needed, including meals. If he was in pain, she'd have to watch his gestures or facial expressions to know. Afraid of being beaten for bothering her, he would not say a word.

Turning five, six months after Dakota became his mom meant starting school. The day of registration she learned he would not be allowed to attend school due to his innoculations being incomplete. None of his required shots had been administered since he was an infant. Those he needed had a waiting period of six months before the others could be given. Therefore, he had to be home schooled.

Dakota took the next eight months and taught him to speak clearly, improved his vocabulary and taught him basic things like colors, ABC's and counting to ten. Enrolling him in a day care for half the day helped to improve his social skills and boosted his self-esteem. Miraculously, he improved tremendously, engaging in conversations that were understandable and made sense.

Starting school would be the next hurdle they'd have to cross. Although it had not been confirmed through testing, Dakota was certain Kenny had learning challenges and needed to be in special education. Frustrated he was forced to bypass kindergarten because of his age, she became determined to make sure he would get the help he needed. Pressing to get him into a special education curriculum was unfruitful. The school system rules did not allow for testing of a child until they failed one grade level.

"I can't let that happen to him," Dakota exclaimed to the principal. "He's already academically behind. Failing will only kill the little self-esteem I worked a year to instill in him. Please help me!" she begged.

Persistence won the principal over. Pleased to see a parent

(especially a stepparent) care so much about a child's education, she agreed to break the rules and have Kenny tested immediately. It took two months to get his results and they were disheartening.

His comprehension, cognitive skills, and motor skills were very behind, barely functioning on a three-year-old's level. As alarming as this information was, Dakota refused to let it stop her belief that he could and would achieve greatness.

Suddenly, sacrificing her dreams to see him achieve his was no longer painful—she welcomed the challenge spending her days helping him improve. Nevertheless she yearned to be a fashion designer. During her downtime (after nine p.m. and the boys' bedtime), Dakota pulled out her sketchpad and drew whatever came to her spirit. If Chauncey was arriving late, she secretly utilized the time to plan the launch of her apparel and accessory line. Never wanting to neglect her children whom she'd become very attached to, she chose to not divulge her plan to Chauncey, afraid he would do what he always does, "make it happen."

"In God's time." She sighed as she stared at the fabulous earrings she'd just sketched.

Well after midnight, the phone rang. Assuming it was Chauncey calling to say he was en route, she answered. The female voice accused her of "stealing her babies" and her man. Flabbergasted, it took a minute before Dakota reacted.

"Listen, I don't know who you are, but don't get it twisted. I can't steal what's not yours. Neither your man nor your babies were stolen. You gave them to me…now get a life and leave ours alone!" Slamming the phone down, she dialed Chauncey, hanging up when she heard him walking up the stairs.

"Baby, you won't believe what just happened." Not surprised to hear the boy's crazy a' mom had called, he listened and reassured her she had handled it properly. Making a mental note to change the number, he immediately focused his thoughts on figuring out how she got it: Didn't take long for him to conclude it was me feeling well enough to be back to my old tricks!

Disappointed, he stared at the bathroom walls in deep thought as he sat on the commode. The money he'd paid to have someone "visit" me at home as I exited my car had not paid off. Afraid for my life, I blabbed what I'd done to a female I had been involved with and swore I would leave her alone. Although it made Chauncey and his boys laugh, he now realized I had no clue the person I was warned to leave alone was him (and his fiancée).

Very content with her life and being a mom, Dakota began to think about her wedding plans. Picking her favorite time of the year to walk down the aisle, late spring, she decided to formally inform her fiancé. With her clothing line on hold, she utilized her time and energy designing her wedding dress and her bridesmaid dresses. Pleased with the contemporary styles she'd drawn, her next free day would be spent looking for the fabric she envisioned.

A month later, fabric swatches in hand, she approached her soon-to-be husband with her sketches, wedding plans, and the date. Patiently Chauncey listened to her "sales pitch" and loved everything she presented—the colors, the dress and tuxedo styles, the décor and even the late-spring date.

However, when she requested he accompany her on the numerous meetings she'd need to attend to "make it happen," he quickly declined her invite, admitting this was one she could "make happen" without him!

Laughing, they lightheartedly chatted about the wedding, the flower girls, and ring bearers. Hoping his only daughter would be included in the wedding, he dropped a subtle hint, but left it alone when Dakota did not bite.

On paper her wedding dress was "to die for." Bringing that vision to life would be costly and time consuming, so Dakota decided to put the date on hold until she was certain she would be able to have her dress completed. The delay did not sit well with Chauncey, a man who had a bomb ticking and set to go off at any time.

A second marriage did not warrant a white gown *and* Dakota was never one to go with the norm, so she chose pewter. Strapless, form fitting, and made of the finest silk organza, Dakota took her time creating her dress, paying very close attention to every detail. It took her two months to intertwine 28,000 Austrian crystal rhinestones into the intricate lacework she'd used to embellish the bodice and the hemline.

With only the veil and headpiece to complete, she set the date. August would give her six months to make her fairy tale wedding come true. Soliciting the help of Jeaune, her former sister-in-law (Jeff's first wife), she secured the Rock Financial Center, Novi's premier banquet facility and began to orchestrate the wedding of her dreams.

White linen tablecloths and very sheer pewter organza over-lays were ordered. Pewter sashes were ordered to accent the white chair covers. Dakota handcrafted rhinestone ribbon and organza tassels to hang from the bow that would meet in the center of the back of the chairs.

Fresh-cut lilac hydrangea floral centerpieces would create a spectacular display, as they stood tall in twenty-four-inch Eiffel Tower vases. White china, set in silver chargers with napkins rolled and cuffed with rhinestone napkin rings, would complete her tables.

Gloved waiters would serve the guests, who would help themselves to Cristal that freely flowed from two champagne fountains located in opposite corners of the room. All the other details that needed to be addressed to ensure her day was unforgettable were turned over to Jeaune so she could focus on a location for her honeymoon.

Chauncey's mom was selected as first choice to baby-sit Kelsey and Kenny while they were gone, but the boys—afraid of her—begged to stay with Dakota's dad instead.

"Plee-eez, Ma!"

Fully aware they would rather eat spinach (something they hated) than go stay with her overbearing, much-too-strict mother-in-law, Dakota played dumb, forcing them to verbalize what they thought was a secret.

"Why don't you want to go stay with your grandmother?"

Reluctant to respond, they looked at each other and smirked. Kelsey spoke up, admitting she frightened him because she yelled all the time. However, when Kenny admitted she hit them a lot, that was all Dakota needed to hear to decide a week with her would be a week in hell for her children.

Later that evening, she discussed what Kenny had revealed with Chauncey and was not the least bit surprised when he defended her.

"Spare the rod, spoil the child," he said casually.

"You know I am not against disciplining them, but remember Kenny came from a home of yelling and beatings. Do you think it's in his best interest to subject him to that again?"

Putting it that way got his attention. Chauncey immediately reconsidered his plans to fly the boys south and agreed to allow them to stay with his father-in-law. Neither he nor Dakota were thrilled about leaving them with Jimmy because of his age and health, but he welcomed the idea, so they agreed.

Thirty-eight-thousand dollars spent and one month to go, Chauncey exhaled as he went over the receipts his future wife handed him.

"All this money for a couple hours of eating, drinking, and dancing," he grumbled as she walked away.

"I heard that!" Dakota teased as she turned the corner to give him a nasty glare. Chuckling, Chauncey assured her he had no problem with the amount she'd spent and was glad he could make her day so special. Blowing him a kiss, she headed to the boys' room to make sure they were getting ready for bed.

Chauncey finished looking at the receipts and then turned his attention to the guest list. Pleased to see Rodney, Val, and I had been excluded; he leaned back in his easy chair and shut his eyes to rest for a while.

Once his fiancée became his wife, he'd find a way to tell her about the looming arrest warrants; with hopes she'd stay with him if he were sentenced to serve time behind bars. For the first time in his life he felt remorse for the things he'd foolishly done in his youth; not because he'd done them, but because when caught for doing them he fled instead of facing the consequences. Now, everything he'd prayed for was in his grasp and he stood to lose it all—thanks to me.

Hearing about the pending nuptials from Elly made me bitter and very angry. Realizing I was left off the guest list infuriated me. Fuming, I took time to meticulously write the method I would use to get back at Dakota. Pleased with what I read over and over, I folded it in half and placed it in the outer pocket of my designer bag.

Dressing, I pulled on wrinkled sweats and gym shoes, took off my fake diamond Rolex and all bling from around my wrists.

Wearing only diamond studs, I removed all makeup and pulled my hair back in a ponytail; taking a minute to check the mirror to make sure none of my weave tracks were showing.

Intentionally portraying every step as being laborious, I walked into the Romulus Police Department and handed my detailed account of how Chauncey "man-handled" me to the officer behind the desk. Instructing me to be seated, he gave me a form to complete while he took my handwritten complaint to the detective on duty.

Carefully reading my version of how Chauncey attacked me when I refused to date him—now that he was dating my cousin, the detective raised his eyes and stared at me. Returning his eyes to the document, he focused on the details that included how Chauncey shook me and tossed me around my home. Fleeing his rage, I ran to my Benz and accelerated; losing control, I crashed into a tree.

Noticeably absent from my story were the punches a man this enraged would have thrown *and* landed. The injuries I listed— fractured rib, bruised sternum, and bruised thigh definitely could be from being tossed around. However, the hairline fracture in my nasal septum and the black eye would match that of a punch, the detective surmised. Yet I never mentioned he punched me. Suspicious of my story, he called me into his office to question me.

"Ms. Jackson, why was Mr. Bentley in your home?"

"We dated a long time ago, and he wants me back," I explained. Not satisfied with that explanation, he continued to query me about other inconsistencies in my story. For example, why and how things became violent and why did I wait more than four months to file a complaint.

Expecting he might ask what took so long, I had an answer

prepared: I was home recovering from my injuries and once I felt better, I came in. Able to give great detail about his personal and professional status, and why things took a turn for the worse, my story came off believable. After an hour of questions and paperwork, the detective assured me he'd look into the incident and get back with me.

"Look into it! You can't arrest him?" I shrieked.

"Ma'am, let us do our job," he responded bluntly, agitated with my presence. A fifteen-year veteran who'd seen many men arrested behind a scorned woman's complaint, he was apprehensive about going after Chauncey.

Not happy with the immediate outcome of this trumped-up story, I left the station angrier than when I went in, vowing to stop Dakota's wedding one way or the other.

The phone blaring woke Chauncey from a light sleep. Agitated with the volume level on the ringer, he reached to turn it down as he answered. Stunned, he held his breath and listened as his sister Carolyn explained the condition his mother was in after suffering a massive heart attack. Although she had been revived, she was in the operating room undergoing emergency heart surgery to save her life.

Even though he was tired, Chauncey did not want to rest before rushing to his mother's side. Forgoing any further details, he hung up the phone and while packing a few things informed Dakota of the situation. Offering to go with him to help drive, Dakota followed him around their bedroom as he tossed things on the bed to pack. Thankful she was concerned, Chauncey promised he'd only be gone a few days and assured her he'd rest en route if he felt sleepy.

Hugging her tight, he held onto her trying to draw from her

strength. Death had never knocked at his door. Being so close
it now frightened him. Not a momma's boy, he never realize
until now how much he'd miss her if something did happen. Tear.
fell, but Chauncey never wept, remaining silent as he leaned down
and kissed his sons who were asleep. Holding Dakota's hand, he
walked back to their bedroom to retrieve his overnight bag.

Kissing her passionately, he promised to call when he had any
news. Standing with the front door wide open, Dakota watched
him back out the drive and waited for him to disappear into the
darkness before closing it. She whispered a prayer for him and
her mother-in-law and then went to bed.

Eighteen hours later, there was news. Chauncey called to inform
Dakota his mother survived the surgery, after dying on the
operating table twice. Lapsing into a coma, the doctors worked
feverishly to save her life. Triple bypass surgery was successfully
performed and they did expect her to wake from the coma and
recover fully. The doctors warned she'd have to quit smoking
immediately and they both agreed that would be no small feat.
A chain smoker, Mo went through two packs a day and never
considered quitting even though her doctor had previously
advised her to do so.

Realizing his mother would remain in the hospital for quite
some time, Chauncey returned to Michigan to take care of some
business dealings before returning to see about her. A phone call
from his sister informing him his mother would remain hospitalized another two weeks, eased the tension he was feeling. Stressed
from her near-death experience and driving more than twenty-
eight hours in less than a week, he needed a break to rest and
regroup.

A day after he'd returned to Birmingham to be with his mother

recuperated, a detective from the Romulus Police
nt stopped by his office, which was locked, and slipped
s card through the mail slot. Two days later, he stopped
ota's father's home after unsuccessfully locating anyone
house in Indian Village. Dakota was visiting her father
the detective arrived.

itely he asked her the whereabouts of her husband. Politely
asked him why he needed to know. The niceties continued
il he revealed the visit was related to a complaint by me.
red of the B.S., she invited him in so she could stop this drama
efore it got started.

Explaining her husband was out of town she asked to see the
complaint. Reading it, Dakota carefully rebutted everything I
wrote and then refuted my words, line for line. The "frosting on
the cake" moment came when she was able to prove he could not
have "man-handled" me on the date I claimed because he was
closing on a real estate venture out of state during the time noted
in the complaint.

Such a claim would be easy enough to verify, so the detective
apologized and left. Less than three hours later he had confirmation of the real estate transaction being completed with
Chauncey being present the entire time and at the exact time I
claimed the assault took place.

Arresting me for filing a false police report would be within
his legal jurisdiction, but the mounds of paperwork that went
along with that arrest was more than he cared to deal with.
Pretty sure Dakota and Chauncey would not want to pursue
this—they had enough to deal with—he decided to drop it, failing to inform me.

After two weeks of daily messages from me, the detective paid a timely visit to my home; the end result being a threat to arrest me if I did not stop calling. My calls ceased immediately, but not because of his threat. I stopped calling because Elly informed me the wedding had been postponed due to Chauncey's mother's illness.

Torn between two emotions—joy, because I would not have to eat crow when my cousin walked down the aisle; and sorrow, because I was not the reason the "I do's" were halted—I sat pensive, deciding what I wanted to do to the happy couple next!

CHAPTER 45

Severely stagnated by the warrant hanging over his head, Chauncey found maneuvering through life on a daily basis a constant struggle. Because he lived in fear that he might be pulled over by a cop, he continuously checked his rearview mirror, looked over his shoulder, drove the exact speed limit, and fully stopped at all traffic signals and stop signs.

"Rolling low" in a conservative Cadillac CTS, he stayed away from the luxury automobile he longed to drive—his namesake, a Bentley; ensuring he would less likely be stopped for DWB (driving while black). Lately, not enjoying the money he worked hard to earn was getting old.

Keeping his secret at bay would not be easy to do once they got married. Dakota's heart was set on a trip abroad for their honeymoon, perhaps Europe. Leaving the United States would require ID that would instantly reveal who he was to the authorities, resulting in his arrest.

Not willing to do the time and not willing to lose Dakota, he chose to resolve the issue by illegally obtaining a new social security number, dropping his middle name, and altering the spelling of his birth name. Even though the entire process took over two months to complete, Chauncey felt relieved; confident he could breathe a little easier.

Now that he had a new beginning, the only thing he worried about was being caught in one of the traps I continuously set for him. Daily he'd have to stay a step ahead of me to make sure he was never taken into custody or fingerprinted. Either would end his freedom.

Murder, though possible, was not probable. Chauncey often daydreamed about takin' me out—actually pulling the trigger himself. But, with his conscience getting the best of him, he could not bring himself to give the okay to Glenn, who got a "hard-on" every time he thought about wrapping his hands around my throat and slowly tightening the grip until my body became lifeless.

However, another year of this madness was not something Chauncey was willing to go through. Almost two years had passed, and in that time I had successfully made his life a living hell. With a new life just months away, he was beginning to get desperate for an end to it all.

Finally able to move about freely, Chauncey began to consider leaving Michigan for peace of mind. In search of a more refined lifestyle, he set his sights on Florida. Airline ticket in hand, he drove to the airport, parked in short-term parking and boarded his flight. Taking his first flight since assuming his new identity, "Chandlery Bentley," was exciting. Comfortably seated in first class, he easily relaxed on the two-hour flight to Orlando.

The realtor he'd contacted met him at the airport and after a light lunch, drove Chauncey to some of the most prestigious luxury living communities in Florida. Located on the shores of Lake Butler, one of nine lakes on the Butler Chain of Lakes, the gorgeous waterfront homes started at $1 million.

Slowly driving the winding streets the realtor pointed out the homes that belonged to a world-renowned golfer, two of the Orlando Magic players, and one that was the off-season residence of a former Los Angeles Lakers star. Although she withheld their names, Chauncey knew to whom she was referring. He had done his research and had intentionally chosen this area and Lake Butler.

Quietly Chauncey took in the lush landscaping, getting lost in his thoughts as he stared at the green golf courses and rich foliage of the nature preserves.

This is it...I would be happy golfing and Dakota would be happy walking the preserves. Fully aware his future wealthy neighbors valued their privacy, he was certain his would be maintained as well. Sold, he waited for the realtor to finish her spiel.

"Mister Bentley, the Butler Chain of Lakes was formed as a result of a typical Florida occurrence known as Karst topography. Limestone, which underlies most of Florida, was slowly dissolved by water to form sinkholes. A series of sinkholes that formed over time produced the sparkling, pristine Butler Chain of Lakes. Many areas within the lakes can be as deep as thirty to forty feet. The chain of lakes, Down, Wauseon Bay, Butler, Louise, Isleworth, Tibet-Butler, Chase, Blanche, Sheen, Pocket, and Fish, have been designated by the Department of Environmental Regulation of the State of Florida as 'Outstanding Florida Waters' due to their excellent water quality and wildlife habitat. Trust me, you and your family will love it here!"

"Sold" was all Chauncey said.

Smiling broadly, the realtor proceeded to find out which home he liked. Narrowing his choices to two, he asked for a couple days to return, bringing his "wife" and children back with him to help make the decision.

Agreeing to meet in three days, the realtor drove Chauncey

back past the two homes he'd selected and then to the airport to catch an earlier return flight. Landing in rush-hour traffic, he decided to stop by his future father-in-law's home to wait it out. Dakota pulled up shortly after he arrived.

"Hey, baby." Greeting her gingerly, he hugged her.

"Hey, yourself! How long you been here?" she asked, pulling away from his embrace and kissing him on his nose. Before he could answer, his two sons tackled him around his waist, both jockeying for his attention. Lifting them, he hoisted Kelsey on his back and held Kenny in his arms. Playfully, they kissed him, pulled his ears, and rubbed his hair.

Laughing heartily, pleased to see his daughter so happy, Jimmy sat down, pulled his white handkerchief out of his pocket and dabbed the moisture that had formed in the creases of his eyes. Offering everyone something to eat, he stood up and reached in his cabinet for plates. Hard of hearing, he was unaware Chauncey had declined his offer. Moving closer, Dakota informed her father they were not eating and then looked inquisitively at Chauncey, waiting on the reason why.

"We're going out to eat," he announced. Assuming that meant McDonald's, the boys began to cheer. Thankful she did not have to cook, Dakota joined them.

Golden Corral was a buffet-style restaurant Chauncey loved, second to Steve's Soul Food. Too hungry to wait in line at Steve's they went there. Settling into her seat, Dakota leaned over and verbally thanked him for the break from cooking and backed that up with a kiss. Embarrassed, the boys covered their eyes and Kelsey exclaimed, "Uu-hh!" Kenny laughed and pursed his lips against his spoon, mimicking his parents' affection.

Tickled, Dakota reached over and playfully poked his stomach.

Kenny burst into a giggle and wriggled in his chair. Lifting his napkin to play peek-a-boo with his mom, he quickly placed it back in his lap when Chauncey walked up with dessert. While the boys ate their vanilla and chocolate swirl ice cream with Oreo cookie sprinkles, Chauncey handed the realty papers to Dakota.

"Look at this, baby."

"Oh wow…these homes are fabulous!" Staring at the photos, she took her time reading the details of each one before she looked up.

"Baby, why did you hand me these brochures?" Chauncey smiled and winked, but reconsidered his normal routine of "cat and mouse." Instead, he explained his desire to leave Michigan *and* me and hoped either home would be enough to convince her to do the same.

Befuddled, she stared at him. Her thought immediately went to her elderly father and his well-being. Reading her mind, Chauncey offered the solution he had already considered.

"I know you don't want to leave your dad, so let's take him with us! There's more than enough room for him and we even have an elevator."

Enough said, standing up, she reached over and hugged him firmly, thankful to be leaving Detroit, cold weather and most of all, me.

CHAPTER 46

I t was Dante's birthday and he'd planned a major thirtieth
bash. Everything was in place with the exception of me. Late
as usual, this time it pissed him off because he'd asked me to
come a day or two earlier to keep this from happening: my coming in last minute, stealing the spotlight from him.

Eyeing me as I sashayed through the door two hours after the
festivities began, he angrily approached, taking inventory as he
did. *Umph! A new St. John…hate it!*

"Dante, happy birthday," I squealed, handing him his gift—a
diamond bracelet—and reaching to hug him.

"Save it!" he barked as he accepted the beautifully wrapped
box and held out a stiff arm to keep me at bay.

"What is your problem?" I asked, genuinely hurt by his actions.

"Try I needed you to be here two hours ago."

Shocked by his behavior, I tried to explain my flight was late.
That did little to soothe his hurt feelings. Too busy to come
when he asked me (because I was f'in with Dakota and Chauncey),
he felt slighted, and my late arrival only added insult to the injury.
Sulking, he left me standing at the door stunned as he sauntered
off and continued to mingle with his guests.

Distraught over his life's recent turn of events, unemployment due to an increasing cocaine addiction, Dante had depended on his friends with means to contribute to his birthday party fund. Moet did, his closest friend *who said she would* (me) did not.

"This is when you find out who your true friends are," he grumbled as he placed his nostril to the mirror and inhaled deeply in an attempt to "vacuum" the remnants of cocaine sprinkled on its surface.

Lately I'd been completely unavailable for him. Although I was not intentionally avoiding him, Dante took it that way; believing I was in love with Benjamin, as in Franklin, and no longer had use for him now that I had plenty of them to keep me company. Distance between us had negatively affected our friendship. Jealousy did not allow him to be happy for my increasing income and popularity when his was on the decline.

An idle mind that is enhanced by the effects of cocaine is a combination that can be lethal. Pondering how to stay afloat, now that money was scarce, Dante found my abundance quite appealing. Certain he could piggyback off my funds to keep his drug lifestyle afloat, he became very indignant when I said no. Wanting what he could not have, he did not care to partake in my lavish spending sprees that routinely benefited him.

In the past, our short trips to Canada to purchase a new fur, or Los Angeles to purchase a St. John from the St. John outlet, were exciting. However, unlike times past, he now showed very little excitement about my desire to splurge and routinely declined traveling with me, even though I seldom walked away without making sure he, too, had something new.

No longer an "A Lister," he felt I snubbed him as most of his circle had. The affluent friends he generally hobnobbed with had begun to treat him with indifference; casting him off to fend for himself. Loose lips do sink ships. Dante's loose lips had cost a well-known socialite her good standing in the community. What goes on in the bedroom stays in the bedroom was a creed Dante's circle lived by. Thanks to his inability to remember this unspoken rule while on one of his drug-induced binges, the happy couple's business made the gossip section of the local paper. He was immediately ostracized.

No one to blame but himself and in denial, the drugs kept him from accepting responsibility for his actions, so he blamed everyone else. I was moved to the top of his "F you" list when he asked to borrow some money to catch up on his bills and I made excuses for not having it. Seeing me wearing yet another new St. John, purchased with the money I should have donated to the cause, infuriated him.

For months, I suppressed my gut feeling that he could be jealous. The fact that he was a man helped to lay that concern to rest. But, every now and then that same thought would surface and the inner battle would begin again. Like now!

The entire evening was a bust. Walking on eggshells to avoid Dante's wrath was miserable. Staying long enough to watch him blow out his candles, I quietly exited the venue and returned to my hotel. Rising early the next morning, I called the airline to change my flight from Tuesday to an immediate departure. Nothing was available until Monday; this being Sunday I was stuck for another day. Disappointed, I hung up the phone and lay down to think things over.

A knock at the door startled me; only Dante knew I was there and I had not yet ordered room service. Peering though the peephole, it was difficult to make out the figure that stood too close to the door.

"Who is it?" I asked cautiously.

"B,' open the door. It's me, Dante!"

Glad to hear his voice, I quickly swung open the door. Flashing the bling I'd given him he hugged me as he walked in with two gorgeous women, one white and one Latina, and a very handsome black man, following behind.

Preferring white men because "brothas were usually hung like a horse," an explanation Dante added when explaining his sexual gravitation toward "anything not black," I did a double-take. I was shocked he was in the presence of another black man that was equally as attractive as he.

Dante liked his men fine, but not so fine they competed with him. Making no qualms about his racial preference, Dante often sang his homemade jingle, "When you go black, you throw them back."

The very sexy Latina woman, I recognized from the last yacht party. In passing, I'd often referred to her as "Latino Heat" because her body was so hot! Surprised to see her, I stiffened when she reached for a hug, but loosened up when the embrace lingered. The other guest, a very tall and buxom blonde, said hello while looking around the room for something she could use to lay out a couple lines of coke. Dante motioned to the handsome black man, who said nothing, to have a seat.

Uncomfortable being around drugs, I asked the blonde not to use them in my room. Undeterred, she ignored me and tooted a line, then offered the straw to Dante. The next line quickly vanished up his nose and he passed the tray to the "Latino Heat."

Shocked to see Dante partake because he'd never done drugs in my presence, but curious about how it felt, I stood in a corner and watched. Assuring me I would enjoy it, Dante encouraged me to try some. Reluctantly I snorted a little and instantly liked the feeling. An aphrodisiac, I wanted more. As the tray made it back around, I snorted the entire line and then reclined back on the bed, enjoying the high.

"Latino Heat" joined me on the bed, lying supine and staring at the ceiling. Shortly after that, the blonde joined us, lying prone and very close to my face. Rolling on her side, the blonde gently kissed me and enjoying the kiss, I reciprocated.

While the two of us swapped spit, "Latino Heat" began to caress my body, starting between my legs. High and very sensitive to her touch, I spread my legs and arched my back, encouraging her to continue. Wasting no time, the exotic dancer pulled down my pajama bottoms and began to lick me softly, while she slowly penetrated me with her finger. Very wet, I began to pant as the blonde continued to kiss me and pinch my nipples through my pajama top.

Ready to explode, they both eased up, denying me the pleasure; I wasn't quite high enough. While I lay on the bed in a euphoric state, they disrobed me. Dante brought the tray to me and encouraged me to do another line. When I did, the ménage à trois continued.

The gorgeous black man rose and pulled out a handheld video camera and began to film the sexual encounter. Unable to think clearly and oblivious to the fact I was being filmed, I went wild. Virgin that I was, I had never had my face or tongue in a woman's crotch, preferring to be the receiver instead of the giver. However, I rolled over and got busy reciprocating both women.

Using toys, the three of us engaged in buck wild sex for two hours. Too high to climax I rolled over and allowed "Latino Heat" to orally take me over the edge, falling asleep after she did.

Hours later when I awoke woozy, there was no evidence anyone had been there. I was alone, lying on top of the covers, butt naked. My vagina, butt, and nipples hurt, and I was extremely thirsty. As I lay there and focused, replaying the events of the morning, I became frightened. Not only had I participated in some wild sexual exploits, I'd done so unprotected.

All kinds of *what-ifs* came to mind. Not ready to deal with them, I suppressed them and dialed Dante's home number. No answer, I tried his cell. Still no answer, I left him an urgent voicemail. If anyone knew the girls' "medical history" it would be him—I hoped!

CHAPTER 47

Bella Vista's elegant home sites stretched along the fairways of several spectacular golf courses. Buffered by lush fairways with panoramic golf, lake, and preserve views, the "members only" atmosphere did not disappoint Dakota.

Swept away by the aura, Dakota strolled the grounds of the luxury-gated community she and Chauncey now called home. Earlier in the day she'd enjoyed leisurely play along Lake Butler and the preserves with Kelsey and Kenny. Before lunch, she took them to play in the glass-enclosed lagoon-style garden and pool at the clubhouse.

Leaving her boys home with their dad, Dakota took time to appreciate the lush landscaping and well-manicured lawns, while paying close attention to the detail of the distinctive homes with their graceful archways and intricate ironwork; rich Mediterranean architecture that met with Spanish-tile roofs.

Afraid of the critters that scattered about, especially the geckos, Dakota stumbled on the cobblestone walkway as one darted in front of her. Flustered she stopped momentarily to regroup and then spotted a beautiful fountain in the distance. Watching its streams of water shoot in a burst of patterns, then separate, and fall back to the base was hypnotic. A couple seconds passed as the patterns of water held her attention. Slowly she continued on the walkway leading to the Tuscan-inspired clubhouse, stopping in front of the day spa to read its hours of operation.

Time on her side, and in need of some pampering, she walked in. The breathtaking fountains offered a cool elegance to the spa's tasteful touches of Honduran mahogany finishes. While she completed her customer profile and sipped on the glass of wine she was served from the enclosed wine cellar, Dakota called Chauncey to let him know she'd be late.

"Baby, I'm at the spa."

Hearing the excitement in her voice, Chauncey smiled, happy she was so pleased with their relocation. Leaving her father behind was difficult, but his promise to visit every two months made her decision easier. Hopefully now they'd live in peace; a peace that could not be interrupted by my meddling and crazed jealousy.

Wasting no time, Chauncey set up an office on the first level of their home and immediately plunged into the South Florida real estate market. Condominium conversions were the latest trend and with the escalating real estate prices, those with means were making out like fat rats. Chauncey intended to be one of those fat rats!

His plan was to invest with a Cuban or Colombian who had a venture capitalist mentality; capturing as many of the condo conversions as possible, before the concept caught on and the prices rose.

Money, lots of it safely tucked away in his "Fort Knox" replica safe, Chauncey felt comfortable enough with his new identity to aggressively put his real estate acquisition plan into action. All he needed to do now was locate a partner. With Dakota planning to be gone for a couple more hours, he had plenty of time to research his options, calling Glenn for his advice and an update on me.

"Keeping an eye on her is like watching a Dr. Jekyll and Mr. Hyde movie," Glenn confided. Certain I needed to be strapped away in a white jacket at a loony bin, he assured Chauncey he'd continue to keep close tabs on his father-in-law and me. Pleased to hear things were going so well for the Bentleys, Glenn promised to squeeze in a weekend of fun, sun and golf when winter hit Michigan.

Getting down to the reason for his phone call, Chauncey explained his real estate concept. Glenn agreed to forward, by e-mail, contact information for the individuals who could best assist him in launching his venture capitalist plan. Tied to a tight-knit group of wealthy Colombians (some rumored to be "connected"), Glenn was certain his cousin would be on top and basking in unbelievable wealth in no time. Equally certain he would win Glenn's connects over, Chauncey agreed that in no time flat, he'd be a force to be reckoned with, and not just in South Florida.

Logging off the computer after printing the information Glenn sent, Chauncey sat at his desk to decipher the encrypted information. It took some doing, but he successfully matched the names with the addresses and phone numbers, and then glanced at the clock. Realizing it would be disrespectful to call at such a late hour, Chauncey tucked the papers in his desk drawer and locked it. Waiting for his "wife" to return, he lit some candles and turned on the Jacuzzi.

Not quite ready to turn the care of her tresses over to a stranger, a white one at that, Dakota passed on getting her hair done. However, after a tour of the salon, she did agree to try the rest of the "salon experience," which included a facial, manicure, and pedicure. Time permitting she would indulge in the spa services, which included a Swedish massage and aromatic body wrap.

Relaxed and feeling amorous, she returned home and joined Chauncey in the Jacuzzi. Sipping on another glass of wine, she allowed him to explore her body in ways they'd long forgotten, thanks to the tension of having me lurking nearby, and now *two* "youngins!" Wet inside and out, Dakota stepped out the tub and with one finger, beckoned him to follow her.

Lying on the bed, spread eagle, she waited for him to join her. They made passionate love most of the night. Before falling off to sleep, she rolled over and kissed him affectionately; thanking him for restoring the life of opulence she so dearly missed.

Keeping his promise, Jimmy came to visit. Dakota's dad could not believe the lifestyle his daughter was living—not that it was new to him. He'd visited her in the past when she lived equally as well with Kevin. But, this was different: she was happy and her life was fulfilled. Everything he dreamed of for his little girl and his grandsons was a reality. Chauncey had done well in making Dakota's dreams come true. Jimmy thanked God for allowing him to live to see his daughter happy once more!

Two weeks of sweltering heat and mosquitoes was enough for Jimmy. As much as he enjoyed the time spent with his loved ones, he was ready to go back to cooler temperatures in Michigan.

Returning from his first visit to Florida, Jimmy could not wait to tell Karen and his son Jeff, how well Dakota and Chauncey were living. Calling Jeff first, he boasted about how his sister was living a life of affluence. Saving Karen for last, he went into great detail about their home, the clubhouse, day spa, equestrian trails, and the fact that they had a maid. I nearly keeled over backward as I listened to his play-by-play account of how well my cousin was doing.

To my dismay, Kevin had not been in touch since my visit to Atlanta for Dante's birthday party, and had completely stopped making deposits into my account. Thankful I had tucked away a large portion of his funds for a rainy day, I did not hesitate to pay the increased asking price of $4,500 to place another listening device on my uncle's phone line. A newer and more difficult bug to locate, I decided my money was well spent as I listened intently to his telephone conversations. Taking notes, I hoped he'd reveal the address or name of the community where the Bentleys were now residing. Even though I was not certain I would be able to wreak havoc on them long distance, I was certainly going to try.

My stomach was in knots as I looked at my notes. *Gated community, 9,000 square feet, six bedrooms, a pool, and clubhouse...*the list was extensive and wealth leaped off the pages. Sickened by Dakota's obvious return to her pedestal, I began to fret. The last thing I wanted to witness was her regaining her status and returning to Michigan as the "reigning prima donna."

"Ain't gonna happen...not on my watch," I grumbled. Of that, I was certain!

The first neighbor to send a welcome basket to the Bentleys was the Chavez family, a handsome Colombian couple with a gorgeous son, daughter, and misbehaved miniature Schnauzer.

Very down to earth, they owned a chain of pizzerias in Miami and Fort Lauderdale, and had practically their entire family from Colombia working in each of their restaurants.

Outgoing Dakota walked over to their front door, rang the bell and introduced herself, thanking them for the basket before leaving. Pleased they were so nice, she returned home and called Chauncey, anxious to tell him about meeting the friendly neighbors. Immediately he felt the hairs on his back rise, wishing Dakota would be more cautious about their privacy.

"You invite them over?" he asked, pretending to be interested in the conversation.

"No, but Barbara…oh yeah, she told me to call her 'Barb'! Barb would like to go walking with me when I get out in the mornings, so right away I got a walking buddy."

Just great, he thought. "Well, that's great, baby, but you know what we just went through with that nut, so don't be too quick to open our doors," he cautioned her hoping she'd listen, but doubting she would.

"Not to worry, baby, what goes on in the house, stays in the house…I learned my lesson!" she squealed. They chatted a little more about nothing of importance and agreed to meet each other in the Jacuzzi later that night.

Barb was very instrumental in helping Dakota settle in. She gave her the times and days for trash pickup, and although a public school advocate, she suggested a couple private schools her children could attend.

"My kids attend Sun Lakes Elementary. It's an A-plus public school, with an excellent reputation. Teachers from all over the United States vie for positions at this school."

"Your kids attend public school?" Dakota asked, failing to hide her surprise.

Thinking Dakota might be more privileged than she imagined, Barbara immediately began to explain why, feeling a need to apologize for not being bourgeoisie enough.

"No, wait…you're misunderstanding my question. My children have always been in public schools. I just assumed the children who lived behind these gates all attended private schools. I'm pleased that's not the case!"

Happy she'd summed her new friend up correctly, Barb offered to drive her to the school the next day so she could complete an early enrollment and avoid the rush when school started.

"Speaking of kids, where are yours?" Dakota asked. Barb explained they were in Colombia with their grandmother and would be home in another week. While they continued to chat, Kenny and Kelsey ran from the backyard and accidentally sprayed Barbara with water from their water blasters.

Startled, she jumped and then burst into laughter. Dakota joined in and they parted company after she introduced the boys. Retreating indoors, Dakota cranked up the A/C to cool the upstairs portion of their home, which had increased in temperature now that the sun was bearing down on the roof. Drained from standing in the sun for over twenty minutes, she guzzled a bottle of water and then fixed the boys lunch.

Four hours away in Tampa, Chauncey called her to let her know he'd be home late, intentionally failing to tell her his whereabouts. With her outgoing personality and chatty disposition, he decided the less she knew the better off they all would be.

Meeting with Sanchez and his partners was thrilling. The fifty-foot yacht chosen for their private meeting was impressive. He, the yacht, and the women surrounding him motivated Chauncey. Not new to the planted distractions during these business encounters and totally committed to his "wife," Chauncey remained focused.

When the conversation turned to real estate investing, Chauncey asked Sanchez to dismiss the women and he obliged, calling Chauncey a very smart man and then complimenting him for not falling into the trap he'd set for him.

Passing the test, Sanchez let down his guard, now comfortable with Chauncey's character. Over the next several hours they hashed out an agreement that would make them partners and very wealthy men, if all went as planned.

Driving home in the dark gave Chauncey a relaxed feeling. In the past, he'd avoided long drives at night, fearful of being pulled over by the cops. No longer feeling threatened, he enjoyed the ride, so much so, that he made the decision to shed his low-key image by upgrading his driving status to his dream car, the Bentley.

"Life is good," he whispered and called Dakota to let her know he'd be home in an hour. He'd share his decision to roll large with her when he got there.

To his surprise, Dakota did not respond as he'd thought. Always practical, she found money spent on automobiles in excess of $80,000, the cost of the average Benz, excessive. When he first mentioned owning a Bentley, it was at the Detroit Auto Show. Familiar with them, she teased and suggested he get her a Maybach, as well. However, this time she was not joking when she asked for one.

"You serious, baby?" Chauncey asked, stunned. Not that he could not afford it or would not get it for her; he was simply shocked she wanted one.

"As a heart attack!" she exclaimed. Looking him in the eyes, she waited for a response.

"Okay, baby, why don't we go car shopping this weekend?" Embracing, they kissed and retreated to their bedroom to seal the deal.

CHAPTER 48

Diversity was a thought process Chauncey learned at an early age from the street hustlers he hung with. None of them risked everything on one endeavor because you never knew when the cops would move in and shut it down. One business, say a numbers racket, might go by the wayside, but their other street hustles, bootlegged items, etc. would go untouched.

Contacting Sonya Lee's husband, Stefan, shortly after moving to Florida to find out how his $100,000 down payment was progressing was informative. During his conversation he learned Stefan and Sonya Lee had separated and the real estate venture was on schedule. When questioned about his marital status, Chauncey lied and told him they were married and living in Michigan. His personal life was in a "need to know" category and that information was something Stefan did not need to know!

With lucrative investments on both coasts, Chauncey felt powerful and invincible. Only one thing kept him on his knees and that was his need to make his life with Dakota permanent. Routinely he went before God to ask for a breakthrough in his marital situation. Pretty sure God would want their living arrangement to be updated from shackin', he patiently waited for the change yet to come.

Not to be deterred from what he wanted most in life, her hand in marriage, Chauncey approached Dakota once more and asked her to set a wedding date. This time she did, but to his chagrin, it was a year away. It made him feel insecure and unwanted, a feeling he did not like.

Revisiting his childhood demons, he fell into a deep depression that lingered for weeks. Withdrawn and unsociable, he stayed away from home, Dakota and his kids, forcing his fiancée to suspect he was cheating. The more she quizzed him about "what was wrong?" the more he withdrew.

Needing some time alone, he lied and said he had to leave town to handle some business. While he was away, Dakota broke her own rule and went through Chauncey's things. Finding no signs of infidelity, she decided to rummage through his office, shocked to find his desk drawers locked. At first it made her more suspicious, but as the day wore on, she shook the feeling and decided to leave well enough alone. Time had always been on her side and if he *was* cheating, time would tell.

Retreating to Sanchez's boat to escape being around his fiancée, Chauncey spent several days and nights there, with an invite to take advantage of whatever he wanted: women included.

The third night of partying, Chauncey entertained sleeping with the buxom brunette on board. Watching her and another female do each other made him hard, but he stood strong. That night when she and her friend climbed into his bed with lines of coke laid out on a tray, he made the decision to go home. Temptation, especially a woman who's high and willing to let you explore any and all orifices, was more than he could handle.

Dakota meant more to him than that, and even though he was currently unhappy being around her, he missed her. On the way home, he decided to be up front and tell her how he felt. Perceptive and very much in tune to her man, Dakota beat him to the punch. When he entered their home just as the sun came up, she greeted him with a kiss and a New Year's Eve wedding date. Only six months away, she explained she still wanted to get married in Michigan, and coordinating that in such a short amount of time would be difficult. Chauncey didn't care. All he wanted was to know she would be in his life for eternity. Saying "I do" would make it so.

Not on my watch! I repeated over and over after learning the B' had once again set a wedding date and was getting married, *in Michigan*, in less than six months. Needing to vent I called Dante and angrily slammed the phone down, after dialing his number a gazillion times with no answer. Limited funds and the Bentleys being thousands of miles away made disrupting their lives impossible, but I would not allow this wedding to take place.

Glenn, now aware the Bentleys were coming home to make it legal, decided to up the ante by tapping my home phone and cell phone. There was no question in his mind I would just as soon see my cousin dead than see her happy. "Not on my watch!" he professed.

Dakota spent weekends in Michigan at her father's home completing her wedding plans. Her niece Seanny, excellent with calligraphy, offered to do the addresses for the invitations. With her help and a few other solicited friends, Dakota got the invites mailed a week ahead of schedule.

Panic set in when I stopped by Elly's to look at the beautiful invite. It *was* really happening *on my watch*, and I was seething. Not wanting to talk about this charade any longer, I abruptly got up, grabbed my purse, and stormed out of Elly's home.

"I'll call you later," I murmured as I slammed the door behind me. Very concerned about my state of mind, Elly called Val and told her what happened.

"You know…that girl needs help!" Val exclaimed. Elly started to laugh, but when Val did not, she realized her statement was serious.

"What do you mean?" Elly asked scared for the first time, remembering the part she played in messing with Dakota and Chauncey. Val went on to explain she used her key to my condo and entered in my absence. While snooping she found proof of bizarre things I had been doing and a note that gave a detailed account of a scheme that included Kevin.

"You and I know that man has been gone for a long time. No way could Rochelle be in touch with him. No one knows where he is! I think she's lost her mind," Val said matter-of-factly. Concerned about the bank slips she'd found in my desk drawer, she asked Elly if she knew where I could get such large amounts of money. Clueless, Elly tried hard to help figure out what I could be doing. Neither could, but both agreed for my sake they would keep trying.

"Got her!" Glenn shouted, as he pulled out of the drive and bolted down the street and into traffic. Pulling off into a gas station, he parked the car away from traffic and carefully sorted through the stack of mail he'd taken from my mailbox. His search ended when he located an envelope with a bank logo on it. Tearing it open, his eyes focused on the large sums of money that had been randomly deposited into my account. Certain this would confirm his suspicion that someone was "sponsoring" my vendetta against Dakota and Chauncey; he set it aside and continued to separate the mail.

Glenn had been monitoring my mail for some time hoping to

find something he could use to force me to leave his cousin and future bride alone. His persistence paid off. Lifting an overnight envelope from the pile of mail, he read the shipping information and then carefully tore it open, emptying the contents on the passenger seat.

Admiring the beautiful penmanship, he smiled, certain it was from a female.

Listen, heifer! Stay away from my man. That's right, Kevin and I are an item and I don't need you making our lives miserable. No more money, so bye-bye fur coats and St. Johns. Now, in case you might be thinking about goin' public with this news…you might want to watch the tape.

Dante

"Dante! Get outta here…no way…!" Bursting into hysterical laughter, Glenn read the note over and over again before picking up the DVD case. It was not labeled, but he was certain whatever the content, it was the ammunition he was looking for to make me "disappear."

"Booyow!" Glenn screamed and started up the car. Heading straight to the airport, he hopped a flight to Florida to watch what was on the DVD with Chauncey.

Reading about the much-publicized wedding in the society page of the *Detroit News* and the *Free Press*, the *Inkster Ledger Star*, and the *Westland Observer and Eccentric* made me nauseated.

"You'd think this cow was Princess Di the way people are talking about her and that wedding!" Sighing heavily, I dialed Val.

"Ma, you see the write-up they did on Dakota's wedding? Can you believe it?"

"Rochelle, I told you before, leave that girl alone. Why do you care what she does?"

Here we go again..."Bye, Val, talk to you later." I snorted and hung up.

Upset my mother was no longer on my side, I began to withdraw from talking to anyone but the voices in my head, who by the way, routinely told me I was doing nothing wrong.

CHAPTER 49

Determined to never let the New Year see the Bentleys married, I set my mind on proving Chauncey was a phony, a liar and into some kind of illegal activity. Going back over all the paperwork I'd kept on his previous banking and business transactions, I searched for something to prove me right. Nothing there, I went back over the real estate paperwork Elly's niece had gotten for me. As luck would have it, I found what I was looking for. There were discrepancies in his name and social security number.

Meanwhile in Florida at the Bentleys home, Chauncey and Glenn stared at the video player in disbelief as they watched me fulfill the ravenous appetite I had for the two women I was getting busy with. When it ended, he and Glenn sat silent staring at each other.

Right about me being a lesbian, Glenn was pleased his "gaydar" was still intact. It had not been tested since being released from prison after serving time for nearly beating a transvestite to death.

Their foreplay had progressed from kissing to caressing and probing, but when Glenn got close to his genitalia the man stopped him, got on his knees and performed oral sex in such a skilled manner, Glenn came in seconds. Not stopping, the transvestite sucked him dry and kept on sucking until he got him hard again. Bending over and hiding his testicles and penis with his hand, he begged to be screwed from behind, which Glenn willingly obliged, frantically pumping his rectum until he saw something dangling where it should not be.

Realizing he was doin' a man, Glenn tried to beat him to death. His horrible screams continued until the police kicked down Glenn's door and pulled him off the man. Unrepentant in court, he vowed to kill the transvestite if he ever saw him again, sealing his fate. And of course behind bars, he had more than enough time to hone his "gaydar"! With the five years they gave him, he did.

In his fiancée's absence, Chauncey and Glenn hatched a plan to permanently get rid of me. Wasting no time, they put it into action.

"Hey, baby, you okay? How's Dad?" Chauncey asked Dakota, before segueing to the topic at hand, his flying to Michigan. Without causing concern, he was able to ascertain she'd be home on Sunday night so he scheduled his flight for Monday morning.

Tucking the video in his briefcase, Glenn stayed over and took an early-morning flight back. When Dakota arrived that evening, Chauncey informed her he'd be flying to Detroit for business the next morning.

"Perfect timing! You can look at the reception hall…"

"Come on, baby…I told you, whatever you decide is fine by me."

Wrapping her arms around him, they embraced and held onto each other for a few minutes. Sensing something was wrong, Chauncey pulled away first.

"What's wrong?"

"I think my dad's phones are bugged again."

"What makes you think that?" Chauncey asked. Dakota explained the strange things that were occurring with her father's phones and Chauncey agreed—it was odd.

"I'll have it checked out while I'm there," he assured her. Leading her to the bedroom, she pulled away so she could check on the boys. Fast asleep and looking like the angels they were, she kissed each on the forehead and joined him in the bedroom.

Tired and jetlagged, she fell asleep the moment they finished making love. Holding her in his arms Chauncey replayed in his mind the diabolical plot he and Glenn had masterminded for me.

CHAPTER 50

Acloset is a storage space for clothes, linens, household supplies or in my case, a sexual secret—one I'd take to my grave before allowing it to surface. The shame and embarrassment my secret would bring to the family name was enough to make me slit my wrists, but the scorn and alienation that would surely follow my admission of being gay was more than I could bear.

Glenn and Chauncey waited for me to pull into my garage. Before the garage door closed, they slid in. Waiting for it to shut, they entered my condo. I was partially nude when I walked into my living room, flicked on the light, and realized I was not alone.

Looking at Chauncey, face to face, with no one else around (or so I thought), frightened me so much I peed on myself. Embarrassed, I looked at him apologetically but did not move.

"Glenn, this ho just pissed on herself."

Laughter could be heard from the stairwell leading to the garage. Chauncey, blocking my front door, stared at me. Disgusted by my masculine build—he grabbed a coat from the closet by the door and tossed it to me. Retrieving it from the floor, I quickly covered myself.

"Sit down!" he ordered.

Handing me the video camera, he ordered me to press the play button and watch the screen. Before my movie debut was over, I vomited and burst into tears. Shaking, I sat quietly and wept.

Snatching the camera from my hand, I flinched, raising my hands to protect my head and face from the blows I thought were headed my way. Backing away, Chauncey informed me the video was going to be plastered all over the Internet and copies would be delivered to each of my friends and family members if I did not leave him and his, alone! Backing up his words, he tossed me a copy.

"There's more where that came from!" he said as he disappeared out my front door. Glenn, bringing up the rear with his gun drawn, pointed it at me and pretended to pull the trigger.

"Bang...you're dead," he whispered and then burst into laughter as I ducked and fell off the ottoman. Before I got up, he, too, had disappeared.

Visibly shaken and covered with pee and vomit, I rose, walked to my door, bolted it and then went downstairs and did the same to the door leading from the garage. Still frightened I picked up the phone to call my parents. Too afraid and embarrassed to tell them what happened and why, I hung up.

Showering off the remnants of the worst day of my life, I let the hot water pick away the pieces of food that stuck to my skin and hair. The water was soothing helping me to relax for a minute. When I did, I realized the video was from the tryst I'd had in Atlanta and that meant my dear friend Dante had betrayed me.

Hurt beyond words, I leaned against the shower wall and screamed "why" before falling to my knees and weeping. There was no doubt in my mind Dante made the tape, but I could not fathom why. Before acquiescing to my forced new "mind your own business" lifestyle, I had to find out.

The red-eye to Atlanta was packed. Seated between a heavy, sweaty man and his very full-figured wife, I was thankful I was a true size four. My tiny frame gave them both the extra room they needed to maneuver in the small seats they were strapped to.

Tired, after a horrendous day, I fell asleep and did not wake until my seatmates stirred to deplane. Groggy, I sat momentarily trying to remember where I was and why I'd come. Dante's name came to mind and I suddenly remembered the reason I had paid double the amount I normally paid to fly to Atlanta.

Usually cabs are in abundance curbside at the airport. This being a Tuesday morning, businessmen were jockeying with me for the few that were available. Managing to hail the last one in sight, I settled into the backseat as he drove off.

Not sure if Dante would be home, I asked the driver to wait. First, I knocked gently on his front door. No answer, I knocked again. Still no answer and now highly agitated, I began to kick and pound his door. Landing one more blow with my foot, I heard the door open when I turned to leave. Dante, still obviously sleepy, answered the door in his boxers.

"What do you want?" he asked dryly.

"We need to talk."

"About what?" he said, his voice rising.

Before I could answer, Kevin walked up behind him. Fear consumed me and I turned and ran from the door. Jumping in the cab, I asked the driver to speed away and he did.

Running through the airport, with the exception of security, I did not stop until I reached the boarding gate. Fortunately, standby was available and I breathed a sigh of relief when they called me to board. Safe for the moment, I tried to figure out what was going on. When did Dante and Kevin hook up and what did this mean for me? Did Dante know about our business dealings?

Did Kevin trust me to keep his secret? Was my life in danger?

Frightened out of my mind, I drove to Val and Rodney's for safety and comfort after landing in Detroit. Looking like a demented person when I walked in, Val decided it was time for some professional intervention. Without my permission, she called the doctor once more and scheduled an appointment. Accepting it was *a mild case of depression* was not going to happen. No, this time I was going to the loony bin where Val was certain I belonged.

Unfortunately, the doctor's office had already closed for the day. The answering service informed Val he was away on vacation and not scheduled to return until a week after the New Year. Desperate, she pressed the receptionist for a recommendation; a means to help me. Her suggestion of taking me to Northville, though possible, was not probable. Rodney would fight Val tooth and nail before he allowed his daughter to be placed in a mental institution.

With few options left, my mom asked me to spend the night so she could watch me and make sure I was okay. Tired and afraid of going home, I agreed and crawled into my old bed, falling off into a sound sleep the instant my head lay on the pillow. Waking in a fright, I screamed for my dad before realizing I was in the safety of their home. Jumping from his bed, Rodney ran into my room in time enough to see me burst into tears.

Val ran to my side and held me, wiping my tears as they fell. Looking up at Rodney with that "I told you so" glare, she waved him off while she held me.

"You want to talk about it?" Val asked. I thought long and hard about telling her I was gay, but couldn't. Shaking my head, I cried some more. Three days passed before I emerged from the room looking drawn and older than my years. Happy to see me moving about Val made me a sandwich and poured me a glass of chocolate milk.

"Here, Rochelle, sit down and eat this. You look like a walking skeleton." Realizing that was not a good choice of words, she covered her mouth as Rodney shot her a scathing glance. Lost for words and unable to stomach the stillness in the air, Val put her foot in her mouth once more.

"You know Dakota is getting married this weekend?" I had forgotten about the wedding and with Chauncey's warning still echoing in my head, I had no desire to hear the details.

"Ma, I don't want to talk about her or it," I responded just above a whisper.

An unexpected response that would have been celebrated just days ago, now made Val more certain than ever, I was mentally ill. Northville was becoming a good choice real fast!

CHAPTER 51

Flittering about, Dakota anxiously waited for her moment, praying nothing and no one, especially me, would mess it up. Her life had come full circle and she was happy!

Spending the morning getting prepared for her walk down the aisle was exciting. Her nieces were her only bridal attendants. Seanny, her maid of honor, and Jai, her bridesmaid, were at her side every second of the day. The three of them laughed and cried together as they swapped relationship and family stories. Having them around was comforting and made the day pass quickly.

Now, just minutes before she was to walk down the aisle, her nerves were getting the best of her, causing her stomach to turn flips. Watching her beautiful goddaughters helped to distract her. Kaylee and Kylee served double duty as her junior bridesmaids and flower girls. Anxious to show off their white floor-length dresses they referred to as "wedding gowns," the twins paced back and forth refusing to sit down because they were afraid to rumple their dresses.

The room was packed with well-wishers and the curious. *Jet* magazine sent a request to Dakota's dressing room for a list of individuals she most wanted them to feature, along with herself, in an upcoming issue. Although she was aware of her RSVP list, she was not certain who actually showed up. Tipping out onto the balcony, she looked down and quickly perused the room.

From behind she could not make out many of the guests who were already seated, but she did recognize the twins' mom, Chauncey's sister and daughter, her brother and sister-in-law, her father and his girlfriend Karen.

Completing the *Jet* magazine request, Dakota asked them to only do a family photo that included Seanny and Jai, Kaylee and Kylee, Kelsey and Kenny, her father and brothers. Fully aware she was dissing her sister-in-law, Elly, she smiled and handed the list to Seanny to return to the *Jet* magazine reporter that was waiting outside the door.

As the guests continued to pour in, the tension mounted for Chauncey. Glenn, his best man, was strapped with a glock and positioned by his side. Kelsey and Kenny obediently stood perfectly still next to their father and held the ring pillows, which were devoid of the actual rings.

At exactly four p.m. the ceremony commenced. Softly the music began to cascade throughout the sanctuary, followed by the opening of the massive oak doors. Jai entered the room first followed by Seanny. Slowly each walked to the front of the church and stood on the left of the altar. Kaylee and Kylee nervously strolled side by side down the aisle sprinkling pink rose petals on the aisle runner as they took their places next to Jai and Seanny. The doors were closed behind them.

Chauncey and Dakota fell in love with the Eric Benet and Tamia duet, "Spend My Life With You," weeks after they began dating, and chose it for the bride's entrance. An exceptional musician and longtime family friend, Clint, played several choruses of the song on the piano before the soloist belted out his rendition which could have easily been a Grammy Award nomination.

Once the solo began, the guests rose and turned to face the aisle, poised to see Dakota make her grand entrance. Ushers slowly opened the massive doors once again. Flashbulbs momentarily blinded the bride as she entered. Allowing everyone to get a good look at the gown that made her so proud, Dakota waited a moment before slowly walking down the rose petal-laced walkway.

The rhinestone-encrusted masterpiece she created was even more beautiful than she'd imagined. Each rhinestone found its own prism of light to reflect off of, and shone brilliantly with each step taken, creating sparkle and shimmer that was breathtaking.

A broad smile enhanced her professionally applied makeup, making her entire face exquisitely stunning. More striking than ever, Chauncey beamed with pride as his gorgeous bride approached.

Reaching to take her arm when she made it to the altar, he stared at her for several seconds before walking two more steps forward to face the pastor. Finally, the time had arrived to exchange vows and he could not have been more elated.

Facing each other, Dakota spoke first.

"When you need someone to encourage you, I want it to be me. When you need a helping hand, I want it to be mine. When you long for someone to smile at, turn to me. When you have something to share, share it with me." Her lips quivered as she smiled and fought back tears.

Taking her hands in his, Chauncey lifted them and cradled them to his chest as he looked in her eyes and said, "Though life may not always be as perfect as it is at this moment, I vow to always keep my love as pure as it is today. I promise to be there to share your laughter and your tears. I will be there in your sickness and your health, in your comfort and your fears because I know that our love is a gift from God."

Pausing to gather his thoughts, he spoke from his heart.

"Baby, we have already been through a lot together, and I believe that God has been preparing us for this moment and for our future. I promise to keep the good memories alive, and to let the bad ones die. I vow not to let the sun go down on our anger, and to treat each morning as a new day to love you, the gift I have been given. I will strive to show you my love for the rest of our lives…" Tearing up, his words tapered off, softly ending with, "This is my promise to you."

Throughout the sanctuary white handkerchiefs and tissues could be seen dabbing eyes, a result of hearing such moving vows. The "I do's" took only forty-five minutes and the kiss seemed to take longer. After a couple seconds of very passionate kissing, the guests rose and began applauding. Lingering on her lips, intentionally prolonging the kiss, Chauncey ignored the well-wishers until his wife pulled away to catch her breath.

Smiling, he pecked her on the lips once more before speaking.

"Mrs. Bentley…that sounds good. May I?" he said as he extended his elbow for her to hold onto as they turned to face the guests. The room erupted in cheers and applause as the pastor presented to them, Mr. and Mrs. Bentley. Slowly they walked the runner toward the back of the sanctuary, stopping at the doorway to turn and wave to the well-wishers.

Exiting the church to retreat to their limo, the Bentleys posed on the steps to allow the *Jet* photographer to take several pictures. Holding Dakota in his arms, Chauncey gently kissed her for the camera. Next he embraced her from behind and held her in a bear hug as he affectionately whispered in her ear, "I love you." As the photographer moved closer to get a cropped shot of the same pose, he directed them to look his way, smile, and say, "cheese."

"Cheese," was followed by *pop, pop, pop*! Chauncey collapsed in his wife's arms, his weight forcing them both to the ground. Spontaneously, Glenn bolted from the doorway with his gun drawn. Hovering over his cousin, he frantically looked back and forth trying to locate the shooter.

Screams and people running in every direction, followed by complete pandemonium, drowned out the moans emanating from Chauncey as he lay on the steps bleeding. Trying to be strong, Dakota held him and refused to cry, speaking life into him.

"Don't you die on me, Chauncey Bentley, you hear me!" she commanded in a whisper. Covered with his blood, she refused to let go of his hand until he was whisked into the ambulance.

Reese grabbed her daughters and dashed to the restroom, bolting the door behind her. Fortunately, Seanny shielded Kenny and Kelsey from everything that transpired by rushing them to the dressing room and locking the door. Although they knew something had happened, what and to whom was not yet known. Keeping them occupied, she allowed the boys to pick fruit and candy from the basket, which had been delivered to Dakota earlier that day.

Noticing an attached card that had not been opened, Seanny withdrew it from the envelope and read the handwritten note. Frightened, she gasped and snatched the contents from the children's hands before they could consume any. Using the wall phone, Seanny frantically dialed 9-1-1 and explained what she'd just discovered. The emergency operator informed her several officers were already on the way, and would be there momentarily.

For the boy's sake Seanny calmed down and remained so until the officers arrived. Handing them the card when they did, she sat with Kelsey and Kenny and waited for further instructions.

The officers moved to the window away from them and read the card:

This will be a day you will never forget. I take pleasure in knowing that. Not on my watch…

No name or signature was included, but the police held the card and basket for further examination and fingerprinting, hoping to find a clue that would lead them to the shooter. Seanny and the children were escorted from the premises to a waiting police car.

In and out of consciousness, Chauncey stopped breathing en route to the hospital. Working frantically, the EMT technicians were able to revive him but he lapsed into a coma. Taken straight to surgery, the doctors were unable to immediately remove the bullet that lay centimeters from his heart, but they successfully halted the bleeding. The remaining two bullets did less damage, one going completely through his lung and exiting on the right side.

His blood loss was tremendous and several pints of blood were transfused to keep him alive during the surgery. Once stabilized, the doctors focused their attention on removing the bullet lying close to his heart.

Dakota, covered with her husband's blood, prayed as she paced the floor in the waiting room. Church had been on the back burner in her life since meeting Chauncey. After Kevin disappeared she returned to the only place she continuously found strength and comfort, church, and remained a faithful worshiper until her husband swept her off her feet. Now, fully aware a miracle needed to take place, she began to pray. Asking for forgiveness from God for not being more committed to Him, she begged Him to spare Chauncey's life.

Ten hours after the surgery began, the doctor emerged to inform Dakota her prayers had been answered. Her husband survived the surgery and his prognosis was promising. Although he was in a coma the medical team was hopeful he'd awaken. *When* was the question.

CHAPTER 52

With confirmation the fingerprints on the card and basket belonged to me, I became the person of interest. As if waiting for the cops to come, I sat stoic in my condo with the gun at my side. Babbling when they took me into custody, I was immediately transported to Northville and kept under watch.

Batteries of psychological tests were run and Rodney and Val were questioned about my mental capacity. Rodney denied I was crazy; Val did not. Because there was no record of my having any previous mental illness, a crazy defense would not work and facing a jury was inevitable.

Even though I was institutionalized and treated for a mental breakdown, I was found capable of standing trial three months later. Charged with attempted murder for shooting Chauncey, the prosecutor levied the same charge against me for the poison found on the contents of the basket.

In Chauncey's absence, Dakota attended every day of the trial determined to see her comatose husband receive justice. Sitting front and center, she routinely glared at me wishing I were dead.

Avoiding eye contact with her, I looked the opposite direction from where she was seated and focused my attention on the rear of the courtroom. Every day I eagerly awaited my parents' arrival.

Staring at the doors, I watched people enter and did not relax until I saw them come in. Being present daily and sitting directly behind me was Val's and Rodney's way of supporting me.

Making eye contact with my mom was a moment I now lived for. In her eyes was the compassion and sorrow I had sought all my life. Realizing Val really cared was a "wind beneath my wings" moment that continuously sustained me.

Today was no different. Looking back as they walked in, Rodney smiled, nodded, and then averted any further eye contact with me. Focusing on Val, our eyes met and she gave me the "I'm so sorry for what I've done" look, before smiling and giving me a thumbs-up.

Fully aware today I would testify on my own behalf, the thumbs-up was to encourage me. That small gesture helped me relax and prepare for my "fifteen minutes of fame" on the witness stand.

Normally after the eye contact was exchanged, I would face forward, but today when I looked at Val I noticed for the first time the burgundy cellophane rinse on her hair made her gray look hot pink. Staring at her hair, I snickered before remembering my attorney's instructions to keep a stoic expression at all times. Facing forward, I wiped the smile off my face, and waited for the proceedings to begin.

The trial moved quickly. In an effort to spare me a lengthy prison stint, my attorney informed the jury my mother had abused me while my father stood by and did nothing. Allowing me to take the stand, the jurors were visibly moved by my tearful testimony of emotional and mental scars sustained from the abuse.

"I have asked myself over and over again, how I ended up here?" Pausing to compose myself, I continued. "Abuse at the hands of my mother and my father's ability to ignore my being abused sent me into a lifelong downward spiral. Fear, insecurity and low self-esteem led me to this point. If you constantly feel you are not good enough for someone to admire, respect, or maybe even love, then it is easy to become a vengeful, envious and jealous person."

I went on to list the elements of my inhumane treatment and then eloquently explained to the jury the turmoil and confusion I lived with daily. Meticulously I gave them a thorough account of the feelings of abandonment I carried, adding this abandonment created a fear that plagued me continuously. However, the one fear that drove me to try and kill Chauncey—being outed—I never spoke about.

"Fear of being disliked, unwanted, and a basic fear of the unknown held me prisoner. For the longest time I repressed all memories of the trauma Val subjected me to, and I idealized Rodney even though he was equally guilty. Later I had no memory of what was done to me in my childhood. However, after feeling good about myself for once in my life, and then watching that superficial installation of self-esteem introduced to me by my cousin dissipate, all those memories came flooding back."

Openly weeping, the judge gave me time to get composed. Blowing my nose, I continued.

"Bitter that Dakota ever made me feel I could be what I was not, I became cynical and she became my target. I blamed her for my hurt…try as I might I could not blame my parents." Like a little girl I bowed my head and refused to make eye contact with Val or Rodney. Shaking. I continued.

"I have always had some sort of resentment, anger and yes… jealousy toward my cousin for being happy. Her integrity was not damaged in childhood. She was protected, respected and treated with honesty by parents who loved her and showed her their love. Her happiness and my lack thereof made me feel unwanted and unloved.

Anxiety setting in, I took a deep breath to relax and then sipped some water before finishing my thoughts.

"That envy took on a life of its own. Watching my cousin enjoy life in ways I could only imagine made me resentful that she had gained something I more rightfully deserved. She had already had a wonderful life. People admired her and liked her…"

As the tone in my voice became ominous, I changed the subject to Chauncey in the middle of my sentence. Lost in the moment, I tried to convince the jury I had done Dakota a favor by shooting him. Repeating over and over, "he's not who he says he is," I accused him of being a "liar" and a "fake" and then glanced at my mother for support.

Fluent in "mom looks," my heart stopped when I saw the apathetic look on Val's face. Devastated when I realized she did not believe me, I nutted up. Facing the jury, I pleaded with them to listen.

"I can't prove it…but he is not who he says he is! You have to believe me…" Certain I'd lost my mind, my attorney objected and requested a moment to speak with me. The judge denied his request and allowed me to continue with my testimony. But he quickly changed his decision when he realized I was very agitated and my testimony had become irrational.

With no prior knowledge I had been treated so horribly, Dakota almost felt sorry for me, *almost* being the operative word. Just when I had her and the jurors eating out of the palm of my hand, I switched gears and began to justify my actions.

Hearing my twisted accounts of why I had to stop Chauncey

instantly slapped Dakota out of any empathy she felt toward me. Learning for the first time in our long history how mentally unstable I actually was left her shaken and sickened.

Reflecting on how much she'd been played by someone she cared about made her furious. She found solace in knowing there was a strong possibility the jury would find me guilty and the judge would send me away for a very long time.

Waking from his coma just three days after the jury delivered a guilty verdict, Chauncey smiled a little when Dakota shared the news with him. After he fell off to sleep she exhaled and went home, praying I would get the maximum sentence. I'd have to wait a minimum of fourteen days to find out.

Unfortunately, discovering she was *not* legally married to the man of her dreams would take much longer!

ABOUT THE AUTHOR

Marsha D. Jenkins-Sanders, motivational speaker and ASCAP award-winning songwriter, was born in Detroit, MI. She received acclaim in the music industry for lyrics written for Keith Washington's freshman album project, *Make Time for Love*. Both "Kissing You" and "Closer" introduced her writing talent and she received award-winning recognition in the R & B genre. "Kissing You" was certified gold and went on to be featured as the background music for love scenes on the ABC-TV soap, *General Hospital*. Her much touted debut novel, *The Other Side of Through*, a fictional account of her defunct marriage to Keith, showcases her crossover into the literary field. This candid insight into the trappings and pitfalls of fame and Hollywood has catapulted Marsha into public speaking, where she utilizes this platform to motivate, encourage and empower others. Following on the heels of *The Other Side of Through* is her sophomore novel, *Jealousy: A Strange Company Keeper*. You may contact Marsha via e-mail: mdjswrites@yahoo.com. Events and tour dates will be posted on her websites:

www.marshajenkinssanders.homestead.com

and

www.myspace.com/marshajenkinssanders

IF YOU ENJOYED "JEALOUSY," LOOK FOR

THE OTHER SIDE OF
THROUGH

BY MARSHA D. JENKINS-SANDERS
AVAILABLE FROM STREBOR BOOKS

Katlyn Kincaid, the quintessential perfectionist, worked overtime to create and then maintain the appearance of someone who "got it goin' on."

Her current interest in interior design lent more fuel to her Type A personality, enhancing her need to ensure that the minutest detail was addressed. For example, the carefully chosen array of framed photos making up the picturescape on the end table had to be angled just so. After a good dusting, she painstakingly and meticulously replaced each photo on the table, making sure they were arranged in the original pattern. However, she couldn't figure out how to apply the same principle to her personal life, which was in total disarray. Try as she might, she could not get all the pieces to line up perfectly.

Katlyn stared at herself in the bathroom mirror; first from a distance, looking at her tiny frame. She had her mother's figure and breathtakingly youthful good looks. Upon closer inspection, she noticed tell-tale signs of her real age, the cupped praying hands that began on the outer wings of her nose and ended just above her chin, framing her mouth. For more than a year now, she'd managed to hide the creases on her forehead by tightly pulling her below-shoulder-length hair back in a ponytail. An instant face-lift, she called it.

As she stared at herself, comparing her likeness to her mother's, tears stung her eyes, forcing them to close slowly. Her mother died on Easter eve. At approximately 8 p.m., her father had answered the telephone and gasped. Nine-year-old Katlyn knew something was very wrong even before he burst into tears. He managed to call a neighbor, a close friend, to come over and sit with Katlyn and her brothers while he retreated to the bedroom to compose himself.

After several minutes passed, Katlyn's father approached the children and informed them their mother had just died of a heart attack. Being the only female left in the home, Katlyn instinctively assumed the "mother" role and immediately felt responsible for taking care of her siblings and her father. At that young age, Katlyn did not understand "heart attack" any more than she understood what a void the lack of a mother's presence and love would cause in her life. In time she'd find out how life-altering both were.

Katlyn splashed cold water on her face, and looked at her red eyes in the mirror. She knew she needed to get ready for the concert, but her mind kept replaying the telephone conversation she'd had with Justin.

"Listen, I'm running late…I'll send the limo to pick you up. Be ready by six. I love you." Justin's fitting had taken longer than expected and he would have to meet Katlyn at the concert hall. The thought of her life, a real fairy tale come true, brought tears to her eyes once more. But she pulled herself together, to dress and do her hair and makeup.

Concerts, award shows and public appearances were the norm for Mr. and Mrs. Justin Kincaid. Katlyn often joined her husband, by default, at one or the other via chauffeured limousine. Most times she went alone and was met at back entrances by his manager or publicist. Like now.

The swarm of reporters and media hounds thrust cameras and microphones in her face as she emerged from the limo.

"Mrs. Kincaid, over here!"

"This way, can you smile for the camera?"

"Any plans to start a family?"

Security pushed through the crowd, creating a pathway for Katlyn to move toward the next mob scene where reporters hovered around Justin.

"You know, it's like a dream. When my alarm went off this morning I awoke to something surreal. I'm probably still dreaming." Justin pinched himself and chuckled, the crowd joining him in laughter. "But listen," he said, raising his hand to silence them and get their attention once more. "Do me a favor, if I'm dreamin', don't wake me. I'm lovin' this." The room exploded into applause as Justin ended his brief press conference.

Eyeing Katlyn, he grabbed her hand and followed security into the green room.

Katlyn knew a few of the "bodies" that sauntered into the green room as well, each working her way to Justin's side, greeting him with a kiss on one or both cheeks. Every time one of them approached, Katlyn searched Justin's eyes to see if they revealed anything. She detected nothing.

Justin was a struggling artist when Katlyn first met him. The most gifted vocalist she'd ever heard. He had a God-given talent that no one had paid attention to, except her. Now his latest single was on top of the charts, going to number one in record time. Katlyn always knew he would be a star—and now, thanks to an excellent PR department, everyone else knew it, too!

Katlyn observed the other couples in the room who were married, shackin' or otherwise committed, and wondered which ones were truly in love and really happy. One that always seemed to be solid and very much in love now had different ideas about where their relationship was headed. The chauvinist husband was an up-and-coming actor, producer and director. His wife, a career woman, was now feeling pressure from him to become a mother first and a career woman *never again!*

Then there was the monogamous two-some who shared each other's bed, but maintained separate residences. The much older headstrong psychiatrist kept her lover's desire to be married and have a family at bay. Routinely hurt by men and well aware *she* needed to be on someone's couch she would only be with him if it was on *her* terms.

Munching on some finger food, Katlyn continued to peruse the crowd. In one corner, a gorgeous black male model, straight off the runways of Milan, was having a heated discussion with the Asian female companion he'd brought along. One drink short of drunk, she was drawing unwanted attention and with the press nearby, he could not afford that kind of attention. In another corner, four half-clad "bodies" were posing for a photographer who promised them copies of the photos in order to get their names and numbers.

At one point, Katlyn's eyes met Justin's; he winked and blew her a kiss as he exited the green room to get ready for his performance. She smiled, pretended to catch the kiss, and mouthed, "I love you." She leaned against a wall and sighed, content and in love with him and their wonderful life.

"What cha thinkin' about?" Sheree, his publicist, asked, leaning on the barstool next to Katlyn.

"How blessed I am."

"Oh yeah, how so?" Sheree asked, pulling the stool closer to sit on.

"Look around the room. Justin could have any and every one of these women in here but he's content with having just me."

"Yeah, I bet any woman in the room would kill to be in your shoes, so don't take them off, Cinderella!" Sheree knew when to exit and she also knew when to leave well enough alone. She did both gracefully as Katlyn's friend Tanya came over.

Suddenly Katlyn caught sight of the most beautiful woman she'd ever seen. She was flawless, a plastic surgeon's masterpiece whose beauty made Katlyn gawk. She caught herself staring and so did Tanya.

"You know you're equally as beautiful as that 'mannequin,'" Tanya said. "Naw—I take that back, you're more beautiful because God gave you your beauty. Trust me, she paid a pretty penny for hers."

Katlyn giggled and hugged Tanya, thankful for her support. The well-timed compliment was just what the doctor ordered. The Mannequin left her off-center; a first and she did not like the feeling.

"How's your project coming along?" Tanya asked, slicing a piece of cheese and sitting down next to Katlyn.

"Which one?"

Tanya chuckled. "I forgot you're a woman who wears many hats. I meant the decorating project for that guy who writes jingles."

"Girl, can I just tell you," Katlyn said. "His home, or should I say my work, has been selected to appear on this local morning show, ummm, I can't remember the name, but it's Chicago's most watched morning show. Can you believe it?"

"Sure I can," Tanya said matter-of-factly, nodding. "You're good at that decorating stuff. My home is a testimony to that. You ever going to get your license?"

"I don't know. I'm still up in the air about where my career is going."

"You miss flying?" Tanya asked.

She and Katlyn had been flight attendants and roommates together in Virginia more than ten years ago. Now Tanya; her husband, Darrel; and their daughter, Lauren, lived in L.A., and Katlyn as well as Justin were glad to have friends outside of the industry. They were "real," a rarity in this town.

"Not even, but I do miss the flight privileges," Katlyn admitted.

"Yeah, but with all Justin's success, money surely is not an issue. Girl, buy a ticket, hop a flight and we'll meet you there."

"Puh-leeze!" Katlyn exclaimed. "The way Justin's tour schedule is running there's no time for fun."

"You *are* going on the road with him, right?" Tanya stared at Katlyn and waited for an answer.

Katlyn hesitated, uncomfortable with her question. She knew where this line of questioning was headed and was not in the mood to go down that road.

"Tanya, I have a life, too! Running two companies keeps me busy twenty-four-seven. If I went on the road with him, they'd suffer." Feeling somewhat pensive Katlyn added, "Besides, I think this time apart would be good for both of us!"

"Really? Are you guys okay?" Tanya asked, holding her breath.

"Not to worry, we're fine." Tanya blew a sigh of relief, as Katlyn continued, "Justin has little time for me and *us* since the new album came out. He enjoys having me around, like at the studio, or here at a concert, but we have very little time alone. Hopefully, on the road he'll miss me and you know the old adage: absence makes the heart grow fonder."

"Well, you're a better woman than me. The old adage that comes to *my* mind is, while the cat's away, the mouse will play! I'm telling you, you should go with him," Tanya said adamantly.

"You know what, I don't have the time to worry about it! Justin and I have six happy years together: six happy years that have not been easy. We worked hard, together, to get where we are. I have never questioned his fidelity before; why start now?" Katlyn stated defensively. "I trust him, Tanya, just as much as you trust Darrel. Remember *him*, the one God forgot to clone before he threw the mold away?"

Katlyn always told Tanya she believed D was the epitome of manhood: handsome with a drop-dead physique, a Southern gentleman through and through and one hundred percent faithful to his wife and family. If only she could be so sure of Justin! With an inward sigh, she excused herself to go to the restroom. Upon exiting, Katlyn was greeted by Justin's head of security.

"It's time to go inside, Mrs. Kincaid."

Katlyn cringed. "Okay, Larry, let's get one thing straight: plee-ee-zz stop calling me Mrs. Kincaid! You make me feel old. Katlyn is just fine."

"Yes, Ma'am."

"Ee-uh-hh," she shrieked. "Not Mam. Now I feel like somebody's Mother! Lighten up. Just Katlyn, got it?"

"I got it. This way, please, 'Just Katlyn.'"

Katlyn laughed heartily and then motioned to Tanya and Felicia to gather the clan and go to the skybox. While her friends made their way to their seats, Katlyn had Larry take her to Justin's dressing room. Whenever she was around, she made it a point to pray with him prior to his going onstage.

"And Lord, make tonight especially blessed, let all his vocal ability be in full range and let him perform his best ever." Justin squeezed her hand and Katlyn lost her train of thought, forcing her to cut the prayer short. "We thank you for all these blessings and we ask them in Jesus' name. Amen."

Justin hugged her and Katlyn lingered in his arms. She was so very proud of him and truly grateful for God's blessings on his career and their marriage. She knew Justin was thankful for her spiritual walk and religious beliefs; since Justin wasn't sure about his own spiritual choices, he chose to lean on hers.

Katlyn hurried to her seat not wanting to miss Justin's entrance. The moment he stepped onto the stage in skintight black leather pants and a six-pack highlighted by a one-size-too-small muscle shirt, every woman in the audience lost it. The screams and applause were so deafening, Justin had to wait to sing his first note.

He worked the stage from one side to another, graciously taking roses from the near-hysterical females. At one point, a woman bolted past security and hurled herself onto the stage, then rushed Justin and held him in a death grip that literally cut his breath off. Security loosened her hold, but not before she tore his shirt off.

That sent the remaining fans who had not yet hyperventilated into a fit; it took Justin's leaving the stage to get another shirt to calm the crowd. Ten minutes later the show resumed. After two hours of swooning ballads, sexy gyrating and hormone-driven females screaming and crying, Justin geared up for the finale.

Justin Kincaid was a five-feet-nine phenomenon. His caramel-brown gorgeous skin flaunted chiseled features usually reserved for Greek gods. A head full of curly, jet-black hair, which he wore close-cut to make it wave, was more than most women could bear. They loved him, he was an aphrodisiac; you always wanted more. Four rows deep, the women lined up around the stage, throwing him roses, money and underwear. They cried, begged and screamed for the opportunity to be near him.

Justin carefully approached the crowd and leaned down to take a rose from a woman he deemed harmless, because of her small stature and controlled behavior. Not! She reached up, grabbed him in a headlock and planted her lips on his. Others in need of the same fix began to grope his body. Justin was helpless.

Katlyn stood up shocked by what she was seeing. When one of the crazed groupies grabbed Justin's oversized gift from God, she lost it! Her three-and-a-half-inch $600 Pradas slowed her attempts to climb over the three seats that blocked her access to the exit. As she finally reached the aisle, Darrel gripped her arm, preventing her from leaving the safety of the skybox.

Even though the ruckus was over in a couple of seconds, for Justin it seemed like hours. The ordeal frightened him, leaving him shaking when he thought about how dangerous the encounter was. He stood stunned for a minute or two, gaining his composure as the crowd one by one rose to its feet and began to chant the title of his latest hit, "Who's Kissin' You?"

Softly, the piano chords began to cascade through the arena. They were soothing to Katlyn. Darrel loosened his grip, realizing she had calmed down. Katlyn sat down and stared at her now half-dressed and visibly shaken husband. "Who's Kissin' You?" was a joint venture between Katlyn and Justin: he'd written the melody and track, and she'd written the lyrics. Even though it was her first attempt at songwriting, this ballad was the biggest hit of Justin's career.

"Who's kissin' you and lovin' you...," Justin crooned. Women raised their arms and swayed to the music as he made love to them with his voice. Tears filled Katlyn's eyes as she watched her husband. She'd done well in structuring her close-to-perfect life. Justin was her prince, her knight in shining armor, her fairy tale come true. People loved him; she loved him. Oh, how she loved him! Theirs was a good Hollywood marriage, of that she was sure.